# SONS OF THE LION

## BOOK ELEVEN OF THE OMEGA WAR

Jason Cordova

Seventh Seal Press
Virginia Beach, VA

Copyright © 2019 by Jason Cordova

All rights reserved. No part of this publication may be reproduced, distributed or transmitted in any form or by any means, including photocopying, recording, or other electronic or mechanical methods, without the prior written permission of the publisher, except in the case of brief quotations embodied in critical reviews and certain other noncommercial uses permitted by copyright law. For permission requests, write to the publisher, addressed "Attention: Permissions Coordinator," at the address below.

Chris Kennedy/Seventh Seal Press
2052 Bierce Dr.
Virginia Beach, VA 23454
http://chriskennedypublishing.com/

Publisher's Note: This is a work of fiction. Names, characters, places, and incidents are a product of the author's imagination. Locales and public names are sometimes used for atmospheric purposes. Any resemblance to actual people, living or dead, or to businesses, companies, events, institutions, or locales is completely coincidental.

Ordering Information:
Quantity sales. Special discounts are available on quantity purchases by corporations, associations, and others. For details, contact the "Special Sales Department" at the address above.

Cover Design by Brenda Mihalko
Original Art by Ricky Ryan

Sons of the Lion/Jason Cordova -- 1st ed.
ISBN 978-1950420254

## Acknowledgements:

First off, thank you to Chris Kennedy and Mark Wandrey for creating such an awesome playground for us writers to play in. While I've been in previous anthologies the opportunity to write a novel in their universe has been an absolute joy. I hope I get to extend my stay here a little longer.

Secondly, the first readers who graciously stepped up to go over this novel, I owe you a huge thank you. Lauren, Collyn, and Kelly are my usual first readers. For this, however, I reached out to the Four Horsemen Fan Community and picked up Jamie, Rene, Pat, Ian, and Dan to help. There are over 25 books in the series and I needed to make sure I had everything straight. They are all awesome people doing a thankless job.

Lastly, to all of you who cheered me on. It was terrific motivation and I couldn't have done it without your support.

Jason Cordova
Clifton Forge, VA

# Prologue

**Izlian Heavy Cruiser *Bird of Prey*, Capital Planet Emergence Zone**

Thorpi knew he was the least likely Veetanho in his race's illustrious history to be in his current position. It was a position of power, almost unheard of for a male to accomplish. The fact it was in a minor Human mercenary company was beside the point. To him, it was the most important job he would ever attain in his young life.

Which was why when his mother's daughter, Leeto, came calling upon him as the Kakata Korps were in the midst of transitioning back to Earth after their most recent successful deployment, Thorpi became extremely nervous. Enough so he looked into his own private dealings and agreements outside the Mercenary Guild and wondered if his plot had already been discovered.

His memories of Leeto were vague ones at best. They hadn't been of the same litter, her being multiple years older than he, and she'd already been gone when he became aware. Thorpi was what the Humans would have called the "runt" of the litter, though in a different sense of the word. It was galling to think this way, but also accurate, he allowed. Humans were an odd bunch but seemed to have a phrase for everything.

He swam quickly through the adjoining tube and into the waiting transport shuttle. Since they were meeting in a ship and not the station, and the Izlians had no use for rotating sections to create any form of centrifugal gravity, the going was fast but a little treacherous. His time served as the Chief Operations Officer of the Kakata Korps had taught him punctuality was everything, even if Leeto made him wait to see her. It was the nature of the beast, experience told him. Even so, he knew being allowed into her presence alone made for an amazing first step. The fact he was being acknowledged sent delicious shivers of satisfaction down his spine and caused his fur to ripple in excitement. His status in the hierarchy of the family was growing.

Thorpi mentally shook himself before his wild fantasies took hold. Caution and wariness were needed when dealing with a temperamental female, he was quietly reminded by an inner voice. The females of his species were far deadlier than the males, and it showed in their domination of both the Veetanho home world and the Mercenary Guild.

At the last stop, he was met by a brooding Jivool, one of the 36 other mercenary races in the Galactic Union. A guard outside Leeto's door wasn't surprising. That the guard was a Jivool, certainly was, however. As far as Thorpi knew, the bear-like knuckle draggers were not the best-suited for a protective detail. But it was not his place to talk, so he remained silent until the piggish eyes of the Jivool focused squarely on his face. He saw some dim sign of intelligence in the alien's eyes, and Thorpi chided himself. Appearances can be deceiving, and the Jivool were highly underrated as mercenaries.

Whiskers twitching nervously, Thorpi waited for some sort of acknowledgement from the guard. Time seemed to pass slowly as he stared at the Veetanho, his expression one of boredom and contempt. Thorpi's skin began to itch as he floated, waiting. He was a Veetanho of action, and being forced to wait in silence was pure, unadulterated torture.

"I'm here to meet with Leeto," he finally said, knowing the Kakata Korps were expected to make their transfer through the gate back to Earth soon. If Thorpi wanted a ride back with them, he would have to hurry. Their ship would not wait around for a single Veetanho. Transition fees had already been paid, and there were no refunds for missing passengers.

The Jivool finally grunted in a surprisingly high-pitched tone and opened the door. Not knowing if he should thank the alien or not, Thorpi instead simply gave the merc a quick nod. Thorpi pushed through the door into a surprisingly large room, where three figures waited.

He recognized Leeto instantly, as she was the only Veetanho present. Two MinSha guards flanked her, both of whom studied him closely with their strange ruby-red eyes. Their narrow, segmented bodies always disgusted Thorpi a little when he looked at them. They wore their standard chitlin armor, though they seemed to lack any obvious weaponry save for their ceremonial staves. It made sense, though. Thorpi didn't know Leeto well, but if she were as paranoid as he had been led to believe, there was no way she would allow weapons in her presence. As terrifying as the mantis-like aliens were, they were nothing when compared to the intimidating form of their mother's favored daughter.

"Greetings, creche sister of our mother," Leeto said and dipped her head at him. Thorpi's ear twitched in shock at the obvious sign of respect.

"I greet thee in return, favored daughter," Thorpi replied and bowed his head deeper. Though she had shown him respect, it was expected of him to show her even more. Not only was she a female, but she was the leading general under their mother. "I am here as summoned, to both pay respects and offer my services."

"You are an odd one, Thorpi," Leeto said as she waved the two MinSha guards away. They left the room without question, leaving the two Veetanho alone. As the door closed, she turned her sleek head and focused intently on him. "Small, a creche sister who passes herself off as male amongst her employers, yet cunning and devious. A planner. You'd be better suited in a logistics role for the Veetanho, did you know this? Perhaps as the senior logistics officer of a small task force?"

The thought had occurred to him, a dream he often fantasized about in the depths of the night when his Human merc companions were sleeping. The first creche sister to be head logistician for the great General Peepo in her crusade through the stars, to further the glory of both the Mercenary Guild and the Veetanho race. It was a job which he lusted for and desired more than anything else in the universe.

However, his time amongst the Humans had taught him almost as much as when he attended school in his youth. The phrase "mama didn't raise no fool" was one which his current employer, Colonel Mulbah Luo of the Kakata Korps, was fond of saying. Leeto was softening him up with compliments and suggestions, which set off alarm bells in his head. The last thing the smaller Veetanho could be described as was a fool. Inexperienced, perhaps, but even this was quickly becoming a thing of the past with every completed contract with the Korps. He had *arrived*, and it was glorious to behold.

"I thank you for the compliment, favored daughter, but I am just another mere Veetanho creche sister in the service of our family," Thorpi stated in a controlled voice, his fur rippling ever-so-slightly at her words. This was not a simple meeting between children of General Peepo but a full-on negotiation, one which would make even the legendary Depik take note of. The immediate problem, however, was he didn't know what was being negotiated. Not yet, at least.

"Nonsense," Leeto scoffed, her tone one of amusement and only mild rebuke. "Our mother did not choose you for this role because you are just another ordinary Veetanho. She picked you because you are an extraordinary creche sister, born of the great General Peepo.

Your other creche sisters were all wastes of matter, suited for nothing more than menial labor and the usual hardships of being one of your kind. You are special, Thorpi. Even among our people, being selected for this task is a sign of expected greatness."

*If you say so,* Thorpi thought as he bowed his head in acquiescence. He really wished she would call him something other than creche sister. He never felt as though it were truly accurate. It was part of the reason he passed himself off as male amongst his Human employers. Too many questions and explanations. Misunderstandings and assumptions were all part of the ploys used against creche sisters by favored daughters, and something he wanted no part of anymore. "I thank you, favored daughter, for your kind words."

"Please, call me something other than 'favored daughter,'" Leeto suggested. "I would not wish to call you 'favored creche sister,' after all. It's a mouthful and wastes time. You have recently received a promotion in rank within your own mercenary company, correct? Congratulations...*Major*?"

*That* little tidbit of information caused him to twitch nervously. There was no way the sudden news of his promotion could have reached Leeto yet, given it happened during one of their normal transits through a gate. It had been over three weeks earlier, true, but the only manner of which Leeto could have learned of the news was if she had someone in the Mercenary Guild tracking the rank structures and payroll of the Kakata Korps. Which meant Leeto was connected almost as well as their mother, and this made him suspicious of her true motives.

"Thank you, General," Thorpi bowed his head a second time. Subservience often meant survival, no matter how distasteful he found it. "Your congratulatory words cause me great joy."

"Tell me." Leeto paused here and casually inspected the back of her paw, examining a stray patch of fur a little too intently. A ruse,

Thorpi recognized immediately, but a very clever one. It was a sign of her indifference to the next question, and it might have fooled him if he had not noticed her ears twitching in nervous anticipation of...something. "How do you like working with the Humans?"

*Careful now,* Thorpi told himself as he gathered the right words. There was much more afoot here than he knew about. Her question had been carefully timed. Even the least intelligent of creche sisters could recognize this.

"They are very interesting to work with," Thorpi stated. That much was true, though the male Veetanho had learnt the various meanings of the word "interesting" in his time with the Humans.

Apparently his mother's daughter had not, for Leeto nodded sagely. "That has been my assessment as well. Very peculiar bunch, prone to do the unexpected. Very adaptable, but also unpredictable, which makes them unreliable in the Mercenary Guild's eyes."

*You mean to General Peepo's,* Thorpi thought. He was beginning to understand where this conversation was going, and he didn't like it one bit. He had moved past caution and was at full-blown trepidation, with a side of dread for good measure. Truth be told, he *liked* the Liberians he worked with. He had never met a more industrious or loyal people in his entire life, and the care they showed for those in their family was something Thorpi felt a Veetanho could learn much from them.

A sudden thought caused his blood to run cold. *Is Leeto aware of the contacts I have inside the Information Guild? Do she or Peepo suspect?*

It wasn't an entirely unfeasible idea. After all, Peepo was renowned for her daughters being as cunning as she. Leeto could very well know who Thorpi was working with on the side, all things considered. His footing felt more slippery and treacherous with each passing moment. He slowed his breathing to almost normal levels, deciding for the time being to allow Leeto to think he was only nervous about the meeting.

"Nonetheless, their success rate for guild contracts recently is over 95%, which is almost unheard of," Leeto continued, unaware the male had already discovered the point she was slowly steering the conversation toward. "They are very profitable, but…" her voice trailed off.

"Yes?"

"General Peepo believes they are positioning themselves to take over the Mercenary Guild," Leeto stated bluntly. This caught Thorpi by surprise, but not for the expected reason. This ruse was not the direction he had anticipated his mother going. Influencers, perhaps, or even falsifying records to trigger an interspecies war, much like what had been done with the Pushtal when they began to try and exert influence over the guild long before. He couldn't hide his body's reaction to the news, so instead of fighting to control his twitching he charged full ahead as a typical, ignorant creche sister would, hoping his apparent over-eagerness would be interpreted as something else.

"Surely they would be mad to believe they can take on the entire Mercenary Guild!"

"We have proof that Humans are flouting Guild Law and spitting in its eye," Leeto proclaimed, appearing to mistake his body posture for something else. "They have elevated a race to sentience and have activated massive war machines of old. They also are creating Canavar, which as you undoubtedly know, is strictly prohibited not only by Guild Law but also by Galactic law."

"I have heard nothing of this," Thorpi admitted, shaking slightly. "Colonel Luo does not do any of these things and keeps the operation small. It saves money."

"Which has come to General Peepo's attention," Leeto nodded, pleased. "Your Colonel Luo is a rare breed, one who puts his oaths first and personal desires second. Our information on him suggests his loyalty to the guild even overshadows his love of Earth."

*That's technically true,* Thorpi silently allowed as he thought it over. Mulbah had little love for Earth, considering the hell which had befallen his people throughout history, as well as the injustices they had shackled themselves with. However, Mulbah had no greater love than what he felt for his nation, Liberia. This was painfully obvious to anyone who spent more than five seconds in his presence. His desire to see his homeland succeed was white-hot and could burn through any other loyalties, pledges, or promises. It had even led to the dissolution of his marriage, a concept Thorpi had only begun to explore as his dealings with the Information Guild grew.

"He is loyal to the guild," Thorpi stated instead, carefully negotiating the unseen minefield as he continued to spar with his mother's favored daughter. There was no way he would allow familiarity to breed contempt in this situation. Leeto was far too dangerous, as well as a shrewd negotiator, for him to allow her to draw him in too easily.

"That is good to hear." Leeto's smile was ghastly to behold, Thorpi realized. It was one of the Human facial traits which had begun to catch on across the known universe, and it had multiple effects on some races. For a Veetanho, it made a rictus death mask on the female who used it, similar to the bliss they exhibited when asserting dominance over a chosen male to mate with right before killing him. Thorpi was shaken to the core by the grotesque sight. "However, with the Four Horsemen flouting their arrogance and believing their own lies of supremacy, the Mercenary Guild has consulted the laws and decided they must be brought to heel. For this to occur, the guild must take full control of the Human home world of

Earth. They are, after all, only provisional members of the Galactic Union."

Thorpi's entire body stiffened at this. If the Mercenary Guild was pulling this stunt now, then the Information Guild's agents were possibly compromised.

"Is this wise?" he prodded gently.

"It is," Leeto nodded, looking down at him with a very curious expression on her face. "Do you not think so?"

"It is...an interesting tactic," he said after a momentary pause.

"You have doubts?"

"More like personal concerns." Thorpi demurred to the superior female as he recognized the barest hints of anger upon her face.

"Peepo's concerns are all we should worry about at the moment," Leeto stated, evidently not pleased with his response. Since he could find no other way to voice his concerns without seeming to attack his mother or her plans, he remained quiet. Leeto took his subservience for something else and continued, the subtle shift of her body language telling him she was pleased once more. "What the general is offering is something that might be of use to your colonel, if he were up to the task."

"Which is?"

"Control over his homeland's western coastal nations," Leeto announced. "In exchange for assisting in quelling any mercenary guilds in the area around the Mediterranean Sea who do not come to heel. The Kakata Korps will also receive a very nice stipend from the guild until cessation of actions and the Four Horsemen are brought to justice. The contract will be in perpetuity, of course."

Thorpi was not the chief financial officer of the mercenary company, so had no say in the matter. He felt fortunate this thankless job fell on the shoulders of Captain Zion Jacobs, 3rd Company Commander. With the Korps' expansion after their first two successful missions, Colonel Luo had purchased more up-to-date armor and equipment, as well as hired Liberians and Ugandans who had recently finished their training at the established Mercenary Service Track school outside Monrovia. After seeing the pay and opportunities provided by being a mercenary, thousands of applicants had sought entrance to the school. It had created a boon for the local economy as well, though it hadn't filtered out to the people yet. Liberia was known for crooked politicians and wayward projects which went nowhere but spent a lot of money somehow. *Very much like the Mercenary Guild,* Thorpi thought humorlessly.

"Do you have a contract prepared so I may bring it to my commanding officer?" Thorpi asked as the mention of "perpetuity" filtered through his head. Typically, the guild did not offer contracts in this manner, preferring to put them on the open market to be bid upon within designated merc pits via the GalNet. However, when they did do this, it meant big money for a mercenary company. Plus, in perpetuity meant guaranteed money until cessation of hostilities, which could be many years down the road. Humans were worse than Goka when it came to eliminating them, not because of any inherent toughness but because Humans were so damned persistent. It was a boon, as well as a curse. Credits could be had by all with this stipulation.

"I had it drawn up and completed before you arrived," she replied. "Check your pinplants. I've uploaded it for you to take to your colonel and have him sign."

"I can't promise he'll sign it, but I will do my best to ensure that he does."

"If he does not sign, then he is in violation of Guild Law, like the Four Horsemen. He will be arrested, summarily tried, and then executed at the guild's pleasure," Leeto warned him. Thorpi's blood ran cold but he kept his expression carefully neutral.

"I do not think he will disagree with the wording of this contract, and will likely sign," Thorpi said and dipped his head lower still as he mentally inspected the language and verbiage of the contract. It all seemed okay to him, but then Guild Law was not his specialty. Moving hundreds of thousands of tons worth of military hardware in preparation of an assault was his first love and chosen profession.

"Very good, creche sister," Leeto rasped with pleasure. Thorpi swallowed and his claws twitched. The longer he remained in the room alone with her, the more uncomfortable he became. It was time to leave.

"When does Earth fall?" Thorpi asked, his voice quiet as his mind raced to find a way to navigate the turbulent waters of the coming storm. He was certain he could spin this in a way so Mulbah did not go on a murderous rampage. It would be difficult with the offer of a free Liberia for the Korps to run, as well as control over the entire coast in exchange for regular work to the north. Thorpi knew of at least a dozen mercenary companies which operated around the large body of water, none of whom even gave a fair shake to the Liberian company. Plus, Thorpi recalled just how loyal Mulbah was to his homeland.

"Soon," Leeto replied.

This wasn't too surprising. Earth, for the most part, was as crooked as a Zuparti conducting a business deal. Corruption ran rampant throughout the government of Liberia, and it was definitely a sore spot for the company CEO. Colonel Luo's dream of a true Liberian paradise would never come true as long as the politicians milked the merc company for every credit they could and then wasted them away purchasing more votes from an ignorant populace. Thorpi schooled his features for perfect calm before looking up at Leeto.

"And how long will Colonel Luo have to decide?" he continued after a moment of silence.

"He has until his arrival back in Earth's system to decide," said Leeto. Thorpi nodded slowly. This made a certain amount of sense, since it would be two more jumps until they reached Earth. As nice as it would have been for the company to remain closer to Earth, the Four Horsemen were the ones who usually received the plum contracts closer to home. Other merc companies needed to go farther out to find good-paying contracts. The Kakata Korps, thanks to how new it was, had to travel farther still to find contracts where they did not lose money. This resulted in them sometimes taking long odds against a superior force, yet Mulbah was clever, and Thorpi was a tactical genius, for a creche sister. The Korps always found a way to win the fight.

This would also give Thorpi a chance to get the contract and information to his contact in the Information Guild. Before this meeting, he hadn't known why his old friend Tookapa had been pushing for more information from Earth. Knowledge cut both ways, and Thorpi had a horrible feeling this was tied in with Peepo's plans for the Humans, and Earth. It was not comforting.

"Earth?" Thorpi asked, swallowing as his mouth suddenly became dry. He needed to know so when he made the pitch to Mulbah the Liberian wouldn't strangle him right then and there. "I need to know *when*."

Leeto bared her teeth in excitement. "Earth falls tomorrow."

\* \* \* \* \*

# Part One

# The Proud Lion

# Chapter One

**SOGA HQ, Sao Paolo, Brazil, Earth**

General Peepo, leader of the Mercenary Guild forces, scanned the latest information brought to her by her chief of staff. Captain Beeko was, as usual, punctual and timely with her reports. The majority of Earth's mercenary companies had made their way off-world in a desperate, last-second escape, leaving behind only the dregs and those who would follow the Mercenary Guild purely for the money. The list of companies still on Earth wasn't impressive, but at least it was mostly comprehensive. Her eyes flicked down the slate screen as she read the names and tried to recall what their specialties were.

*Varangian Guard.* Proud, but slow on the uptake. Not considered elite. Better at intimidation and crowd control than first strike contracts. Decent defenders, however. They had accepted the Mercenary Guild ruling Earth without too much question. For the time being, they were providing site security in Sao Paolo for the Mercenary Guild as it strengthened its grip on Earth. Their commanding officer really liked the credits which were flowing into his coffers now. She saw a little side note warning about their negotiation tactics and chittered softly in amusement. *How very Flatar of them.*

*Middle Kingdom Dragon Guard.* Peepo shuddered at the memory of her earlier meeting with the diminutive Human woman. There was an active and open hostility between the Dragon Guard and the Golden Horde. Some historical reference the Veetanho did not fully understand between the Horde and the Guard involving who had the right to rule or some such nonsense. The Dragon Guard had agreed to accept the guild's pay, even if some of the fallout from the bombing of the Golden Horde's HQ site had impacted the region where the Dragon Guard recruited from. The strange little woman from the Guard had taken everything in stride, looking at Peepo with those cold, lifeless eyes.

Peepo paused as she came to the third and final company on her list. It was the least known of the three, despite having a Veetanho on its staff. One of her children even, though Thorpi was a mere creche sister. But still...Peepo could think of no reason why the information detailing the company was so sparse. They were still relatively new to the mercenary business, but their success rate was phenomenal. Their losses were always under 5% of their full strength, and their profit margins were through the roof. She swiped left and peered at Colonel Mulbah Luo's information profile and was quickly able to discern just why they were financially successful in spite of being so small.

*An accountant and inventor who passed his VOWs,* she realized as she continued reading. The company had actually not been one of the Human groups she had believed would work with the guild, which made their acceptance of the deal more than a little suspicious. After all the fighting and delaying tactics by the mercenary companies before they had left Earth, Peepo had believed the Kakata Korps would follow the lead of the Horsemen.

According to Leeto, Thorpi had claimed the Korps wanted no part of the Horsemen's rebellion against the Merc Guild. Peepo had her doubts about both the Korps and the creche sister. Still, they were going to be confined to operations in the Mediterranean Sea and southern Europe, as well as pacifying western Africa. With her spawn guiding them, they could undoubtedly be a huge asset while remaining safely occupied and out of the way. Once their operations against the remaining mercs were done and her final plan was executed she would then have the Korps eliminated. After all, they were not necessary in the final scheme of things. The Horsemen were the key to it all.

"General?" Captain Beeko interrupted her reading as she poked head through the open doorway. Peepo looked up in irritation but stopped the quick rebuke as she saw the look on other Veetanho's furry face.

"What is it?"

"We've captured Sansar Enkh!" Beeko informed her, excitement bubbling forth. Peepo stared at her chief of staff for a long moment, concerned.

"Captured?"

"Well," Beeko looked down, mildly embarrassed, "she showed up downstairs fifteen minutes ago and surrendered."

"I see," Peepo nodded, even though she did not. *What game is this?* "Where is she now?"

"Being taken to a holding cell to await guild justice," Beeko stated.

Peepo held up a paw, considering. "Bring her to me first," Peepo said as she looked around the former secretary general's office. It would do to serve as a reminder to the Human just who ruled this planet now, a point she planned on driving home shortly. "Make sure she arrives in one piece and in relatively good health, Captain."

"Yes, General!" Beeko disappeared from the room and Peepo's shoulders relaxed.

The goal had been to decapitate the leadership of the Four Horsemen and bring the rest of the Human mercenary companies to heel. The plan hadn't worked out quite the way she had planned but holding one of the Four Horsemen commanders was better than none at all. It would make the trial and eventual conviction better if one of them were there in person, instead of all of them being tried *in absentia.*

For the first time since she had set foot on this repulsive planet, things were starting to look up.

\* \* \*

**Möller Interstellar Consortium Vessel *Jörgummund*,
Emergence Point, Sol System**

Colonel Mulbah Luo backed himself into the chair and looked around at his gathered senior staff. He was pleased with what he saw gathered before him, even though the topic at hand was not the most desirable one. Running his fingers along the trim of his unadorned black beret, he could feel the edge of the nasty scar hidden beneath. This scar had not been earned in combat though. No, that would have been honorable and not forced him to order a uniform change for the entire Kakata Korps.

Thrashing about in his bunk one night, Mulbah had not strapped himself down tightly enough following the company's first contract and had split his head open wide upon the edge of the bunk. Embarrassing as hell, the mess had been even worse to clean up. Blood in zero gravity got everywhere. It had amazed him to find blood in his compartment three weeks later, after he had sanitized the berthing area five times. His three senior officers had teased him mercilessly, which forced him to action. The berets were ordered for all members of the Korps, with him wearing the black beret. His officers wore blood red, with a logo for each of their companies, while enlisted wore blue with the matching company patch.

In hindsight, Mulbah found the color combination was actually a stroke of genius. It helped the new recruits to quickly figure out the rank structure, and since there were only five officers in the Korps for the time being, it enabled Mulbah to establish a solid senior NCO rank structure based solely on experience and merit. Following the ranking structure of Cartwright's Cavaliers had paid off in huge dividends. Mulbah inwardly smiled at this. In order to be the best, one had to beat the best. Emulating the best was a step in the right direction.

Of course, this had led the Liberian government to cry foul and demand he promote those who were related to politicians faster. Stubbornly, Mulbah had refused. His mercenary company, his rules. The Mercenary Guild law stated as much. Rather politely, he had pointed this out to the now-former president Teah Njie during their last meeting before the Korps had shipped out on a new contract. Soon after, the Liberian government had raised taxes on all businesses where 90% of their business took place outside the country's borders.

This blatant attack on the Korps, which was the only business in the country which was still turning a profit at this point, was almost too much for Mulbah. His homeland held a special place in his heart, and he wanted more than anything to see Liberia rise up to take its place among the greatest democratic nations on Earth. It soured his stomach to watch the insipid greed of his fellow countrymen hamper the country's natural development.

As he listened in on the arguments around the table, he thought about the two ways to handle the situation. The first was obvious: leave Liberia and re-establish the Korps' HQ in another country. However, pride prevented Mulbah from taking this easy way out. The desire to be Africa's premier mercenary company kept him in Liberia. No other country on the continent, save perhaps Egypt, had the infrastructure necessary for a mercenary company to succeed. He had no desire to move his company over 7,500 kilometers to a country where he had absolutely zero contacts. Cairo, while being a potential location for a starport, was simply too much of a cesspool to actually be of use.

The second option was attractive but potentially dangerous. It was also the reason for the current staff meeting with his senior officers.

"I'm not asking for your decision on the matter," Mulbah said, interrupting the argument between Captain Samson Tolbert of the 1st Company and his counterpart in 2nd Company, Captain Antonious Karnga. The two officers had started out as mere mechanics for the company Mulbah had bought out but had been pressed into being CASPer drivers after it became apparent the Korps would not be able to afford to hire new ones. They had performed admirably and later been promoted when Mulbah brought in new hires.

"Then what are you asking, *bass*?" Samson asked in a respectful tone. He waved a hand in front of his face, his expression dark. "The way the guild says it, the Horsemen had turned their backs on Earth and broken Guild Law. But would they really do that? We do not know them very well, *bass*, but I do not think they would betray Earth."

"Greed makes people do strange things," Antonious interjected as he glared at his counterpart. They were friends, true, and fought well together in battle. They were also prideful men, and they constantly jockeyed with one another for superiority. It was a rivalry Mulbah didn't feel the need to quash, not yet at least. If it began to affect their performance in the field, only then would he step in. Antonious continued, "We could have gotten to know them better, *bass*. Laziness on our part."

Mulbah inwardly winced at this. It had been his fault he hadn't built up much of a *tête-à-tête* with the major mercenary companies of Earth. Building a company from the ground up was time consuming, and it left little time for much else. It was part of the reason why his now-ex-wife was living with her new boyfriend in Baltimore and had a generous alimony package to boot.

However, he did have one contact in the Winged Hussars, albeit a loose one that not too many people knew about. The only problem was he hadn't heard from Wendy since the Korps had accepted the sublet contract months before. He had no idea if the Sanders girl was alive or dead at this point. If the Hussars had fled Earth to try and save it later, surely they would have sent out a message to all Human mercenary companies about what was going on and would have provided some sort of evidence to back up their claims. It was this lack of evidence—or even a message to the Korps, really—which was swaying Mulbah toward believing the Mercenary Guild. He had a gut feeling Antonious shared in his suspicions.

Mulbah already knew where Thorpi stood on the matter. The Veetanho had been the one to bring the contract and proposal to him, along with the suggestion the Korps rule not only Liberia, but every country along the coast from Ghana to Senegal under one common nation. It was an interesting idea, far grander than anything Mulbah had thought about, but he had little patience for governing that much area. The number of tribes in Liberia alone made his head spin, and their conflicts continued to spill over and create new civil wars. Considering the last two had resulted in the deaths of almost a half million people, it was a road he was not yet prepared to travel. This aspect of the proposal in particular was something he had kept from his senior staff...for now.

Next to the Veetanho, the Korps' Chief Financial Officer was going over notes via his pinplants, staring off into the distance. Captain Zion Jacobs was an intelligent man who had a better education than Mulbah did, though he rarely flaunted it. Given command of the support unit, 3rd Company was typically filled with men who ascribed to Zion's pragmatic views on everything. Overly cautious and a fastidious planner, it would be Zion who could change Mulbah's final decision.

"The numbers look good, boss," Zion informed Mulbah, his eyes coming back to reality. The CFO blinked a few times and rubbed his face with his palm. "There's some sketchiness with the term 'in perpetuity,' since that could be forever, or they could declare a success tomorrow and not pay us at all, leaving us holding the bag and landing us on the bad side of everyone still on Earth. I'd get that part changed. As for policing the mercenary companies of southern Europe, that should be easy. From what I've seen, most of the other merc companies ran the moment General Peepo and her fleet showed up. The ones remaining are either on her side, too poor to leave, or are actively working to subvert the Mercenary Guild."

"*Bass*, whose side are *we* on?" Samson asked, leaning on the table. He peered at Mulbah with dark eyes. "I don't trust the aliens. No offense, Thorpi."

"It is wise to never trust anything at face value," the Veetanho said shrugging off Samson's apology. "I was the one initially presented it from an individual I know, and *I* am skeptical of the sincerity behind it. However, the contract does look good, and with the exception of the perpetuity clause, I think it's an honest contract."

"*Menh*, I don't like it," Antonious chimed in as he used the rubber band on his wrist to tie his dreadlocks back. "I don't want to fight Human mercs. Isn't it obvious to anyone else? If General Peepo doesn't want to fight them, then why should we?"

Mulbah conceded the point. "True. But what happens when they bring in the Besquith to pacify them, and then they come at us for not helping? This isn't about destroying the merc companies but about the survival of Earth. What happens when they decide Humans aren't worth the risk anymore? I don't know about you, but accidents happen on a frighteningly regular basis in the Galactic Union."

The comment caused all the men in the room to fall silent. Africa was a continent where the term "accidents happen" held a far darker connotation than elsewhere in the world. Far too often, presidents were "accidentally" killed fighting rebels, or protestors "fell ill" during transportation to a local jail. Even the occasional general who "committed suicide" by shooting himself 27 times in the back was a cautionary tale about how "accidents" occurred.

"General Peepo could also call in Tortantulas to 'pacify' Earth," Mulbah added, driving the proverbial stake home with a single, vicious blow. "We can prevent a potential slaughter by taking the contract. We can protect Earth by doing this."

Everyone shuddered at the idea of pacification by Tortantula. Spiders the size of a small car were not something even the most hardened of mercs wanted to face on a regular basis. Not to mention, the Flatar who rode them into battle were not to be taken lightly either. Letting them loose on a civilian populace was probably the worst thing imaginable.

"*Bass*, I still think we're getting played here," Samson murmured and rubbed a hand over his bald scalp. He looked away, almost ashamed. "But if you think this can keep more people alive, then we do it."

That settled it. "Zion, get the contract fixed, and I'll sign it. Everyone else, ready your companies for action. I have a feeling we're going to be deployed a lot sooner than we'd hoped once we're back in Liberia."

Unbuckling their safety harnesses, the trio of company commanders left the meeting room, leaving Mulbah alone with the Veetanho. Thorpi was looking at him with what Mulbah called his "curious" expression. However, the alien appeared almost embarrassed by something that was on his mind. Mulbah raised a single eyebrow at him.

"I couldn't help but notice you left out the mention of the Korps ruling all of the coastal countries around Liberia," Thorpi observed, his tone neutral. It wasn't accusatory, but something between surprise and curious. Mulbah did not fault the Veetanho's caution. He had to play a dangerous and delicate balancing act between his loyalty to his employer, his guild, and his people. He was much like Mulbah, in this regard. The Veetanho flicked an ear and cocked his head slightly. "Why did you choose not to reveal this information?"

"Instinct," Mulbah replied. Thorpi motioned for him to explain further. After a moment of introspection, Mulbah clarified for the Veetanho. "Humanity has been at war with itself since the dawn of time. The first murder occurred when there was only four people on the planet, supposedly. We are born and bred for conflict. However, Africa—my people and all the peoples of Africa—have a special disposition to violence and conquest of one another. Before and after the white Europeans came and enslaved us, we were doing it to one another."

"But that doesn't explain…" Thorpi's voice trailed off, apparently at a loss for words. Mulbah smiled. It was confusing to someone who didn't know the region, the tribes, or the ancient conflicts stretching back generations.

"Did you know that everyone on the command staff is Liberian?" Mulbah asked him. The Veetanho nodded eagerly. "Did you know that none of them are from the same tribe?"

The Veetanho blinked, his sleek and furry features showing confusion. Mulbah understood the bewildered look all too well. Many Americans he had tried to explain the same issue to while he was going to school had looked at him the same way. It was a common mistake amongst Westerners, assuming just because someone was of the same country meant they were all the same people. Sometimes Mulbah wished everyone thought in the same positive manner as the Americans he had known.

"Liberia is made up of ethnic tribes," Mulbah explained. "Think of it like families, and then tribes, and then the nation itself. Nobody is going to put nation over tribe. The sense of community that drives, oh...Canadians and Americans? Africa doesn't do this. I feel we *can't*. We are divisive, conflictive, and, generally, we never trust anything or anyone outside that tribal circle. That is the African way. People are easier to rule this way, so politicians don't preach unity outside of the tribe. They might argue otherwise, but when the cards are down and all the chips are in the pot, a tribal group will save its own, even at the cost of its country."

"I...don't understand this at all," Thorpi admitted as his claws dragged lightly across the table top. "Everything we Veetanho do is to further our species, and the Galactic Union."

"Yes, but if you had to choose between your species or the Galactic Union, which would you pick?"

Thorpi said nothing as he unbuckled his safety harness. Pushing away from the meeting table, he glided toward the door leading back to his private quarters. As he reached the doorway, however, he stopped and half-turned to look back at Mulbah.

"I did not mean to cause offense, sir," the Veetanho said. "You have just given me much to think about. Permission to be excused?"

"Of course," Mulbah told the alien. Thorpi nodded and pushed his way through the doorway and down the long hall. The CEO of the Kakata Korps watched him go and gazed down the corridor for a long time after, deep in thought as his mind began to draft plans for dealing with Human merc companies without actually wiping them out.

\* \* \*

**Möller Interstellar Consortium Vessel *Jörgummund*, 900km Above Earth, Sol System**

"Load 'em up!" Captain Karnga shouted as the men of 2nd Company hurried to their drop shuttles. He stared and waited for a few stragglers, the last of his men. Their CASPers moved more slowly into the shuttle than he would have preferred. Antonious looked over at First Sergeant Victor Oti and grimaced. "They were a lot faster during the drills, *menh*."

"Ya, *bass*, they were," his Top agreed. Master Sergeant Oti had been with the company since they returned from their first successful contract and had proven to be an able leader of enlisted personnel, which had led to him being rapidly promoted through the ranks. When it came time to form the companies within the Korps, Antonious had snagged the former fisherman as quickly as he could to serve as his senior NCO.

They made for an interesting duo. Antonious was skinny, wiry, and good with the ladies. Victor was tall, broad, and rarely talked to women in any manner. Antonious wasn't sure if the larger man was shy around women or simply not interested in them. However, he also did not want to pry, so he'd left it alone and allowed Victor to whip the boys of 2nd Company into shape.

So far, the men of 2nd Company were not performing up to expectations. They had experienced the most losses during their recent contract, with two killed and four wounded. One of those injuries could very well lead to a medical retirement, which was not something Antonious was particularly proud of. However, Colonel Luo hadn't been too concerned, since he had established a very generous retirement package for anyone who survived 25 completed contracts as well as a retirement package for combat-related injuries. The combat readiness of the company, however, had been brought up by the colonel as being "suboptimal."

Antonious had his doubts early on when Colonel Luo had purchased the failed mercenary company *Mercenarios Ojo de Tigre* and renamed them the Kakata Korps. The first meeting had not gone very well but the first contract had been successfully accomplished. Completed, perhaps, but they had lost Antonious' oldest friend, Khean Waring, while protecting the alien Korteschii from the mysterious lizard raiders. From there they had transitioned the company to Liberia, where they had almost lost their owner in a partially botched contract which had ended well for the company. It also earned them a fat payday, courtesy of the Winged Hussars. From there, the successes—and newer equipment—continued to pile up as Mulbah Luo carefully guided the Korps through contract negotiations.

"Remind the boys we only get paid if we can get our jobs done on time, Top," Antonious muttered over his personal frequency to the First Sergeant.

"Ya, *bass*, it done," came the quick and easy reply. Antonious nodded. Despite Victor's barely passable English he was an effective first sergeant. He had no doubts the enlisted men of 2nd Company were about to have their hides verbally flayed in a pidgin mashup of English and Kisi.

"Be gentle on them," Antonious suggested. Victor snorted over the radio and gave his boss an incredulous look. Antonious shook his head and smiled. "Right, stupid idea. You handle it, but *after* the drop is complete and the fighting is over."

"Ya think fight, *bass*?"

"I don't want one," Antonious admitted as they boarded the combat dropship and looked around. Eight CASPers stood waiting for their command team to take their places in the hold. The duo moved to opposite sides of the dropship and the magnetic locks secured them in place. Antonious exhaled and continued his private conversation with Victor. "But just because I don't want one doesn't mean we won't get one, *menh*."

"Ya, *bass*," Victor agreed. The first sergeant switched frequencies and addressed the men of 2nd Company. "*Menh*, listen. We go down, only shoot if they shoot. They wan' fight, we fight. Kill they fighters. Get pay. You *ken*?"

"*Paint the sky!*" roared the rest of the company. Antonious grinned inside his CASPer and switched frequencies. "Lion Six, this is Jackal Six, over."

"Jackal Six, this is Lion Six," Mulbah's voice came over the radio. "Probably don't need to remind you, but I'm going to anyway. Only fire if they fire, Captain. I don't want to kill Humans if I don't have to."

"Roger that, *bass*," Antonious acknowledged. His grin remained wide upon his face. "We're ready to go. See you on the ground, *bass*."

"Copy, Jackal Six," Mulbah replied. "Paint the sky, over."

"Roger, Lion Six. Paint the sky. Jackal Six, out."

Antonious took a deep, calming breath as the weight on his chest steadily grew stronger with each passing moment. The dropship rocked slightly as it entered the atmosphere. The captain kept his eyes on the Tri-V inside the cockpit of his Mk 7 CASPer, marking their descent the entire way. A small countdown timer emerged on the lower half of his screen. The G-forces grew stronger as the dropship accelerated and began to pull out of the steep dive.

He could faintly make out a man howling from somewhere near the front of the company. Antonious couldn't blame him, not really.

They were pulling almost five Gs for longer than they ever had before. Even the battle-hardened captain was beginning to feel the effects of the combat drop as the edges of his vision began to blacken. Pushing down with his gut, he struggled to force his blood to circulate so he would not pass out.

"You train for dis!" First Sergeant's Oti voice cut through the darkness. "Don't be *craw-craw*. Do your job. Get pay! *Ken?*"

The force on his chest began to lessen as the dropship leveled out. Wobbling slightly, the craft stabilized and continued to slow as they approached the target drop zone. Antonious looked at the bright light to his left where the rear ramp was. It was still red, but he knew it wouldn't be much longer. It was time for them to bail.

"Drop positions!" he ordered the men of 2nd Company. "Shuttle control, this is Jackal Six. Release magnetic clamps."

"Releasing magnetic clamps, Jackal Six," came the immediate reply. "Good hunting."

*I hope not,* Antonious thought. "Copy, shuttle control. Jackal Six, out."

Freed from the magnetic clamps used to secure the CASPers during a combat drop, Antonious slowly moved to the ramp. The rest of the company followed their captain's example and carefully made their way to the rear. The vibrations of the shuttle increased violently as the ramp hatch slowly opened, exposing the bright blue Mediterranean Sea below. In the distance, he could make out the familiar boot shape which was Italy, as well as the island of Sicily just off the "toe."

The light suddenly changed from red to green and Captain Antonious Karnga, 2nd Company, Kakata Korps, made his first combat drop onto Earth.

\* \* \*

**Möller Interstellar Consortium Vessel *Jörgummund*, Near Earth Orbit, Sol System**

Colonel Mulbah Luo watched on his Tri-V display as the second of his three companies dropped to Earth. 3rd Company had dropped earlier, on schedule. 2nd Company had been slower than the rest boarding their dropship. This bothered him greatly. It had become something of a trend ever since the botched kidnapping of the Zuparti crime lord at Troubadour Station. They were constantly running behind on just about everything since Mulbah had broken down the organization into a traditional military model, and it had more to do with Mulbah's choice of commander for the company than anything else.

Mulbah really did like Antonious personally, but it was becoming painfully obvious to everyone else on the command staff why the captain had been a mechanic early on. He needed to attend some sort of leadership school, but given the current state of affairs on Earth, it simply wasn't an option anytime soon. He could replace Antonious as CO of 2nd Company but considering the working relationship he had with his men, Mulbah could potentially be facing an even bigger problem. Not mutiny, but something close enough to cause the entire Korps to not function as efficiently as it once had.

No, for the time being, Captain Karnga would remain the 2nd Company's CO.

Mulbah switched frequencies as his Tri-V shifted the view to the second dropship. "Leopard Six, this is Lion Six, over."

"This is Leopard Six," Captain Samson Tolbert of the 1st Company replied. "Go Lion Six."

"2nd Company is in position and dropping," Mulbah told him. "Commence your drop now."

"Copy, Lion Six," Samson confirmed. "Leopard Six, out."

Unlike Antonious, Mulbah had complete and utter confidence in 1st Company and its captain. Samson had proven himself to be more than capable of command and had kept his losses to only one casualty in eight missions. That had been a broken leg, which was later fixed in no time, and the merc in the CASPer had been battle ready for the next contract. It had surprised Mulbah after he learned Samson seemed to thrive as being the Korps' "Tip of the Spear" when it came to battle. Despite the odds, Samson's perfect combat record remained intact, which made the faults of 2nd Company all the more apparent.

*You can't compare the two when you look at their histories,* Mulbah mentally chided himself. While Antonious had been from a decently wealthy family in the States and had played his way through high school and his VOWS, Samson had been one of the thousands of child-soldiers left out to die when the fourth Liberian civil war ended. However, unlike most of his fellow former slaves, Samson accepted the teachings of the Christian missionaries and was a quick study. His VOWS scores had been average, which meant nobody had really gone after him in the recruiting department. The only reason he had taken the job as a mechanic for the Spaniards was because it paid better than most of the merc positions he was offered. Until Mulbah hired him as a CASPer driver, at least.

Plus, Samson had two children and a wife at home, whereas Antonious liked to joke with the rest of the men he had three kids "somewhere." Samson was grounded in his faith, his family, and his life. Mulbah wasn't certain whether it was because Samson had children, or a faith that nobody else could match, which made him such an effective combat leader. In the end, it really didn't matter, as long as he continued to work for the Korps.

A voice cut in over the comms. "Colonel?" Mulbah sighed and killed the view of his Tri-V. It was time for him to execute his part of the mission. It was the most dangerous part as well. He'd rather be in combat in the safety of a CASPer than face what was to come.

"Yeah, Thorpi, I'm ready." Mulbah exhaled and got up from behind the desk. He floated to the entry into his personal office and paused. The Veetanho was giving him a very strange look. "What is it?"

"I just…" Thorpi paused and scratched behind one ear. "Are you sure you don't wish to bring the command squad with you, in their CASPers and ready to fight, Colonel?"

"I *do* wish to bring them," Mulbah stated, a wry smile upon his face. "But then the Presidential Guard would think we're there to start a coup, and things will go to shit in a hurry."

"But, Colonel…*aren't* we there to start a coup?"

"Yeah, true. Probably," Mulbah acknowledged as he shrugged hesitantly. "Doesn't mean they need to know until it's over, though. Plus, we could get lucky and not need one. I really hope this is the case."

Thorpi bared his fangs ever so slightly. "You think too much like a Veetanho, Colonel. It is downright scary at times."

"Besides, Major, if it does go to shit, I need the command squad to come in blasting everything they've got, just like we planned," Mulbah reminded him. "We show up looking for a fight, we're going to get one. I'd rather they come to the negotiation table peacefully. Well, appearing peaceful."

"What about Captain Jacobs and 3rd Company, then?" Thorpi pressed. "Why do you have them in CASPers but so far away from the potential combat?"

"Zion has his own mission to complete," Mulbah reminded the Veetanho. "It was your idea for him to do this, remember?"

"Yes, but that was before I knew you were going into the capitol without even a single CASPer backing you up!"

"I know." Mulbah nodded as the duo began to head toward the sole remaining shuttle onboard the *Jörgummund*. "If I had told you what I planned to do, you wouldn't have let him go to secure our HQ in case things go sideways. You would have him flanking me, probably in Chocolate City or something, ready to jump into the fight at a moment's notice, since it would be the last direction they'd expect him to come from."

"You're absolutely right!"

"Now do you understand why I didn't tell you?"

"Unfortunately, I must concede your point," Thorpi said, his voice miserable. The Veetanho's ears twitched slightly as he looked at Mulbah. There was genuine concern in his eyes. "You will use caution, Colonel?"

"If I used caution, Major, I wouldn't be going down with my ass hanging in the wind," Mulbah reminded him. "But since I like living so much, I'll be extra careful. I'm glad you care so much, Major."

"I don't have job security if you're dead," Thorpi reminded him. "Stay alive, sir."

* * *

### 15 Kilometers above Taranto S.R.L. Mercenary HQ, San Pietro Island, Italy District, Earth

"Jackal Six, Golf Four. *Bass*, got eyes on the prize," Corporal William Noah announced as they continued to plummet through the thick cloud cover over Italy. "Landing in two minutes."

"Confirmed, Golf Four." Antonious checked his altimeter. They were passing fifteen kilometers and would be groundside precisely when Corporal Noah stated. *So far, so good,* he thought. "Stay safe, *menh*. Jackal Six, out."

Outside his suit, the wind howled as it whipped past. Antonious was nervous since this was only the second time the company had done a kamikaze drop. The first time had been done to the colonel's satisfaction, but thanks to the amount of deployments the Korps had been on over the past six months since, he had not had the opportunity to keep his company up-to-date on the training regimen. He knew he had to do it eventually, there just hadn't been enough time to do it before all this happened.

"This sucks, *menh*," Antonious muttered as the landing zone came into view. The flight line just outside of Taranto S.R.L.'s main compound was chosen for their LZ before they moved into the base proper. Antonious had no idea if the mercs inside would surrender and submit to Guild Law, though he really hoped they would. The idea of killing another Human merc company just didn't sit well with him.

Truth be told, none of it was fine by him. He hadn't said much on the matter when Mulbah had presented the guild's case to them, but since then his mind had been in turmoil over the matter. Antonious knew he really didn't understand politics or politicking the way the other company commanders did. He'd done well enough on his VOWS, true, but he'd always been inclined to simply live and let live. Backroom deals involving one person pledging loyalty to another in exchange for money while publicly denouncing the person paying them, always confused the hell out of the Liberian.

Jump packs screamed as the rocky ground of the island just off Italy's coast came rushing up to meet him. Antonious felt the suit right itself and he landed gently on the sandy beach a mere fifty meters from his anticipated spot. Using his pinplants he began to tag every CASPer as they landed, identifying them and marking their locations as a secondary backup for each squad's NCO on the Tri-V inside his suit. He knew from experience that Master Sergeant Oti was undoubtedly doing something very similar, and he fervently hoped the squad leaders were as well.

"Jackal Six, Jackal One," Oti's voice crackled in his ear. "Good drop, *bass*. All okay. Orders?"

*Holy shit, we all lived,* was Antonious' instinctual first response, but he decided saying so out loud would be highly unprofessional. He decided to stick with something Colonel Luo might say. "Good work, Top. Have the squads move into position. I've got to make contact with the Italians, over."

"Ya *bass*, on it. One, out." Oti clicked over to start barking orders at the men of 2nd Company while Antonious prepared to do the hard part.

Settling down, he transmitted on an open frequency to the members of the Italian merc company inside the complex.

"Attention mercenaries of Taranto S.R.L.," he began, reading the script which was helpfully displayed on his screen. It had been written by Mulbah and Thorpi, with Zion going over the finer details to ensure they didn't screw it up. Not for the first time did he wish Samson had been the one chosen to do this part of the mission. "This is Captain Antonious Karnga, 2nd Company, Kakata Korps of the Mercenary Guild. You are in violation of Guild Law Article Fourteen, Section Seven, Paragraph Twenty-two: violating a guild directive by not responding to a guild missive in a timely manner, thus causing the guild to file a formal protest on your lack of compliance, which in turn forced the guild to file a missive to which you did not respond to in said manner. You are hereby subjected to guild justice and are ordered to turn yourself over for judgement within the hour. Please respond."

Antonious clicked off the comms and stared at the script. He took a deep breath and tried to read it a second time. He failed to understand a single word of what the Italians were being accused of. He muttered under his breath.

"What the hell did I just tell them?"

\* \* \*

**Inside Taranto S.R.L. Mercenary HQ, San Pietro Island, Italy District, Earth**

"What the hell did he just say?" Chief Sergeant Major Umberto Meloni asked as he looked around at the gathered men and women of Taranto S.R.L. Mercenary, one of the three government-sanctioned Mercenary Guild units within Italy. Unlike their Italian brethren who had fled when the general alert and evacuation order from the Four Horsemen was received, Taranto S.R.L. had neither the funds nor inclination to abandon their island base. It had been decided by near-universal agreement to remain behind, to act as the eyes and ears for the rest of the companies. Plus, they had been commanded to hold down the fort by the Italian government and, since their now-missing and presumed dead leader was a distant cousin to the Prime Minister, their hunkering down to wait out the storm had been an easy decision to make.

"I think…I think we're being punished for not answering a letter," First Corporal Major Mario Bonucci answered, confusion etched upon his craggy features. "We're in trouble for not answering?"

"No, we're in hot water because they were forced to send out an official notice to our non-compliance to their letter, which caused them to write…another letter?" Chief Sergeant Major Maloni suggested as he looked back at the gathered CASPers outside. "That's pure bureaucratic bullshit right there."

"Who are the Kakata Korps?" Corporal Major Alia Guigliana asked as she consulted her pinplants. After a moment she began shaking her head, a slightly bemused expression on her face. "They're a *moolie* company from Liberia."

"They let the *moolies* have CASPers?" Chief Sergeant Major Maloni asked in surprise. "The guild must be getting desperate."

"I don't know," Corporal Major Guigliana said as she delved deeper into their combat records. "They look pretty good. I wonder why the Horsemen didn't tell them to leave, too? Oh, I see. They were off-world and their comms were dark. Cheap bastards."

"They're *moolies*, Alia," Chief Sergeant Major Maloni stated, finality in his tone. "Why would any of the Horsemen mess with them? Tell First Squad to suit up. We'll teach them how proper mercenaries fight." He activated his pinplants to respond. "Kakata Korps, this is Chief Sergeant Major Umberto Maloni, Taranto S.R.L. Get off our lawn, *moolie*."

\* \* \*

**Outside Taranto S.R.L. Mercenary HQ, San Pietro Island, Italy District, Earth**

"What the hell does that even mean?" Antonious muttered as he stared at the facility. Only fifty years before, the island had been a luxurious vacation spot for wealthy Europeans, with lovely views of the port city of Taranto across the bay on one side, and equally pleasant views of the Mediterranean on the other. He changed frequencies. "Oti, it's Tony. You know what a *moolie* is?"

"Like *kaffir*," Oti answered immediately. "Bad name. No kill, can beat them hard?"

"I'm tempted," Antonious growled as he recalled where the term *kaffir* had come from and the history behind the derogatory word. His blood began to boil but he forced himself to remain calm. "Don't shoot unless they fire first, though. *Bass* doesn't want to kill Humans, even if they are full of *biggity, menh*. Over?"

"Okay, *bass*, no kill," Oti confirmed. "One, out."

"Stupid *biggity*, cocky, ugly Euros…" Antonious muttered as he switched frequencies once more. "Taranto S.R.L., this is your second warning. Surrender to the Korps and prepare to accept Mercenary Guild justice or face the consequences. Please comply, over."

\* \* \*

### Inside Taranto S.R.L. Mercenary HQ, San Pietro Island, Italy District, Earth

"They're smoking something if they think we're going to surrender without a fight," Chief Sergeant Major Maloni grunted as he stubbed out his cigarette. He turned in his seat and looked at Corporal Major Guigliana. It was obvious to the experienced senior NCO she was concerned. "What?"

"Chief, they are *very* good at assaults," she pointed out as she shared the information via pinplants. "They've only been around for a few years, but they are solid. They've even survived a Besquith contract with almost zero casualties!"

"They're *moolies*, Alia," Chief Sergeant Major Maloni reminded her, ignoring the data. "Look at their history. Of course they're good at assaults. It's the simplest tactic in the history of mankind, outside of defending a walled structure. Charge head-long into something and smash it in the face."

"Chief…"

"I've heard enough, Corporal," Maloni warned. "Have First Squad deploy as soon as they're suited up. More than likely the *moolies* will either back off, or we'll start shooting, and they'll be cut down. Oh, and get Tsolmon Enkh up here. He's going to want to see this."

"Yes, Chief," she answered miserably and turned back to her pinplant to give the command for First Squad to move out. The corporal wondered if the chief remembered all they had was First Squad before shoving the question aside. It wasn't her place to second-guess her superior's commands, after all.

\* \* \*

**Outside Taranto S.R.L. Mercenary HQ, San Pietro Island, Italy District, Earth**

"Well, that's different," Antonious commented to nobody in particular as he watched the solid concrete blast doors begin to open. The large bunker was undoubtedly tough and went underground, since there was no way they could cram more than fifteen CASPers into the small area he could see from his position.

He clicked over to 2nd Company's channel. "Jackals, this is Jackal Six. Be advised, we got movement over here. Master Sergeant Oti?"

"*Bass?*"

"Have the men ready, but remember not to shoot unless they shoot first, over."

"Yeah, *bass*, you say already," the man reminded him.

"Just…making sure," Antonious said. "Six, out." He changed frequencies and contacted Captain Tolbert. "Leopard Six, Jackal Six, over."

"This is Samson, go ahead," came the quick reply from roughly 42,000 feet overhead.

"*Menh*, they're coming out from the look of things," Antonious said as the large doors started moving. He could hear loud noises from within and swallowed nervously. "They didn't sound happy when I told them to surrender."

"I heard it when you were broadcasting, *craw craw* boy," Samson chuckled. "1st Company is on standby. Just give the word, over."

"I swear to God…" Antonious growled, irritated. "One time! It was one time, and the cream made it go away!"

"Okay, Jackal, okay. I'm sorry. I won't tease you anymore about them Ghana girls," Samson apologized.

"Thank you," Antonious breathed in relief.

"But I said nothing about them girls from Guinea…" Samson roared with laughter.

"Shut the hell up, *menh*," Antonious said in an irritated voice. Leave it to Samson to remind him about the other time, which had required pills and multiple doctor visits to clear up. He silently vowed to never brag about his conquests in the bedroom again whenever Samson was around. "Jackal Six, out."

He killed the connection before Samson could get in one final joke at his expense, and focused on the noises coming from within the concrete structure. The sounds were obviously being made by CASPers moving across a concrete surface, but for the life of him he could not figure out just what they were doing. If they were coming out to fight, then he would have expected them to come pouring out of the building like ants when one kicked over the anthill, not to toy around in the darkness simply to build suspense.

"What are they doing?" Antonious hissed as he waited impatiently for something to happen.

An engine rumbled loudly from within the darkness and Antonious' guts clenched up nervously. Whatever the noise was, it was definitely *not* a CASPer. It almost sounded like a tank, but ever since the advent of the Mk 5 CASPer, tanks had become obsolete. Surely the Italians wouldn't try to fight them in tanks? Something was up.

From out of the darkness a massive shape emerged. Antonious yelped in surprise as the huge form of a semi-trailer truck came barreling out of the concrete structure, its roof barely clearing the ceiling as it drove out onto the hard pavement at breakneck speeds. The semi was pulling a long flatbed behind it, and Antonious suddenly realized just what the Italians had planned, even though he had no idea how they had managed to get a semi into a building which was half its size.

On the back of the flatbed were fourteen Mk 7 CASPers, each with a MAC on one arm and a lightweight cyclic energy weapon on their opposite shoulder for balance. They leapt off the flatbed and landed heavily on the pavement before fanning out. Their heavy steps shook loose a few small stones which had been piled up next to the small artificial berm near the water's edge.

Antonious watched as the Italian CASPers turned and aimed their weapons at individuals in Antonious' company who were not behind hard cover. He felt a tiny bead of sweat begin to run down the side of his face as his guts churned. They were in a standoff, and with Antonious under strict orders not to fire first, he was probably going to take some casualties if the Italians decided to start blasting at the Korps. He still retained some hope it would not come to a shootout, but those hopes were quickly dwindling by the aggressive tactics shown by Taranto S.R.L.

"Stand down," a voice broadcasted from one of the CASPers. It was heavily accented English, but still understandable for Antonious.

"Stand down, or you will be destroyed. The guild has betrayed humanity."

"The Four Horsemen have betrayed us!" Antonious called out in reply. "They broke both Galactic and Guild Law, then left us to hold onto the planet while they ran off! How can you be so stupid?"

"The Mercenary Guild has betrayed us!" the CASPer countered. "Surrender now or be destroyed!"

"Naw, *menh*, you surrender, or we'll destroy your base," Antonious threatened, though he wasn't too sure how he could accomplish this. If a semi could drive out of a concrete building which looked to be only fifty feet long, then he had no clue as to how far underground the true complex burrowed. More than likely it would take quite a bit of time to actually destroy the base, which would probably mean flooding it with the Mediterranean Sea.

"Last warning, *moolie*," the voice warned. Antonious' eyes narrowed.

"Who you calling *moolie*, you stupid Euro?"

A single shot from a MAC echoed out, missing Antonious' head by three inches. The Liberian instinctively ducked as the tension suddenly ratcheted upwards. Every single member of the Korps was now targeting one of the Taranto S.R.L. CASPers with both MAC and shoulder mounted K-bombs. Only the strict discipline instilled upon them by Mulbah Luo and a general fear of Master Sergeant Oti kept them from returning fire.

"That was a warning shot," a cold voice informed Antonious. "The next one won't miss."

"Leopard Six, Jackal Six. You hear that, *menh*?"

"Copy, Jackal Six," Samson replied, all business now the Italian CASPers had crossed the unspoken line. "Inbound now. Leopard Six, out."

Sonic booms cracked overhead as eleven objects fell from the sky at a terrifying rate. All of the Italian CASPers turned to look up. Antonious' suit tracked their descent and saw the flatbed was their impact point. Taranto S.R.L. quickly realized this as well and began to move away from the truck as quickly as possible.

The lead drop pod crashed through the flatbed, utterly destroying it, while driving portions of the steel frame into the concrete below it and into the island soil beneath *it*. The next pod impacted half a second later, the drop pod crushing the hitch joining the semi to the trailer. The force of the impact lifted the cab high into the air before it slammed back down to the pavement. The windows of the semi shattered from the impact and the engine crashed through the radiator grill in the front.

Nine more drop pods hit the ground around the trailer, forming a nigh-impenetrable ring around the center pod. The doors dropped open and Mk 7 CASPers from 1st Company stepped out and trained their MACs onto the defending Italians. It was quickly apparent to all involved on the Korps side there was no way for Taranto S.R.L. to win if they tried to shoot their way out.

"*Alonzo!*" a voice cried out from the CASPer in front of Antonious. The suit took a step toward the destroyed semi-truck then stopped. The CASPer driver turned and pointed his MAC directly at Antonious' chest. "*Cazzo di merde, bastardo!*"

The first MAC round punched straight through the CASPer's chest armor and into Antonious' shoulder, causing him to fall flat on his back as the force of the impact drove him off his feet. He gasped in pain as two more rounds punched through the legs of his suit, missing his legs by inches as they were diverted by the armor as they impacted. The rest of the rounds chewed up the pavement near his head as the Italian tried to finish off Antonious.

"Open fire!" Antonious heard Samson call out. Suddenly San Pietro Island became a chaotic maelstrom as 1st Company shot Taranto S.R.L. from one direction and 2nd Company hit them from another, the crossfire destroying every Italian CASPers in seconds. Not a single shot was wasted by the Korps, nor a round errant. 2nd Company might get a bad rap for suffering more casualties than any other units within the Korps, but their abilities in a fight had never been questioned by Mulbah or the others.

Someone knelt down next to Antonious and injected nanites into the suit to accelerate the healing process. He looked up and his Tri-V informed him it was Specialist Jon Taylor, his company medic. Struggling to breathe, Antonious began to thrash inside his cockpit. The medic quickly disabled the haptic relays within the suit so he could administer first aid.

\* \* \*

Around them, the Korps began to take stock of the situation as a few began to sort through the dead. Fourteen ruined CASPers lay strewn about the pavement, smoke and dust rising from them as their systems failed one by one. The men and women inside had been torn to shreds by the magnetic accelerator cannons the Korps used as their primary weapons when laser rifles were simply not enough. There were no survivors. And, somehow, other than Antonious, not a single member of the Korps had been wounded.

Captain Samson Tolbert sent men out to establish a perimeter near the entrance of Taranto S.R.L.'s base before walking over to check on Antonious. He saw his old compatriot was badly wounded but would likely survive. However, since the situation had escalated into a shooting match, Samson, as ranking officer at the scene, would have to report to Mulbah that his goal of not harming other Human mercs had failed.

One thing he could not figure out was why the Italians decided to attack once it was clear to all involved they were ensnared and hopelessly outgunned. He looked at the mangled and ruined truck which had been carrying the flat trailer and walked around to the driver-side door. Using the additional strength of the CASPer, he grabbed the broken door and wrenched it open. It stuck, so he applied more power to behind his grip and ripped the door clear off the hinge. Tossing the ruined door aside, he looked in the cabin.

There was a broken, crumpled body of a boy, perhaps fifteen, inside. It was obvious the teenager was dead from the amount of trauma on the body. A large chunk of metal had somehow broken off from the engine block and speared him clean through the heart. Blood had splashed everywhere in the interior, a testament to the force at which the boy had been struck by the rod. Samson seriously doubted the kid had even felt it before he died. He sighed, understanding now just why the Italians had attacked so quickly after he had dropped. This one was his fault, not 2nd Company's or its captain. He had screwed up, bad.

"*Bass*," one of the suits from 2nd Company said as he approached. His pinplant showed the speaker as First Sergeant Victor Oti, Antonious' "Top" in 2nd Company.

"Yes, First Sergeant?" Samson asked as he stepped away from the ruined semi. He looked down at his hand and saw blood had stuck to the armor. He flicked his hand a little but the liquid clung defiantly, mockingly.

"*Bass*, more underground," the first sergeant said in a very heavy accent.

Samson sighed. "Master Sergeant Oti, let your pinplant translate for you," he instructed. The first sergeant was silent for a moment before he tried again.

"Sorry, *bass*, I never knew about that," he said, much clearer this time. "That's very handy. I always felt a bit hamstrung by the limits of my English."

"Now try again."

"*Bass*, there are more of the mercs from Taranto S.R.L. inside their concrete bunker. They only sent out about one-third of their reported strength. We need to go into the bunker and clear them out. It's going to be a nightmare under there, *bass*."

"We're not going down there, First Sergeant," Samson told him as he began to look around. The island was only a few feet above sea level, and the entrance to the bunker was only about 100 feet from shore. He was pretty sure if they could keep the concrete doors open, flushing out the mercs of Taranto S.R.L. would be a breeze. "I've got a better plan. Pass the message to 2nd Company to start digging a trench, eight feet deep and four wide, all the way to the shore."

"*Bass*, won't the pavement keep the water from flowing into the bunker?" Master Sergeant Oti asked.

Samson shook his head. "Let me handle that problem."

"Yes, *bass*," Oti briefly snapped to attention before hurrying off. Samson sighed and took stock of the situation.

*It's not going to get any easier from here*, he thought as he closed his eyes. Taking a deep breath, he thought of what was still to come. *Even if we get them out, they're going to be pissed. Word will get out, too. The Portuguese mercs out of Lisbon are proud, very proud, and don't like being overshadowed by the assault capabilities of Asbaran Solutions. They'll fight harder than the Italians did.*

*Such is life,* he thought as he wandered away from his team a little to make the call to his boss. Mulbah was not going to be happy about this. Not one bit.

\* \* \*

**The Lion's Gate, Freeport of Monrovia, Liberia District, Earth**

"This is absolute bullshit," said Captain Zion Jacobs, 3rd Company, Kakata Korps. He growled dangerously as he eyed the two government-hired security guards. The men cowered as he looked at them, though it was not because of his steely gaze. Zion, for all his abilities, was not an intimidating man, standing barely five and a half feet tall, and before his ophthalmic upgrades, had needed glasses.

The two Mk 7 CASPers standing behind him, however, did the intimidating for him. Part of the Korps' original five combat suits, they had been retrofitted to carry heavier armor and magnetic accelerator cannons on each arm, as well as a cluster of K-bomb launchers on each shoulder and mounts for small, laser-guided missiles, allowing Zion's company to serve as a heavy weapons support company. These Mk 7s could dish out a lot of punishment from a distance; they were practically mobile artillery platforms the Korps could use in engagements.

Mobility was the enemy of 3rd Company, however. Zion knew from experience he would have to make changes to the overall setup of the armaments. He loathed losing the heavy armor, so something else would have to go. The laser-guided missiles wouldn't be much of a loss and would lessen the load of each CASPer by almost 18%. The reduction in weight would allow them to regain some of their lost maneuverability.

The four MACs were pointed directly at the heads of the two men currently intruding in Zion's personal space, and only orders from his boss were preventing him from eliminating them on the spot. That and because the subsequent cleanup of splattered Human remains would be tedious. Even so, it was a very tempting idea.

"I'm sorry, Mister Jacobs…" the man on the left whined in a heavy coastal accent. Zion pegged him immediately as being from Salone, and his distaste grew. He really did not like the area, though if pressed he could never exactly say why.

"It's Captain Jacobs, Kakata Korps, 3rd Company Commander, sanctioned member of the Mercenary Guild," he said his official title as he stepped forward menacingly. "And your presence here is beginning to irritate me. If you leave now, I won't have the boys behind me start shooting."

"That would be illegal!" the second squeaked. Zion eyed him and nodded.

"Shooting *at* someone is illegal," he corrected. "As a lawyer, registered as such in both the United States and Liberia, I will remind my clients that shooting *randomly* is perfectly legal and within their rights as members of the Mercenary Guild who happen to be testing their equipment. However, if two government *gawnnas* accidentally wander into their firing range while they are conducting their tests…there's no way we can be held responsible for an accident, *ken*? Guild Law protects us in this regard. Guild Law usurps any law of Earth, *menh*."

The two men shared a look and quickly left the premises, leaving a very disappointed Zion behind. He turned and looked at the duo in the CASPer suits.

"Okay, secure the compound and make sure they didn't 'appropriate' anything in the name of the government," Zion ordered, sighing deeply. "Have the rest of the men double-check the outside fence. I need to find out what happened to our site security."

"Yes, *bass*," Master Sergeant Christian Nuhu, his senior NCO, said from within his CASPer. "Want someone with you?"

"I'm fine," Zion told him as he pinched the bridge of his nose, a pained expression on his face. "They're not hanging around, and word has spread already that we're back. They'll be running like rabbits."

"What do you want us to do, *bass*?" Nuhu asked.

Zion sighed. "I'm not happy with what the government was doing here. I want to find out why they weren't in their designated areas, what they probably stole, and where our hired help went. Not necessarily in that order."

"Got it, *bass*," the master sergeant said and turned to look at the other CASPer. "Sergeant Bayed, you heard the captain, break into teams of three men each. I want Sergeant Kepah on perimeter, you secure the warehouse, and have Corporal Williams start inspecting the seals on all the boxes. I'm going to check the armory."

As the two CASPers lumbered away, Zion felt the beginnings of a headache form in his frontal lobe. Blaming stress, he walked through the disheveled warehouse, taking particular note of what had been ransacked and what had simply been destroyed by the looters.

Zion's first sign of trouble as they had approached the Kakata Korps headquarters was when he spotted the graffiti on the massive stone lion Mulbah had put up at the former main gate. The Liberian flag which had hung from it was also gone. Only after some inventive swearing and cursing did he notice the sentries who were supposed to be guarding the Lion's Gate weren't there. The Korps were assigned a relief force, courtesy of the Liberian government, to watch over their main base and storage site while the mercenary company was off-world. There were also supposed to be hired guards the Korps had paid for out of its own pocket, none of whom could be seen anywhere. Dismounting from the transport, Zion ordered 3rd Company to spread out while he investigated the guard shack just outside the gate.

Unsurprisingly, all the radio equipment had been ripped out. The slates, which were to be used by whoever was on duty at the time, were both gone. Even the motorized gate opener had been stolen, leaving the chain-link fence perched precariously on the rail, and could only be opened manually by Zion and his men. The security cameras on top of the posts, as small and innocuous as Galactic tech could make them, had been pilfered as well.

Once they opened the main gate, 3rd Company proceeded onto the base, covering a lot of ground in a hurry. When they reached the warehouse, they stumbled upon two men in the process of ransacking a small crate of unidentified goods Zion was almost certain had once been filled with slates. This angered him, since the crate of slates alone had been worth the national GDP of the five neighboring nations around Liberia.

Zion wanted the storage warehouse secured first, since everything in the Korps HQ building was under gene-lock and could only be opened by one of the Korps' five officers. The warehouse, where everything which made the Korps capable of deploying on a contract within hours, was far more vulnerable. It was most of the reason why they had agreed to the government's proposal of national guardsmen on their base. Not leaving the Korps much of an option in the matter, since not-so-subtle threats of "economic sanctions" had been tossed around by the sleazy representative from the Treasury Department, Mulbah and Zion had been forced to acquiesce.

As Zion prowled through the ruins of the warehouse, he began to wonder if those aforementioned sanctions would have been cheaper than replacing everything that had been destroyed by looters and only God knew who else. Given the fact quite a few of their goods—which had been stored on pallets—were all gone, including said pallets, suggested the Liberian government had probably been in on the theft as much as the regular criminals had. That was pure speculation, however, since thievery on a scale as grand as what had happened here could be accomplished by either side, as long as they had the proper tools and a flatbed truck to haul it all away in. Which was upsetting, Zion found as he walked along.

Sometimes the only difference between what type of crook the Korps dealt with was whether the individual was elected or not.

Times like this were when Zion had to reach down deep inside himself and find a quiet place, lest he go crazy and start butchering politicians in the streets. With a CASPer and a company of men backing him up, he could potentially turn Liberia into an anarchist's paradise in short order.

Breathe, he told himself. Just breathe. At least we're not Somalia. Not yet. Just breathe or you're going to stroke out.

"Goshawk Six, this is Goshawk Four Romeo," a voice came over Zion's pinplants.

"Go ahead, Four Romeo," Zion responded as a mental image of Corporal Koffe Dayo was helpfully brought up by his pinplant, as well as his position in Second Squad. The rage was fading slowly into the background as his mind focused on something other than bloodshed and dismemberment.

"*Bass*, we caught some looters near the back of the warehouse," Corporal Dayo informed him. He sounded troubled to Zion, which was odd. The NCO from Burkina Faso was not a man who was disturbed by much, as he was one of the many who had seen his home country go to hell in a hand basket at an early age.

"Handle it," Zion said in a terse voice.

"I can't, *bass*."

"What?" Zion blinked, confused. This was not like the corporal at all. "What's wrong, Corporal?"

"*Bass*...I don't know how to handle this. Requesting official assistance, over."

Zion blinked. The men of Kakata Korps were getting better at their radio discipline, but as far as he knew nobody had ever requested official assistance on any matter while in 3rd Company. Mulbah gave his officers quite a bit of leeway to handle issues as they cropped up, and Zion had taken this tactic and applied it to the unusual formation of his company. It had proved to be an effective tactic in team building and caused many previously unheralded privates to ascend the ranks. He trusted his NCOs almost as much as Mulbah trusted Zion's command of 3rd Company.

"Copy, Corporal," Zion replied as he brought up a mental image of the warehouse. He pinged the GPS on Corporal Dayo's CASPer and found him almost immediately on the opposite side of the 50,000 square foot warehouse. He swore softly. "Be there in five. Hold them prisoner until I arrive, over."

"Roger, *bass*. Dayo, out."

"I wonder what the hell is this all about?" Zion whispered as he began the long trek to the other end of the massive warehouse. Warehouse Zero was one of the few buildings the Korps had left standing when they bought the old shipyards from the government; they had left the name alone while doing a lot of work around the property and beyond. Even a small starport had been built, albeit with the reluctant approval of the now-former president and his congress. The bribe alone had been enough to fund the government for almost six entire months, before the first run of increased taxes had kicked in.

Of course, none of the citizenry outside of Monrovia's city limits had seen any of those credits. Zion wasn't about to point fingers and blame anybody, but he had spotted Liberia's previous president's newest personal yacht just off the coast before their last deployment, and it happened to have been filled with many young, beautiful women, so he had plenty of suspicions. The argumentative contract lawyer in him screamed bloody murder every single time the Liberian government ratified a new levy on Earth-based mercenary units who happened to headquarter in Liberia. Lo and behold, there just happened to be only one such company who was stupid—or patriotic, Zion could never be sure—enough to do this. Color him shocked at this random and completely surprising development.

Zion sighed. If his anger kept growing at its current rate, he was going to have a difficult time looking the former President of Liberia in the face the next time they met without punching the bastard. Like he needed to create a bigger diplomatic incident than the one which was already looming over their heads after this fiasco.

On second thought, he corrected as he rounded a large cluster of empty boxes and found a CASPer standing guard over a darkened corner, if they lump it all into one punishment, maybe I should just go ahead and punch the asshole. I could claim Guild Law and request a trial through them. That...might get me out of serving prison time on Earth, at least. The idea made him feel slightly better.

"Corporal," Zion announced himself as he drew closer. The CASPer unit took a step back and the overhead light illuminated the corner better. Zion slowed, then stopped as he saw a group of four young children huddled there. At their feet were some of the prepackaged MREs the Korps used while on deployment. One or two had already had their covers torn open and the kids were eating them cold. All were clearly malnourished. Zion stopped dead in his tracks, stunned.

"What the hell?"

"*Bass*, I didn't know what else to do," Corporal Dayo proclaimed, his voice shaky over the pinplant. He waved one of his CASPer's arms at the foursome. "They were cold and hungry. I didn't...I just...well, look at them!"

"It's okay, Corporal," Zion replied, thinking fast. He needed to get control of the situation before Dayo went out and administered justice on his own. "Good idea, making sure they stay in a corner where it's warmer. I didn't notice how cold it was outside when we first got here. Since I'm here, why don't you go over to Section Eight and find some of the winter clothing we have stored. Those boxes still looked sealed when I passed by them earlier."

"Ye—yes *bass*," the corporal stammered slightly and moved his CASPer away, leaving Zion alone with the four children for the moment. He waited until the corporal was out of earshot before questioning the children.

Zion tried English first. "You understand me?" All four children—three boys and a girl he discerned after a brief inspection—nodded. Zion sighed in relief. He didn't speak the mashup up of English and Liberian which dominated the country, and he highly doubted the kids understood French, though there always was a slim possibility since it was a popular language with the Christian missionaries who ran the schools out in the bush. He continued slowly, in plain English. "Okay. You're not in trouble...well, not in trouble *yet*. But I need you to answer some questions. Be honest and don't lie to me, and I'll let you eat all you want and give you clothes. Agreed?"

He wasn't about to deny these kids food, but he also understood how their minds worked. Food was one hell of a motivator. Slowly, the children nodded their heads. Zion took a deep breath and stomped down hard on the anger boiling within. He knew who these kids likely worked for and why they had been sent back after everyone in Monrovia undoubtedly knew the Korps had returned to

Earth. It pissed him off to an extent he hadn't felt in about three minutes.

Zion really needed to watch his blood pressure. A coronary would not be the way to go, not as a young and relatively healthy mercenary.

"Who sent you in to steal from the Korps?" he asked. All four children stared at him with terrified expressions. Zion frowned slightly. He needed confirmation of his suspicions before he could execute Guild Law and arrest the crime lord on its behalf. There could be no doubt. The children remained silent, so he tried a different tactic. "Have you ever wanted to be a mercenary? Fight for the colonel and the Korps?"

Only the little girl nodded. The three boys refused to budge, reminding Zion of frightened rabbits when cornered. His only hope would be the girl. *So be it.* He'd dealt with worse situations in his life, though he couldn't think of any at the moment.

"*Bass?*" Corporal Dayo's voice interrupted his brief interrogation. Zion looked over his shoulder and saw the corporal had decided to bring the entire wooden box filled with supplies, instead of trying to dig through them and pull out packets individually. "There are sweaters in here, *bass*. Also some MREs. The good ones though, not the sh—*ken*, stuff the government tried to sell us."

"Good work, Corporal. Keep an eye out and watch my back for a moment."

"Got it, *bass*."

Zion looked at the three boys and tried to give them a friendly look. "That box has sweaters and MREs. Clothes and food. You can take them with you if you want, no questions asked. These MREs are the good ones. Those you had with you when the corporal…ah, *found* you taste bad cold. The good ones taste fine without being heated. You can have the sweaters, too. Last night it got pretty cold, didn't it? Go ahead and take one or two for each of you."

The boys moved to the box, warily watching the CASPer looming on the other side and reached into the container. When the boys took two sweaters each instead of one, Zion didn't say anything. He merely watched as they pulled the sweaters on, doubling up before they began to snag as many MREs each as they could. Once they were full-up, they looked at Zion expectantly.

"Remember, the Korps are here for Liberia," Zion told them. "You don't need to steal from the Korps. If you ask, we will help. Understand?"

The three nodded, slowly, their eyes never leaving the CASPer standing watch. Zion sighed. The boys wouldn't be able to help him, not at all. They were either too afraid of what would happen to them if they did, or they didn't know who sent them in, only the promise of food was too alluring to pass up. It was just one of those things which made Zion long for Philadelphia. While the city had its sore spots, even the worst neighborhoods in the City of Brotherly Love were better than the majority of what he'd seen in Liberia and the surrounding countries.

"What about you?" he asked the girl. "Sweater?"

"The big *bass* gives food and clothes to kids, too," she retorted, still eyeing him nervously. It was clear to him there was very little trust in the girl's mind. He couldn't blame her, not really. "Then he take everything...*everything*."

Zion gritted his teeth and tried not to snarl. "I promise not to...take anything if you want a sweater or two, or even food. Please? It's yours. I just need to know who the boss—your *bass*—is."

She stood up slowly and Zion suddenly realized she was older than the three boys by a couple of years. He had expected a girl of ten or so, but the girl standing before him was a tiny, malnourished teenager at least. The three younger boys continued to watch her as she slowly walked to the box, grabbed some of the smaller sweaters, and pulled them on. Bundling up, she ignored the food before moving back to the corner. She sat down on the warehouse floor and continued to eat the cold MREs which had already been opened.

"You don't want the ones over there?" Zion asked, mildly surprised. She shook her head.

"Don't want to waste these," she replied in a quiet voice and continued to dig her fingers into the MRE packet, pulling out what looked like sweet and sour pork and popping a piece into her mouth. Her eyes never left Zion, though, even while eating. Not sure what else to do, Zion sat down across from her. He pulled his knees to his chest and simply waited until the girl was ready to talk.

"What's your name?" he asked her after she had finished off the first MRE packet and started on a second.

"Sunshine," she responded around a mouthful of what looked like Salisbury steak or simply a hamburger patty smeared with brown gravy. Zion couldn't be certain.

"That's different," Zion said before checking himself. His mother had named him "Zion," after all. Who was he to criticize anybody else's name?

"The major general *bass* man gave it to me," Sunshine replied, chewing her food noisily as she continued to eye him. Her eyes were unusually colored, green with smatterings of brown. Her hair had a hint of red in it, which confused him a little. It suggested her family was from out in the bush somewhere east, but it didn't match her accent or personality. Her skin was as dark as his, yet there were enough differences in her face to suggest she was not even from Liberia. If this were the case, then where had she come from? Ghana, perhaps?

"The major general?" Zion asked, suddenly hopeful, as a piece of the puzzle was revealed as well as where it could possibly fit. There were only a few of the self-stylized "generals" who roamed the streets of Monrovia with their little gangs. They wanted to be warlords like those of old, but had only managed to succeed at petty theft, protection rackets, and running prostitution rings. Basically, small men with big dreams, he realized as a plan to crush them came to mind.

Sunshine nodded. "Major General Sparkles gave me my name. He say I remind him of a bright day."

Armed with a form of identification now, Zion's pinplants began a search for any information on one Major General Sparkles. As absurd as the name was, he'd seen and read worse. Unlike some of the others in the Korps, Zion had a college education, which meant at some point he'd learned to do his own research outside of the classroom. The history of his parent's homeland had been something he'd been interested in during his first year of college, when it quickly became apparent his upbringing was far different than the typical Liberian home.

He found Major General Sparkles quickly enough. The police department of Monrovia had an extensive list of crimes he was accused of but, unsurprisingly, no charges had ever been filed. Nobody wanted to testify against him, and nothing ever seemed to stick. He was the worst sort of street scum, a degenerate who preyed upon the weak and young to do his bidding, using their malleable minds to commit heinous acts while he kept his hands clean. Keeping control of his "soldiers" through various drugs, the major general was the kind of man Mulbah and the Korps would gladly stomp out of existence.

Zion swallowed, hard. His throat felt tight. His voice was raspy as his tumultuous emotions caused bile to rise up into his throat. He'd never felt anything like this before. This was beyond pain, beyond anger. It was pure, righteous rage. It took him multiple attempts to clear his throat before he could speak.

"3rd Company, meet in the briefing room, one hour. We have a mission."

\* \* \* \* \*

# Chapter Two

**SOGA HQ, Sao Paolo, Brazil District, Earth**

"Are you certain about this?" General Peepo asked her chief of staff as she set the slate down on the conference room table.

"Yes, General," Beeko said, nodding. Peepo's chief of staff was very excited. "Our models suggest that with a little nudging, we can encourage more Humans to take the VOWS and then they would be willing to work for us. This is most exciting."

"Indeed," Peepo nodded, though she was not entirely convinced. "Offer higher pay for those who would take the VOWS. Rewards, sweets, whatever motivates them. We need humanity on our side if we truly wish to rule this world. If the population of this planet obeys us, then the Horsemen will have nothing worth coming back to. This will crush their spirits and their will to fight."

"Yes, General," Beeko nodded. "One final note: Sansar Enkh has arrived safely at Capital Planet and is currently being held in the cells below the Mercenary Guild. Her trial is set to commence soon."

"Good," Peepo nodded, pleased. "Ensure the execution takes place soon after."

While not everything was going according to the plan, this was one area she had been most worried about. Getting Sansar Enkh in front of the Mercenary Guild council for judgement was tantamount to her plan's success, as the only way to ensure the total ruination of the Four Horsemen and to bring Earth to heel was through a guilty conviction of at least one of the Horsemen. She knew *that* was already set. Now it was only a matter of time.

"Very good, indeed."

After Captain Beeko left the office, Peepo heard a slight rustling behind her. Instead of looking around, she merely waited for the visitor to reveal itself. It was one thing to deal with a Grimm via comms, but quite another in person. She would never let the alien know how much it disturbed her.

"General," the SooSha hissed in a quiet voice. The skeletally-thin alien folded its arms across its chest and nodded politely.

"Administrator," Peepo replied in kind.

"The Information Guild agrees to your proposal," the mysterious alien informed her, not wasting any time for nuances or pleasantries. "You have forty-eight hours from the time we receive confirmation."

Peepo nodded. "And no information will get out, save for our own?"

"That was the bargain," the SooSha cocked its head and peered at the Mercenary Guild leader curiously. "Do you wish to…alter the deal?"

"No," Peepo said sharply. "I'm concerned about the Human Aethernet allowing information out which could harm the guild or the union."

"It is linked through GalNet," the SooSha reminded her. "Which means it is controlled by our guild. We decide what gets through, and what does not. Throttling their pathetic excuse for information transfer is…less than nothing."

"Excellent."

"And in return, you will tell us about the current location of the TriRusk world?" the SooSha asked, perhaps a little too eagerly. Peepo's eyes narrowed.

"The location of where they were seen last," Peepo countered. "This was the deal. It is your job to deal with the Peacemaker presence and the fallout afterward."

"I understand the difference perfectly, General," the Information Guild Administrator confirmed, not even the least bit abashed at the mild rebuke. "The Trade Guild is firmly on board with us. Just give the word and the countdown will begin. But…only for forty-eight hours, General. Any longer and some will grow suspicious."

The SooSha disappeared and Peepo shook her head. She hated dealing with the Grimm in any capacity, but given the importance of the meeting, she had been forced to. Even so, the Information Guild could make a potentially powerful ally in the coming war.

If the Mercenary Guild was going to save the Galactic Union, they would need everyone on their side. Before she could accomplish this, however, she needed to deal with the irritating, pesky Sansar Enkh, as well as the rest of the Four Horsemen.

Fortunately for the Mercenary Guild, she had a plan.

\* \* \*

**Executive Presidential Mansion, Monrovia, Liberia District, Earth**

Mulbah parked the car in one of the few open spots in the lot and looked around. A warm breeze blew across his face and the scent of saltwater filled his nose. Overhead, circling gulls cried out as they fought amongst one another for scraps of food and trash. The sky beyond was gray and cloudy, though he could just make out a few hints of sunlight peeking through. His pinplant suggested today would warm up eventually, but the mid-morning air was just brisk enough to suit him.

Looking across the street, his eyes rested on the ancient Capitol Building, built almost 150 years before. It was in dire need of a renovation, he realized. He was shocked to discover he was able to see the cracks in the mortar from so far away. Parts of the roof had been replaced with bright blue tarps to cover holes, and someone, within the past few months since he had last been here, had stripped away the gold-painted metal that had once topped the three domes of the building. In its place there appeared to be simple ceramic tile.

He made a mental note to hire some contractors privately to pay for the reconstruction of the Capitol Building. Outside of the president's mansion and the Korps' HQ, the Capitol Building was possibly the most important structure in modern-day Liberia. As bad as the politics of his homeland were, the edifice still meant something to the millions living within the country's borders. Not just as a symbol of hope, but of a nation which remained Africa's oldest republic. It had been built as a promise to the homeless, the destitute, of freed black men and women who left America behind to start a new life elsewhere. He would be damned before he let corrupt politicians lining their own pockets ruin the dreams of his ancestors.

*At least they finally poured the concrete for the parking lot,* Mulbah noted as he checked his uniform. He hadn't wanted to wear it but historically he was required. Even though the Kakata Korps was a private entity, his rank within the Liberian military was very real, albeit truncated. As a mere colonel, he normally wouldn't gain access to the

President of Liberia whenever he wanted. However, as Mulbah had proven time and time again, he was no ordinary colonel.

His dark green CADPat battle dress uniform, based off of the old Canadian design, had been pressed and ironed to the point where he was almost certain the starched creases on his sleeves could open a man's throat. A matching green belt and gold buckle secured his waist. On his right hip he carried his standard-issue Malketh Model 17 laser pistol. The black leather holster was shined bright enough to cause retinal damage if light reflected off of it at just the right angle. He wore his black commander's beret, black boots shined as properly as his holster, and the ribbon rack on his chest had been updated before he made the trip. Traditionally, the highest award given by the Liberian government went before all the others, but given his current mood and the point he was trying to make, all of his Mercenary Guild ribbons had been placed above his honorary Liberian ones. This included the CASPer marksman qualification ribbon. If the president had an eye for awards, it was surely going to drive Mulbah's message home.

If not, well, screw him, Mulbah thought as he walked toward the mansion. *I could always back a coup and depose him.*

Unlike the building across the street, the Executive Presidential Mansion had been extensively upgraded over the past few months. The most obvious were the wrought-iron gates protecting the entrance. Tall enough to deter most people, they were also thick and heavy. Mulbah was fairly certain they could stop most cars.

The grounds were also immaculate, a stark contrast to the rest of Monrovia he had seen on his way in. Even the flagpole had been recently painted, he noticed. On top of the pole flew the Liberian flag, so very similar to that of the United States. It reminded him that while he was one person, he had two distinct heartbeats. One beat with the compassion of his childhood in America, the second beat with patriotism for the land of his birth.

Guards stood on either side of the entrance wearing the Class "A" uniforms of the Liberian Presidential Guard, which had been instituted when former President Teah Njie was elected to office. They looked ridiculous to Mulbah, who favored the traditional camouflage design of the older Liberian National Army. Still, the bright blue uniforms and white plumed hats definitely caught the eye.

The two guards watched him as he approached, their eyes locked onto the Model 17 on his hip. They both carried ceremonial rifles of some design, though Mulbah was almost certain they weren't loaded. The rifles were painted white to match the feather plume stuck in their dress hats. Mulbah nearly laughed. What had been designed to impress visiting dignitaries and citizens of Liberia seemed to be worth nothing more than a humorous chuckle for the mercenary veteran.

A third guard stepped into view from behind a raised pedestal, halting Mulbah's approach. He was a big man, as tall as Mulbah but wider in the shoulders. It was obvious to anyone he worked out vigorously. Mulbah, who spent quite a bit of time in his CASPer suit, didn't hit the gym nearly as much, and it showed. He'd developed a little bit of a pooch over the last deployment. It was something he vowed to fix, eventually.

"Visiting hours are from ten until four, Monday, Wednesdays, and Fridays," the burly guard said in a terse tone as he looked Mulbah over. It was apparent to Mulbah the guard was not impressed with the uniform or the ribbons. "Today is a Tuesday."

"I hadn't noticed," Mulbah admitted. He often lost track of the days while off the planet and readjusting to Earth's schedule was a bit difficult for the first few days. "I need to see the president. I have an appointment, I believe."

"Name?" the guard said as he pulled out his slate from the pedestal. Mulbah could almost hear the disbelief. It was insulting.

"Colonel Mulbah Luo," he replied. The guard's head snapped up and he inspected him a second time. After a moment of this, the guard snorted in disbelief. *It's the pooch,* Mulbah decided.

"Sure you are," the man said and slipped the slate back behind the pedestal. Mulbah frowned, pulled out his universal account access card, and handed it to the guard.

"Here's my yack," Mulbah said irritably. "Check it."

The guard reluctantly brought his slate back out and scanned the card. A moment later his eyes widened in surprise as he handed back Mulbah's card. Then the guard snapped to attention and saluted. "My apologies, Colonel." Mulbah saluted back and the guard dropped to parade rest. "I was told you…well, I thought…" his voice trailed off.

"You thought I'd be seven feet tall, muscles on top of muscles, and with so many medals I wouldn't be able to stand upright?" Mulbah asked before laughing. The guard nodded his head sheepishly. "I'm a merc. We come in all shapes and sizes. Even if I am a bit out of shape at the moment."

"Yes, sir," the guard nodded. "Sorry for the delay. I'm new to this detail, sir. Do you know the way?"

"Yes, I do. Thank you," Mulbah said and waited for the guard to step aside. Mulbah thanked him once more, slipped him a business card for when the guard left the military, and entered the mansion proper.

Mulbah noted they had changed the carpet as he walked through the large, silent area. Since the legislature wasn't in session and no public tours were being given, the mansion was decidedly emptier than normal. There were a few office doors open with secretaries and aides talking quietly within. It felt more like a funeral parlor to him than a presidential home. He'd been to the White House in Washington, DC once as a kid. The president hadn't been there that day, but even then it had seemed more alive than this.

Mulbah had yet to meet the new president of Liberia. The election had been decided the day before the Korps had been shipped out to Krollenord, the dog-like Krolls' home world, on a protection and defense contract. It had surprised many, including Mulbah, to learn the People's Democratic Future Party had taken the presidency in spite of not earning a single seat in the legislature.

As crooked as Teah Njie had been, Mulbah at least had an understanding about how the former president worked. Bribery, then compromise, then a final bribe, and then the job would get done. It was a pain in the ass but at least he knew he could get results. *Probably,* he amended as his pinplants dug up more information on Liberia's current president, Justin Forh.

He blinked in surprise. President Forh, his pinplant informed him, was very distantly related to Charles Taylor, a former president of Liberia who had been deposed and later convicted of war crimes. In an odd campaign, the newly-minted president had run on the good memories of his ancestor, focusing on the growth of infrastructure and education for all. Which, if anybody had studied history, was not something Taylor had been known for at the time. History was oftentimes too kind.

Mulbah shook his head. In the end, politicians all promise the same thing.

As he approached the Peach Room, he had a moment of melancholy. Oval Office. Peach Room. 10 Downing Street. RCR 7. Each residence of a nation's leader held a certain mystique to it. Mulbah had always enjoyed the ambience of the Peach Room, even when the former president was threatening his company with economic sanctions. There was just something about being in the room that made him happy.

Striding purposefully into the waiting area, he quietly took a seat. Mulbah was a bit early for his appointment. Instead of bringing out his slate to see what was going on in the world since the Korps had left, he decided to enjoy the surroundings. Being patient would give the new president the impression Mulbah was eager to meet him. A lie, but not a bad one.

The new décor of the Peach Room suited Mulbah's sense of style. It was muted, a far cry from the loud and celebratory feel it had when Teah Njie had served as the nation's president. There were three paintings on the walls, and the wait allowed him to inspect them all in great detail.

The first was a bust of Liberia's first elected black president, Joseph Jenkins Roberts. It was a marvelous painting, Mulbah thought as he looked at it. The painter had somehow managed to convey the difficulties and trials of establishing a new nation into his eyes while setting the mouth in a manner which suggested determination. The colors on the right were dark and shadowed, almost predicting the bloody wars Liberia would face in the future, but the left featured more light and suggested hope for the people.

The second was an idealist's vision of a future Liberia, though not Mulbah's. It showed everyone working in a field, happy, singing, with the word "UNITY" printed along the bottom. Bright colors abounded, and the painting was clearly made to catch the eye. It was pure propaganda, Mulbah knew, but it was effective for the non-educated denizens in the slums of Monrovia. Zion would have laughed at it and called it Soviet propaganda, and Mulbah knew his financial officer wouldn't have been far off the mark.

The last painting was the one Mulbah liked the most. It was actually on his hard drive back at HQ, since he had been the one who took the picture over a year before while in his CASPer. The artist had stylized the look of the alien in the recording, primarily because Besquith are difficult at best to capture on film in the middle of a fight. It showed Captain Tolbert holding the Besquith out at arm's length, disemboweling the massive alien with the blades on his CASPer's arms. The artist had done an excellent job of capturing the tension in the scene. Mulbah made a note to find out who the artist was and to hire him to do more stylized recreations of some of the crazier fights they'd been in during their three years as registered mercenaries. A series of portraits would look amazing on the walls of their offices at HQ.

"Colonel?" A small, petite woman stuck her head out of a separate office door near the other side of the room. Mulbah stood and walked over to the door. She waved him inside but then stopped him, frowning as she looked at his belt. "I'm going to have to ask you to leave your weapon."

"Guild Law states that I am allowed, as a member in good standing within the Mercenary Guild, to be armed at all times unless otherwise stated by the Guild Council," Mulbah recited by rote. It had taken four visits and multiple rescheduled appointments before the previous president had finally relented on the "no weapons" policy when it came to mercenaries. He hoped with this president it would be a lot sooner.

"My predecessor mentioned you were a hard man to negotiate with," a warm voice said from beyond the door. The secretary sighed and opened the door wider, allowing Mulbah the opportunity to see his country's newly elected president for the first time.

President Forh wasn't an imposing figure the way Samson was, but he was definitely taller than Mulbah. Dressed in a nice but not overly expensive suit and a well-groomed beard, the younger man made a positive first impression on Mulbah, if appearances were anything to judge a man by. He offered his hand, which Mulbah gladly accepted as he continued to look the new president over.

"Congratulations on your election, Mister President," Mulbah stated as the other man nearly dragged him into a quick hug. Mulbah, startled, pulled back quickly as soon as President Forh allowed him.

"Sorry, sorry," the president apologized. "But you are a celebrity, *menh*. Never in my wildest dreams would I have imagined ever meeting Colonel Mulbah Luo, owner of the mighty Kakata Korps!"

Mulbah blushed slightly and coughed, embarrassed. "I'm just a merc, sir."

"Ha! 'Just a merc,' he says." President Forh motioned for Mulbah to sit in one of the two proffered chairs. Once he was seated, the president took the chair opposite him. "You've created a legacy here in Monrovia, and Liberia on the whole. You've helped establish a new Mercenary Service Track school here and ensured it doesn't have half the corruption its predecessor did. Then you actually hired mercenaries who passed their VOWS! My political opponents claimed you were running a tax evasion scam, but not I. I believed in the Korps; I still do. The people do as well. And because they believe, I was elected by them."

Mulbah wasn't certain that had been the reason. Rampant corruption had plagued the former president's staff and his tenure in office. That probably had more to do with the landslide victory for Justin Forh. However, Mulbah was skilled enough in diplomacy at this point to leave this little tidbit out of the equation and give the president his moment.

"Thank you, Mister President," Mulbah nodded slowly, thinking. He had not expected this type of reception when he had made the appointment. After years of dealing with a trumped-up blowhard, Mulbah had not anticipated a politician who actively wanted to do what was best for Liberia. It was...refreshing. And, Mulbah had to admit, a little terrifying. "I was trying to establish schools for children as well—free of course—but was met with reluctance by your predecessor."

"How many schools do you wish to establish?" President Forh asked, leaning forward. "My Education Minister will do what I tell him, and I can write an Executive Order giving him carte blanche over the educational reforms in the private system. It's not public education, so the legislature can't complain about that now, can they? Plus, funding won't come from government coffers, so they can stuff it, *ken*?"

"Two at least," Mulbah admitted. He wasn't sure what exactly he was feeling at the moment, but the best he had to offer was hope.

The meeting was going far better than he had imagined in his wildest dreams. "More if we can…" his voice trailed off as he realized he had almost let slip the offer from the Mercenary Guild.

"More if…?" President Forh prodded gently. Mulbah swallowed and decided to see what the new president's mettle was made of.

"The Mercenary Guild asked the Korps to, ah, help settle down the issues with our neighboring countries," Mulbah said quietly, uncertain as to who might be listening. "They've offered the countries from Ghana to Senegal for us to rule, if we can bring peace to them."

"Us as in Liberia, or us as in…?" President Forh motioned at Mulbah, who nodded. The President of Liberia steepled his hands before him and leaned forward. He wore a troubled expression on his face. "Correct me if I'm wrong, but those are democratically elected countries. It is not proper for us to consider usurping their own democracies to enforce our will."

"According to the guild, Earth is not capable of ruling itself," Mulbah said, recalling all the information he had received from Thorpi prior to accepting the contract. It was helpfully stored on his pinplants. "They've determined it is in Earth's best interests for the guild to make the majority of the decisions. It's why the head of the guild is currently at the Secretary of the General Assembly's office as we speak. After all, Earth is merely a probational member of the Galactic Union."

"I had not heard," President Forh admitted. "Why do they wish for you to rule western Africa?"

"I think they were trying to tempt me with a prize if I put down any remaining mercenary companies here on Earth who won't play ball with the guild," Mulbah stated, a sour taste in his mouth as he finally admitted it out loud. "The Horsemen did break guild law, but this? I think this is an overreaction to the problem."

"The charges laid upon them by the guild are very steep," President Forh reminded him. "Violating galactic law is a way to get our membership revoked, is it not?"

"Which is why I accepted the guild's offer," Mulbah declared. "If the Korps can keep a lid on Africa and bring the other merc companies in without bloodshed, I can help protect Earth. Not from itself, but from the aliens."

"This is your plan then?" President Forh asked.

"It's all I've got," Mulbah admitted. "It's the job nobody else was willing to do. They ask for noble sacrifices in their fight to be heroes. They want people to rise up and battle on, against impossible odds, on planets far away from here. The problem, though, is the Horsemen have ignored what's most valuable about our planet, what makes us *Human*."

"What is that?"

"Our love of all Human life."

\* \* \*

After the meeting, Mulbah checked his messages and saw he had missed a call from Samson. He quickly brought up the message and all his hopes of saving lives and avoiding needless bloodshed sank as he listened to the shaken man.

"Colonel," Samson began speaking, a hitch in his voice which Mulbah was not used to hearing from the calm and placid individual. "I screwed up and it led to the deaths of fourteen mercenaries from the Taranto S.R.L. There's still some mercs down there and they're refusing to come out. They're underground so I'm going to flood them out. I think they have an underwater tunnel leading to the mainland, though. One wounded, but it's Antonious—uh, Captain Karnga, *bass*. Took a MAC round in his upper chest, near the shoulder. He's stable for now but the medic says he needs a trauma doctor. He's on his way back to HQ now. We're continuing with the mission."

The video message ended, and Mulbah sighed and looked out at the Atlantic Ocean. He'd wandered out to the rear of the mansion after the successful meeting with the president to contemplate his next step. The first and most obvious would be to find a trauma doctor who could look at Antonious and determine the extent of the damage from his wound. Captain Tolbert would be next, since Samson obviously needed some sort of encouragement. If the mission in Liberia wasn't so important, he'd drop everything and head to Italy in his CASPer.

No, he would have to stay in Liberia for the time being. There was too much work to accomplish. However, he could tell Samson to continue his work with the Italians while having 2nd Company bring Antonious and his CASPer back to Liberia. Then Antonious could get decent treatment in the base HQ and perhaps come away with all body parts attached. Mulbah knew what a MAC could do to flesh, even with the armor of a suit in the way.

He pinged Zion to let him know he had wounded incoming, but the 3rd Company commander's comms were isolated. *That's weird,* Mulbah thought as he tried again. No response. Frustrated, he grumbled quietly under his breath as he switched channels.

"I'm gone for a few hours and everything goes to hell. Major, are you there?"

"Yes, Colonel," Thorpi replied almost instantly. "How'd it go?"

"I'll tell you in a bit," Mulbah answered and eyed his surroundings. "Can you run a trace on Zion?"

"He's out on Bushrod Island," Thorpi informed him. Mulbah bit back an exclamation as the alien continued. "He told me he was going dark to take care of an issue, and he would be back on in an hour, two tops."

"Copy," Mulbah growled, displeased. "He could have at least…no, he knew where I would be. He went to you next. He followed the chain of command. Good on him. What's next?"

"Captain Tolbert needs to speak with you as well," Thorpi said. "He says it's rather urgent."

"I got the message," Mulbah said. "I'll call him next."

"Yes sir. Colonel?"

"Yeah?"

"Go easy on him," Thorpi suggested. "Accidents happen, especially in combat, no matter how well-trained you are. Remember his past, and your own, sir."

The comms went dead, and he stood alone for a long moment, staring off into the distance. Thorpi was right. There was a time to berate a junior officer and a time to teach. This was a teaching moment, as well as a way to try and console the man. He knew of Samson's past. This was tough for anyone to deal with, doubly so for the former child soldier. Mulbah made a promise to keep this in mind as they talked.

"Captain? It's Colonel Luo," Mulbah said as he activated his pinplants to return Samson's call.

\* \* \*

**Bushrod Island, Monrovia, Liberia District, Earth**

Zion walked calmly down the unnamed street, one of hundreds scattered between the random homes. The dirt roads were endemic of a larger problem in Monrovia, which was a lack of modern infrastructure. Many of the homes had plumbing at least, but not all. Running water during the summer season was hard to come by as the rivers which flowed through the region slowly dried up. It was even worse further inland, away from the city.

In this part of the city, gangs were a huge problem. However, they weren't gangs in the same sense as Zion had dealt with back in the United States. Here the gangs were usually little children running around, trying to steal stuff from people walking down the street with their arms full. They would approach, use little knives to slash open pockets, bags, or anything else they could get their hands on, then scatter before the victim could do anything. The little thieves would then take it back to their boss, who might feed them in exchange for the stolen goods. More often than not, though, since poverty was so high in the area, all the kids received were beatings for not bringing back anything worthwhile. Or they were robbed by bigger, stronger kids for what they were carrying.

Zion had forgone his CASPer suit, though the men in First Squad were backing him up and were fully equipped. He had left Master Sergeant Nuhu back at Korps HQ with Second Squad to finish cleaning up the mess left by the looters. The Senior NCO had not been happy about it, but with First Squad in their CASPer suits and Zion not backing down one iota, the master sergeant had relented. Mostly.

While he was not in his CASPer, Zion had donned body armor which had the ability to stop nearly every type of chemically-propelled small arms fire on Earth. It was a concession Zion made for the master sergeant, and Christian had not been about to let his company's commanding officer walk around Monrovia without body armor of some sort. Reluctant at first, 100 feet from the secured grounds of Kakata Korps HQ he had come to see the wisdom behind the master sergeant's demands.

Zion had been sheltered from the roughest parts of the city when he and Mulbah had travelled between headquarters and the president's residence. For the most part, he had spent the time looking into the data and the new tax laws the legislature had passed on the Korps after each successfully completed mercenary contract. It was only when they pulled into the parking lot that he would come out from within his pinplants and realize where they were. It had unintentionally prevented him from seeing the destitute and poverty-ridden streets.

This was one of the many things which both baffled and concerned him. It was the law for every Human being on Earth to receive a Basic Living Allowance, courtesy of the taxes collected by the General Assembly from every mercenary company. This money should have been enough to lift nations like Liberia, Burkina-Faso, and even Sudan out of poverty. However, just as people have proven time and time again throughout history, a government cannot be trusted explicitly by its populace. Liberia, while not the worst offender, was still plenty guilty of adding on their own taxation, after the fact.

Zion crossed a small "street" which was devoid of vehicle traffic and began to look for the house Sunshine had described. The young girl was adamant about not going with him, which told the merc far more than anything else she had said. She was afraid of this Major General Sparkles, and Sunshine struck him as a girl who did not fear much. Zion was not going to let any child live in fear, not as long as Mulbah and the Korps were trying to make Liberia better. It would be a slow process, but he was a patient man. Mostly.

To either side of his current position, and making their way down streets just out of view, Zion could hear the CASPers of First Squad ensuring the lawyer-turned-merc wasn't flanked by any of the Major General Sparkles' "troops." They were more for overwatch and intimidation than for any actual fighting, with First Squad's Sergeant Abraham Kepah leading the way to Zion's left. On the right was Sergeant Kepah's assistant squad leader, Corporal Mbutu Williams. Both men led three CASPers each as backup, though Zion doubted very much they would need them. This was a show of force, something he'd wanted to do for a while now.

He was scanning the dilapidated homes for the distinctive red front door covered in glitter, so Zion almost missed the wannabe-warlord's little spotter sitting on the roof of the one abandoned houses. It was only when the boy, no more than six years old, accidentally knocked off a piece of the tin roofing did he notice. Zion looked at the boy, who had a slate in one hand and wore a fearful expression on his face. He wondered just how much trouble the child was going to get into for failing to stay hidden. The mercenary hoped to deal with the issue of Major General Sparkles before the boy was punished by the wannabe-warlord.

"First Squad, be advised, I've got eyes on a spotter," Zion murmured as he connected his pinplant to the rest of the squad. *Hell, was that slate one of ours?* he wondered as Sergeant Kepah helpfully tagged the location of the boy for all the others, which saved Zion the hassle of trying to maintain situational awareness while playing around with the program. "Williams, bring your team over this way; I think we're close."

"Copy, sir," Corporal Williams replied into his ear. Zion was glad he had grabbed the old-fashioned radio to communicate through his pinplants, otherwise the only thing he would have been able to do was listen. He had no idea how Mulbah was able to juggle both the incoming and outgoing calls with only his mind to track everything, though he strongly suspected the Korps' CO had gone ahead and had his pinplant completely upgraded to the maximum somewhere along the line. *Which suggested Mulbah had dealt with one of the mysterious Wrogul at some point,* he thought. He shook his head. It was time to focus on the task at hand.

The Mk 7s moved carefully between the run-down houses and joined Zion in the dirt street. Bushrod Island had turned into a veritable ghost town with the arrival of the Kakata Korps, as though everyone knew precisely why the mercenary company was there. It would explain the abandoned houses they'd seen along the way, though it might have more to do with their target than their arrival. Either way, this allowed the CASPers to move with a little more freedom than they would normally have in a busier section of the city.

Unsurprisingly, it wasn't the red glittery door of the house which told him he was at the right location, but the two young boys standing guard outside, each surprisingly well-armed with late model AK-15Ks. Why Zion wasn't surprised at seeing the ancient rifle here in Libera, he could not say. It was one of those odd factoids in life, like dialing a phone or saying one was throwing down the gauntlet.

The two boys, no older than twelve at the most, were attentive and held their weapons in a safe manner, Zion noticed with no small amount of surprise. This suggested whoever Major General Sparkles was, he made certain his young lackeys knew which end of the barrel the bullet came out of. Zion wasn't sure if he was comforted by this newfound knowledge or not.

"Hey, *menh*," Zion said, jerking his head up in greeting. He knew it sounded weird to their ears, since it felt strange coming out of his mouth, but he needed to get them to at least listen to him before they tried to shoot him. His armor would probably stop the AK's rounds, but he really didn't feel like testing it. "Your *bass* in?"

The two boys exchanged a look, and they shifted their feet slightly. Not a lot, but enough to tell Zion they were apprehensive about answering truthfully. Which meant the man he was looking for was there, Zion decided.

"*Bass*, how do you know this is the right guy?" Corporal Williams asked him. "I don't see a red sparkly door."

"Well, either way, we're talking to a criminal today," Zion said. "But I'm pretty sure this is the right guy."

"How?"

"Ever seen boys with AKs and glitter eyeshadow before?" Zion asked rhetorically. "Yeah, this is the right spot."

"*Ālek'awi izīhi yelemi,*" one of the boys said as he stepped forward. Zion's pinplant immediately translated it for him. "The *bass* isn't here."

"*Kezīhi t'ifa,*" the other instructed as his finger drifted toward the trigger guard. The tone and edge to the boy's words allowed Zion to figure out the meaning of the words as fast as his 'plants could translate them. "Get lost."

Zion took a step forward and said, "It's very important that I talk with Major General Sparkles."

In a flash the rifles were pointed directly at his chest. Zion raised his hands and shook his head, pointing with a finger at the CASPers behind him. He then drew a finger across his throat. Even with the language barriers his warning of what would happen if they continued down this road was plain. "Don't be stupid, kids. Go get your boss."

One boy lowered his AK and stepped inside the darkened doorway. The second kept his weapon pointed at Zion's chest armor but, the merc was happy to see, the boy's finger was no longer on the trigger. It appeared he might go another day without having to test the combat armor.

"*Ālek'awi wede wisit'i megibati inidemīchili negerewi,*" a voice called out from within the darkness a minute later. The boy guarding the door lowered his rifle but still looked at Zion distrustfully. The merc captain looked back at Corporal Williams.

"They're letting me in. Keep an eye out for rooftop snipers. Have your team spread out and cover the entrance. Direct Sergeant Kepah's team to form a perimeter around the place. Maintain comms with one another at all times. I'm relaying everything to you in case I need backup. Understand?"

"Yes, *bass*, I got it," Corporal Williams replied.

"Here we go," Zion whispered and stepped past the lone guard at the door.

The pungent stench hit his senses immediately. It was the ripe smell of unwashed bodies and stale sweat, mixed with smoke from whatever drugs they were doing in the house; it reminded him of burnt Brillo pads. The other boy was waiting for him inside the darkened room. His AK was slung over his shoulder, but the barrel was pointing at the back of the kid's head. Zion wanted to say something, but he didn't want to upset the kid, so he remained silent on the matter. It was an issue which could potentially be solved afterward.

Assuming the petty little major general didn't try to shoot his way out of this, Zion groused to himself as he eyed the kid.

"Come," the boy said in heavily accented English, motioning with his hand. "Come."

Zion looked around the room as his eyes slowly adjusted to the dim light. What he saw sickened him. Laying on soiled sofa cushions strewn about the floor were young boys and a few girls, all in various stages of undress. Fortunately, it didn't look like anything else was going on besides a decided lack of clothing options, but he was able to quickly discern from the odd, distant look in the eyes of the kids that they were high on something. Probably the latest psychotropic, but there was a litany of drugs to choose from, all of which were easily accessible within Monrovia and on Bushrod Island in particular. Whatever could be smoked and easily attained, Zion silently bet as he looked around and frowned. Opium, perhaps.

A lot of blame for this could be laid at the feet of the corrupt governments which had ruled Liberia for the past hundred years. Exports and imports were the primary reason the Liberian economy had managed to stay afloat from its founding all the way into the 21st century. With the arrival of the Galactic Union and the technology it offered, almost everything exported from Liberia had dropped in value. Meanwhile, the cost of stuff the country imported shot up exponentially, creating a massive trading deficit from which the country had yet to recover. This in turn led to massive poverty as business in Freeport dropped to almost nothing.

Mulbah's goal, Zion recalled as he tore his eyes away from the kids on the floor, had been to remedy this by creating employment opportunities for citizens of Monrovia working for the Korps. The biggest problem had been the natural corruption which ran rampant through the region. Even Antonious, a positive idealist if Zion had ever met one, knew Mulbah's goals would be damn near impossible until something changed within the mindset of their government.

As he moved into a smaller room off the main area, Zion took one final glance at the children which Liberia had failed in the past and wondered: was the Korps enough to change the future?

"Big merc!" came a loud, boisterous voice as soon as Zion stepped inside the room. It was brighter here due to a butane lamp hanging from the ceiling and another on a filing cabinet in the corner. Instead of a desk, a large chair dominated much of the room. It was gilded with gold paint and designed to look like a throne of some sort. Along the wall on either side of the chair were rows of neatly organized AK-15Ks, identical to the ones the boys guarding the front door carried. There were ammo boxes piled up haphazardly next to the filing cabinet and magazines wrapped together with oversized rubber bands on top of them.

Seated on his throne, barefoot but dressed in pleather pants and wearing a horrible leopard-print suit vest, was Major General Sparkles. There was no mistaking his braided hair and purple twists coated with dye and glitter, or the copious amount of glossy eye shadow, worn in exactly the same manner as the boys outside. Around his neck were three gold chains, though they looked pretty thin to Zion; he'd seen bigger on the lowest hustlers in Philly. *This guy's a fraud,* Zion thought with disgust. *He'd last a day, maybe, back home.*

"Big merc man, hello," Major General Sparkles said and smiled wide. His lower teeth were capped in gold, but his uppers were a strange mishmash of colors, almost like candy had been glued to them. *No, not candy,* Zion realized, struggling to hold in his laugh. *Are those plastic toy gems for kids? No, no way.*

"Do I call you 'major general,' or 'General Sparkles?'" Zion asked. Two more guards filed into the room behind him, making the tiny, crowded room feel even smaller. There were too many unwashed bodies in the room. The smell of burned metal pads and smoke made his eyes water.

"You? You can call me *bass*, big merc man," General Sparkles' grin didn't budge. Zion narrowed his eyes as he saw something in the self-proclaimed general's face which set his teeth on edge. He quickly sent two pings to the troops outside via his pinplant, warning them to be ready.

"I already have a boss," Zion said in a mild tone.

"He not the *bass* of my island, though," General Sparkles insisted. "Here, *I'm bass*."

"If you say so," Zion muttered. If the drug lord wanted to verbally spar with him, it would be his funeral. While a contract lawyer by training, he still had the chops to run verbal circles around any drugged-out man with candy for teeth. Zion continued, louder this time, "Mister Sparkles, I caught some children stealing from the warehouses at the Korps headquarters. We know they work for you. We want to know why you would steal from fellow Liberians? Why you would risk the wrath of the Mercenary Guild and the Kakata Korps to steal food? We would give it to you if you asked."

"I don't ask for nothing," the warlord spat as he slammed a fist onto the arm of his chair. The cheap material flaked off the armrest, revealing cheap plywood beneath the thin, gold paint. "I am *bass* here. I will take what I want."

"Yeah, that needs to stop," Zion told him. General Sparkles' eyes narrowed dangerously. Zion ignored the look and continued. "If it doesn't stop, we—meaning the Kakata Korps—will have to take drastic action. You know what that means, right?"

"You tell me what to do, on my island?"

"Son, I'm going to give it to you straight," Zion said as he laid on his best law school accent. Not for the first time did he appreciate the slight southern accent he had picked up while attending Tulane University. "You're on Kakata Korps' turf now. The only reason you're still alive is because we've been off-world fighting aliens, killing them, and then reaping bountiful rewards for doing it. I, personally, have killed Besquith, Goka, some lizard alien that we still haven't identified, Zuparti, and even an Oogar. *Once.* You would steal from us? From the Korps? Boy, are you out of your goddamned mind?"

Major General Sparkles fairly leapt from his gilded throne, snarling. His fake plastic gemstones glittered in the light and the gold grill adorning his bottom teeth almost fell out. Spittle flew as he yelled at Zion.

"You think you're big? You think you're bad?" General Sparkles stalked over to his wall and grabbed one of the AK-15Ks with one hand and one of the curved magazines with the other and then slammed it into place. He pulled the bolt back to chamber a round and pointed it at Zion's chest. "I show you who's in charge. I am the *bass*!"

"Corporal Williams, I sure as hell hope you can hear all of this," Zion said as he stood calmly in the center of the room. He took a deep breath and tried not to cough from the rank stench which flooded his mouth and lungs. "Blow it."

"Blow what?" General Sparkles questioned loudly in anger and confusion.

The wall to Zion's left suddenly exploded inward as Corporal Williams burst through the wall, his MAC up and ready. Dust, combined with the pre-existing smoke, obscured everyone's vision, save the CASPer driver. The gas lantern which had been hanging from the ceiling fell to the ground, dangerously close to the ammo pile. Zion jumped back and pressed himself against the interior wall as the roof above the CASPer began to buckle and collapse.

*"Baku!"* General Sparkles screamed as he turned his gun toward the mech suit and opened fire. The fully automatic weapon poured an inordinate amount of ammunition into the CASPer at near-point-blank range, but not a single shot from the thirty-round magazine did anything more than scratch the paint.

It did, however, cause ricochets to bounce wildly around the room. Zion swore and tried to duck as one of the stray rounds smacked into the dirt floor next to his foot. Another struck the wall where his head had been moments before, and a third glanced off his chest armor. He swore in surprise at the close call.

Corporal Williams pivoted and aimed the MAC at the obvious threat in the destroyed room, a quick five-round burst. The MAC rounds split Major General Sparkles asunder like wet tissue, painting the knock-off throne, the wall beyond, the ceiling, and the floor with the warlord's blood. The force of the multiple rounds drove the skinny criminal boss off his feet and into the wall. He slid down to the ground, dead.

Kids began to scream and run, the sound distracting the CASPer pilot and throwing everything into utter chaos. Zion, unsure what to do, tried to step in the doorway to block any of the kids from seeing the utter carnage Williams had made of their former provider and drug lord. He glanced back and grimaced at the sight. *That's a lot of blood.*

Unexpectedly he felt the sharp bite of a knife sliding along his ribs. Reacting instinctively, he rolled away quickly, kicking out with his right leg as he did so. He hissed as the sharp pain which grew as he stumbled against the wall. Glancing back, he saw his attacker was a boy, no more than nine or ten, armed with a tiny knife no bigger than Zion's middle finger. He felt blood seep into his undershirt and stumbled away, nearly colliding with Corporal Williams. The CASPer turned his MAC onto the boy but Zion yelled and pushed the arm of the mecha up and away.

"No!"

Corporal Williams refrained from firing. Zion, however, noticed his hands were now bleeding as well. He looked up at the arm and saw he had pushed at one of the extended blades of the suit with his unprotected hands. "Shit," he muttered, suddenly woozy as his palms began to *hurt.*

His hands were sliced open, exposing meat and tendons. Zion stared dumbly at the white thing inside the cut. *Is that the bone?* The pain wasn't so bad once he got used to it. That, or he was beginning to slip into shock. The mercenary commander wasn't completely sure which. He blamed the second-hand smoke from all the drugs out in the main area of the ramshackle house.

"Hang in there, *bass,*" the corporal told him as he stood protectively over the prone figure. More of the roof began to fall in and children poured out of the ruined house, running for their lives, believing the Korps mercs were there to kill them all. "Sergeant! One of the little bastards knifed the *bass!*"

Outside, Sergeant Kepah came to a halt after running the final one hundred meters to the house. He had observed the children fleeing and, assuming the worst, had quickly made his way to where his commanding officer was. Hearing Williams' statement, he almost fired on them until he recalled Colonel Mulbah's standing orders about the children of Liberia.

Accessing the situation, he barked out a new set of orders.

"Wallace! Clear the house! Make sure all the kids are out. Utu, Kromah, go to the back. Williams? Get the *bass* out of there!"

"He's hurt, Sergeant," Corporal Williams called out. "*Bass* is bleeding everywhere."

*Shit.* Sergeant Kepah realized Master Sergeant Nuhu was going to beat him senseless for this massive screwup. If he was lucky, Nuhu would get tired before he killed Kepah. "Get him out anyway. That fire is spreading, and it's going to cook off all those rounds, *menh*. You *ken?*"

"Yeah, on it," Corporal Williams replied. Using the suit's armored back to keep the debris from the collapsing roof off the captain, he gently grabbed his CO by the arm and tried to drag him backward. However, debris was blocking the way, and the corporal couldn't see how he could get the captain out without harming him further. "Sergeant, I have no safe exit for the *bass*."

"I'm on it," Sergeant Kepah said as he waded into the damaged house. The fire was growing, and the entire structure was going to be engulfed in a matter of minutes. Flames licked greedily at the debris on the ground, which appeared to be highly flammable. The sergeant knew they did not have much time before the ammo rounds cooked off in the heat. The entire neighborhood was at risk.

He tossed aside some old tin, which had once been the roof but was now blocking Williams' exit path with the captain. Moving quickly, the sergeant pushed the fallen filing cabinet away and kicked a few of the ancient rifles. Corporal Williams now had a path out of the burning structure, and he towed Zion out into the street to relative safety.

"Wallace? Grab Utu and knock down the building next door," Kepah ordered. "Make sure nobody is inside first. Pile up the debris in a circle around the fire. Keep finding empty houses and build a wall around the fire so the bullets don't hit anybody."

"Yes, Sergeant," they called out in unison and quickly began to dismantle the two closest housing structures. Both had been abandoned for a long time and the ruined skeletal structures were weakened by weather and age. In almost no time the two suits had taken the houses down and had a large pile of rubble before them.

Working as a team, they quickly built an artificial barricade. They stacked it as high as they could, erecting a thick, two-meter-tall barrier around the fire. It did not help stop the fire. However, they soon heard a *pop!* from one of the rounds cooking off, but it did not make it through their hastily built structure. The barrier would hold for the time being. Sergeant Kepah nodded in satisfaction and knelt down to check on his captain.

The hand wound looked bad, but Sergeant Kepah was more concerned about the stab wound. It was a deep cut, sliding just between the armor plates which protected Zion from the random gunfire. It had managed to go between the ribs as well, but other than a cursory scan there was nothing he could do. They had stupidly left the company's medic back at HQ, not even considering they would need him for this operation. A round might not be able to pierce the armor but a knife could apparently slide between the plates, Kepah noted. With as filthy as the street was, on top of the viciousness of the cut, the sergeant's experience told him a wound such as this could very well become infected in a hurry. They needed to get back to the Korps' secured HQ building and get Zion treated, and quickly. With luck, their captain would only have scars and a terrific drinking story to share later, when they were all out in a merc pit somewhere, drunk to the point of blacking out. Kepah radioed ahead for the company's medic to prepare to receive wounded.

Of the children who had been working for the late and unlamented Major General Sparkles, there was no sign. It wasn't as though Kepah could blame them. Even in the slums of Monrovia, everyone knew shit always flowed downhill.

\* \* \*

**Outside Taranto S.R.L. Mercenary HQ, San Pietro Island, Italy District, Earth**

Samson looked at the situation and nodded in satisfaction. The transport shuttle had landed and retrieved Antonious an hour before, leaving Samson in overall command of both 1st and 2nd Companies. It was a first for him, being in charge of so many mercenaries at one time. So far, everything was moving along like clockwork.

The CASPers of 2nd Company had found the tunnel leading away from the underground bunker rather easily. Once they knew what to look for, the underwater tunnel connecting the mainland to the island had been found within ten minutes. It was a mere thirty meters underwater at its deepest point, so Samson went ahead and had 2nd Company follow it to the mainland and seal the entrance on the mainland's end. He then continued digging the trench which would allow the sea water from the Mediterranean to flood into the underground compound on the opposite site, where the flatbed kept the bunker's blast doors jammed open.

In hindsight, Samson thought this structure's design was one of the dumber ideas out there. He wondered if the Italians trapped below had come to the same realization. Hindsight always improves one's vision, he had found over the years.

The surviving members of Taranto S.R.L. had attempted to barricade the concrete doors shut but their plan had been stymied by the Korps simply pushing the rear half of the flatbed trailer into the entrance. Given the front end of said trailer had been destroyed by the two drop pods, it had been relatively easy to move. The doors had tried to shut and almost succeeded, but the steel frame of the trailer held it open by a full meter. While not enough room for a CASPer to fit inside, it was more than enough to slowly flush them out.

"Chief Maloni, you and the rest of Taranto S.R.L. have five minutes to come out of the underground bunker, unarmed and out of your CASPers, or I'll have to do something I really don't want to," Samson declared across the open radio frequency. Around him, 1st Company waited expectantly for any signs of trouble. The Italians didn't reply, so Samson continued. "Your men and women will be treated in a respectful manner and will not be harmed. You will be turned over to the Mercenary Guild and placed in a detention center until a trial can be arranged."

"Go to hell, *moolie*," came the short, terse reply.

Samson sighed. "Fine, be that way, *menh*," Samson growled and killed the comm. He turned and looked at his men. "Sergeant Washington!"

"*Bass?*" 1st Squad Leader Sergeant Seku Washington wandered over.

"How's the tide?"

"Coming in now, *bass*."

"Perfect," Samson nodded. Scanning the depth of the trench 2nd Company had spent almost a full hour digging, he saw they'd done it perfectly, with a two-degree downslope from the edge of the water to the concrete bunker. The only thing left was to smash the pavement at the entrance, then patiently wait for the Italians to recognize the inevitable conclusion to the situation. Saltwater had already filled the trench to the brim and the rising tide, combined with the downward sloping angle, would fill the base in hours. It would be a slow, torturous besiegement. He tried one final time to get through to the Italian mercs.

"Chief Maloni, I don't want to drown you and your mercs," he said. "Just come out. Nobody else needs to die today."

Nothing. Samson sighed. He had known the men and women of Taranto S.R.L. were a stubborn and tenacious lot but this was absurd. He switched frequencies. "All right then. Master Sergeant Oti, knock down the last barrier."

"Okay, *bass*." 2nd Company's Top trotted quickly over to the concrete barrier preventing the water from the trench from going through the doors and into the underground bunker. The first sergeant leaned against the ruined flatbed and began to kick at the barrier, hard. After four solid strikes the concrete fractured. Oti bent over and began to scoop the crumbled material out of the trench. Slowly but with ever increasing speed, water began to flow steadily into the bunker.

As the water really started to pour in, Samson had his CASPer try to gauge the flow of water. From the looks of things, over ten gallons a minute were headed into the underground bunker. While he still wasn't sure how deep the bunker was, he figured it couldn't go much further down than the underground tunnel. It would take a few million cubic gallons of saltwater to fill the bunker but then, it was why it was called a siege, he knew. Things like this weren't instantaneous.

"Tick tock," he whispered as water continued to pour into the dark. The Italians were now on a timer. Samson knew eventually they would be forced to come out. The question was whether would it be peacefully, or if there would there be more unnecessary deaths?

* * *

### Inside Taranto S.R.L. Mercenary HQ, San Pietro Island, Italy District, Earth

"They're insane," Chief Sergeant Major Maloni muttered under his breath as he looked at the gathered mercenaries around him. It was far less than what the Korps had anticipated, since most had gone with the company's CO in the flight from Earth with the South Africans from Dood Wraak. Only a handful had remained behind, to be the eyes and ears in the region. The Korps had no idea just how badly they had hurt the numbers of Taranto's rear guard with their assault. And it wasn't as though anyone from Taranto S.R.L. was interested in telling them.

"How long until they force us out?" Corporal Major Guigliana asked, worried. She hadn't seen that much water in Level One since the underwater tunnel had sprung a leak soon after it had been installed. It had made her nervous then; this was terrifying.

"Ten hours, maybe nine," Chief Maloni acknowledged. He, along with the others who had been left behind, were all in their CASPers, though they knew if they walked out of the compound suited up they would get slaughtered by the Korps.

It was horrifying to watch their brothers and sisters in arms be disposed of so quickly. However, they also noted the Korps only opened fire after one of the Taranto S.R.L. mercenaries had shot first. This hadn't made any of them feel better, though. In fact, it made everything worse. The Korps, from the look of things, had gone out of their way to try and not get into a fight. Still, the bastards outside had killed their comrades, and only blood would repay blood.

First, however, they needed to get out of the situation they were in.

"What do you think our odds are, taking them head-on?" Maloni asked. He was looking at the monitor. There were multiple hidden cameras set up around the island. All but three had been knocked out by the Kakata Korps as they sought to deny them information. The chief was irritated at the utter ruthlessness of the Korps. He really hated dealing with professionals sometimes.

"Not good, Chief," Guigliana admitted. "They have something like twenty CASPers up there. Mk 7s, sure, but still pretty tough. The worst part is they know how to drive them."

"Escape tunnel?" the chief tried again. Guigliana shook her head.

"They blocked it off the moment they found it, remember?" she informed him. The chief cursed and looked at his slate.

"Out of options, I take it?" a quiet voice asked from the darkened corner. Chief Maloni looked over at the slight man, who also happened to be one of the main reasons why Taranto S.R.L. had held out in the first place. They were supposed to be the eyes of the Horsemen in Europe, yet had been discovered quickly. The man dipped his head. "There is no point in more needless deaths, Chief. There is no shame here, even if they are...what did you call them? *Moolies?*"

Maloni grunted. "I might have underestimated them a bit."

"No shit, Chief." Guigliana said in a sour voice. "I tried to warn you."

"Yeah, enjoy the gloating while you can," Maloni snapped back. He heaved a defeated sigh. "Shit, you're right. You were right. I'm going to go ahead and send out the terms for our surrender. I hope they'll listen."

"Let's hope they aren't carrying a grudge for shooting their guy," Guigliana added in a humorless tone.

\* \* \*

### Outside Taranto S.R.L. Mercenary HQ, San Pietro Island, Italy District, Earth

One by one the six remaining members of the mercenary company filed out of the bunker, their hands clasped atop their heads as they came. Samson and those of 1st Company who were available were covering them, their MACs trained on the approaching men and women. Samson knew his men weren't looking for a fight, not after the bloodbath they had participated in earlier. Still, it was a bit nerve-wracking for them all.

Samson did not expect a fight, not at this point, but he would be damned if he let them get the drop on his and hurt one of his men like they had managed to do with Antonious.

The leader of the group stopped and looked up at him. The Italian was not an ugly man, Samson decided as he inspected him, but the expression he wore upon his face was twisted and angry. Still, he had surrendered without any more deaths or injuries. It was enough for now.

"Chief Sergeant Major Maloni?" Samson asked. The man before him replied with a short, curt nod of his head. "I am Captain Samson Tolbert, 1st Company, Kakata Corps. You are hereby placed under arrest on order of the Mercenary Guild, and you will now be taken into custody. Do you have anything to say?"

"No," the man responded through gritted teeth. Samson understood this level of anger. He'd been there before, a long time ago.

Shoving those memories aside, Samson continued, "You will be kept in a secure facility until the date of your trial. I have been assured by the Mercenary Guild that your safety is important, and you will not be harmed in any manner."

"We need to look good for our show trial," a soft voice muttered from behind the chief. Samson shifted his CASPer slightly and identified the speaker. It was a short, skinny Asian man of indeterminate age with a very bland expression on his face. Samson could easily tell he was a merc. There were multiple scars running the length of his arm and the captain could see the pinplants just behind the man's ears. Samson blinked as he accessed the data storage system in his brain and came up with nothing.

"I don't have you on file," Samson admitted after a moment. "Are you a new recruit to Taranto S.R.L.?"

The man laughed sympathetically. "You could argue this, though I know where my true loyalties lie."

"Yack?" Samson asked. The man shrugged his delicate shoulders. "Misplaced it."

"C'mon, *menh*," Samson sighed tiredly. He was in no mood for games. It had been a long day and he was tired. "Don't toy with me."

"I am Lieutenant Tsolmon Enkh," the slight man told Samson after a moment of silence. "Golden Horde."

Samson blinked. "You lying, *menh*?"

"No lies," the man replied. "I remained behind to assist Taranto S.R.L., as ordered."

"You look kinda short to be in the Four Horsemen," Samson observed. "I heard they were all giants."

"That's Cartwright's Cavaliers," Tsolmon corrected with a wry smile. "Their commander is, ah, a tad overweight. A big boy."

"You really are in the Horde," Samson breathed. He looked around but none of the other Korps members were listening in. Taking a slight risk, he leaned in closer to the man. "Did you really betray Earth and do all the things the guild said you did?"

Tsolmon squirmed slightly before responding. "We did do some things which might be considered violating Guild Law, if strictly enforced and none of the other races in the guild weren't doing the same thing. Other than that, I cannot say."

"Fair enough," Samson nodded and stood upright. He scanned the other three surviving members behind Chief Maloni and Tsolmon. Two women, and two men, one of which who had a very nice prosthetic for his leg. He wondered where the injury had occurred before shaking his head. Questions could be asked later. For now, he needed to contact the guards who would be taking care of the prisoners.

"*Helios* One, this is Captain Samson Tolbert, Kakata Korps," Samson radioed. He knew somewhere overhead the Zuul transport shuttle was waiting to come down and transport the prisoners.

"This is *Helios* One," came a quick reply. "Do you have prisoners in custody?"

"Affirmative, *Helios* One," Samson confirmed. "Six prisoners ready for transport."

"Only six, Captain?" a voice came back over the radio. It almost sounded like a whine to Samson's ear. "We were hoping for more."

"Yeah, so was I," Samson muttered, thinking back to the ruined CASPers his men had spent the better part of the day removing from the island. Each would receive a proper burial on the mainland unless their families wanted something else. It was the least he could do for them, given the circumstances. They might be traitors in the eyes of the guild, but they were still Humans. He keyed his radio to transmit. "Confirm six prisoner pickups, *Helios* One."

"Fine," the voice came back, exasperated. "Touchdown in three minutes. *Helios* One, out."

"*Puk janga craw craw...*" Samson muttered once the link was dead. He was really beginning to hate dealing with aliens. Perhaps Asbaran Solutions had the right idea? What was it again? Kill aliens, get paid? Much simpler.

"Where are they taking us?" Tsolmon asked, curious.

"I'm not actually sure," Samson admitted after a moment of silent contemplation. "Possibly a jail near SOGA HQ in Sao Paolo? I don't know."

"Captain," a new voice interrupted them. It was Specialist Taylor, the 2nd Company's medic. "Status update. Captain Karnga is safely back at HQ and receiving treatment. The surgeon says he'll live, but he will probably lose his arm."

"Thanks, doc," Samson acknowledged and closed his eyes. As much crap as he gave Antonious over the years since they had first started working together in Spain, he considered the wounded man as close to being a brother as anyone could. The worst part of it was the 2nd Company was already showing signs of fraying with the loss of their CO.

The VTOL shuttle screamed overhead, making a quick pass over the island as it looked for a spot to land. Thirty seconds passed before the shuttle circled back around and slowed. It hovered over a large open area behind the concrete bunker entrance into the underground base and settled down, the shocks of the landing gear absorbing the heavy load of the shuttle easily.

The rear door dropped down and a squadron of Zuul in combat armor poured out, their laser carbines pointed at the six prisoners from Taranto S.R.L. as they hustled forward. The dog-like aliens looked uncomfortably at the gathered CASPers which were currently guarding the prisoners.

"Captain Tolbert?" a Zuul with a gold insignia on his chest called out as the Zuul approached. Samson raised an armored hand and the Zuul altered his course slightly. "I'm Subcommander Jisloon. I'm here to take charge of your prisoners."

"They're all yours, Subcommander," Samson said as he looked back over at Tsolmon Enkh. For some reason he decided not to mention the inclusion of the Golden Horde member in the prisoner roster. "Can I ask what you're doing with them?"

"You can ask, but I will not answer," the Zuul stated in a cold voice. "Your job was to subdue and apprehend. Mine is to transport."

"My contract was to arrest them, not to suffer you or your pissy attitude," Samson snapped back. "Take your prisoners, Pup."

The Zuul bristled but said nothing as he realized his squad was vastly outgunned. The alien's ears were back and flattened against his head.

"Don't get cocky, Human," he finally growled. "Your time will come, just like all the others."

Samson ignored the jibe and motioned with his hand toward the shuttle. "Those prisoners better arrive at their destination intact and unharmed, *menh*. You *ken*?"

The Zuul gave Samson a nasty snarl, pivoted, and walked off. Samson calmly waited as the prisoners were rounded up and guided toward the shuttle. Tsolmon Enkh cast one final glance over his shoulder before he was shoved into the shuttle by another Zuul mercenary. Once everyone was on board, the doors closed and the thrusters began to burn white-hot. The VTOL engines lifted the shuttle off the ground and the nose pointed out toward the Mediterranean Sea.

*I'm sorry I couldn't do more for you, Tsolmon,* Samson thought as he watched the shuttle take off and claw for altitude. It angled slightly to the southwest and rapidly disappeared from view. He tracked it via the CASPer's Tri-V monitors until it was beyond the horizon, his heart unhappy about the Korps' victory at San Pietro.

"I feel like I've done something wrong," Samson whispered quietly to himself. Unfortunately, there was nobody else there to help him feel otherwise.

\* \* \*

### Kakata Korps HQ, Freeport of Monrovia, Liberia District, Earth

Mulbah looked at the man standing before him. He was confused, and for a good reason. It was rare to see a white man in Liberia these days, especially one dressed as well as the individual who sat across from him. In addition, the businessman did not have any bodyguards, which was almost asking for trouble while roaming the streets of Monrovia. Mulbah glanced back down at the antiquated business card in his hand and frowned.

The air in his office was chilly in spite of the midday heat, thanks to the central air conditioner he had installed before they had left for Krollenord. The day promised to be a scorcher across Liberia, and the next wasn't going to be any cooler. It wasn't even summer yet.

*Gregory Donahue,* Mulbah read as he accessed the databanks via his personal slate. Former mercenary captain who'd gone into the defense contractor business at Mattis Aeorspace Solutions. They, in turn, had been around for roughly 75 years now, supplying mercenary companies with top-notch equipment. They were no Binnig, sure, but Mattis was definitely up there in quality and cost.

"How can I help you, Mister Donahue?" Mulbah looked back up at the contractor. Donahue was a big man, easily almost six and a half feet tall, and carried himself like a veteran merc who had seen many battles and was expecting another to start up at any given moment.

That could explain why he didn't bring any bodyguards, Mulbah thought as he reassessed the situation. Someone would have to be dumber than a jocko in heat to try to steal from this monster.

"It's how Mattis Aerospace can help you," Donahue corrected, a smile plastered upon his face. On anyone else it would have looked fake and insincere, but the smile seemed genuine to Mulbah. The big man gave off an aura of geniality. "We've been watching the Korps for quite a while now and have been impressed with your record. We've noticed some of your equipment, while outdated, is still performing at or above expectations. We would very much like to arrange a business partnership with you, Colonel."

"You don't have new CASPers, do you?" Mulbah asked.

Donahue chuckled as he shook his head. "We have some old Mk 7s that have been retrofitted for scouts," Donahue explained as he motioned at the chair opposite of Mulbah's desk. The colonel nodded and the contractor sat down. "But Mk 8s? Not yet. We've been in the process of assisting newer companies such as yours with getting older equipment to accomplish today's mission."

"I would literally give an arm for a few extra Mk 8s," Mulbah muttered.

Donahue nodded. "With some of our tech, we could either regrow an arm or have one hell of a bionic prosthetic made," the defense contractor confirmed. "It'll be better than the original. Tougher, more durable. Could probably hide a small laser pistol inside it, too."

"It's why I said that…" Mulbah's voice trailed off as he pursed his lips, suddenly thoughtful. "I appreciate your company's time, Mister Donahue, but I don't really see how you can help us in any way, save for a prosthetic arm. I happen to be in need of a high-end one at this time."

"We'll throw it in as a token of goodwill," Donahue nodded, evidently pleased he was making inroads with the mercenary commander already. "Whoever the individual is, I can have it fitted and shipped within the hour. But the real reason I'm here is a simple one: how long?"

"Excuse me?"

"How long until the Mercenary Guild decides your company is ripe for the plucking?" Donahue clarified for him. "Imagine it, if you will: your highly successful merc company has been making waves. You've already helped them take down one company which was violating Guild Law. That's good and all, but how long until they decide *you* have broken Guild Law? *Quis custodiet Ipsos custodes*, Colonel?"

"I think we're done here," Mulbah said as he abruptly stood up. Donahue's words struck too close to home with his own feelings and misgivings. It was something the colonel was not yet prepared to hear from someone he didn't even know. "You may leave at your earliest convenience. Thank you for coming by."

"My apologies," Donahue said as he followed suit. "I didn't mean to offend you. My job is to ask the tough questions and offer solutions. Let me make it up to you. No costs, nothing. I'll fit that prosthetic you were asking about for your merc. Consider it the beginning of an apology."

Mulbah paused, uncertain. Donahue seemed to share some of the same concerns as Samson did, and while Mulbah would readily admit the 1st Company commander had a point, he had no obligation to listen to some salesman there to sell weapons. Not yet, at least.

"That works. Antonious needs a bionic."

"Very well. Thank you once again for your time, Colonel," Donahue said as he stuck out his hand. He didn't seem upset to Mulbah, merely disappointed. The Liberian could live with this.

"I'm sorry you've wasted your time here," Mulbah said and shook the man's hand.

"On the contrary, I learned much," Donahue said as he released the grip. "I'm just happy to help your merc in need. I have a briefcase which was left outside your office at your Veetanho's insistence. In it I have the tools I need to fabricate the prosthetic. If you show me where to go, I'll gladly help."

"Um, sure," Mulbah said as he walked to his office door and escorted the salesman out of the offices. They quickly descended the stairs and walked across the warehouse floor to the medical ward, which currently housed a single mercenary.

The infirmary was quiet as they entered. Antonious was propped up on his bed, and his eyes were closed as his head swung rhythmically back and forth. It took Mulbah a moment to realize the merc was using his pinplants to listen to music in his head. How this didn't give him a headache Mulbah would never know. Prolonged pinlink use gave Mulbah a splitting migraine.

"Captain," Mulbah said as he tapped Antonious on the shoulder. The other man's eyes popped open and he looked at them in confusion for a moment before grinning. "Music?"

"Podcast, *bass*," Antonious corrected. "It was on a commercial break though and had some good music."

Mulbah nodded. "Captain, this is Gregory Donahue. He works at Mattis Aerospace, a defense contractor who deals with merc companies. He's going to fit you for a prosthetic."

"You mean I'm getting a new arm already?" Antonious asked, eyes wide. "I thought it would be a month, *bass*. I only lost lefty three days ago!"

Donahue spoke for the first time since they entered the ward. "The faster you get fitted for one, the less likely you are to 'forget' how to use those muscles. Your neural pathways are still fresh, if damaged, and the nerves are still working. It's why your arm hurts sometimes even when it's gone. The nerves think there is trauma and are trying to stimulate the healing process. Eventually it fades into a background ache and becomes nothing more than psychosomatic pain. Getting your prosthetic now will avoid the process altogether."

"*Bass*, does that mean I can still fight in my CASPer?" Antonious asked, surprised. Mulbah shook his head.

"The Mk 7s aren't equipped to deal with a prosthetic, not exactly," Mulbah admitted with reluctance. "I'll need to get my hands on an upgraded Mk 8 command suit that uses full pinplant interface to drive it. The Horde uses them, and a few others as well. I'll ask around. Once this happens, we can get you up and running again. The Jackals are already missing their *bass*."

As Donahue began taking measurements and talking to the captain, Mulbah stepped back and considered what Donahue had said earlier. While he did not want to believe the defense contractor, he definitely had a point about the gaze of the Mercenary Guild inevitably turning back onto the Korps. It was something Mulbah was not willing to talk about with anyone not in the Korps, though.

*No*, he decided as he watched Antonious' face light up like a kid on Christmas morning as the 3D printer began to print out a robotic hand. *I'll talk it over with Zion first. No more hasty decisions.*

\* \* \* \* \*

# Chapter Three

**SOGA HQ, Sao Paolo, Brazil, Earth**

General Peepo looked over the reports one final time, fur bristling, exposing her irritation at the situation. Keeping any of the prisoners in the building's converted holding cells might be an ideal short-term solution, but she was well aware the lack of proper defenses would make for a very short siege if any rescue attempt was made. She already had plans to upgrade the building's systems, but it would be easier to split the attacking forces into different groups to chase the bait and focus her own defenses here than to try and withstand a singular massive assault.

No, it would need to be somewhere else, she decided after a long pause. Using her slate, she quickly flipped through hundreds of sites which could potentially serve as a location for the mercenary prisoners currently being rounded up all over Earth. The Korps had managed to capture six in Italy, killing the rest, which amused her to no end. She hadn't thought they had it in them to kill their own kind, but Leeto's assessment was correct. Colonel Luo had no love for Earth as a whole. His sole loyalty was to the guild.

"That makes using you so much easier," she thought out loud as she identified a location which could potentially suit her needs and plans. It was an older facility in Nigeria, currently in use by some sort of drug warlord as a holding and torture center. It was disgusting, but also fairly defensible at the entrance, which meant the CASPer drivers had to abandon their suits before entering due to the narrow entrance. It was also solid enough so the issues which plagued the Taranto underground bunker on San Pietro wouldn't come into play in Nigeria.

The largest problem was the only Human merc company loyal to her and the guild within fifty thousand kilometers was the Korps. She had no problem sending them out to do her dirty work, after all, but the prospect Colonel Luo might balk at the proposal almost gave her pause. However, his psychological profile suggested he hated the warlords which had plagued Africa throughout history. In fact, Peepo was beginning to suspect there was very little on Earth the colonel appeared to like. Thorpi had suggested to Leeto this was the case, but Peepo had discounted it initially. Now, though, it was a different story altogether.

*Perhaps this is a blessing in disguise,* she thought as she messaged the colonel. He could clear out the compound, then her Zuul mercenaries would be able to come in and hold the position until it became untenable. *But how to ensure the Four Horsemen would attack the facility later without it seeming too easy or suspecting a setup,* she wondered.

A devious idea came to mind. She picked up her slate and began making plans.

\* \* \*

### Kakata Korps HQ, Freeport of Monrovia, Liberia District, Earth

Mulbah slowly walked around the storage facility, his mind awash with doubts and questions. For the first time since he had bought the company and moved them to Liberia, he was truly second-guessing the wisdom of his decision. Wearily, he brought up the contract information which had been forwarded to him by Thorpi earlier in the morning.

It had been very quiet since the 1st and 2nd companies had returned from Italy. For the past three weeks the Korps had recruited and trained from the growing population of Liberia as more and more people from neighboring countries came for the promise of schooling and jobs. They weren't mercs, not until they finished the MST and took their VOWS, but they could still work for the Korps. Monrovia was exploding with opportunity as the nation's president fulfilled his promise of less government graft and more money for infrastructure.

The mere fact that President Forh kept his promises still floored Mulbah. He had heard similar empty promises in the past and had learned to take anything a politician told him with a bucket of salt. But Liberia's president held true to his word. He had even managed to convince three of the countries General Peepo had suggested they conquer to instead enter into talks of a free trade zone—no tariffs, no fees, nothing. This had shocked and amazed Mulbah. It was an exhilarating time to be in the country, to be a Liberian.

There were downsides, however. Despite the wealth pouring into the country via merc contracts and trade, the ranks of the Korps were not growing with actual mercenaries. Thousands of people were taking their VOWS and failing, which caught Mulbah off-guard. In fact, the only person who had passed their VOWS at either of the established MST schools in Liberia thus far had been Zion's rescued orphan, Sunshine. Since there was currently no way to have her fitted with pinplants while in-country without significant risks, Mulbah wasn't certain how she would be able to drive a CASPer as well as the rest of the Korps until he could get her over to the United States. He had a spare suit, coincidentally, since Antonious was semi-retired from CASPer service due to losing his arm, but the option simply wasn't there yet.

Mulbah still needed a Mk 8 Command CASPer, however, for Antonious to come back. Without it, Antonious would struggle in his command role in 2nd Company as he tried to use the suit in ways it was not designed. If there were any suits in the world, Mulbah had no idea where they were. Rumors abounded. Alaska, Spain, Portugal, Egypt…all were locations where spare suits were rumored to have been stashed when the Four Horsemen left. None of the Zuul mercenaries who had been sent to find them had been successful, which was disheartening. Then again, Mulbah knew just how sneaky Humans could be. It was entirely possible the various locations were hidden and gene-coded to reveal themselves when Humans were near. He had used something very similar when encoding the doors to the inner sanctum of the Korps' HQ.

Distracted, Mulbah thought back to the message General Peepo had passed him via Thorpi. The orders read, "Obtain the prison known as New Ikoyi Prison in Lagos, Nigeria, to serve as a detention center for any and all captured mercenaries." Unlike past contracts he had dealt with, this had come down directly from General Peepo herself, which surprised him. There had been no bidding process or assessment waiting period, simply orders.

This did not please Mulbah, since he'd been promised a small amount of autonomy when it came to operations in Africa. The fact he hadn't been *asked*, merely *told* to go, irritated him. Still, it would be an easy contract with a fat payday, which offset the problematic nature of the deal a bit. This didn't answer the question about how

Nigeria would feel with the Korps tromping around in one of its bigger cities, but it was something he would be left to figure out, along with Thorpi. However, it still didn't solve the current issue plaguing one of his companies.

2nd Company was on HQ security as Mulbah tried to figure out who to promote as temporary replacement for Antonious. The obvious choice would be Master Sergeant Oti, except the senior NCO had already declined the offer. In fact, every single NCO in the entire Korps had declined the promotion so far. Everyone believed Antonious would continue to lead the 2nd Company and they were reluctant to step in to replace him, even if it was temporary. The captain sure wasn't telling them not to take his spot until he was back up at full speed. Mulbah was beginning to consider alternative ways to handle it, part of which involved his chief operations officer.

Thorpi, while nominally a member of the Mercenary Guild, had never actually shown any aptitude for combat. The alien had explained his kind weren't suited for fighting, which Mulbah had found to be a bit odd. Males fought all the time. It was genetically ingrained into their biological makeup to fight for mating rights at the basic level, Mulbah knew. Even Veetanho males had to impress and woo the dominant females somehow.

*Right?* The colonel was forced to admit he really didn't know much about Veetanho culture or societal norms, or for that matter even the true dynamics behind the council which ran the Mercenary Guild. Everything he had once thought to be crystal clear was now murkier than a brown stream flowing rapidly through the poor part of town. Mulbah continue to mull over his options for how to handle 2nd Company as he monitored the restocking of the warehouse.

He could always roll them up into the command squad and make a company. This was probably the easiest solution, but he really had no desire to take on the burden of being both the CEO of the Korps and 2nd Company CO as well. There would be so much going on it likely wouldn't work out well. Plus, he recalled as he finally reached the bio-locked door which led into the main part of the Korps' HQ, he wasn't overly fond of 2nd Company as a whole. There was just something about them which made him uncomfortable, and it was a feeling no company-level commander should have with his mercs when they went into battle.

He pressed his thumb against the scanner pad next to the door and waited as the gel-like substance formed a vacuum seal around it, checking his pulse, body temperature, and fingerprint. Satisfied the person holding the thumb was attached to the proper owner the door unlocked and Mulbah stepped inside. He turned and closed the door behind him.

The inner sanctum of the Korps HQ was something of a joke. There were more slates scattered around for operational planning purposes than there were actual users. Every single one of his company commanders got their own office and attached apartment, which had driven the contractors crazy when he had demanded it. So far, only Mulbah and Zion seemed to use their apartments for the designed purpose. Antonious, up until he lost his arm, never spent the night with the same woman more than twice, though his clothing and uniforms were stored on base, and Samson lived off base but nearby with his wife and children, as well as his wife's niece and nephew, both of whom were war orphans. Mulbah had hopes the children, who were already tearing it up in the school programs he helped establish in the country, turned to the Korps whenever they passed their VOWS.

Mulbah's office was sparse and had very little in it, outside of a desk and four chairs. There was no need for filing cabinets, not with the popularity and ease of use of slates. He didn't even bother with a potted plant or pictures on the walls. It wasn't as though he wouldn't have decorated his office, had he the time. No, the problem was he was never actually in his office to begin with.

He walked past his office and stopped at Thorpi's. The Veetanho actually preferred plush pillows more than anything and, with the slates scattered around in his office haphazardly, Mulbah thought it reminded him more of an unruly teenager's room than a battle-hardened mercenary's. However, it wasn't his office, so he let the alien do as he pleased.

"*Menh*, got the plan for the prison break yet?" Mulbah asked as he knocked on the Veetanho's door.

"You're beginning to talk like them," Thorpi stated without looking up from his slate. The faint sounds of the alien's nails on the device's screen were barely audible over the cool breeze of the central air conditioning, another demand of Mulbah's during the conversion of the rundown facility.

"Like who?"

"Like the men under your command," Thorpi explained. "As for your 'prison break,' yes, I have a plan. You do realize this isn't a prison break as much as it's a type of prison appropriation, right?"

"Prison break sounds far more interesting," Mulbah pointed out. "Besides, we need to move all those prisoners already there to somewhere else, and we really haven't consulted the prison guards yet. That, technically, makes it a prison break."

"I'll concede the point, for now," Thorpi nodded. "Thanks to their civil unrest a few months back, Nigeria's prisons are actually well below their maximum occupancy. Who knew mass executions could be so beneficial to our current needs?"

The Veetanho was alien and simply did not understand Humans sometimes, which meant Mulbah needed to be patient with his COO. "Thorpi..." Mulbah paused, closed his eyes, and took a deep breath. Exhaling slowly, he continued, "It's not necessarily a good thing. Some of them were simply tossed in prison for having the wrong political beliefs."

"I thought your General Assembly charter prohibited this?" Thorpi looked at him, confused. The alien tapped a few commands on the slate, then flipped through the screens. After a moment he began to nod. "Yes, see? Right here it says that political discrimination against any minority party will be dealt with in a harsh manner."

"White people laws." Mulbah waved his hand in the air, dismissing the argument. "Good for Europe and America. They write each other sternly worded letters and bitch about it in the General Assembly, but nothing comes of it. When they come to Africa, the General Assembly simply waits until we're done killing each other before stepping in and declaring peace—well, most of them do. Then they say they created peace, while causing more shit with their foreign troops who are supposed to enforce the peace, sometimes violently. They'll pick the side which lost, claim it was victimized, and then we start all over again because of old tribal grudges while they step back to watch all over again."

"This sounds inefficient," Thorpi acknowledged. "Why not kill them all? One of your greatest military leaders once said, 'I shall make a desert and call it peace,' did he not?"

"'To ravage, to slaughter, to usurp under false titles, they call empire; and where they make a desert, they call it peace,'" Mulbah quoted as he closed his eyes. As much as he hated Roman history while in college, the quote from Gaius Cornelius Tacitus had always stuck with him. Mostly because the professor had been adamant it was the only way for absolute peace.

"It sounds far more Veetanho than I thought a Human could," Thorpi admitted after a moment of silent contemplation.

"It does," Mulbah grunted. "Which is why I decided to accept the proposal from the Mercenary Guild when you first brought it to me."

"Sir, I must say Humans…are really *weird*," Thorpi stressed the final word, his ears twitching slightly as he spoke. "I don't know if the word came out correctly or not."

"It was the correct word. Yeah, we're very weird," Mulbah nodded. He shifted gears. "So, how goes Operation Prison Break?"

"It's not…fine," Thorpi relented with a very Human-like smile. "Operation 'Prison Break' is going to require both the 1st and 3rd Company to pull off. Not because of the prisoners in the prison itself, but the guards. According to this brief I received from General Peepo's chief of staff, the prison has been taken over by a drug-trafficking warlord by the name of Moses, who appears to have the full support of the current Nigerian government and, more importantly, their military."

"Moses?" Mulbah asked, raising an eyebrow.

Thorpi nodded. "Yes, Moses." The alien looked at Mulbah, confused. "Is something wrong?"

"No, just...forget it," Mulbah told him as he shook his head. "Ready for the mission briefing, then? I can tell Samson and Zion to meet in the briefing room in ten."

"Sounds good," Thorpi agreed. He looked back down at his slate. "I also have a proposal for the problem with 2nd Company you might be interested in."

"Oh?" Mulbah said. He stepped into the office. Closing the door behind him, he leaned against the wall. "Go on."

"I know performance issues within the Jackals are worse than we'd hoped they would be," Thorpi began, his eyes locked on the slate in his paw. "They seem to suffer the most casualties out of any other company, but it's actually not Captain Karnga's fault. They are typically deployed into combat situations first almost thirty-two percent more than the other companies, even though Captain Tolbert's company has the reputation of being the most combat ready unit."

"Really?" Mulbah asked, surprised. He hadn't known about that.

"Oh, yes, Colonel, it's obvious once you notice the trends," Thorpi nodded and swiped right on his slate. "I just sent you the data. You tend to put the Jackals into dangerous positions more often than the others, even if it's not apparent during pre-deployment drops. This isn't through your fault, or Captain Karnga's. It's simply bad luck."

"Then what do you propose to do about fighting off bad juju?"

"Juju? Oh, bad luck. I like that word. I will use it in the future. First off, we rotate them back here and keep them around as base security until Captain Karnga is back on his feet," Thorpi said as he motioned for Mulbah to look at his slate. "We switch out the company numbers, which is easy enough. Captain Jacobs and the rest of his Goshawks become 2nd Company in terms of deployment rotation. Captain Karnga gets a promotion and becomes the S-1 for the Korps while remaining here at HQ, with the rest of his Jackals providing base security. This way we don't have an understrength company out on contracts while leaving a fully-crewed one here."

"Hmm…" Mulbah pursed his lips, a thoughtful expression crossing his face. Antonious was fairly popular in town, even with his womanizing ways, and the loyalty showed to him by the Jackals *was* pretty high, even with all the hits they'd taken to their personnel. Mulbah was forced to admit that while the man had never actually been through any sort of officer's training program, his natural charisma seemed to bring about a certain level of leadership ability. Plus, serving as an S-1 would allow Antonious to assist with the maintaining of personnel in the Korps, while teaching him different ways to become a better leader without it feeling like a lecture. The more Mulbah ran the idea through his head, the better he liked it.

"Do it," Mulbah decided. "Antonious only has nine mercenaries in his company at the moment, counting himself, but they can easily maintain security on the base from here on out. Make sure they still receive combat bonuses, though. I don't want them to think they're being punished. I'll explain to the other companies that we'll be rotating everyone through HQ security eventually, but right now it's going to be the Jackals until they get up to full strength."

"Which might be never," Thorpi added as he looked over the recent VOWS results. "Have you seen these numbers?"

"Horrible," Mulbah agreed. "I'm sort of surprised, though. The scores in North America and western Europe are actually lower than ours are."

"I wonder…" Thorpi's voice trailed off.

"What?" Mulbah prodded.

"Oh, I was just thinking. If I wanted to subvert an occupying force from using our own people against us, I'd do something about it," Thorpi shrugged his narrow shoulders. "I'd make sure the populace resists in a way where they don't even realize they're resisting at all, like corrupting data in VOWS results to lower the scores or by making the test impossibly hard."

"Since when did you start calling the Mercenary Guild an occupying force?" Mulbah asked, surprised.

"When I accepted it for what it is," Thorpi said. "And because General Peepo accidentally let that bit of information slip in her missive through Captain Beeko. As smart as Peepo is, her subordinates aren't up to her level. This, we can be thankful for."

\* \* \*

### Three Kilometers from New Ikoyi Prison, Lagos, Nigeria District, Earth

"Move it," Samson called out as the CASPers of 1st Company bounded out of the transport shuttle's rear. He waited until the last man was out before he followed suit, jumping from the shuttle and landing on the ground fifteen meters below. The CASPer's legs absorbed the impact and he stumbled forward, his MAC warmed up and ready for anything while he swept the scene with his laser rifle.

The outskirts of Lagos were no prize, and they made the streets of Monrovia look clean by comparison. Small ramshackle houses built with nothing more than a few sheets of metal and tarps dotted the area, and small puddles filled with feces dotted the edges of the worn path Samson guessed was supposed to be a road. A few faces peered out from the shadows of their homes, eyes wide in surprise as they took in the sight of the Korps' CASPers.

The ground was surprisingly squishy beneath his CASPers feet, slick and not unlike some of the back alleys in the worst parts of Monrovia. Samson made a silent promise to not look down and see precisely what he was standing in. He focused instead on his surroundings. It was eerily silent save for the noise created by 1st Company as they moved around. This bothered him. Knowing the people had been cowed by the warlord running the prison and actually seeing the results of his handiwork were two entirely different things.

Around him, the rest of 1st Company established a secure perimeter. Samson grunted in satisfaction upon seeing his First Sergeant, Julius Simbo, had already prepared the mercs for the next part of the plan.

"Top, are we ready to go?" Samson asked.

"Yes, *bass*, we're ready," Julius acknowledged. "No word yet from Captain Jacobs?"

"Not yet," Samson grunted. He'd been more than a little surprised at the restructuring of the Korps, but in hindsight it made sense. He missed his friend out in the field, but until they figured out a way to purchase one of the Mk 8 CASPer suits for Antonious, he simply would not be able to fight the same way, pinplants or not. Zion and the 3rd Company were good, but Samson didn't have nearly as much experience working with the lawyer as he did with Antonious.

"Contact!" Corporal Alonso Dau called out over the comms. "Two AMX-30 tanks, range fifteen hundred meters and closing. Sending coordinates now."

*So, it begins,* Samson thought as the two tanks suddenly appeared on his Tri-V screen.

"First Squad, engage," Samson ordered. "Second, provide support in case they send in air."

"*Bass*, did someone forget to tell the Nigerians we were coming?" Julius asked as the confirmations came rolling in from the company.

"No, Top, they know we're coming," Samson stated. "This is all from the guy we're taking the prison from."

"They let that crazy *junda* have tanks?" Julius asked, his voice incredulous.

"There's no real government here right now," Samson reminded him. "It's nothing more than a provisional government. Plus, those tanks are over one hundred years old. We'll be fine."

"*Bass*, the AMX-30R has a modified railgun attachment on the turret," Julius reminded him. "They've had those for fifty years. These models might have them, too."

"Damn," Samson muttered. "Leopards, this is the captain. All personnel, spread out and keep moving. Don't let yourselves be an easy target."

Samson sprinted to his right as 1st Company reacted to his orders, moving into a half-circle and spreading further out with each bounding leap.

Samson zoomed in on the lead tank and saw it was, in fact, one of the upgraded turret designs with the rail gun. He targeted the AMX with his MAC but slipped on the ground as he struggled to stop. This threw his CASPer off-balance and he dropped to one knee, his free hand slamming into the ground to keep him from falling over.

The barrel of the railgun oriented on one of his mercs from first squad and fired. A suit in the lower left-hand corner on his Tri-V display suddenly turned red. Samson swallowed as he recognized the red marker for what it was.

"Hit those tanks!" Samson roared and reoriented himself. His MAC turned green and he let loose at the same time as the rest of 1st Company, every shot targeting the tank which had killed their brother. Three hundred MAC rounds ripped through the armor of the tank as though it were paper, slaughtering the occupants inside. A moment later a fire broke out as the oil from the engine compartment leaked into the crew compartment.

"More contacts!" Private Morgan Asselmo stated loudly, targeting the new arrivals on the Tri-V for all to see. "I see four more tanks and mobile artillery moving into position!"

Samson was confused. *What the hell kind of hornet's nest did we stick our dicks into here?* They had expected *some* resistance, but it appeared the entire Nigerian Army had shown up to welcome them to their country in the most violent manner possible.

Normally one for a good fight, he preferred it to be against aliens, not his fellow Humans. *Just shows the colonel's plan for pacifying Africa sucks,* he groused as he tried to target the other tank. Not seeing a good angle, he moved to his left. *The guild's going to bleed us dry, then hit us when we're weak. Just watch and see.*

The second AMX, upon seeing the death of its partner, backed up and used the blazing wreck as cover. The turret shifted and suddenly three shots belched out in rapid succession. Two more red suits appeared in his Tri-V, as well as a yellow. *Two kills, one wounded. We're getting murdered out here.*

"Lion Six Actual, Leopard Six," Samson called. As he began to run again, he targeted his MAC on the partially-covered tank and let out a quick volley. Most of the rounds bounced off the angled turret armor, though one did appear to punch though the command hatch. Uncertain if he caused enough damage, he stopped firing and dove as a round from the railgun went blazing past him at five times the speed of sound. Sliding on his stomach in the muck and bodily waste, he flipped onto his side and tried to find some cover, but the suit's size and lack of sturdy buildings hampered him. Out in the open, he was a sitting duck for the rail gun. "Colonel, we're getting hammered out here. Requesting assistance, over."

"Copy, Leopard Six," Mulbah's voice came over the radio. "Help will be there in five. Copy?"

"Roger, *bass*. Leopard Six, out," Samson replied and switched frequencies. "All Leopards, this is Six. Keep moving, keep fighting. Help is on the way, *jockos*."

\* \* \*

### One Kilometer Above New Ikoyi Prison, Lagos, Nigeria District, Earth

"Be there in five. Copy?" Mulbah said as he looked at Captain Jacobs and the rest of the newly-minted 2nd Company. He couldn't see the men's faces inside their CASPers, but he could almost feel their grim determination upon hearing their brothers in the 1st Company were dying out in the field.

"Roger, *bass*. Leopard Six, out."

"Zion, get everyone in your company ready to drop," Mulbah ordered as he looked at the four men from his command squad. He switched frequencies. "Change of plans. The five of us are going into the prison, alone. Watch your backs and make sure your combat armor is secure."

"Yes *bass*," they replied in unison. Mulbah switched frequencies once again. "Thorpi, Mulbah. Executing option 'Kraken.' Acknowledge?"

"Copy, Colonel," Thorpi replied over the radio. "Executing option 'Kraken.' Adjusting flight path now."

Mulbah felt the change in G-forces as the dropship changed course and rocketed back out to the edge of the city, where 1st Company awaited their arrival. The CASPers of 3rd Company moved to the rear entrance as the ship arrived on location fifteen seconds later, circling the battlefield from an altitude of 100 meters. Anti-aircraft fire erupted from the ground as flak and tracer rounds flew past and exploded around the ship.

In the rear, the instant the light turned green 3rd Company was out the back, heading toward the Earth like avenging angels from on high.

"All suits clear. Back to the prison, Thorpi," Mulbah instructed as the last CASPer departed the rear of the dropship and the door was secured.

"Yes, sir," the Veetanho replied from the cockpit. The ship was back over the prison in almost no time at all, free from the added weight of the CASPers. It paused for a moment as the VTOL engines began to howl, allowing for the dropship to land in an open area near the main entrance of the prison. The two MACs on the wings pivoted and blasted something Mulbah couldn't see. Subsequent secondary explosions suggested it was a large target, however.

"Two guard towers down," Thorpi called. Mulbah grunted. *That explains a lot,* he thought as the Veetanho continued. "Dropping rear ramp now. Be careful, sir."

"Always, Thorpi," Mulbah replied as the command squad hustled down the ramp and made their way to the prison entrance. The dropship remained on the ground, covering their approach with occasional fire from the MACs on the wings whenever a threat emerged.

Mulbah reached the concrete entrance to the underground portion of the prison and saw, as the plans had suggested, that it was too narrow for a CASPer. Relieved he had left his suit behind at HQ, Mulbah pressed his back against the rough concrete and waited a moment to catch his breath.

"I hate running," he muttered as his detail caught up. He glanced over at Staff Sergeant Casimir Ange, who was breathing just as heavily as he was. "CASPers make this running shit easy."

"Yeah, *bass*, this *craw craw* running shit is bad for your health," Casimir laughed between gasps. Everyone else in the command squad was either a runner by nature or simply too nervous to joke around with him, Mulbah decided. Casimir grinned humorously. "You run and all you do is die tired, *bass*."

"Breach, then clear," Mulbah decided as he looked at the entryway. He didn't see any obvious boobytraps, but experience told him this meant little.

"I'll check," Corporal Herman Adrazgo volunteered and immediately leaned around the corner to look into the darkened entrance.

"Wait—" Mulbah tried to stop him but a loud shot echoed out from the darkness. Herman's head exploded into a fine red mist and the body of the late corporal tumbled to the ground. Mulbah leaned away from the entrance and began cursing as blood began to pool beneath the body, staining the concrete steps below. "Fuck."

It only made sense something big was down there waiting for them. This was a guy who owned tanks, after all. Mulbah growled and scratched his unshaven chin, thinking. There were other options available. He just wasn't sure if playing the card this early in the engagement was worth it or not.

"Grenades?" Casimir suggested. Mulbah mulled it over for a second before he nodded.

"Fuck 'em up, *menh*," Mulbah agreed and pulled two grenades from his belt. Casimir and the two remaining enlisted men followed suit. "Eight grenades should be enough. On the count of three, pull the pin and tossed them inside. Don't linger out in the open again, *ken?*"

"Yes sir," came the quiet reply.

Mulbah readied his first grenade. "Okay. One, two, three, now!"

The first four grenades were tossed inside and bounced across the concrete floor below. A second later the next wave followed. Explosions ripped through the defenders. Mulbah, his ears ringing from the concussive explosions, leaned forward slightly and brought up his laser carbine.

"Lights?" he directed and Private Mele Ibara stepped forward and flicked on his flashlight. The two million lumens lit the entrance of the prison. Two pairs of mangled legs could be seen, as well as a ruined .50 caliber sniper rifle which appeared to be older than the prison, judging by the wear and mud caked on it. Beyond the massive rifle, it was pitch black.

No more shots echoed out from the darkness. Mulbah looked over at Casimir. "Sergeant?"

"Private Ibara, down that hole and secure the entrance," Casimir ordered. The young Liberian swallowed and nodded, an identical carbine matching Mulbah's resting against his shoulder. Ibara descended into the darkness, then Casimir quickly followed. Mulbah counted to four before he entered the underground prison as well, with the last surviving member of the command squad, Corporal Adrian Obassi, bringing up the rear.

\* \* \*

### Three Kilometers from New Ikoyi Prison, Lagos, Nigeria

"*Move your asses!*" Samson screamed. More artillery rounds hammered the ground around the CASPers as they struggled to move through the hailstorm which was falling upon them. The rockets from the mobile artillery units were absolutely shredding the run-down shacks of the civilian populace. Fortunately, the moment the fighting had started, people living in the area decided it would be a terrific idea to be somewhere else.

The arrival of Zion and 3rd Company had made short work of the surviving tank, and momentarily turned the tide of battle to the Kakata Korps' favor. However, immediately after that, mobile artillery rockets found their range.

Over half of 1st Company was showing yellow, but Samson felt fortunate they had suffered no more fatalities. 3rd Company was showing two yellow but no red, which meant every one of them was still in the fight. Samson brought up the tactical overlay and tried to find the rocket artillery site. It wasn't easy, all things considered. However, it only took the Reaper drone, launched hours before, minutes to locate it.

"Zion, it's Samson," he said as he ran to the east, toward the prison. He tried to keep his breathing steady as he vaulted over an old rust-bucket faintly resembling a car mounted on cinderblocks. "I've got the rockets' location marked. You're closer; handle them. Leopards are moving to secure the outer prison grounds."

"Copy," Zion responded immediately, wheezing over the comms. Samson would have normally laughed and teased the lawyer about being out of shape, but it didn't feel like the right time considering how much it was taking him to keep his own breathing under control. Perhaps if they all lived, he would give the CFO of the Korps a hard time about it. "Goshawk Six, out."

"Leopards, head east two kilometers," Samson ordered his company. "Watch for mortars."

Artillery rockets screamed overhead as the men of 1st Company sprinted toward the prison. Samson really wanted to kill those artillery rockets but with Kraken in effect, it would be Zion's job to neutralize them. Samson was now responsible for securing the prison grounds, since he had suffered the most casualties on the battlefield. Zion would handle the artillery and, with luck, would arrive at the prison in time to create a larger ring around the perimeter to maintain control. Only then would the Zuul come down and establish a presence as the prison administrators.

"Stupid pups," Samson growled and wondered if the Korps was being bled on purpose. The Zuul mercenaries currently on the planet far outnumbered the Korps, yet it seemed the Liberian company was doing all the scut work. "That's all *chokla, menh*."

Samson had no love for aliens, even though he had enjoyed meeting the Korteschii on his first actual contract in a CASPer. He had a particular dislike for the Besquith and Goka, though he would never admit to anyone the giant werewolf-like aliens terrified him as much as they did. The Goka, to him, were simply disgusting, oversized cockroaches. While he wouldn't call himself xenophobic, the idea of Earth being run by something which resembled dinner to his grandfather irked him.

The bombardment of the artillery rockets began to slow, then ceased all together as Zion did his job quickly and effectively. Now it was time for the Leopards to do theirs.

Young men began pouring out of buildings at the edge of the prison, armed with laser rifles and shoddy pistols. Most couldn't hit the broad side of a building, Samson noticed as they fired wildly, but a few were taking practiced, well-aimed shots. Their problem was that their rifles could not penetrate the CASPer frontal armor.

Wanting to conserve his MAC rounds in case any more armored surprises showed up, Samson switched to his laser rifle. Unlike most CASPers in 1st Company, which had K-bomb mounts, Samson had gone with the laser rifle in case he ever ran into a horde of lightly armored enemies, especially after dealing with the miniature lizard creatures who had been hunting the Korteschii. He hated wasting MAC ammunition for something like this.

Rifle in hand, Samson began to target the hundreds of soldiers firing at him. Around him, the remainder of 1st Company did the same, their MAC rounds, K-bombs, and laser fire cutting through the warlord's soldiers with relative ease. It was almost too easy once the tanks and artillery had been destroyed.

A suit on his Tri-V suddenly went red. Another dead merc. Samson blinked, confused. He'd seen nothing which would indicate the soldiers facing them had anything that could take them down. "Bravo Four, this is Six, over."

Nothing.

Samson tried his battle buddy. "Bravo Three, this is Six Actual, come in, over."

"This is Bravo Three," came the quick reply. He sounded frightened. "*Bass*, Doré just got killed by a sniper or something. We're being *hunted*."

"What do you mean, hunted?" Samson asked. "Explain, Bravo Three."

"There's something out here, *bass*. Something not Human, shooting at us."

Samson's heart skipped a beat at this revelation, though he couldn't be sure just what the young man was talking about. The possibilities were endless. Was there an unseen alien on the field of battle, taking out individual CASPers? Or was there something more insidious going on? Samson couldn't say. Whatever it was, though, he needed to put a stop to it.

Locating Bravo Three on his Tri-V, Samson quickly headed in his direction. Bravo Four and Three had both ended up near the edge of the slum, where the overgrown underbrush of the Nigerian jungle threatened to overrun the area. There were a few shanties there, each looking as though they would fall over from the gentlest of breezes.

Samson settled down next Bravo Three, which he quickly identified as Corporal Har Baranga. Looking around, he spotted the fallen

CASPer. Oddly enough, there was a single, neat hole in the center of the cockpit. Samson saw it was a perfect kill-shot, the high-powered laser easily penetrating the suit's armor and killing the CASPer driver with a round straight through the heart.

He turned and looked around but there was no sign of an obvious enemy. Samson swallowed slightly and looked at Corporal Baranga, who was still looking outward toward the jungle. "Corporal, fall back to the prison. We don't need to be here."

"Yes, *bass*," Baranga replied, perhaps a little too eagerly. Samson did not blame him one bit. Whoever—*whatever*—had killed PFC Doré, it was long gone now.

Still mildly shaken from the mysterious death, Samson and Baranga headed quickly back to the prison, where the rest of 1st Company were mopping up. Samson could see the average age of the men with the rifles was older than he had experienced back in the day, but they still were too young to be stupidly charging CASPers and dying by the droves at the whims of some hopped-up drug dealer with delusions of grandeur.

"Some things never change," he whispered to himself as he joined in on the butchery.

\* \* \*

### Inside New Ikoyi Prison, Lagos, Nigeria District, Earth

The stench in the prison wasn't horrible, but it was far worse than anything Mulbah had smelled in recent memory. Spending too much time indoors while at HQ and in a sealed vehicle during his travels to the executive presidential mansion in Liberia had insulated him from the worst environments, not to mention his time in a CASPer meant it was rare for him to be exposed to the elements at all. Being in Nigeria was a rude reminder for Mulbah as to just how bad most of Africa, even the civilized parts, still were.

His command squad, sans the deceased Corporal Adrazgo, were covering as much of the hallway as they could, clearing every room before moving on. Most of them were prison cells converted to drug labs, which seemed a bit of an overkill to Mulbah. The interior of the prison was dark with only the occasional dim lightbulb showing them the way. The rank smell Mulbah had thought to be Human feces grew stronger as they moved deeper into the prison.

"Body," Corporal Obassi called out as he pointed to a small room. Mulbah peeked in. Inside the tiny supply closet was a malnourished man, obviously dead and horribly decomposed. The mercenary colonel tried to quiet his stomach as it rolled around dangerously in protest. The rancid stench assaulted his senses and sent waves of nausea crashing over him. He looked away and barely managed not to vomit.

"Keep going," Mulbah said, his throat hoarse. The humidity was awful, and the smell of rot and decay permeated through everything. He heard Corporal Obassi suddenly throw up on the floor and curse under his breath once he was finished. The sound almost set Mulbah off. Only an iron will and determination not to vomit in front of his men kept him from following suit.

A small, red light was blinking in the corner at the end of the hallway. Ibara took careful aim with his carbine and snapped off a shot. The camera exploded in a shower of sparks. Mulbah nodded and motioned for Obassi to move forward and scan the last set of rooms in the corridor.

Mulbah heard the familiar sounds of heavy objects being hastily moved about in the room to their left. Moses and his men were attempting to create a barricade to fire from. They wanted to use their impromptu cover to keep themselves safe. He would have laughed had the situation been any different.

"Remember what Moses looks like," he told his squad. "Orange mohawk. Don't kill him if you get the chance. Kill everyone else holding a weapon."

"Got it, *bass*," Casimir murmured back. He looked at the others. "You heard him. Obassi, Ibara, first through. Stay low. If they're firing on full-auto the barrels will track high."

The young mercenaries both nodded jerkily and waited. Mulbah looked over at Casimir, who pulled out a few more grenades. Mulbah raised an eyebrow at him but the staff sergeant merely shrugged.

"I always keep a few extra," Casimir helpfully supplied. "Just in case."

"You're a dangerous man," Mulbah muttered. "Might as well use them."

"Just what I was thinking, *bass*," Casimir agreed. He pulled the pins, counted to two, then tossed them far into the room. Twin explosions ripped apart the men inside and dust filled the corridor.

"Go!" Mulbah ordered. Ibara and Obassi moved into the room and split up, each moving to corners as they began firing at the barricade and the men hiding behind it. Mulbah waited a moment before he barged in and charged directly into the center of the room. He dove onto his belly as someone fired a full burst at him.

As he had expected, the shots all went high. He could hear faint cries of surprise and pain as the drug warlord's soldiers lost sight of

Mulbah. A few stood up and tried to shoot at him from over the barricade but Ibara, Obassi, and Casimir cut them down with ease.

Panic ensued among the defenders as they struggled to decide who to shoot at. The trained mercs of the Kakata Korps had no such compunctions and began to scythe down the opposing force, using their superior training and firearms to make short work of the remaining defenders.

As the dust cleared, Mulbah saw a familiar orange mohawk cowering in the corner. Mulbah waved away the dust and saw it was indeed their target, Moses. Obassi moved forward to ensure there were no more of the drug lord's men hiding behind the barricade while Ibara covered the other side. Casimir had turned and was now covering the entry in case any reinforcements arrived, though Mulbah was fairly certain anyone who could potentially assist Moses was probably dead at this point. Still, only a fool wouldn't watch his back, he knew from long experience.

"Moses," Mulbah called out to the drug lord as he grabbed the cowering man's collared shirt. Moses was sweat stained and smelled of ripe cabbage, though it was a vast improvement over the stench surrounding them. He hauled the scrawny man to his feet and looked him in the eye.

Or tried, rather. One of Moses' eyes was missing and had been replaced by a prosthetic at some point. The pupil must have been knocked asunder during the gunfight and was pointed in the wrong direction entirely. Mulbah ignored it and focused instead on the drug lord's good eye.

"The Mercenary Guild is seizing this prison and evicting you and your ilk," Mulbah informed him. "You are to be tried for war crimes and crimes against humanity. Have you anything to say?"

"*Mon*, I don' *ken* dis t'all!" Moses stammered as he looked wildly around with his one good eye, his accent heavy and slurred. It was obvious he was as high as the child soldiers he had sent out to be slaughtered, if not more. "Dis boolsheet!"

"You've said enough," Mulbah said and slugged the drug lord in the mouth, hard. Moses cried out but didn't say anything else. Mulbah looked over at Casimir. "Staff Sergeant? How're we looking?"

"Good, *bass*," Casimir replied instantly. "Ready to extract."

"Perfect," Mulbah nodded as he manhandled Moses out of the corner and threw him into the barricade. The man yelped in pain as he landed on broken furniture. Mulbah clicked his radio and waited a beat before speaking. "Leopard Six, Lion Six."

"Yeah, *bass*?" Samson replied almost immediately.

"Package secured," Mulbah told him. "How're things up there?"

"It's…handled," Samson said after a momentary pause. "ETA on the shuttles is ten minutes, over."

"Roger," Mulbah grunted. "Be up in five. Lion Six, out."

"*Bass*, what are they going to use this prison for anyway?" Ibara asked as he kicked aside some of the debris. He looked around the room and shook his head. "Not like this is going to be worth much. It's filthy."

"The orders were to take the prison, not clean it," Mulbah said as he eyed the drug lord. He prodded the man with his foot. "Hey! How'd you get all this military hardware?"

"Fuck off," Moses told him. Mulbah kicked the man in the gut, hard.

"I asked nicely," Mulbah said as he reached down and unstrapped his knife from its pouch. He flicked the blade open and tried to cause the blade to reflect what little light there was in the room into Moses' good eye. "Next time you don't answer me, I start cutting. I'll start small, then work my way up to something you might actually miss. Now I'm going to try again. Where did you get those tanks?"

\* \* \*

This time, Mulbah ensured the men of both 1st and 3rd Companies were aboard their transport shuttles before the Zuul mercenaries came down to take control of the prison. He had heard from Samson just how close he had come to punching one of the dog-like mercs, and the last thing the Kakata Korps CO wanted was for something like that to occur and void their contract.

Six dead. Eleven wounded. Those were more casualties than the Korps had ever taken in one operation. The artillery and tanks had come as a surprise, though the fact that the Nigerian government had sent along trained troops to provide security to the drug lord had been a shock.

The suits were all recoverable, three of which looked as though they could be repaired. The others would simply be scrapped or parted out to repair others. By his estimation, they might be able to get all the wounded back into action within six months except for one or two. Mulbah wasn't sure yet but he thought there might be a medical retirement in there for one of Samson's troops.

The shuttle jetted out over the Gulf of Guinea, leaving Lagos and Nigeria behind as it climbed high into the sky. Mulbah and the rest of the command squad were near the rear of the shuttle, with the survivors of 1st Company toward the front. They had been brutalized by the tanks and artillery of the Nigerian Army, and all the men of the unit had damage to their suits. Everyone in the shuttle was quiet, their thoughts on the mission and of absent comrades.

All except for the drug lord Moses. He was chattering away at whoever would listen, which was beginning to drive Mulbah nuts. The Kakata Korps CO stared ahead, his eyes unseeing as he mentally went over the death toll. The loss of suits didn't bother him. Those could be replaced now, courtesy of the credits they had earned for completing the mission. No, it was the loss of CASPer pilots which hurt more than anything.

They were his men. Sure, they served under the command of Samson, but at the end of the day it was Mulbah who signed their paychecks, paid out their death benefits to the grieving families, and had to console his own officers when they lost mercs in their companies. It was rough and he wasn't sure just how military generals of old managed. He thought back to the brutality of the Somme Offensive during World War One and repressed a shudder. That series of battles had featured a body count which, fortunately, humanity hasn't seen since.

He stole a look at the drug lord and wondered why he hadn't killed the man while they had been in the underground prison. Moses seemed oblivious to his gaze, focusing instead on mocking the surviving troops and reminding them they could not hurt him. It angered Mulbah more than anything ever had in his life, which he found to be surprising. Never had he felt such a rage toward any one man.

Before he was consciously aware of what he was doing, the colonel was on his feet and walking toward the drug lord. Moses had but a moment of incomprehension before he was bodily hoisted to his feet by his stained shirt collar. Mulbah dragged the drug lord toward the rear drop ramp and slapped the green activation button. Alarms buzzed as the pressure in the cabin dropped suddenly, though not enough to suck them out into the sky.

Moses had a panicked look upon his face as Mulbah walked him to the edge of the ramp. Turning him around, Mulbah positioned Moses so he could look out into the great blue nothing. The merc kept a tight grip on the back of the drug lord's shirt.

"Nobody's going to miss you, *menh*," Mulbah shouted into Moses' ear. "You won't even be a footnote in history. I'll make certain of this."

Mulbah released the drug lord's shirt and took a step back. Moses began to turn around but before he could, Mulbah's foot lashed out and impacted solidly on the other man's chest. Moses cried out and stumbled backward. He tried to regain his balance but was unable as his foot slipped off the edge of the ramp.

Screaming and flailing his arms, Moses fell from the shuttle. Mulbah shuffled carefully to the edge of the ramp, grabbing hold of a ready bar to look down. His eyes tracked the brief fatalistic flight of the drug lord as he descended quickly from four kilometers to the ocean. The bright orange mohawk contrasted sharply with the dark blue water below, allowing Mulbah to watch Moses for the entire trip. There was a small splash in the middle of the ocean, then nothing as the mercenary lost sight of the body.

With a satisfied grunt, he turned and walked back into the interior of the shuttle. He closed the ramp's door and looked at the CASPers gathered around. He knew they were watching him, however, none of them stood up to help the drug lord, which told Mulbah they approved of the impromptu trial and sentencing.

"Only Humans get trials," Mulbah announced loudly to all. "Scum like that gets nothing but a quick flying lesson. You get me?"

*"Paint the sky!"* the mercs roared approvingly in response.

\* \* \*

### Six Kilometers Southwest of New Ikoyi Prison, Lagos, Nigeria District, Earth

After what felt like an eternity, the Blevin gingerly removed the ghillie blanket which had protected her from both visual and thermal imagery. The elongated laser rifle, with a range of up to ten kilometers, was carefully disassembled before being put away in the carrying case. The ghillie blanket went into her small pack, folded and organized.

Task completed, the brown-skinned alien looked around and admired the view from her perch atop the towering skyscraper, one of three which dominated the downtown Lagos skyline. The atmosphere was a little wet on Earth but otherwise perfectly charming, save for the Humans who lived upon it, of course. The planet had the perfect combination of legitimate businesses and corrupt black markets for those who simply took the initiative. For a Blevin, it was almost like being back home.

*I will never understand why Peepo said to target the lowest ranking Human mercenaries first,* she thought as she tapped in her homing signal to request pickup. She received confirmation within moments, so she took in the beautiful views of the nearby ocean as she waited.

Still, 20,000 credits to kill only a single target? Fastest money I've ever made. Plus, those CASPers are very easy to see from this range.

\* \* \* \* \*

# Part Two

# The Thorn & The Paw

# Chapter Four

**SOGA HQ, Sao Paolo, Brazil**

General Peepo's Chief of Staff, Captain Beeko, was in a foul mood. There were many factors which helped contribute to this general malaise, but it was fairly easy for her to figure out the order of importance in which these events took place.

The biggest one, however, was that she had been deliberately left out of the meeting between General Peepo and General Chirbayl, much to the captain's chagrin. Peepo had always said she trusted her longtime chief of staff to get the job done, but she had not let the captain sit in on the meeting. It was an important one as well, since it was a briefing on the incident at Capital Planet. It also covered the successful escape of the Cavaliers from Karma, which was a double injury to the goals of the Mercenary Guild.

Beeko chuffed, irritated. No matter what Peepo and the guild did, the damnable Horsemen always seemed to wiggle their way out of every cleverly laid trap. It was enough to drive any Veetanho to distraction.

Fortunately, the pacification of Earth was going swimmingly. Sinai Steel, the Egyptian mercenary company who had remained behind on Earth to spy on the guild with Taranto S.R.L., had been rounded up and executed by MinSha troops. Taranto S.R.L. had been almost wiped out to a man by the Kakata Korps, leaving behind only a handful. The capture of Tsolmon Enkh, one of the

Golden Horde members, had been a welcome surprise, though Beeko had little idea how it would help further the guild's plans for Earth. Tsolmon was not one of the higher-ups in the Horde, that was certain. And there were scattered groups still causing problems around the planet, with Sinclair's Scorpions being the largest issue. They were, at last guess, somewhere in the United Kingdom, though General Peepo hadn't seemed too concerned at the time. No, the general seemed to be far more interested in the continent of Africa and the problems there.

Beeko frowned as a map of Portugal appeared on the slate's screen. While technically outside the zone the Kakata Korps were being requested to patrol, it was close enough to warrant their presence. At least, this was how the chief of staff saw things. Besides which, it was a smaller mercenary company, one which had suffered severe losses in the months leading up to the Mercenary Guild's occupation of Earth.

*Desbravadores de Lisbon* were the last Portuguese mercenary company on the planet, Beeko knew from previous reports. Poor even for a Human company, they had fallen on hard times when they were nearly wiped out while on contract. They were almost not even worth going after, yet they were recruiting in South America, which irritated General Peepo to some extent. This was reason enough to send the Korps in the take care of the issue.

The Kakata Korps had quelled almost every warlord and slave trafficker within 6,000 kilometers of Liberia. They had also, with the guidance of their country's president, led the western states to form a defense union the likes of which hadn't been seen on the continent since the days of colonialism. It was a heady time to be in Liberia.

Slowly but surely, the country was shifting from third world hellhole into something *more*.

Normally a source of good news, the Veetanho knew this was bad for the guild's overall plan.

No, Beeko thought as she flipped through the slate. The problem isn't the country, or the Kakata Korps. The problem is their entropy-cursed president!

It had started off as something small and inconsequential. A word here, a comment there, and the millions and millions of people who flocked into Liberia in the past three months cheered wildly for the president of the country. Later came the condemnations of the guild controlling the world, depriving people of their freedoms, and even jailing the mercenary companies his own people had participated in. It was mind-boggling the mental gymnastics Humans put themselves through in order to feel they were doing the right and noble thing.

Beeko thought about how to handle the problem without bothering General Peepo. It would be an excellent opportunity to show the type of leadership the Mercenary Guild leader looked for in her underlings, as well as take care of a potentially pesky problem before it blew out of proportion. Typing a command into the slate, Beeko smiled as she changed the Blevin's primary mission.

Presidential assassinations were nothing new in Liberia. *What was one more dead president, anyway,* she wondered, her mood markedly improved. Better still, getting rid of a pest such as the Portuguese would make her more worthy in the eyes of the general.

\* \* \*

## 40 Kilometers North of *Desbravadores* HQ, Odeleite, Portugal District, Earth

"Target is in sight," Mulbah said quietly into his mic as the two transport vehicles rumbled into view on the other side of the bridge. His command squad clicked confirmation. No one spoke. There was no need at this point. Each of them knew their jobs.

Around him, the dry landscape of southern Portugal reminded Mulbah a little bit of the deserts of Mali as the sun began to slowly rise to the east. The steep valley the old road traversed just past the wide bridge had been selected as the perfect ambush point along the entire route between Odeleite and the town of Beja. It was remote enough not to draw any unwanted attention as well as to provide enough of a window for his team to escape should the alarm be raised.

He shook himself. After the horrible and wasteful deaths in Nigeria, as well as the near-death of Antonious in Italy, Mulbah had decided to take only his command squad out for this one. Every single bit of intelligence Thorpi had dug up on the *Desbravadores* showed they had maybe ten mercenaries left after their transition accident in the Ch'sis System months earlier. Mulbah knew if they were armed with the proper tools, the Korps could easily take the Portuguese company without having to kill anybody.

Everyone agreed with using non-lethal tactics to take the Portuguese down. Nobody wanted a repeat of New Ikoyi Prison. After some searching, Zion had come up with a solution which made everyone happy. They would simply hit the *Bravadores* with tranquilizer darts and kidnap them.

The transports slowed as they rumbled carefully across the two-lane bridge. Mulbah checked his combat armor one final time and waited. Though they had rehearsed multiple times over the past few days, it was still nerve wracking to be out doing it. The execution was simple enough. The trick, Mulbah had discovered during the planning phase, was simply to be in the right position at the right time. This meant they needed to get the *Desbravadores* out of their headquarters and encourage them to flee.

The task had seemed insurmountable at first glance. The Portuguese mercenary company, abandoned by its government as well as its private supporters, had simply barricaded themselves in their base. Mulbah, not wanting a repeat of what had happened in Taranto, had decided to lure them out. The question was how.

Thorpi had figured it out, using his contacts in the Information Guild. Mulbah never asked for the details, even though he was immensely curious, but Thorpi had passed some data to the *Desbravadores*. Mulbah didn't know what, precisely, but whatever it had been was enough to force the company's hand into moving north. With a Reaper drone high overhead providing surveillance, Mulbah and his command squad had watched as the mercs loaded up into two transports and left their HQ in a hurry not an hour before.

If he had not already known which way they would go, the ambush would have been impossible. Thorpi, however, assured him they would take this road north to Beja and not into Spain. Mulbah had been doubtful, but once again, his faith in Thorpi was rewarded.

"Ready," Mulbah whispered as he took a deep breath to remain calm. From here, it was up to Staff Sergeant Ange, who was perched nearby under a ghillie suit with the only potentially lethal weapon in their collection. The subsonic rifle, combined with a suppressor, should not be heard by anyone when fired. He smiled grimly as the truck finally reached the designated spot. "Send it."

The rifle shot was almost inaudible to Mulbah, even though he was less than twenty feet from it. The front left tire of the lead vehicle blew apart as Ange's perfectly placed shot shredded it. The vehicle wobbled slightly before pulling to the side of the road and turning on its flashers.

Four men piled out of the lead vehicle, weapons drawn as they scanned the area. Mulbah and his command squad remained still, using their camouflage to hide from suspecting eyes. Every scenario they had gamed suggested they would need more than the command squad if they attempted to subdue the Portuguese the moment they were out of their vehicles. No, they would wait until their guard was down, and the mercs were just about finished changing the tire on the vehicle, before the Korps struck.

As expected, the second vehicle stopped behind the first and five more mercs climbed out, each one armed with a carbine Mulbah couldn't immediately identify. Their eyes were focused outward, scanning for any signs of danger as the driver began to inspect the damage. Thanks to the subsonic round's fragmentation, though, the tire was pretty well shredded, with no obvious sign of a bullet hole.

The next part was the hardest. The Korps simply lay there and watched as the tire jack was dug out of the back and the vehicle raised so they could change the tire. The mercenaries began to relax, their eyes turning inward. Their talking became less agitated and moved onto more inane topics, exactly as Mulbah had hoped. A few even lit cigarettes and stood around smoking.

Mulbah double-clicked his mic and counted to five before clicking it three times in rapid succession.

Four shots whispered out from compressed air guns, the miniscule darts flying true through the open space between their concealed positions and their targets. More darts followed, and within thirty seconds, ten men were unconscious in the middle of the road.

"Shuttle *Aristotle*, this is Lion Six," Mulbah murmured into his throat mic as he pushed his ghillie blanket away and slowly approached the downed men. "Bagged ten mercs. Requesting retrieval, over."

"Copy, Lion Six," came the immediate reply. "Down in thirty seconds."

"Lion Six, out," Mulbah confirmed and killed the comms. Moving faster now, he pulled out his zip ties and began securing the captured mercenaries' hands behind their backs. The process took less than thirty seconds, and he was able to check on the status of his squad before the shuttle landed.

A perfect op. There was no other way to describe it. He had been a part of many ops throughout his years as a mercenary, and not one had ever gone perfectly to plan. Not until now, at least. Exhaling sharply, he looked around, concerned. Nothing had gone wrong? He shook his head.

"That's just strange," he muttered as the shuttle landed ahead of them on the road. Zuul clambered down the rear ramp, their eyes carefully on the road, not the members of the Korps. *Which is a good thing,* Mulbah thought.

The last thing Mulbah wanted was to tempt fate one too many times.

* * *

### Mother Bea's Tea Tavern, Chocolate City, Liberia District, Earth

"I like you, Captain Tolbert," Gregory Donahue said as he sipped from his mug, his blue eyes closed as he enjoyed the spicy flavors of the local tea leaves. He set the drink down before continuing. "You are very much like your venerable colonel, Mulbah Luo. Did you know this?"

"So I've been told," Samson replied with a dry chuckle.

The captain had accidentally run into the defense contractor on his way home from the Kakata Korps' headquarters the day before as the contractor was inspecting some of the larger buildings within Chocolate City. Worried the westerner would be robbed, or worse, by local toughs, Samson had invited him to his house. Once he realized just who he was, however, the captain began to doubt their meeting was any sort of accident at all. It was part of the reason he had insisted on taking the defense contractor out for tea at a local tavern, away from his family. Not because of the potential danger the westerner faced, but for privacy. His neighbors were both nosy and gossipy. Rumors were sure to spread.

"Unlike your stalwart colonel, I believe the Mercenary Guild will turn on the Korps eventually," Donahue said as he stirred his tea with a pinky. The heat of the liquid didn't seem to bother the man, Samson noticed. "I did a little research on their history before the Information Guild began to clamp down on what passed between Earth's Aethernet and the GalNet. They...have a reputation of doing this to races who belonged to the guild. Nothing concrete, mind you, but some of the allegations are serious enough to warrant an investigation, if there was anything in the Galactic Union that could stand up to them."

"I don't get it," Samson said with a shrug. He looked at his empty cup and decided he had enough tea for the day. "Why would the guild do this?"

"Hard to say," Donahue admitted as he swallowed the rest of his hot tea in one gulp. Sighing with satisfaction, he set the empty mug down and looked across the table at Samson. "I think part of it is that the colonel has put a lot of faith into the Mercenary Guild. It's done wonders for your nation and your company, after all."

"Still," Samson paused for a couple of heartbeats, considering. He thought about it and decided both men were correct. The possibility of the Mercenary Guild turning on them once everything had calmed down was definitely there, while the colonel's reasoning why they wouldn't was also sound. He grunted. "Still, the *bass* always says to be prepared. I'll talk to Zion. He's the man who controls the bank, *menh*."

"I promise you, your boss will thank you later for this," Donahue assured him. "I'm a former merc myself, you know. I've seen the 'justice' and 'fairness' doled out by the Mercenary Guild firsthand."

"Who were you with?"

"Morgan's Morticians," Donahue said as he leaned back in his chair. He put his hands behind his head and sighed contentedly. "God, those were the days. Suicide drops from assault shuttles on worlds where the sun is too far away to cast anything other than pre-dawn light, toxic worlds where the air was filled with oxygenized acid, aliens that can eat you in two bites, aliens who were venomous,…"

"You are a twisted person, *menh*," Samson chuckled and shook his head. "That sounds like no fun, *ken*?"

"It wasn't," Donahue admitted with a wry smile, "but it paid well."

"You have no CASPers we need at the moment," Samson stated as he brought the conversation back to the original point of their meeting. "You have no assault shuttles. Yeah, *menh*, I looked up your company. No spaceships. What do you have we *can* use?"

"Ever heard of the Patriot Advanced Capability missile?"

"No," Samson admitted, digging into his pinplant for some information. What he found was very limited. "Who makes it?"

"We do," Donahue grinned. "We developed the PAC-VL when we got our hands on some Galactic tech. We made a surface-to-air missile that has almost zero heat signature when it launches. It doesn't use radar but is instead guided into position by a dummy missile from a control unit. Neat stuff."

"Why…?" Samson paused as he thought his question over. The only feasible way for the Mercenary Guild to attack the Korps without violating Galactic Law would be through assault shuttles. The overland route was swampy and horrid, while around the capitol and Chocolate City there were spots where one could land a shuttle without difficulty. Without telling Mulbah, the former child soldier had already begun to identify potential landing zones.

Samson still had serious misgivings about the Korps working for the guild and arresting the other Human mercenary companies. His natural distrust of all aliens, even Thorpi, was nearly impossible to shake. There was just something in the way they looked at Humans which set the mercenary on edge. It was as though they were constantly and silently judging humanity.

Samson tugged on his ear and considered. He would have to bring Mulbah around, and quickly, since Zion would go to their CO the moment Samson asked for credits.

Launch sites would be dispersed around the city so identifying them would be difficult. Finding a spot for the command vehicle would be tricky, as would getting someone trained up enough to actually run the command site. The SAMs would definitely be an unwelcome surprise to any pilot who had been under the impression Liberia was a backwards country with no defenses.

"Can you get your missiles into the country without alerting the Mercenary Guild?" Samson asked the defense contractor.

A sly smile began to grow on Donahue's face. "Getting it past the aliens was fairly easy."

"Good, I was worried about—wait, was?"

"You didn't think I'd come all this way and not be prepared, did you?"

\* \* \*

### Kakata Korps HQ, Freeport of Monrovia, Liberia District, Earth

"Easy," Zion said as he helped Sunshine out of the CASPer suit. "You handled it well, considering."

"I don't feel good," she gasped and promptly vomited all over the concrete floor of the storage warehouse.

They had been going at it for almost twelve hours straight, with Sunshine refusing to give up on the training exercises Zion had designed for her. Despite her relative inexperience in the machines, she had initially taken to it like a duck to water. As time progressed, however, it became clearer to the CFO of the Korps the young woman was in dire need of pinplants. Not so she could keep up with the suit, but so the suit could keep up with her.

"Let it out," Zion murmured, not knowing what else to say to the sweat-soaked teenage girl. Sunshine had put more hours into a CASPer than anyone else had over the past few weeks.

Mulbah was still incensed the Nigerian government had given the drug warlord their mechanized units, complete with trained crews. Nobody knew just how deeply the rot went, but Zion had a sneaky feeling that if the country's leadership did not right itself soon, the Korps would be making a second trip to Nigeria, and it would not end well for the current regime.

Sunshine crouched down and stared hard at the puke-covered concrete floor. Zion gave her another moment to spit out the last taste of bile and catch her breath before he reached down to pull her back upright.

"Let's go, back into the suit," he instructed, hating himself for it but following her request to push her harder than he did anyone else. "Your breaktime is up."

"Ugh," Sunshine groaned but quickly climbed back into the suit. Sealing herself in, she began to simulate a cold-start. Moments later the CASPer came back online. "Private Sunshine, reporting for duty."

"Don't vomit in the cockpit or you'll be cleaning it out for weeks," Zion warned as he brought up a new simulation within the CASPer. He searched through the options on his slate until he found one in particular he felt was challenging. "Okay, the objective in this mission is to protect the primary. He is marked blue on your Tri-V display. There are an unknown number of hostiles in the area. You have some air support but the rest of your team is down. Get him to the evac site and off-world before they catch up with you."

"Time?" Sunshine asked, all misery and pain gone from her voice as she became hyper-focused on the task at hand.

"Eleven minutes and counting," Zion said, checking the timer off on his slate. "Starting now."

The young girl went to work.

* * *

"She's coming along well, sir," Zion told Mulbah two hours later as the duo sat in the briefing room. Both wore the typical dark green jumper of the Korps' standard uniform, though neither wore the beret which Mulbah preferred. Zion shook his head. "Hell, she's better in a CASPer than most of the men. The problem is the suit doesn't respond as quickly as she does."

"Thinks too much?" Mulbah asked as he scrolled over the assessment report Zion had sent him of the young girl.

"Thinks too fast, Colonel," Zion corrected. "Her mind processes the simulation and comes up with a plan within seconds. It's terrifying, sir. None of the other prospects tested as high as she did during her MST. For a girl who was nothing more than a thief and property of some wannabe drug boss, she's almost too good to be true."

"You're thinking she's a plant of some kind?" Mulbah asked, his eyes narrowing suspiciously. "If you think that, why recommend her for the procedure?"

"I don't think she's a plant, no," Zion said. "I'm just saying that if we push this ahead, she'll be able to access stuff on the GalNet. It's one thing to succeed in the classroom, but it's another if she realizes just how big space really is."

"Final assessment?" Mulbah said in a tired voice. If he allowed the lawyer-turned-merc to dither around with the decision, they would be there until the end of time.

"She's ready, and we should foot the bill for the procedure," Zion declared. "We're flush with credits right now and if we wait, we could miss out on a window we might not get again."

"Meaning?" Mulbah probed.

"Thorpi doesn't like the feel he's getting from the Mercenary Guild of late," Zion said. "He thinks there is something afoot which will cause us problems, but he doesn't have any leads just yet. Plus, Samson brought something to my attention I think you should really consider."

"I'll talk to him later," Mulbah promised. He tapped in a final series of commands and sent it to Zion's slate. "Schedule her for the operation. The doc's in Miami, Florida. It'll take a full day, so I'm going to get her put in for the day after tomorrow. Does she know how painful it'll be?"

"I've warned her," Zion nodded, though he was not quite fully convinced. "But I don't think she believes me as to just how hard it could be."

"She was a slave who was beaten and abused by people her entire life, Captain," Mulbah reminded him. "If she says she can handle this, then she can handle it. You of all people should know this."

"Call it my protective streak of all children, drunkards, and fools," Zion chuckled.

"I always wondered why you became a merc," Mulbah said. "Now I know."

"Why, to protect Earth and the children of it?"

"No. To keep idiots like me alive."

Zion laughed and got to his feet. Though it was early in the afternoon, he was exhausted from working with Sunshine all morning. He half-turned and looked at his boss, all humor quickly vanishing as he changed the subject. "One thing still bugs me after reading the after-action review from New Ikoyi."

"The laser shot which killed PFC Doré," Mulbah finished for him.

"I went over the visual feed and everything," Zion stated as he smoothed out a small crease on his rolled-up sleeve. "There's literally nothing around which could have made that shot from the angle it did. Not for kilometers around. The only location the shot could have come from was from almost seven kilometers away, near downtown Lagos. The R3 Galactic building, actually."

"Want to investigate it?" Mulbah asked, frowning. Zion shook his head.

"It's the beginning of the wet season," he stated. "Any evidence that might have remained is long gone. It just...bugs me we don't know who killed PFC Doré, or even why."

"Whoever made the shot, they knew the precise spot to hit," Mulbah reminded him. "It's not hard to get a really good sniper rifle these days, especially one that has the hitting power of a .577 and almost zero drop at up to ten kilometers. I know we've made enemies, both here and off-world. Hell, I wouldn't be surprised if this was retribution for Italy."

"If it was, they sure picked one hell of a time to do it, sir," Zion shook his head. "No, sir, it doesn't add up at all."

"Okay then," Mulbah decided as he stood up as well and pocketed his slate. "Keep it on the down low and investigate it on your own time. Meanwhile, go prep Sunshine for her trip to Miami. Sign out a shuttle from Major Thorpi and check his availability as a pilot. I'm fairly certain he's free the rest of the week."

"Where are you off to?" Zion asked.

Mulbah smiled slyly. "Meeting with President Forh in an hour," he answered. "I think I know what he's going to ask, which would be terrific, but I'm also a little afraid of it as well."

"Hey, the West African Defense League was a brilliant idea," Zion countered. "He's not thinking of changing it, is he?"

"Not that I'm aware," Mulbah reassured his CFO. "If anything, he might be adding more nations to it."

"Well, this is good news, isn't it?" Zion asked.

Mulbah shrugged. "When was the last time you saw a Liberian politician willingly cede power of any sort of magnitude?"

"Uh, didn't former President Njie do that?"

"He only did it because I warned him if there were *any* problems with transference of power, the Korps would come and take care of him," Mulbah stated. Zion's eyes grew wide with surprise. Mulbah chuckled. "I did say 'willingly,' you know."

"I would never have pictured you as a king-maker," Zion muttered.

Mulbah grunted. "I never wanted to be one," he said. "I'd rather be looked at differently than the man who led a coup against a coup to defeat another coup in order to restore democracy."

"That made my head hurt."

"Should've tried saying it. I think I sprained my tongue."

* * *

### Executive Presidential Mansion, Monrovia, Liberia

"Colonel Luo! Thank you for coming on such short notice."

The President of Liberia greeted him as soon as he cleared the last set of guards.

Mulbah was impressed with the security upgrades. As much as he loathed needing so many defenses to protect the president, the recent uptick in legitimate threats to President Forh meant precautions had to be taken, especially as more and more people moved in from the bush to live in the capitol city itself. The city, which was once called home by 1.5 million people before the influx, was now bursting at the seams as various indigenous tribes and people lived amongst one another.

Old rivalries died hard, though. The overworked police force in the capitol were barely keeping up with the arrival of over 800,000 new people. Knifings were becoming more and more common. Arrests were up, though, and the general feeling in the city as a whole was a positive one. It was something Mulbah, five years ago, would have given his left eye to achieve.

Now, though? He wasn't so sure. When theory met practice, oftentimes the results were far more dangerous than originally believed.

"It's not a problem at all, sir." Mulbah nodded respectfully. The president stepped forward and embraced Mulbah in a giant hug. Surprised, Mulbah could do nothing as the man hoisted his feet off the ground a few centimeters before setting him back down.

"Please, I know how busy you are," President Forh stated and motioned for him to walk alongside him. Mulbah obediently complied and fell into step next to the man as they made their way to the spacious rear lawn behind the mansion. "Since the threats against me have multiplied in recent weeks, I've been forced to remain within the mansion more and more often. I hate this, because it deprives me of being able to walk among the citizens of this nation as one of them. Instead I am coddled, swaddled in protective layers, and cocooned. It's very frustrating."

"I can only imagine," Mulbah agreed. He'd been in a similar situation when former President Njie had been in charge.

"I made certain I can enjoy my walks out in the garden at least," President Forh stated as they walked down one of the wide stone paths.

"It's a lovely garden," Mulbah said. The president laughed and gave him an amused look.

"I admire your attempt to humor me," President Forh stated. "This? This is pathetic. I've wanted to make this place beautiful, so I can spread this atmosphere out into Monrovia and beyond. This is a pale imitation of what a garden should look like, but a brilliant mind once remarked that all great journeys begin with a single step."

"I didn't know you were a fan of Lao Tzu," Mulbah admitted, impressed. The president looked at him in confusion.

"Who? I read it on a fortune cookie one time when I visited Spain."

"Ahh...okay. Still, it's a good quote." Mulbah shrugged and smiled. "It's fitting in these times."

"'These times' are precisely why I wanted to speak with you," President Forh admitted as they passed one of the many stone benches which lined the path. Overhead the blue sky was bright. For once there was not a cloud in the sky, Mulbah noticed. The wet season might be at hand, but it still didn't mean the sunny skies weren't unwelcome every once in a while. The president paused and turned to look at Mulbah. "Let me ask you something. How hard would it be to roll the Korps into the Liberian National Army?"

"I—huh?" Mulbah blinked. That wasn't what he had expected the president to ask him. He slowly began to shake his head. "With all due respect, sir, the mercs under my command wouldn't respect anyone who hadn't passed their VOWs or attended an MST. Plus, the pay of the army doesn't even come close to what I pay my mercs. I'm sorry, Mister President, but the idea wouldn't work."

"I didn't think it would, but the legislature has directed me to propose it to you anyway," President Forh admitted, a sour tone in his voice. "In fact, they're pressuring me to nationalize the Korps on the whole."

Mulbah nearly exploded. "Are they out of their freaking minds? The Korps alone provides almost fifteen percent of the nation's taxable income! If they try to take my company I will take all our revenue and resettle somewhere else."

"That's kinder than what I thought you'd say," President Forh said calmly. "I figured you would simply launch a coup and kill the legislators."

"The thought did cross my mind," Mulbah grumbled.

President Forh held up a hand. "Which is why *I'm* the one talking to you. I feel we have mutual respect, and I greatly admire what you've done here. I feel an agreement of some sort might be reached, though it's not the one the legislature thought of."

"What exactly were you thinking?" Mulbah asked, intrigued despite his earlier outburst. He knew the man before him had a cunning mind. One could even argue devious.

"How hard would it be to roll the army into the Korps?"

Mulbah started to reply off the cuff but paused, considering. Standard combat body armor was cheap, and he had thousands of sets laying around in his warehouse. One didn't need to pass VOWs to attain a set. They also served well in case a riot broke out, except for knife attacks, as Zion had proven during his run-in with Major General Sparkles.

"That's...possible," Mulbah allowed, mulling the idea over. "I would need some time to go over the numbers, as well as present the idea to Zion and Thorpi. Their advice is invaluable to me."

"Thorpi...is the alien who works for you, yes?"

"Yeah, he's a Veetanho," Mulbah confirmed. "The only male I've ever heard of leaving their home world. Good worker, excellent planner."

"And he is the same race as the leader who occupies Earth?" President Forh asked, his voice clipped and short.

"Well, from a certain point of view—" Mulbah tried to explain but the president cut him off.

"They occupy the office of the Secretary General," President Forh stated firmly. "It means we are being occupied."

"Well...yes, I guess so."

"Was that so hard to admit?" the president asked, slightly surprised.

"Honestly? Yes," Mulbah nodded.

\* \* \*

**Winners' Chapel, Monrovia, Liberia District, Earth**

Perched atop the dome of a converted house of worship wasn't where the Blevin assassin preferred to be, but it was the only structure within ten kilometers, not within the Kakata Korps' compound, that was tall enough to see over the buildings between her and her target.

The pay was bad, the timing was horrific, and Kl'arn couldn't help but feel as though this was being ordered by someone other than General Peepo. While the missive had the general's name attached to it, the Blevin had done some of Peepo's wet-work in the past. This job felt rushed.

There were better angles if the stupid Human would leave the compound, but recent events had increased security at the president's residence. This alone would typically have prompted the Blevin to wait until a later date, when the target was out in the open and multiple firing angles could have masked the direction of the shot. If she took the shot now, it would be obvious from which direction it had come from.

The order had been specific, though. It had to be today, which meant the Blevin had doubled her normal rate. The fact that it had been paid without even a quibble had alerted her that not all was right. However, the credits were in the account. Doubt only went so far, but then cold, hard currency took over.

She stilled herself and entered *xialintae*, the trance-like state where a Blevin could temporarily cause both hearts to stop beating for up to ten minutes. It allowed the senses to sharpen and the muscles to go slack, as well as ensure there wasn't so much as a tremble on the trigger of her rifle. Perfect, absolute stillness was only attained during *xialintae*.

A slight gust of wind from the ocean drifted over her position, blowing the ghillie sheet slightly off her rifle. In her present state, however, she wasn't aware the rifle's long barrel was now exposed, as was her spotter's scope, a sleek and ancient metallic tube which had been passed down in her family for generations. Sunlight reflected off the metal, a bright beacon nobody would have noticed unless they were looking right at it.

However, at that precise moment, Mulbah Luo, CEO and Commanding Officer of the Kakata Korps, happened to be looking in that exact direction.

\* \* \*

### Executive Presidential Mansion, Monrovia, Liberia District, Earth

Mulbah saw the flash of light and instinctively grabbed the president.

"Down!" He roared as he pulled the president behind one of the many stone benches. A smoking hole appeared in the grass where the president had been standing a second before. Mulbah pushed the heavy stone bench onto its side and pulled the president behind the makeshift barricade. He immediately triggered an alert via his pinplants. "Active shooter! Position is atop the old Winners' Chapel near the training pitch, one kilometer to the northwest. Korps, Lion Six Actual! Reactive response team to pinged location, now!"

The Presidential Guards began hustling out onto the grounds as Mulbah risked a quick peek over the edge of the bench. Two more shots had struck the bench, but the five-inch-thick marble and the angle deflected them away, leaving nothing but a greasy burn mark in the stone. Mulbah's eyes narrowed as he realized the burn pattern around the mark was similar to the one which had killed PFC Doré in Nigeria.

"Stay down, Mister President," Mulbah ordered as the Presidential Guard took up positions around the duo, their eyes scanning for threats. Mulbah pointed in the direction for them to look. "One known shooter, that direction. Possibly more. Keep him covered."

"What are you going to do?" the president asked, his eyes wide.

"I'm going to hunt the bastard down," Mulbah growled.

\* \* \*

### Winners' Chapel, Monrovia, Liberia District, Earth

"Well, that's not good," Kl'arn muttered to herself as the familiar whine of CASPer jumpjets filled her earhole. During her near-hypnotic state, her ghillie sheet had blown off, exposing her to the planet's harsh sun. This in turn had somehow alerted the damnable Kakata Korps commander of her presence. Bad luck all around, but now was not the time to dwell upon the details of the blown op. It was time to leave.

Unfortunately, she had not counted on the speed at which the Korps would respond to the shooting. She hadn't planned for the possibility that she would be seen, considering how far away she was from the target. She glanced to the north and saw six CASPers bounding down the street. They would be on her in moments; there wasn't nearly enough time for her ship to arrive and extract her.

With no other options available, and a strong desire to continue to live, there was only one thing she could do. Sighing, she carefully packed away her equipment and climbed down into the old, abandoned chapel. She raised her long arms into the air in a position of surrender and walked out the front door.

"I surrender," the Blevin said meekly as she found herself staring down the barrel of a magnetic accelerator cannon. For once, she was glad she could not see the faces of those before her. There was very little evidence suggesting she would be comfortable with what she saw.

\* \* \*

### Kakata Korpa HQ, Freeport of Monrovia, Liberia District, Earth

"We've never had a prisoner before," Captain Antonious Karnga admitted to his boss as they led the alien into the converted holding cell. Originally intended to be used as a freezer by the warehouse's previous owner, it now served as a temporary holding cell until Mulbah could figure out what to do with the alien Blevin.

Mulbah had heard of the humanoid aliens before, though he'd never actually seen one. They were considered scum, ranking almost as low as the Pushtal or the Zuparti when it came to being a member of the criminal element. This one, though, did not come off as anything more than a hired gun. It was a strange distinction, but Mulbah had learned to trust his gut over the years. It had brought him mostly success.

"Keep the zip ties on him," Mulbah decided as two men from the rapid response team shoved the alien into the converted cell.

"Her," the Blevin corrected. "I'm a she."

"I could give a *jungo* about it," Corporal Har Baranga spat. "You killed my friend. I hope you rot in there, *asalewandi*."

"My translator did not pick that up," the Blevin said in a calm voice. "Will you re—"

Corporal Baranga slammed the door in the alien's face, cutting her off before she could finish the sentence. He looked at Colonel Luo before dipping his head.

"Sorry, *bass*," the young man apologized. "Won't happen again."

"I know," Mulbah said gently. "Go find First Sergeant Simbo and ask him to come down."

"Yes, *bass*, right away," the corporal braced to attention before quickly striding away, leaving Mulbah alone with the alien.

"Why did you send him when you could have used your pinplant to contact your first sergeant?" the Blevin asked through the thick door, her voice muffled. Mulbah walked to the comms button and flipped the switch to On.

"It gives the young man something to do besides brood over the alien who killed his best friend," Mulbah told her. He took a deep breath. "There are two ways this can go for you. One, you tell me who hired you to kill President Forh and why, and your death will be quick. Or two, I beat you senseless until you tell me who hired you to kill President Forh and why, and your death is slow and painful. Choose."

"There is no need for threats, Colonel," the Blevin stated. "I am more than willing to share everything I know."

"You are?" Mulbah asked, incredulous. *Could it really be this simple?*

"You let me leave here alive, and I will even give you the proof you would require upon hearing my accusations," the Blevin continued. "My name is Kl'arn, and upon the memory of my ancestors I give you my word that I will share all…after, of course, a reasonable exchange."

"You killed one of my mercs," Mulbah growled.

"Humans are fragile things," Kl'arn observed. "A Besquith might have been able to continue to fight with that shot. You see, my aim was off. I was five centimeters below the heart."

"You are not helping your case," Mulbah said irritably.

"I did not know I was on trial."

"It started the moment you were taken in custody," Mulbah informed her. "You're not ignorant of our customs, otherwise you wouldn't have taken this job."

"You are observant," the Blevin replied. "I applaud this."

"I'm recording this conversation via pinlink," Mulbah informed her. "However, until First Sergeant Simbo arrives, this is nothing more than a very informal conversation. When the time comes, I will require your full confession."

"And then I walk away, never to return to your planet?" Kl'arn asked.

"We'll see," Mulbah answered after a moment. "But not likely."

"Then we are at an impasse," Kl'arn stated. "Until I have guaranteed safe passage off your world, I am unable to tell you the full depth of this conspiracy against your president. Or you. Or…Earth."

"I've never met a Blevin before," Mulbah said as he ignored the alien's lure for the moment. "Is it true you can enter some kind of trance and freeze your body for long periods of time?"

"The *xialintae*, yes," Kl'arn corrected for him. "It is a state of heightened awareness which sharpens a single sense, but also creates a blissful ignorance of the others. Both a blessing and a curse, as proven today. If I hadn't been in *xialintae* I would have noticed the ghillie sheet had fallen off my old spotter scope. You would never have seen me otherwise."

"You made a mistake," Mulbah shrugged. "You screwed up."

"Yes, I did," the Blevin agreed. She did not sound angry at this fact, Mulbah noticed. It simply was. "You have not yet convinced me I will walk out of here alive."

"You haven't convinced me you should," Mulbah countered. "I know there are people who want to kill me. It's a hazard of the job."

"It is a hazardous universe in which we live," the alien agreed. "Everything is trying to kill us. Time, space, matter, oxygen, water...even now our bodies are fighting the entropic embrace of death."

"Very poetic," Mulbah said. "For a Blevin."

"Our kind were artists of great renown for many years," Kl'arn replied. "It's genetic at this point in our existence."

First Sergeant Simbo arrived at last. "Sorry it took so long, *bass*." The short, rotund NCO was sweating slightly despite the cool air inside the warehouse. "I was moving equipment. What do you need, *bass*?"

"A witness," Mulbah told him after killing the speaker into the converted holding cell. "The Blevin inside has information that could be of use. Guild Law says for a valid confession to occur on a planet under guild administration, there must be two officers and an NCO present during the recorded confession, or their race's equivalent. I already pinged Captain Tolbert."

"Got it, *bass*," Simbo nodded. "You think he knows anything worth knowing?"

"She, and possibly," Mulbah corrected as he looked back at the jail. He wished he could see the Blevin's face, though he really didn't know why. It wasn't as though he could read the alien's features. Mulbah shook his head. *For all I know, though, the Blevin could lie and say you ordered the assassination attempt on the president.*

"If I had done it, *bass*, it would have been with a shaped IED alongside the road, two pronged," Simbo stated in a quiet voice. "Or just hit the mansion with a missile. Alien sniper? That's not how anyone we know thinks."

"I'm thinking the same thing," Mulbah said nodding in agreement. "But again, there's nothing firm until I have proof. She could lie in order to save her life."

"She better not survive this, *bass*," Samson growled as he arrived. The 1st company captain appeared to be in a foul mood. Mulbah couldn't blame him. "We know the alien in there killed Doré. Even if she told you the secrets to the Galactic Union, if you let her go free then all the boys will lose respect for you."

"I hadn't planned on letting her go, even if she does have information we can use," Mulbah said as he turned to look at his old friend. "But I won't kill her just for the sake of it."

"You had no problem kicking Moses out of the shuttle," Samson reminded him. He motioned toward the makeshift prison cell. "Why are you worried about killing an alien when you didn't even blink killing another Human, *bass*?"

"That was different," Mulbah tried to explain.

"Of course it was, *bass*." Samson said, snarling at his commander. "It's always different. We kill the Humans for the aliens to take their money, but now we're not killing the aliens who kill Humans? The boys listen to you, *bass*, and they trust you. But this shit? This is stupid, *menh*."

"What? No," Mulbah shook his head, confused. "The Blevin may have files on Peepo and what she's doing here. I need those."

"Then what, *bass*?" Samson asked, looking away. He picked at his uniform's collar, frustrated. "Then we wait until Peepo comes to kill us all?"

"What are you asking me, Samson?" Mulbah asked, growing. "I can't say to the universe 'this is difficult for us, make it easy,' can I?"

"You can make it easier for us by killing the alien in there," Samson snapped back. "If you don't, I will."

"No, you won't," Mulbah said and moved between the captain and the prisoner's door. Though Samson towered over Mulbah, the colonel didn't budge. "I need that damn info."

"What you need is to remember where you're from," Samson retorted. "Move, *bass*."

"No."

"*Bass*, I don't want to hurt you, but the Blevin has to die."

"*After* I get those fucking files," Mulbah growled in a low voice. "Samson, don't make me do something you'll regret."

"I can snap you like a twig," the big man reminded him. "Move."

"I'm not moving," Mulbah replied. "So snap me like a twig."

Samson looked away, his hands balled tightly into fists. "Why you let her live, *bass*? Why? Why we kill those Italians? Why didn't we run with the Horsemen?"

"Because I didn't think they were right at the time," Mulbah said in a quiet voice. "I was wrong."

"We can still make it right, *bass*," Samson whispered and closed his eyes. "Let me kill her."

"Not yet, Captain," Mulbah said. "I need those files."

"Why though, *bass*?"

"I know we're not getting off-planet again, not as long as the planet is under the guild's administration," Mulbah said as reached out and grabbed the bigger man's arm. Samson opened his eyes and looked at his commander. "Peepo will make sure of this. The information still can, though. If we can get it into Peacemaker hands, Earth has a chance. For this to happen, I need to get the files first."

"The Peacemaker Guild?" Samson asked, shocked. "You…already knew the Merc Guild would turn on us, *menh*? Why didn't you say?"

"Thorpi knew," Mulbah said, his tone calm and neutral. "I was in denial. Thorpi knows how the guild runs, how Peepo thinks. He said they would turn on us once we fulfilled our tasks. We've done it. The only thing we can be now is a threat. I promise you will have your revenge for Doré. But it has to be *after* I get the information, *ken*?"

"Yes, *bass*," Samson acknowledged after a moment. He looked away, ashamed. "I'm sorry, *bass*. I wasn't thinking."

"We all screw up, Samson," Mulbah replied. "I should have listened to the Horsemen. I think now they were right about the guild. But would it have made things different? Probably not. I would have stayed here and made sure the aliens didn't kill everyone just to make peace. Only thing it would have changed is how fast the guild turned on us."

"What now?" Samson asked.

"We do our jobs," he told him. "First Sergeant Simbo?"

"Yes, *bass*?" Simbo asked.

"In ten minutes, get two more armed guards from 2nd Company and bring the Blevin to the briefing room," Mulbah instructed. "Nobody from 1st Company, you understand? Get with Oti and make sure he knows you're borrowing some of his guys. Captain Tolbert?"

"*Bass?*" Samson asked.

"Let's get ready for the meeting," Mulbah told him. "We need to be on the same side, and the Blevin needs to see it if she's going to break and give us what we need. After we record the confession, we'll get her up in the conference room and put her on a show trial. We have to be on the same page for this, though."

"Same page…yes, *bass*," Samson nodded. "That's easy."

"And next time, if you have a problem with me, don't bring it up in front of anyone else," Mulbah warned him. "We need to be seen as united by the men. If they think we're fighting, they lose faith in our ability to lead."

"Yes, *bass*," Samson nodded sheepishly. "I won't do that again."

"Good." Mulbah grunted. "Now, let's go make our visitor feel most unwelcome."

\* \* \*

Twenty minutes later, Mulbah was seated at a conference table in the unsecure briefing room inside the Kakata Korps headquarters. Next to him, Samson was staring at his personal slate. The two men had decided to make the alien assassin across the table from them sweat nervously and wait in the silence.

*Do Blevins sweat?* Mulbah wondered idly as he stared at the blank slate in his hands. The reptilian alien across from him couldn't see what he was looking at, since the angle was wrong, but her imagination was obviously filling in enough to make her extremely agitated. He made a show of swiping the slate and set it on the table, face down, and folded his hands. Leaning forward, Mulbah gave the Blevin a curious look.

"Nothing I've found matches what you claim," he began, his voice perfectly neutral. "Care to elaborate?"

"It's there if you know what to look for," Kl'arn responded, her thin-slit eyes darting between Mulbah and Samson nervously. "I have the data stored somewhere safe."

"You uploaded it to the GalNet?" Samson asked, incredulous. "You wouldn't be that crazy."

"No, somewhere even Peepo would never think to look," the Blevin responded, her voice sour.

Mulbah chuckled. "I know where you put it. Ballsy."

"What?" She turned her head to look at Mulbah in surprise. "There's no way you could possibly know where I put the data."

Mulbah smiled at her. "You uploaded it to one of Earth's Aerthernet storage sites."

"How…?" her voice trailed off as Samson, grumbling to himself, pulled his wallet out of his back pocket. He pulled out an old dollar bill, printed over one hundred years before, and handed it over to Mulbah. The merc commander waved Samson's payment of their bet away before continuing.

"You're very calculating," he told the Blevin as Samson repocketed the bill. "You know Peepo well, and I'm guessing you consider the leader of the Mercenary Guild to be arrogant. So what better place to hide data which could ruin her than right under her nose, the one place she would never think to look?"

"Humans are ingenious little tinkerers," Kl'arn said as she settled back uncomfortably in the chair. It was designed for Humans and did not fit the ungainly alien. She tried to make it work anyway. "It is why the guild despises your kind so. They want obedience. Humans are...anything but."

"It's an evolutionary thing," Mulbah smirked. "Survival of the wittiest."

"I have not heard that before," the Blevin noted.

"Look, we're not going to punish you for your assassination attempt on the President of Liberia," Mulbah promised her. "You missed, no harm done there. But we need the data if we're going to truly get back at the Mercenary Guild."

"You swear?" Kl'arn asked, confused. "No punishment for shooting at your president?"

"None whatsoever," Mulbah said as he held up an open palm. "I swear upon it with my life you will not be punished for attempting to kill our president. Now, help us help you."

"When you release me, I shall give you the dropbox it's stored on," the Blevin countered, evidently pleased by Mulbah's desire to not kill her. "If I give it to you beforehand, you'll just kill me."

"Wrong," Mulbah told her. "We'll keep you here until it's safe for you to leave. It's better than us killing you, wouldn't you think?"

"Safe?" the Blevin asked incredulously. "You think I'd be safe anywhere on this entropy-forsaken planet? Ha!"

"You stay here, nobody knows what happened and everyone assumes you're dead," Mulbah told her as he leaned back in his chair. "Peepo won't be hunting you to find out why you missed the target."

"Let me go," the Blevin countered. "I'm much better on my own."

"If I let you go, Peepo will eventually find and kill you," Mulbah reminded the Blevin. "In fact, I could just let it slip out onto GalNet you were captured by a Human merc company on Earth, assassinating its political leaders on behalf of Peepo and the guild. Who knows what would happen then? I might die, the Korps might get attacked, but…I wonder what your lifespan would be after this interesting bit of information got out?"

Kl'arn hissed and drew back from the table. Her six fingers drummed on the table, a telltale sign the alien was nervous. The Blevin was probably not used to being manipulated like this. Mulbah could see her discomfort and tried to withhold a grin.

Years at the corporate level had taught him it was all about an individual's buttons, and when to push them. Skilled negotiating tactics were something he had been forced to develop as his startup had struggled to compete with the mega corps on the galactic scale. He'd shown Kl'arn the bad, and painted the worst possible picture he could imagine. It was time to show her some of the good.

"Or, you stay here, as our prisoner, and we let slip the assassin died after a failed escape attempt," Mulbah offered, dangling a different sort lifeline in front of her. "Peepo wouldn't bother looking for you. Meanwhile, you could build a new persona and get off-world at your convenience. Or, conversely, we could just execute you and dump your body into the bay. Sharks around here are pretty aggressive, and any evidence would be quickly eaten. It would be unfortunate, but an acceptable loss."

The Blevin blinked rapidly and looked away, lost in thought. Mulbah gave her enough time to consider all the options which were on the table before she began to nod, slowly at first but with increased enthusiasm.

Next to him, Samson helpfully chimed in. "You haven't seen a shark feeding frenzy, have you? Pull one up on the GalNet sometime. I heard one of the clips was bad enough to scare the Besquith, who promised to never set foot in our oceans."

"Enough," Kl'arn growled, her yellow pupils narrowed. Knowing what he did of the Blevin, Mulbah guessed he had struck a nerve. She continued, "I'll remain here, in your 'safe' custody. No information on GalNet about my arrest, none of your sharks. I'll download everything I have, raw data and otherwise, in exchange for my life."

"I knew we could come to an agreement," Mulbah nodded as he looked at First Sergeant Simbo. "Grab two men and take her back to the cell. Try to see about making it more comfortable. In the meantime, we need to have a general staff meeting."

"Oh yay, more staff meetings," Samson said as he rolled his eyes. Mulbah ignored the comment.

"First Sergeant, you're dismissed," Mulbah said. He looked at Kl'arn. "Simbo will help get your information downloaded and safely stored. We thank you again for your generous assistance."

"I like living," the Blevin countered. "This was my best option."

"I'm glad you see it the same way we do," Mulbah said as the Blevin stood. Simbo and Kl'arn left the room and Mulbah waited a few moments before he continued. "As soon as we have the information, dump her ass in the bay with a bullet in her brain."

"You're breaking your word?" Samson asked, surprised. Mulbah shook his head.

"No," he countered as he flipped the slate over and played with the edge of the device with his fingernail. "I said I wouldn't kill her for attempting to assassinate the president. I never said a word about her shooting PFC Doré. I made sure it never came up."

"Ruthless," Samson observed. Mulbah grunted.

"We exist in a universe where everything can kill us pretty easily, Captain," the commander of the Kakata Korps replied. "If humanity can't be ruthless, we won't survive."

\* \* \*

**Cahill Memorial Hospital, Miami, United States District**

Thorpi looked at the Sphen-Eudy standing atop the bench with no small amount of trepidation. What the sleek, black-feathered alien was proposing was insane, and the odds of the Information Guild's plan succeeding were almost zero. Yet the simple fact remained, it was the only feasible way to transmit the information Mulbah had sent him off-planet without the Mercenary Guild catching wind of what they were doing.

The Sphen-Eudy's brows went higher, the yellow tufts of feathers an obvious sign of the agent's exasperation. Thorpi had known all along he was playing a dangerous game, working for both the Mercenary and Information Guilds. It was now time to turn the tables on Peepo and her ilk, for better or for worse. He hoped what he was about to do didn't come back to bite him later on.

"And you're absolutely certain she has enough?" Thorpi pressed, nervous. He actually liked the young girl, crass attitude and all. She reminded him of a rebellious creche sister, which pleased him to no end. Creche sisters who made the lives of favored daughters entropic were impossible to find. Especially in his family. He continued after a breath. "The Korps are inordinately fond of the girl. As am I."

"Some slight variations from the other subjects we've tested," the Sphen-Eudy offered with a delicate shrug. Its white feathered belly ruffled, then flattened against its body. "Typical in Humans. My uncle states the differences in Human DNA sequencing between their various tribes is minimal at best. No, it won't affect the information or the storage amount."

"And the Wrogul?" Thorpi pressed.

"Ray says it'll be a snap," the Sphen-Eudy replied. "He's oddly excited about this."

"Odd creatures, Wrogul," Thropi muttered. "What will she remember?"

"Pain."

"She can handle it," Thorpi said. "We still are looking for a way to get her off-planet before the feces strikes the rotary impeller."

"I can't help you there," the aliens replied.

"I thought your people were smugglers?"

"We're independent commercial and industrial financiers," the Sphen-Eudy corrected with a sharp snap of its beak. "There is a difference."

"Payment will be made once the connection is established," Thorpi told the small alien as it hopped off the bench to the tiled floor. The Sphen-Eudy grunted in an odd pitch.

"There are so many different ways Humans are living, breathing weapons," the alien casually noted. Thorpi's ear twitched unwittingly forward but he quelled the movement before the smaller Information Guild agent noticed. "The guild is excited about their potential."

"Let's just hope they survive whatever the Mercenary Guild has in store for them," Thorpi cautioned the creature. "Whatever Peepo is planning, she aims to ensure they are firmly under her control when the time comes."

The Sphen-Eudy began hopping back down the hall toward the operating suite before it stopped and turned its head almost completely around to look at Thorpi. The dark eyes of the alien bore into his. "Has it not occurred to anyone else the Veetanho seem to control the most dangerous of the mercenary races?" it offered before shaking its head slightly. "No, a Veetanho wouldn't notice this. But I find it…unsettling; the MinSha, Tortantula and Flatar, and the Besquith all seem to do the bidding of the Veetanho without hesitation. Perhaps there are other reasons, ones nobody has considered, which drives Peepo along her path? I shall leave those thoughts for others with time and money to ponder. I am far too busy. Good day, Thorpi, and good luck."

Thorpi didn't watch the Sphen-Eudy leave. Instead, he hurried back into the surgical suite waiting area, where he found Zion half-asleep in his seat. The Veetanho slid into a second chair without the Human noticing and pulled out his slate. As far as he could tell, the 3rd Company commander had not noticed he had left the room at all.

\* \* \*

Zion waited patiently in the surgical suite, his eyes half-closed as he stared off into nothing, his mind scouring the GalNet for any information he could find about the current state of events on Earth. There were a lot of blocks in place, but he was still able to use the guild codes, courtesy of General Peepo and the Mercenary Guild. This was supposed to have ensured their loyalty, but the more Zion explored, the worse it became. It wasn't looking good for humanity, which made the Korps' current situation untenable in the eyes of the rest of the mercenary companies who were Earth-based.

Word on the street was that the Izlian were backing away from the current war against humanity, but nobody could tell Zion why. Using his codes to dig deeper into the GalNet told him nothing except something big had happened involving the entire Izlian race and a time of mourning. Zion understood how phrasing worked, and using this new information was able to deduce that the Izlian's most popular and successful admiral, Admiral Omega, had somehow died. In combat or just simply from old age, though, Zion couldn't say. Even with his access levels, the information was restricted.

As to why this information was being restricted, Zion couldn't say. He suspected it was partly due to the remaining elements of the Horsemen who were still hiding out on Earth and using the GalNet to pass messages along. A niggling little voice in the back of his mind, however, suggested something else.

Zion looked at the slight alien seated across from him. Thorpi, who had taken an interest in Sunshine as well, had come inside the hospital with them and decided to wait with the mercenary. The Veetanho was quiet as he read his slate, using his nails to flip through the screens at a rapid pace. Now that Zion actually had time to consider it, he decided the whole situation was strange. Thorpi was the first male Veetanho any Human had ever seen, and yet they knew almost nothing about him, even after three years of working with him.

"Can I ask you something?" Zion asked the alien. Thorpi looked up and set his slate aside.

"Please," Thorpi said, evidently happy with the interruption. "This wait is driving me to distraction."

"Do you have any family?"

Thorpi's face scrunched up into what Zion could only describe as a Veetanho's version of a grimace before answering. "I do. My family situation, however, is…rather complicated."

"I have two younger sisters up in Philly," Zion said as he scratched his head. "Thought about stopping by up there to say hi, but…I love them, but distance works best in our relationship."

"I could say the same about my sister," Thorpi admitted after a brief pause. "All my sisters, actually. The primary daughter of my mother is…difficult, to say the least."

"I get that," Zion nodded. "I went to Tulane for my undergrad, law school at Denver, passed both the Bar and the CPA exams, and my sister is still better in my parent's eyes because after she graduated from Harvard she went back to Philly to become a community activist. I mean, really? I've actually achieved something in my life, but because she went back home to help other immigrants, she's more successful, according to my parents."

"I am the first…of my kind to leave the creche," Thorpi said quietly, his whiskers twitching as he spoke. "In my mother's eyes, I am nothing more than an anomaly. The primary daughter of my mother is the future for her, for all of our family."

"What's a creche?" Zion asked. He shook his head and grimaced. "I mean, I know what the word means, but what does it mean to you? Is it like a nest or something?"

Thorpi took a deep breath before responding. "A creche is a name for household, but much like your feudal system in ancient times. There are five classes of Veetanho in the creche—high mother, brood mothers, favored or primary daughters, creche sisters, and males. You are born into this and there is no changing your status."

"That's...pretty strict," Zion muttered. "I don't mean to pry, but can you explain them to me?"

"I can try," Thorpi stated after a moment of contemplation. "Some concepts are difficult to fully explain in just words, but I shall endeavor to do my best.

"The high mother is just that. She decides the role of the creche and the future path. Her decisions are law within the creche and we all obey. Usually the smartest and strongest, she is also responsible for ensuring the primary genetic sequencing of the creche is passed along. She is what you Humans would call the queen of the family, I suppose, though that term isn't really accurate either.

"Brood mothers are sterile females who remain behind on our home world to raise the young and care for the creche. They are the ultimate authority figures in the creche and if you like living, you don't cross them. They enforce the will of the high mother. If you are born sterile but otherwise are normal, it is almost certain are you will become a brood mother. Our creche had five when I was growing up. It was...unpleasant at the best of times.

"Favored daughters are what you would call the warriors of the creche," Thorpi said after taking a breath. It was obvious to Zion this was a sensitive subject for the Veetanho, but for some reason the alien seemed to want to talk about this more than Zion had anticipated. "My mother's favored daughter is the sibling in question I have...difficulties with. They are the ones who will later take over the creche and become the high mother. If there are multiple favored daughters then a creche war will break out to fight for the high mother position. This war cleanses the gene pool and ensures future generations are stronger, faster, and smarter. Only the weak succumb."

"Brutal," Zion observed. "And here I thought growing up in a Liberian household was rough."

"Veetanho culture is a very interesting thing," Thorpi admitted. "I have learned during my time with you Humans that 'interesting' can have many connotations. This, I believe, is interesting in the Chinese sense of the word."

Zion chuckled. He understood the meaning behind it as well.

"Then there are creche sisters," Thorpi said, squirming uncomfortably at this part. "They are born smaller than most females and typically are what you would call mentally challenged. They exist for only one purpose—to serve as prey to favored daughters as they come of age."

"Holy…you *eat* one another?" Zion asked, eyes wide with shock.

Thorpi quickly shook his head. "No. It's more of an intellectual hunt. The favored daughters are expected to torment, abuse, and generally make a creche sister's life hell. This ensures the favored daughter understands what cruelty is, and ruthlessness, in order to ensure the creche survives and grows stronger."

"What happens to the creche sister?" Zion asked, perturbed.

"They almost always die before they come of breeding age," Thorpi said in a quiet voice. "If they live past that, which is exceedingly rare, they usually assist the high mother in anything they need."

"Damn," Zion grunted.

"Yes, very," Thorpi said. "Most creche sisters are indeed damned. Then there are the males, who have one sole purpose in life—to breed. They fight for supremacy amongst one another for the chance to sneak in while the high mother is nesting and submit themselves to her will. If she approves of them, she will allow the mating to occur. If she does not, she kills them by rolling on top of them and smothering them. Fortunately, thanks to the size difference, it's a rather quick death."

"Size difference?" Zion asked, surprise on his dark features. He chuckled and shook his head. "A high mother must be enormous."

"No," Thorpi shook his furry head. "A male is just very small."

"I don't understand."

"Not many outside of our species know this, but the typical Veetanho male is about the size of your pet sugar gliders," Thorpi explained. "Males are tiny and fragile things."

"Wait...are you a female?" Zion asked, shocked.

Thorpi shrugged his shoulders. "In a way, yes," the Veetanho corrected. "I am a creche sister."

"But...I thought you said..."

"Creche sisters are mentally challenged?" Thorpi finished the question for Zion before chuffing slightly, amused. "Creche sisters are very mentally limited, yes. I was born different for some reason. I was able to outsmart the best of the favored daughters in the creche, which drove my siblings to despair. Only the last favored daughter, the sibling of which I spoke of, survived the high mother's displeasure at my besting them. More than once did I have to fight off their attempts to simply kill me with their superior strength and size. The high mother of my creche saw value in me, however, and decided I would have a different role other than bait. Eventually, I accepted your job offer and left my creche."

"And you've never been back?" Zion asked. Thorpi shook his head. "If you are a creche sister, why do you call yourself a male?"

Thorpi laughed at this. "It's much easier to state that I am a male, rather than a genetically inferior female. It appeases my high mother, as well as allows other Veetanho to ignore my status in Colonel Luo's company. If I were to state my status as a creche sister and was open about this, then they would constantly seek to challenge me and your company to prove their own worth. This way I can exist and live without appearing to be a threat to future high mothers."

"That's crazy," Zion muttered.

"Not in the least," Thorpi said. "You have Humans who do this as well, yes?"

"Yeah, but..." Zion's voice trailed off as he struggled to elucidate his argument better. "It's just weirder here. I mean, they don't do it for survival. Usually. Hell, I don't know, they could be doing it to stay alive. Maybe. Ugh, this is one of those things where growing up in American culture clashes with my Liberian heritage and norms. No wonder my parents didn't want to go back to Liberia."

"As I said, it is easier for all involved to accept me as a male," the Veetanho said. "I'm sure your people feel the same."

"Do you...want me to keep it a secret?" Zion asked carefully, not wanting to offend the alien.

"It would make functioning easier amongst the enlisted mercs," Thorpi admitted, his furry face scrunched up in thought. "But for the officers, it doesn't matter. I...have a personal preference of being called a 'male,' however, for the simplification of things. 'Creche sister' just seems like a bit too much."

"Fine with me. It's not like we could tell the difference if you hadn't said anything. Changing the subject," Zion said with a nervous titter, "are you blocked from the GalNet? I mean, do you have full access?"

"No," Thorpi said as he picked up his slate and checked. "Very curious. I wonder why access is limited?"

"I was going to ask you the same thing," Zion stated. "It's almost like Peepo wants to limit the things we can search from Earth."

"It would be difficult for the general to accomplish that, but not impossible," Thorpi pointed out, though he was careful as to what he shared. There was only so much he was willing to tell anybody, especially given the divisions in both the Mercenary and Information Guilds. "The information is outside the control of the Mercenary Guild. The Information Guild would throw a fit if anyone tried to control the GalNet or thwart the flow of data."

"Could they be bought?" Zion asked.

"Everyone can be bought," Thorpi said as calmly as he could manage. Humans were too perceptive at times, and it drove him crazy. It was time to shift the conversation away from this avenue. "Look at me. I'm working for a Human mercenary company."

"Point," Zion nodded.

"But typically, the Information Guild is the most demanding with their loyalty," Thorpi continued after a moment of contemplation. He could offer them something without it seeming as though he was hiding more. "Information is vital to making the universe function. The Mercenary Guild might want to clamp down on information, but it would fly in the face of the Information Guild's self-proclaimed ideals and could cause friction. I doubt Peepo would want to irritate the Information Guild."

"Why is that?"

"Because the loss of information can cut both ways."

"Ignorance isn't always bliss?"

"Ignorance is bliss until it kills you," Thorpi confirmed.

The door leading back to the surgical suite opened and a Human doctor in scrubs came out. He looked tired but pleased, which gave both Veetanho and Human hope. Thorpi was particularly happy the Wrogul hadn't tagged along.

"She's out of surgery," the doctor said, shaking his head. "That girl is tough. This surgery was very invasive, yet she never complained, not even when we created the storage data area within the folds of her brain. There's no way to block the neural pain, so the fact she didn't even wince tells me more about her than I care to know."

"How long until she's ready to return to Liberia?" Zion asked. The doctor shook his head.

"Her recovery process is long," the doctor explained carefully. "I know you mercs have the tech to speed up her recovery, but I'd be more comfortable with her remaining in the hospital for two or three days. I've been watching the news, and I see Liberia isn't safe right now."

"What? The attempt on the president's life?" Zion asked, surprised. "Sure, national news in America. That's just a typical Tuesday in our country."

"She will be under my care, as well," Thorpi stated, looking up at the doctor. "Sunshine will be well-taken care for."

"Well, I was hoping you'd agree with me," the doctor stated. "But she was saying as soon as the local anesthetic wore off she wanted to go home."

"Well, let's get going then," Zion said as he reached out and shook the doctor's hand. "Thanks again, Doc."

The doctor muttered something under his breath and walked back toward the surgical suite. A few moments later Sunshine appeared in a wheelchair pushed by an orderly. Zion struggled not to laugh as he listened to the teenager rip the orderly apart.

"You stupid, *menh*, I can walk!" Sunshine protested loudly as she half-turned and glared up at the woman pushing the wheelchair. "Walking is easy."

"The doctor said you can walk when you are no longer on hospital grounds," the orderly said firmly. Sunshine launched into a tirade of swear words which could have blistered paint. Some of them were new to Zion, who had thought he'd heard it all. Apparently, he'd been mistaken. Even Thorpi appeared taken aback by Sunshine's verbal assault upon the orderly.

The Veetanho looked at Zion. "Is that even anatomically possible?"

"I hope not." Zion winced as mental images flooded his mind unbidden. He shook them off and decided the young private needed a reminder as to the order of things. This was as good of a time as any to begin her training. "Sunshine! As a representative of the Kakata Korps, everything you say can reflect poorly upon the *bass*. You remember this, *ken*?"

This seemed to deflate the teen a little. She looked down at the floor, embarrassed. Zion knelt down and took her hand in his.

"I'm not mad. But if you want to be a member of the Korps, you have to remember how to treat other people in public," Zion explained as gently as he could. "You have a problem with someone, you go to one of your NCOs. If they can't fix it, the problem will eventually reach me. If I can't help, I go to the *bass*. We call it the chain of command."

"Yes, *bass*," she acknowledged quietly. Satisfied for the time being, Zion stood back up. As he did so, he received a small ping through his pinplant.

"I just got a message from the colonel back at HQ," Zion said as he walked back to his seat and picked up his slate. He looked back and saw the alien had his slate already in hand.

"I received a message as well," Thorpi informed him as he looked at his own comms device. The Veetanho looked at Zion, a malicious glint in his eye. "Time to head back to HQ. Colonel Luo has called a general staff meeting. He has something very interesting to share with us. And it's one of those 'interesting' things which makes certain we keep earning money."

\* \* \*

**Kakata Korps HQ, Freeport of Monrovia, Liberia**

Mulbah slid the slate to the side and looked at the gathered officers in the room. The atmosphere was grim.

"Thorpi and Zion just landed and will be in here soon," Mulbah said as he folded his hands on the table's smooth surface. "We'll begin as soon as they arrive."

"*Bass*, mind giving me a heads up what this is about?" Antonious asked as he played with his prosthetic arm. It pained Mulbah to see the high-tech device, but it didn't appear to have slowed Antonious down too much.

Mulbah was surprised to find he missed having Antonious and the rest of his Jackals out in the field. As much as they drove him nuts with their lack of strict decorum, the Jackals also had the most direct combat experience. After the butchery at New Ikoyi Prison and a severe reassessment of the Korps' overall capabilities, Mulbah realized not all of his companies fit the bill the same way, and he would need to be far more flexible when deploying them in the future.

Mulbah cleared his throat. "I could, but then I'd just have to go all over it again when they get here. But I can tell you that it involves the assassination attempt on the president."

This satisfied Antonious for the time being. Samson, on the other hand, only grew more excited.

"I knew it," the 1st Company commander growled in a fierce voice. "We got info, *bass*?"

"Hold on," Mulbah said as he heard footsteps coming down the long hallway. A few moments later, Zion and Thorpi appeared, the former looking tired and haggard. Zion plopped down in a chair and promptly heaved a deep sigh while Thorpi carefully situated himself in the open seat next to Antonious.

"How's the patient?" Mulbah asked.

"Tough little girl," Zion replied. "Didn't complain at all until the hospital tried to make her stay longer."

"According to my translator, she invented certain curse words which 'blistered paint,' I believe the term is," Thorpi added humorously.

"So you don't think she's going to need the typical three days for recovery and integration?" Mulbah asked Zion.

The captain shook his head. "Doubt it," Zion admitted. "One, two at most. She's been through seven different types of hell already, sir. The fully integrated pinplants? That was nothing."

"Good," Mulbah grunted. He shot a querying ping via his pinplants to Thorpi, who confirmed the question with a single word, before he continued. "We're going to need everyone available, soon. Even you, Antonious."

"Huh?" Antonious looked at Mulbah, confused. "What you mean, *bass?*"

"I have a recorded statement from the assassin who missed taking out the president," Mulbah began, sending the files to each of the officers gathered via slate. "Take a look, listen to the Blevin's claims, then discuss."

The office became silent as the officers listened and parsed through the files. It was a long time before any of them spoke.

"They try to kill the *goma* because of us, *bass?*" Antonious asked, slipping into his native accent due to the shock. "It's like they think we *greegree* and kill the aliens?"

"Worse," Mulbah told them. "They wanted us to turn Liberia into a warzone."

"But why?" Samson asked. "It makes no sense, *bass.*"

"Perception," Thorpi said quietly as he set down the slate. He looked around the table. Mulbah motioned for him to continue. "It's all about perception."

"What you mean, *menh?*" Samson asked, looking at the Veetanho.

"Humans are being shown as a backward, violent species who cannot govern themselves within the Galactic Union," Thorpi began, his eyes partially closed as he spoke. "Flaunting Galactic Law and doing whatever they will. Part of what the Mercenary Guild—more importantly, what General Peepo is doing—is showing everyone that humanity must be managed. If they succeed, then humanity and her colonies would be placed under direct control of the Mercenary

Guild in a sort of guardianship. It's happened before. Many times, actually."

"Thorpi, when they came to you with the proposal, you said you knew the individual and that it came from a trusted source," Mulbah said. "Who was it?"

"I don't believe I used the word 'trusted,'" Thorpi corrected. "I said 'reliable.' There is a difference."

"Still, who gave you the contract?"

"It was a Veetanho by the name of Leeto," Thorpi said and exhaled slowly. "She is our mother's favored daughter and heir to my creche."

"Your sister?" Zion asked, cocking his head as he thought back to the discussion they had while still in Miami. "Wait…is this the one you told me about who survived the war in your house?"

"Yes," Thorpi nodded. "She is…the favored daughter of General Peepo."

*That* revelation drew gasps from the gathered Humans around the table. The outbursts were almost indecipherable as the African men around the table began swearing and cursing in their pidgin mashup of English and Liberian. Thorpi slumped in his chair as they directed their surprise, shock, and anger at the Veetanho.

Only Mulbah remained silent, however. The commander of the Kakata Korps had a pensive expression on his face as he waited for his officers to get the griping out of their systems before he tackled the problem. He had always suspected there was more to Thorpi than the alien was letting on, though being the offspring of the Four Horsemen's greatest enemy was something even *he* hadn't considered.

Mulbah raised a hand and slowly the noise died down as the company commanders all looked at their boss for guidance.

"First off," Mulbah said, "I've known all along General Peepo was the individual who wrote the contract for us, though she used a proxy to do the actual dirty work. I didn't think she'd use her own daughter. I also knew there was something Thorpi wasn't telling us. I figured it was the fact Thorpi kept referring to himself as a 'he' when it was obvious he was a smaller female. I'd never heard of a creche sister but I'm sure—" here he looked at Thorpi—"I'll get some sort of explanation shortly."

"So what now, *bass*?" Samson asked quietly.

"Before the Blevin took her shots at the president, President Forh asked the Korps to take overall command of the entire Liberian Army," Mulbah informed them. "I told him I would consider it, but there would be problems."

"Yeah, like generals not wanting to listen to some nobody colonel, *menh*," Antonious chuckled darkly.

Mulbah nodded. "That's one thing. Another is the fact I don't have any idea how to command 125,000 soldiers. Dozens of mercs? Fairly easy, all things considered."

"You let your officers lead the way, *bass*," Samson murmured as he ran his open palm across his sweaty bald head. It was obvious to everyone in the room the former child soldier was uncomfortable talking about this. "You let them generals lead their men, but they follow your plan."

"You think we can do it, don't you?" Mulbah asked.

Samson nodded. "Yeah, *bass*, I think we can."

"Them generals will not be happy," Antonious added, a sour look on his face. "But they listen to the president. If he tells them what to do, they do it, *bass*."

"Why do you think it'd be a good idea if we did this?" Thorpi asked. "I'm not saying it's impossible, just that it doesn't make sense."

"Keep reading the information I sent you," Mulbah instructed the Veetanho. "You'll find it eventually."

"Is this real?" Zion asked a few minutes later. "All of this? Is this…real?"

"As far as I can tell, yes," Mulbah nodded. "All of the Blevin's story checks out. At least, what we can find. A lot of circumstantial evidence supports her files, though, and for a common criminal, she keeps meticulous records. Peepo was either sloppy or simply didn't care enough to hide the evidence."

"Or didn't think you'd look," Thorpi suggested.

Mulbah nodded in agreement. "Or that."

"Doesn't it bother you that your own mother didn't tell you what she was doing to the company you worked for?" Zion asked the alien.

"No," Thorpi admitted calmly. "As I told you before, the abuse of a creche sister makes the potential high mother stronger. This is common."

"Veetanho are *cray*," Antonious grunted.

"Could be worse," Thorpi admitted. "I hear the Tortantulas eat one another."

"Okay, that's just…wrong," Zion said as he paled slightly.

"Aliens," Thorpi stated. Mulbah nodded.

"*Bass*," Samson rumbled in his deep voice. "What do they want to do? They trying to set off war in Africa?"

"It's all part of their plan to destabilize the world," Mulbah stated without any doubt in his tone. "Peepo believes her primary objective is subduing Earth. She's only half-right though. Earth is the center of humanity, but not as important as she believes. The files the Blevin dug up shows Peepo thinks that humanity is defeated since she—and the Merc Guild—controls Earth. She doesn't have any idea just how wrong she is."

"The general thinks linear," Zion added. "Humans don't. It makes pacifying Earth next to impossible, and forcing Humans to step in line is difficult at best. There are some ways to do it, and the Tri-V disruptions and rewards for snitching on people shows she is adapting."

"She's learning, *menh*," Antonious chuckled darkly. "Don't mean she got it yet."

"Exactly," Mulbah nodded. "We have an opportunity to prepare. We already know she's going to come for us. I just don't know when."

"We better be ready then, *bass*," Antonious said.

"We will be," Mulbah promised them all.

"What you thinking, *bass*?" Samson asked.

"I'm thinking it's time Peepo learns just how hard it is to tame the wilds of Africa," Mulbah said, a ruthless smile upon his face.

\* \* \* \* \*

# Chapter Five

**SOGA HQ, Sao Paolo, Brazil, Earth**

It felt odd for Peepo to even contemplate it. Take away the basic luxuries of the western districts of the world and they riot. Offer to give the poorest parts the riches of another and *they* threaten to riot. Granted, one of their most popular leaders had survived an assassination attempt, but it wasn't as though she had killed the Secretary of the General Assembly or anything. He was a third world leader, at best. Plus, there was absolutely no way anybody could pin the attempt on her. After all, why should the leader of the Mercenary Guild hire a lone assassin when she could bring in an entire army of alien mercs?

Still, it was something she would need to talk to Captain Beeko about. The attempt had been sloppy, even for a Blevin.

She let out another sigh and looked around the former SOGA's office. The Jeha had done an excellent job repairing the damage, as well as removing the blood stains from Zeke Avander, Brantayl, and the other MinSha guards. One could hardly tell a large bomb had detonated in the office, save for a few faint scorch marks left on the ceiling near the door, which she would get around to repairing eventually.

*No,* she decided as she peered out the large window and out over the large city. In spite of the attack, life in the megapolis continued onward, its citizenry ignorant, fat, and content with life. Humanity was simply bizarre. *These Humans are becoming more and more irritating with each passing breath. Perhaps the best option would be to wipe the species out as a whole?*

They were a nuisance, these Humans, and they were continuously doing things to annoy her. While they persisted in making a hash of things, it wasn't enough to derail her entire plan, though.

Peepo sat down at her desk and grabbed her slate from the table. The Middle Kingdom Dragon Guard were situated near the ancient Three Gorges Dam, in the town of Sandouping in the China District across the massive Pacific Ocean. The extraordinary power requirements of the mercenary company had forced the Chinese government to base their HQ there. The dam had seen much repair over the years and, typical of the bureaucracy that had befallen its communist builders, substandard materials and shoddy engineering had been used when repairs had been made. It would be almost nothing to send in a fleet of mini drones armed with missiles to take out the dam without alerting anybody as to just why it failed. By the time anybody began to suspect foul play, the planet would be fully under guild control for all time.

This left Liberia, and here she paused, thinking. How was she supposed to handle a region Humankind itself had left to the dregs for centuries? She wasn't certain, but historically the area was prone to civil war. However, the Kakata Korps had done an excellent job of securing the area and pacifying most of the major crimes without actually deposing the current leaders. They were the product of their own success, and this was not what she'd had in mind when she offered them the opportunity to quell the region. Worse still, somehow they had all joined some allegiance to promote civil defense and shared information. How could she possibly trigger a civil war when everyone was working to ensure one could never happen again?

"Hello, Peepo." Alexis Cromwell suddenly interrupted her musings from the center of the office.

* * *

### Kakata Korps HQ, Freeport of Monrovia, Liberia District, Earth

"I've never seen so many soldiers, Colonel," Zion admitted as he watched the next division take their position in line for equipment distribution. He shook his head and looked at Mulbah. "This is *insane*."

"Tell me about it," Mulbah agreed as he checked the supplies status through his pinplants. They were on track to equip every single soldier in the Liberian Army in advanced combat armor by the end of the week and, given the usual amount of graft that occurred in every army, he was pleasantly surprised to see the losses so far were well below the expected norm. Typical threats of court martialing had little effect on these soldiers. The threat of summary execution under Guild Law, however, was an entirely different matter.

"How long do we have, do you think?" Zion asked quietly. "Before they come for us?"

"A month, tops," Mulbah admitted.

The news out of China was grim. Over two million civilians dead when the ancient Three Gorges Dam had finally buckled under the immense pressure of the Yangtze River. Investigators were on the scene but already this was being hailed as the worst man-made disaster in Human history.

Coincidentally, of course, the Middle Kingdom Dragon Guard mercenary company had been wiped out to a man, caught unaware in their downstream headquarters when the dam broke. Many lamented their bad luck and the horrible timing of it all, but Mulbah suspected something other than an accident. It would be well within Peepo's capabilities to drop a dam and kill two million people just to rid herself of a loose end.

He cursed his own stupidity and egotistical nature for the tenth time. Peepo had played his own prejudices and fears against him, using his desire for a free Liberia and distrust of others to ignore the warnings which had been sent by the Four Horsemen. Believing every lie he had been fed, Mulbah even helped eliminate quite a few of their competitors while assisting Peepo to strengthen her hold on Earth. There was much blame to be had, and he was responsible for a lot of it.

Mulbah's comms chimed, interrupting his self-indulgent pity party. He pulled up his slate and he saw a message from the president. With a sigh, he answered the call.

"Good afternoon, President Forh," Mulbah greeted the Liberian president as soon as his face appeared on the slate's screen. He felt Zion shift next to him as the captain quickly realized who Mulbah was talking to.

"And to you, Colonel," the president replied. The busy man got straight to business. "How goes the armament program?"

"Quickly," Mulbah admitted. "The soldiers are better trained and have better commanders than I expected. I estimated it would take two months to equip everyone, but we're close to wrapping it up already. I predict, unless something strange happens, we'll be ready by the end of the week."

"I wanted to inform you the Defense League proposal was passed within the AU this morning," President Forh stated, referring to the African Union. It was a holdover from the early days of African independence, when the countries first began to govern themselves.

"Really?" Mulbah was surprised. His best guess was the majority of the northern African countries would reject the proposal outright, half of the remaining would dicker about how many troops they would have to send, with the rest saying they would join and then never following up. To have the bi-partisan support of over a dozen nations was tantamount to a miracle, Mulbah realized.

"You do realize this means you might have to equip an additional quarter million soldiers, right?" the president asked. Mulbah swallowed and nodded, unsure whether or not they had that much combat armor on hand. In theory they could equip almost 500,000 soldiers, but history had proven expectations didn't often match reality. They'd been lucky so far, but Mulbah did not want to push it.

"I'll have to have more ordered," Mulbah admitted as he did some mental calculations. Assuming the lack of theft would not keep, he estimated a 10% loss of armor. This meant he should probably order 75,000 more sets of the top-grade combat armor. Remembering his last budget meeting with Zion, he winced at the hit he was about to take.

"Also, the Nigerians are clamoring for access to CASPers," the president admitted in an unhappy voice. "I told them I would consider their proposal."

This was an easy refusal. "Can't do it unless they've passed their VOWs and graduated from an MTS program," Mulbah said. "I have current records of all who have managed to, and, trust me, sir, every single one of the Nigerians who have passed are already in my employ. It's a guild rule, so you can ignore their complaints. You can tell them to kiss my ass...uh, sir."

President Forh laughed. "I'll make certain to pass that along."

"Please don't, Mister President," Mulbah sighed and pinched the bridge of his nose. "The last thing I want to be responsible for is another diplomatic incident."

"You are more tired than I thought if you couldn't understand the joke," President Forh lamented. It took Mulbah a full minute to process the information.

"I'm sorry, sir," he finally answered as his brain caught up. "The past few weeks have been hectic."

"I understand," the president stated. "The Defense League is meeting next week here at the Executive Presidential Mansion to sign the accords. I would like you, Colonel, to be in attendance."

"Me, sir?"

"Yes, you," the president affirmed. "You're the reason they all agreed to it. I ignored those fools in South Africa and their Boer merc company, and argued the Egyptians are more Middle Eastern now than African, to point out you are the first and only truly *African* mercenary commander registered with the guild. This fact alone got everyone on board to sign the accords to create the Defense League, so your mercenary company may grow, all the while remaining within the rules of the AU."

"But sir, we're not, though," Mulbah protested. "We don't follow or even acknowledge the rules set by the AU."

"I know this, you know this, and the other countries? They all know this," President Forh said. "But it makes the people happy. They believe you work for the AU. That's what matters at this point."

"If you say so, sir." Mulbah grunted. "Next week, eh?"

"Next Monday," the president confirmed. "I'll forward you all the details."

"Mind if I bring a guest?" Mulbah asked as a sudden flash of inspiration struck him. *Make me do a dog and pony show, will you?*

"I don't see a problem with it," President Forh said after a momentary pause. "Are you coming in dress uniform, or work?"

"Work uniform, sir," Mulbah answered with a smile. "It's pretty...utilitarian. Plus, we don't have a dress uniform. No need."

"Whatever works for you, Colonel," the president agreed almost too quickly. "I appreciate you taking the time to do this. I know how pressing the equipping of the troops is, but you know how politics work. Sometimes you have to do what is necessary to get what you want."

*Be glad I decided not to be Julius Caesar and treat the Saint Paul River as my own personal Rubicon,* Mulbah thought as he recalled the original plan of seizing control of Liberia years ago. He was glad it hadn't come to that, because the last thing he wanted was a civil war in the midst of everything Peepo and the Mercenary Guild were trying to pull at the moment.

"Yes, sir, I understand fully," Mulbah agreed.

"Thank you again for all your hard work, Colonel," the president said as he cut the call.

Mulbah stared at the slate for a moment before he slid it into his jumpsuit pocket.

Zion nudged Mulbah elbow to get his attention.

"Trap?" Zion asked.

"Trap," Mulbah affirmed. Zion shook his head.

"Yeah, but who's setting the trap?"

"I don't think the mouse cares who set the cheese in the last moments of his life," Mulbah murmured as he turned to look back across the expansive warehouse. "Only that the steel bar across its neck is killing him."

\* \* \*

### 152 Kilometers Northwest of Timbuktu, Mali District, Earth

"Move your asses!" Samson shouted as the new members of 1st Company struggled to keep up with the veterans. He dimmed the light exposure through his canopy to make it darker inside his suit as the display of his Tri-V brightened slightly. "First Sergeant Simbo! Any man falls behind you and he gets beat, *ken*?"

"Yes, *bass*!" Simbo replied, just as loud. The command had been broadcast across the entire 1st Company frequency and though the veterans knew precisely what the captain was doing, the new recruits did not and were suitably terrified. Their pace increased.

Integrating the new recruits into 1st Company was taking longer than Samson and Mulbah had liked, so the Leopard's commander suggested taking them out into the middle of nowhere and forcing the recruits to find their way back to civilization. Mulbah had then proposed he take *all* of 1st Company, and Samson, seeing an opportunity to build up the teamwork necessary for them to be efficient mercs, had readily agreed.

They had left headquarters three days ago. Three days of running inside their Mk 7 CASPers, stopping only to refuel their suits at designated spots and for a quick bite to eat and some water from their packs. No showers, little rest. The men inside the suits were tired and angry, but functioning as a unit. This was important because of the storms looming on the horizon, ready to lash down on the Korps.

*We truly are the lions now,* Samson thought as they began to bound past one another, using a standard two-man fire and movement tactic used by soldiers from around the world. Bounding overwatch was effective when not in contact with an enemy. It was a doubly effective maneuver when two CASPers used it to lay down the pain and offer suppressing fire for one another as they moved.

Samson had considered early on just using the sims but then realized the new recruits weren't ready for integration through simulation just yet. It hadn't taken much to get Mulbah on board with the enhanced training ideas, either, which meant the Korps commander knew an attack was imminent. The problem? Nobody knew precisely *which* alien race it would be.

Samson was determined to train against all possible threats. He knew Zion and, to a lesser extent, Antonious were both preparing in similar manners. With the flood of new arrivals, Antonious had been fitted for a new-ish Mk 8 CASPer with a fully integrated pinlink Mattis Aerospace and the ever-helpful Mister Donahue had found somewhere. The one-armed merc could be a pilot once more and command the Jackals out in the field, where he belonged. His old CASPer, after being patched up, had been assigned to the only woman in the entire Korps, Sunshine.

A yellow suit warning appeared on his Tri-V. He read the screen and saw the cooling system in one of the new recruit's CASPer was beginning to fail. Samson waited for the panicky call from young private. Sure enough, eight seconds after Samson detected it, the call came.

"Uh, Leopard Six? It's Private Fields," the voice said nervously over the company frequency. Samson rolled his eyes and flipped over to a private frequency.

"Alpha Five, this is Leopard Six, go," Samson ordered. He made a mental note to work on comms discipline at the next refuel stop.

"Sir, I've got coolant issues with my suit, over."

"Have you informed your squad leader yet, Private?"

"Uh…no, sir?"

"Best get on that, Private," Samson stated. "Leopard Six, out."

He killed the comms and waited a bit as he listened to the new recruit struggle to create a private frequency between the 1st Squad Leader and himself. Samson shook his head as the private fumbled his way through the problem, which the squad leader rightfully kicked up to First Sergeant Simbo. The sergeant had the solution to the issue within seconds and the orders came back down. Samson smiled but said nothing more as more instructions were relayed. Alpha Five stepped out of the bounding cover maneuvers to work on the problem in his suit.

Samson checked the external temperature and found it to be a rather placid 112 degrees Fahrenheit. Given the time of year and location they were running through, he had expected it to be markedly higher. Yet if this mild of a temperature was causing some foul-ups in the suits, then there was no telling just how bad it could get when it truly got hot.

There had been many reasons he had selected the Tanezrouft region of the Sahara Desert for this sort of bonding/training exercise, but the overall heat in the dead of summer was his primary reasoning. Most of the men were from Monrovia, so they were used to the combined heat and humidity. Water was never a problem there, though sometimes it was suspect and chock full of bacteria. Dysentery was still a problem in Liberia, even after mankind had traveled to the stars. Training in the barren wastelands of the Tanezrouft meant water was more precious than anything else. Cover and shelter were also needed, and the maintenance the mercs of 1st Company performed on their CASPers before they went out was beginning to show.

"Leopard One, this is Six, over," Samson said as he bounded after the lead element of the company, using his jump packs to vault forward fifty meters at a time.

"Copy. *Bass*?"

"We're five klicks from the last refuel point of the day," Samson said as he consulted his GPS locater on the Tri-V. "Recommend we take the long way."

"Let them learn to love the Land of Thirst, eh, *bass*?" Simbo laughed boisterously. Samson couldn't help but chuckle at Simbo's "embrace the suck" mentality. It was very much in kind with what Mulbah liked to preach, and what 1st Company had adopted. "Copy, Six. One, Out."

Samson grinned as he listened to the first sergeant order a new set of commands on the company frequency. He could hear the groans of the men, particularly from the new recruits, but they followed the first sergeant's lead anyway. Samson nodded and watched the procession continue the bounding overwatch.

Practice makes perfect, he thought.

\* \* \*

Later, as the sun set and the men of 1st Company were settled down for the evening, the sky began to burn.

Samson watched in awe as meteorite after meteorite fell from the heavens, blazing a brief, bright trail across the sky before disappearing. Dozens fell by the minute and the Liberian could only watch the splendor which was the universe. He had traveled across dozens of worlds and seen many alien sights, yet nothing called to him more than his own planet. There were many mysteries yet to be uncovered.

For the first time since being hired by Mulbah, he understood just what the commander meant. Earth was different in a way no other alien species could hope to understand. It had spawned a race unlike anything the Galactic Union had ever seen. Slowly, as he watched the beauty of the night and the stars race overhead, Samson came to realize this was why the Mercenary Guild had taken control of Earth. Not for the safety of the planet, nor because of the Four Horsemen allegedly breaking Galactic Law. No, it was out of fear. Fear of what humanity was.

Of what it could become.

"First Sergeant?" Samson called as he sought out the company's senior NCO. Outside of his suit, he found the desert beauty came at a price. It was colder than he had expected, but otherwise not too unpleasant. Some of the other men, however, had elected to sleep in their CASPers to stay warm. Almost all of them were the newer recruits. The veterans had opted to sleep outside their suits to enjoy the nighttime views.

"Yeah, *bass*?" Simbo appeared out of the darkness as if by magic. Samson never took his eyes off the stars above.

"You think the *bass* know what he do?" Samson asked, slipping into the familiar pidgin mashup he had been raised with. It was comforting, but it also felt slightly wrong. He had been using his translator in his pinplants for too long. His accent was beginning to fade. "He *ken* good idea, but this?" He waved a hand around the desert, and he switched back to standard English. "Is this worth it? Is all of this worth our possible deaths?"

"It's not for me to decide, *bass*," Simbo answered as he looked up at the sky. "I do what I'm told. If you or the *bass* say go and fight, I go and fight. But you want to know the truth?"

"Please."

"I don't like to fight," Simbo admitted. "But this merc job pays better than anything, and I can feed my family. My mama didn't have food. It's why I ended up with you when we were kids. The general, he feed us, but he beat us, too. This? This is like...responsibility, *ken*?"

Samson nodded. Loyalty he understood. It had been loyalty which had kept him onboard with the Korps after his friend Khean had died defending the alien Korteschii on their first contract. Samson's word was worth something, which was one of the many lessons he wanted to impart on his children before he left the world for good.

"I think we misnamed the company," Samson said after many long, silent minutes of reflection.

"What're you thinking?"

"Mulbah—Captain Luo, he named his platoon the Lions," Samson said. "I took Leopards and Antonious took Jackals. It fit too well. Heh. Zion took Goshawks, which I can understand a little. But you know what? We are all under one banner. We should have called ourselves Sons of the Lion."

"The fabled lost lions of Liberia," Simbo nodded in understanding. Every boy knew of the stories of how the lion was once mighty and proud, prowling the delta of what would later become Liberia. The Christian parable of the mouse and the lion was always at the forefront of their minds because legend had it the lion was from their part of Africa, enslaved and abused for the amusement of its Roman masters. "I never told you about the time I saw a lion out in the bush, did I?"

"No, never," Samson admitted. Simbo sighed and crouched down. He found a small rock in the sandy basin and brought it up for a moment. The merc played with the stone, rolling it across his rough, scarred palms.

"I ran away from the CLPA when I was ten," Simbo said, lost in his memories. Samson listened, fascinated. He never knew how Simbo had arrived at the old general's camp. Simbo had shown up one day and been proficient with a weapon. The fact Simbo had been a child soldier for the Christian Liberation People's Army was surprising, since they had been wiped out to a man when UN peacekeeping forces clashed with them. "You remember how bad they were? The rumors? The rumors were *nothing* compared to the reality of it. The *bass* there was mean and liked games. He called himself General Pontificus, like some great Roman general. Said he was the African Caesar, and every great Caesar needed his gladiator pits. He had a game he liked to play. He would throw two boys into a murder pit and let them try and kill one another. The winner got to eat, the loser became dinner to the lion he kept in another pit. It was always scary, but also...fun. Looking back, it was horrible, but at the time it just didn't seem real. You know what it's like."

Samson nodded. He did understand. The warlords always kept the children under their command addicted to drugs and in a constant stupor. It was hard to run away when you were dependent on a drug only the general had.

Simbo continued. "Then one day my time came. I knew it would happen. I was always the smallest, *ken*? Fought hard but got beat by the bigger boy. I was supposed to be thrown into the lion pit but then we were attacked. I ran into the bush in nothing but my pants and an old dress shirt I stole from some dead boy.

"For three days I walked around. I was lost. My feet were bloody and my teeth were loose, *ken*? I could barely see. I was in withdrawal. I was starving, but I knew I couldn't go back to the CLPA. They'd kill me. But I didn't know what else there was. The drugs had worn off by then, so I was hungry and sick. Everything hurt. I kept throwing up the water I drank. I knew I was dying, *bass*, but I wasn't afraid. It just was supposed to be.

"Then I saw it. It was a night like tonight, far away from the city lights. I saw a lion standing on a rock, looking at me. It might have been a dream, I don't know. It was a big lion, *bass*. His mane was gold, his eyes glowed in the dark. His fur looked as if it had been dipped in bronze. Maybe it was the drugs changing the way I saw things? It jumped off the rock and started walking away. I followed it. All night I walked, staying just behind it. The lion, *bass*, was strange. He never looked back at me, not once. Just kept walking, like he was leading me somewhere.

"At sunrise I lost sight of the lion. It just disappeared in the bush. I was crying because I was still alive. I thought I was dying and the lion was taking me to heaven, *menh*. The sun grew brighter and I wanted to die so much. I thought I earned the good death, *ken*? But...then I saw the general's camp. I made it to the gate and they let me in. He recruited me and fed me. I lived when I knew I should have died. Two weeks later we were freed by them Christian missionaries. I never had to fight for him.

"But even now, I wonder if I really saw a lion. I want to say yes. I want to believe God sent that lion down to guide me so I could do things later. When I heard about the Korps I signed up. I knew how to fight, even though I didn't like to. Still don't. But the *bass*, Captain? He give us something to fight for. This is why I fight for the Lion. He wants Liberia to have *hope*, *menh*."

The officer and the NCO sat quietly for the remainder of the night, each lost in their own thoughts as they watched the stars rain down upon the great Saharan Desert.

\* \* \*

### Mangrove Island, Chocolate City, Liberia District, Earth

"This is the best you got?" Donahue complained as he looked around the barren, swampy muck of the island. He tried to lift his foot out of the thick mud and almost lost his boot. "Once the missiles get placed here, the vehicles aren't going to be able to move again. You'll be stuck in there good."

"If everything happens the way it appears to be headed, then we're only going to get a few chances at launching," Thorpi reminded the defense contractor as he nimbly made his way through the muck and grime. "This island offers a clear flight path in all directions with zero barriers for your missiles. The hardest part will be hiding them from above."

"Let us handle that," Donahue reassured the diminutive Veetanho. Pushing his brown hair from his eyes, the contractor set his sunglasses firmly in place and placed his hands on his hips. "Yep, we've got inflatable buildings which can be popped up and pulled down within seconds. We already know when satellites pass overhead, as well as the platforms, and there's a good four-hour window every morning just before dawn. Hiding won't be too much of a problem."

"If you say so," Thorpi said and kicked at a rather large clump of grass and mud. It splattered against the toe of his boot as well as against the side of the off-road utility vehicle Donahue had driven them in. The COO of the Kakata Korps looked at the two mercenaries flanking the vehicle, providing security in case a local decided they made a tempting target, and sighed. "This will work. The assault shuttles will need to be targeted first. Don't waste time on the fighters, if they send any. The mercs being dropped need to be targeted, not the fighter."

"I was a merc once too, remember?" Donahue reminded the Veetanho, his tone sour. "You can bomb a culture back to the Stone Age but it doesn't matter if you don't have boots on the ground to hold it. We've learned this lesson the hard way many times over. Humans…well, we are very good at killing."

"So I have noticed," Thorpi said without much humor. "Everyone in the Galactic Union knows by now."

"What type of assault shuttles do you think they'll bring?" Donahue asked as he surveyed the muddy isle with a careful eye. The more he looked around the better it appeared. The grounds would dry out as they moved out of rainy season. The island would rejoin the mainland when the river diverted after the seasonal storms dissipated. This could be both a blessing and a curse, though.

"I have no idea," Thorpi admitted, annoyed at the fact he was missing vital information once more. It was beginning to grow tiresome. "I would assume they would be Zuul shuttles, though, so what you Humans would call *Excelsior*-class assault shuttles. Besquith and Tortantulas are similar in design, but larger."

"Small exhaust ports, bulky things, decent armor," Donahue murmured as he began to flip through his slate and scroll through the data. "Yeah, the PAC-VL's would do wonders against them. What about other mercs though?"

"Besquith and the Tortantulas are still reeling from the biological attacks, last I heard," Thorpi stated. "General Peepo is most displeased by this, and is trying to keep it quiet at how far back this sets her. Unfortunately for her, she has made enemies everywhere. Other than that, she doesn't have many options. The Horsemen are keeping the rest of the guild busy around the galaxy. One of the few times I will admit to being thankful for them."

"Why do you hate them?" Donahue asked, turning to look at the Veetanho. "I mean, they didn't do anything to you, did they?"

"I don't hate them," Thorpi stated after a long, pregnant pause. He looked off into the distance, his eyes unseeing. "It's envy, sort of. Luck, too. Luck is not a strategy, yet each one of the Four Horsemen have had more than their fair share of it, altering the tide of battle far too often in their favor. Luck which many other mercenary companies, Human and non-Human alike, have not been blessed with."

"I hear you," Donahue grunted. "I had a guy in my old company who walked through fifteen drops without a single scratch on his

CASPer. Luckiest son of a bitch I ever met. Retired when he made enough money to buy his own company but settled off-world somewhere, fat and wealthy. But you know what? The reaper comes for us all, eventually."

"His luck ran out, I take it?" Thorpi looked over at Donahue, who nodded.

"Died on his wedding night," Donahue stated. "Married a girl who was young and energetic. By that point old Julian was pushing well into his eighth decade. Heart attack in the middle of his wedding night, ah, *celebration*."

"It is...darkly humorous, and is terrible of me to feel as such," Thorpi admitted, his voice uncomfortable. Donahue chuckled.

"Welcome to the club," the contractor replied. "We laughed our asses off at his memorial service while tossing back drinks in his memory."

"His poor wife," Thorpi sighed. Donahue's grin widened.

"She made out pretty well," he told the Veetanho. "Legally married, and inherited quite a large fortune because of it since she didn't violate the pre-nup. Julian was big on contracts, but he didn't expect to die in the middle of...well, you get the gist. Before you say she had it easy, however, bear in mind it took the first responders thirty minutes to pull the body off of her. Julian was...extremely hefty."

The Veetanho laughed, his fur rippling at the image of an old, retired merc dying while trying to mate with his new spouse. It was dark but humorous, which summed up his own feelings toward the coming fight against the Mercenary Guild. While he knew they were going to get hammered at the hands of Peepo and her mercs, it brought him no small amount of joy knowing they were going to bloody her face.

"How many missiles can you spare, Mister Donahue?" Thorpi asked.

"How many do you need?"

"All of them."

"It...could be arranged."

"How fast can you have them delivered?" Thorpi asked.

"Tomorrow, if we're going to miss the overhead satellite. Why?"

"The sooner we get everything set up, the better."

"Oh, one last thing," Donahue said as he smiled as the small Veetanho. "I found a way to upgrade the new CASPer we found for you...without permanently damaging the structural integrity."

\* \* \*

### Kakata Korps HQ, Freeport of Monrovia, Liberia District, Earth

"One more time, *bass*," Sunshine insisted as the VR program ended. She was breathless and Zion knew the girl was exhausted, yet she continued to push herself harder. "I know I can do it right!"

This was part of the problem, Zion realized as he stared at the slate in his hand. Sunshine *could* easily beat the program if he didn't continue tweaking the difficulty to make it damn near impossible to defeat. Her aptitude for all things CASPer-related was downright frightening, and her grasp of the intricacies on how to run a squad was damn near implausible. If he didn't have her results in his hand, he would have suspected someone had doctored them to make her results embarrass everyone else.

As it was, he could barely believe what he was seeing. Zion had been well aware Sunshine had scored high enough on her VOWs that if the Four Horsemen had been around on Earth, they would have thrown a lot of money at her to try to recruit the young girl. *No, you can't keep calling her that,* Zion mentally chided himself as he booted up another program. *She's legally an adult now. She's not some girl. She's a full-fledged merc.*

"Last one for the day, Sunshine," Zion warned her as he checked the time. They'd been at it since midnight the night before, and Zion really needed to sleep if he was going to be in any shape for the next day's workups. Samson and the rest of the Leopards were due back in about two days, so Zion had decided to use the urban environments around the older parts of Chocolate City to drill his men—*and woman,* he reminded himself—mercilessly. It would allow the 3rd Company to stay close enough to HQ should the inevitable occur sooner than Mulbah believed.

"Which one, *bass*?" she asked him. Zion frowned and decided to leave the difficulty of the last simulation on normal. It was one of those which had been designed to mimic the ill-fated assault on Moloq by Bjorn's Berserkers. The Berserkers had won, Zion knew, but the cost had been almost too bloody. Every single time someone else ran the simulation their casualty rate was upwards of 90%. Zion had no idea how Bjorn Tovesson III had managed to do it with a mere 33% casualty rate. The lawyer-turned-mercenary suspected some wizardry and more than a little bit of luck had come into play.

"It's a surprise," Zion replied as he fired it up. "Just do the best you can, Sunshine."

"Got it, *bass*," she exclaimed. "Gonna paint the sky with these fucks!"

He couldn't fault her enthusiasm; that much was certain. Still, he wondered just how she would react when she ended up losing the majority of her troops to the alien Jivool as the surprise reinforcement. Would she become morose and blame herself, or would she accuse him of cheating the system? There were many ways how this could play out, but he doubted any of them would be boring.

Hearing footsteps behind him, Zion half-turned and spotted Mulbah approaching. Stifling a yawn, he gave a respectful nod to his boss. Mulbah was staring at the Mk 7 CASPer Sunshine was running the VR simulations in with interest. Zion smiled.

"She's been going at it for almost twelve hours now, Colonel," Zion informed him in a quiet voice. "I've had to bump up the difficulties on all the scenarios to a rate where they almost crashed my slate. I didn't think it was possible."

"She do the Bridge over River Kwai one yet?" Mulbah asked, referring to a no-win scenario he had designed himself the year before. One lone company of thirteen CASPers were to hold a bridge against a horde of Zuul mercenaries and not take more than 50% casualties. Mulbah was rather proud of the scenario, since it was a barometer of potential leadership for all who took it.

"Smoked it," Zion said as he looked back at his slate. "No KIAs, one WIA. Seriously kicked its ass."

"What?" Mulbah looked at Zion, shocked. "That's impossible. Only one wounded?"

"Yeah," Zion nodded. "I thought it was a glitch and made her do it again. Same thing. I thought maybe she had hacked it. No cheating, so I watched the replay."

"And she met the objectives?" Mulbah pressed. Zion grinned, knowing his boss was not going to be happy at having his record smashed.

"Well, not a single Zuul crossed the damn bridge, I'll tell you that much," Zion offered. Mulbah whistled.

"Did she blow the bridge? That'd constitute a failure in the scenario."

"She blew *part* of the bridge," Zion corrected. "Created a large enough hole that the Zuul had to come across three wide at most. The bridge was still useable by vehicles, though it was a one-lane pass."

"Damn," Mulbah chuckled, impressed. "I didn't think about that."

"That was when I decided I needed to bump up the difficulty levels for her," Zion continued. Mulbah grunted.

"What's she doing now?"

"The Moloq Massacre."

"Ouch," Mulbah said. "You think she's ready for it?"

"I have no idea at this point, sir," Zion admitted after a moment, his eyes tracking the data as it appeared on the screen. "But according to this, she's running neck and neck with Bjorn himself right now."

"What?"

"Of course, the Jivool reinforcements haven't hit yet," Zion added. "It's going to be one hell of a surprise."

"I had another reason why I came down here instead of simply using the radio," Mulbah said as he glanced over at Zion. "I didn't want anyone listening in, just in case you weren't in a suit. Frequencies have a strange habit of getting picked up by random young women inside their CASPer suits these days."

"Oh?" Zion asked. "I miss the days when it was just the five of us, like when we were helping the Kertoshii on...what was the alien planet's name?"

"I couldn't pronounce it, but Bob the alien called it Hot Ball of Fiery Piss when I asked what it translated to," Mulbah laughed. Zion joined in as he remembered the odd little alien blob *thing*. As the laughter died off, Mulbah sighed. "Simpler times, that's for damn sure. Never got involved in politics. Just take contracts and go fight amongst the stars."

"Hey, boss, this is what you wanted," Zion reminded him. "Remember? Liberia is one of—no, it *is* the wealthiest nation in western Africa now because of your work. The country had a democratic succession without bloodshed, and the population is growing. Our GDP is higher than it has ever been, and corruption is starting to go down. You, Mulbah, are the primary reason for this. You gave the country a chance, and it has responded in a way my parents could never have dreamed of."

"It's weird," Mulbah admitted. "I thought it would be different. I don't know, maybe easier?"

"Responsibility is a bitch, sir," Zion declared in a firm voice.

"Regardless, I'm here because I need to talk to you about Sunshine," Mulbah stated as he looked back at the CASPer. "How good is she at staying quiet?"

Zion laughed. "Sunshine? Quiet? Not what I would ever use to describe her."

"Let me phrase it differently," Mulbah tried again. "You think she could handle a function at the Executive Presidential Mansion?"

"In or out of the CASPer?"

"In, actually."

"Yes," Zion said without hesitation. "Take her out and she's...ah, Sunshine. Inside the suit she's completely different. It's difficult to explain, sir."

"Understands decorum in the CASPer; doesn't give a damn when she's not?"

"Ah...*not* so difficult to explain, I guess," Zion shrugged. "That's pretty close."

The slate suddenly beeped, interrupting their conversation. Zion lifted it and looked at the screen. His eye didn't quite bug out of his skull but it was a near thing. He shook his head and handed the slate over to Mulbah.

"60%," Mulbah muttered as he read it. "And that's using our Mk 7s, not the Berserkers' more advanced Mk 8s. Jesus."

"If she can do this in the field, I think you might have found your 4th Company commander when the time comes," Zion suggested.

"Okay, I'm switching her to the command squad," Mulbah decided after a moment of thought. Zion opened his mouth to protest but Mulbah stopped him. "I already know what you're going to say, but think it over for a second. If I bump her up to lieutenant and leave her in your squad, she'll usurp Master Sergeant Nuhu and it could cause some minor issues, even if she becomes your XO. It'd make 3rd overpopulated as well, bringing you up to fourteen CASPers while 2nd still only has ten. There's no way I'm sticking her with the Jackals. They're too unorthodox and she would probably stick a knife into Karnga's ribs the first time he tried to hit on her. If I put her over in 1st, Samson would probably try to quash her enthusiasm a little. Not on purpose, of course, but he's not the happy-go-lucky merc. We don't need that. If I promote her to lieutenant and put her in *my* squad, however, she won't even be the XO because that's nominally Thorpi's job. Plus, I have a spot open after Corporal Adrazgo died during the New Ikoyi op."

"Yes, sir," Zion agreed. Mulbah cocked his head and looked at the other merc.

"Not happy with my decision?"

"That's not it, sir," Zion said as he struggled to explain. "I'm more concerned about Sunshine, and how she'll react."

"React to what?" a female voice asked from the CASPer. The two men looked and saw Sunshine had popped the cockpit open. "That last mission, *bass*? Fucking hard. You didn't say Jivool were coming."

"You never asked," Zion said, hiding a smile. "I need to get these sim runs looked at, Sunshine. The colonel wanted to ask you a few questions. I'll talk to you later. Sir?"

"Dismissed, Captain," Mulbah said. "Good work."

"Thank you, sir," Zion responded. "But she's the one doing all the good work. I just monitor and report."

Sunshine blushed at the compliment and Mulbah noticed for the first time the young woman actually had freckles. He laughed softly and waited as Zion left the two alone before turning his attention on to the new recruit.

"Zion told me how well you're doing in the CASPer," Mulbah said as a way to break the ice. It was the first time he'd actually spoken with the young woman since he had hired her on after her VOWs results had come in. It felt strange. "You might not have the field experience yet, but you definitely show potential. Do you think you could lead a group of men if called upon?"

"Squad leader?" Her eyes lit up. Mulbah chuckled.

"Think bigger."

"There's nothing bigger, except…" her voice trailed off as her eyes widened. "No, *bass*, I can't do it."

"You can't command a company?" Mulbah asked, surprised. He waved the slate in his hand. "You were doing a very good job in the simulation."

"No, *bass*. I mean, I won't replace one of the others as *bass*," she clarified. Mulbah realized she had assumed he was talking about replacing one of his current commanders. His opinion of her went up a notch.

"Your loyalty is admirable," Mulbah observed. "But that's not what I meant. Major Thorpi and I are hoping to stand up a fourth company in the coming year and we need a captain to command it. If this is something you might be interested in, I'd like to explore the possibility."

"Yes, *bass*!" she nearly shouted in excitement. "I want to fight! I want to show them boys how to fight back right!"

"Before you do, though, you have to prove yourself," Mulbah stated. "You'll be assigned to the command squad and I'm promoting you to the temporary rank of lieutenant. You do well there and by the end of the year you'll have the new unit I plan on creating. In the meantime, I have something else for you to do."

"Yes, *bass*?"

"Have you ever been to the Executive Presidential Mansion?"

* * *

### Kakata Korps Tertiary Zone, Freeport of Monrovia, Liberia District, Earth

Antonious looked at the final positioning of the artillery piece and sighed. The 155mm Palmaria-Fiero piece had been one of fourteen which had been salvaged from the shattered ruins of the Nigerian Army after the Korps had assaulted New Ikoyi Prison. All had been damaged to one extent or another, and it had been the captain's job to figure out which vehicles could be salvaged to be used in defense of Liberia. Considering almost every single piece had multiple holes punched through their thin armor, Antonious had whittled down the dozens of potentials to ones which actually looked as though they had not been made into Swiss cheese.

Quick welds and some fresh paint covered most of the damage, and the Liberian recruits who had been embedded with the Korps were looking forward to using the massive artillery pieces. The Liberian Army had the US variant of the 155mm howitzer, but the opportunity to play with other equipment was something no military personnel ever passed up. As irritating as it had been to move them, Antonious had enjoyed using the captured artillery pieces.

Antonious shoved the last bit of camouflage atop the artillery's main body, leaving only the barrel exposed. Painted red, it looked like a chimney smoke stack amidst the ruins of a run-down shack. Stepping back, he admired his handiwork.

At ground level, it wouldn't fool anybody, he determined as he walked around the ruined "house." However, when viewed from above, he decided it would pass muster. The angle of the "chimney" was tilted enough to fool a combat shuttle's scanners when they flew overhead, and the sheet metal piled on top of the armored carriage would mask the energy signature of the engine. It would only be after they fired the massive 155mm cannon that the ruse would end. Antonious predicted he would either be dead or victorious by then, so he wasn't worried about it.

"Jackal One, Six," Antonious called out to his senior NCO. "Status?"

"All set here, *bass*," Oti replied. "First Squad just finished with the last of them."

"Copy, Oti," Antonious said as he checked his Tri-V. He grunted. *So far, so good,* he thought. "Give them one last pass and make sure the army knows to stay away from them, then head back to the barn."

"Copy, Six. One, out."

Antonious missed Oti's heavy accent. Speaking through the pinplants just made everyone sound so generic. He switched frequencies and pulled up Zion.

"How's guard duty?" he asked once the link was established.

"This sucks," Zion complained. "How the hell did you do this with only ten suits and not lose your damn mind?"

"When the boys aren't patrolling, I have them run combat sims," Antonious laughed. "It helps pass the time and gets our scores up, *menh*."

"How's the project coming along?" Zion asked, careful to not mention precisely what it was 2nd Company was working on. The manufacturer had guaranteed their comms were secure but nobody in the Korps was taking any chances, not these days. There was no telling just how good the Mercenary Guild's technicians were. The Korps hadn't even let the regular army in on their frequencies yet, something which bothered the generals in charge to no end.

"All done here," Antonious confirmed. "Heading back now."

"Copy, Jackal Six. Goshawk Six, out."

Antonious brought up the overview of city and marked off the position of the artillery sets. Thorpi insisted when the inevitable invasion occurred, the alien mercs would land just inside Monrovia and move to the capitol buildings to secure them. Another wave would hit the Korps' HQ to decapitate the primary source of resistance. Mulbah agreed with the assessment and assigned Antonious and his company to handle it.

As much as he wanted to discount Thorpi's plan, it made a lot of sense. When the Mercenary Guild took Sao Paolo, they swooped in, hit the city with mercs, then took the SOGA HQ with almost zero casualties. The Liberian chuckled as he realized this time around there would be more than enough resistance for the guild to deal with.

Satisfied, he brought up all the Jackals and saw he was the last one outside of the base gates. Moving quickly, he bounded toward the base to finish the final preparations.

*I don't expect to survive this shit*, he thought, *but they're gonna know who hit them.*

\* \* \* \* \*

# Chapter Six

**SOGA HQ, Sao Paolo, Brazil**

General Peepo looked at the two mercenary leaders she had called to her office an hour before. Kitted out in armor and ready for battle, they were an imposing sight to any Human who might try to stand in their way. She approved of the duo standing before her.

The Zuul was a magnificent example of its species, with black markings patterned across the creature's muzzle contrasting sharply with the grey face. The rest of the Zuul's body was decorated similarly, though Peepo could see the mercenary was not enjoying the wet winter of Brazil. Where they were bound next, however, the Zuul wouldn't have to worry about winter at all. The mercenary would be happily miserable in the summer heat in Africa.

The Besquith, however, was a terrifying example of evolution gone horribly wrong. Standing over two meters tall, it was a mass of fangs, fur, and rage. Peepo was well-aware every Human mythology on the planet whispered horror stories about creatures which resembled the Besquith. She was counting on this to subdue the Humans fully when the mercenaries attacked.

"Commander Griss, do you have the new Mercenary Internment Facility ready?" Peepo asked the Zuul. Since they had been placed in charge of the captured prison the Kakata Korps had helpfully provided, Griss and her mercenaries had been given a total of thirteen prisoners so far. Peepo expected the number to climb sharply in the near future.

"Yes, General," the Zuul nodded. "It was fixed the way you asked, and I have dozens of guards posted there now."

"Good," Peepo was pleased. "I've been following your progress reports with some interest. How are your mercenaries faring in the African heat?"

"Summer is tolerable," Commander Griss allowed, her eyes flitting occasionally to the towering Besquith. Peepo recognized the distrust for what it truly was: fear. At a core level, all Zuul distrusted the Besquith. "The winters are wet, but other than watching out for the ticks, it's not bad."

"Ticks?" the Besquith laughed at her. "You're bothered by *ticks*? In the United States District they have these horrible little things called chiggers. They get under your skin and cause you to itch all the time. Poor little pup. Maybe you need a flea bath?"

"Enough," Peepo commanded, interrupting the brewing fight before it could get going. The two rivals looked back to the guild leader. "You are wasting my time. This problem in Liberia needs to be shut down, hard."

"Liberia?" The Zuul cocked her head. "The Kakata Korps?"

"Their country's president, to be more precise," Peepo continued. What passed for a very Human-like scowl crossed her features. "He is advocating for Earth to expel the 'alien occupiers' and is demanding the Secretary of the General Assembly be reinstated as custodian of Earth. The Mercenary Guild will not allow this, of course. However, there is newfound evidence the Kakata Korps have turned their backs on the guild, and we are left with no option but to subject them to guild justice. They have been tried and convicted. You are to carry out their sentencing."

"Which is?" the Besquith asked, though the expression on his face suggested he already knew.

"Their complete and utter annihilation."

* * *

### Executive Presidential Mansion, Monrovia, Liberia District, Earth

"I never thought I'd see fourteen different protective details working together to provide security at an event in Monrovia," Mulbah stated as he scanned the gathered crowd. Diplomats from all over western Africa had gathered to discuss and sign onto the West Africa Defense League. Every diplomat appeared to have brought his or her own security detail as well, which Mulbah guessed had driven the presidential guard to distraction.

Still, it could be far worse. The biggest issue thus far was the fight over who was going to be the second signatory on the document after President Justin Forh, the architect and primary force behind the agreement. Smart money suggested it would be the President of Burkina Faso, but Mulbah had his eye on the feisty president from Côte d'Ivoire. There was no way the former professional football player was going to allow his rival from Burkina Faso to sign above him.

"*Bass*," a timid sounding voice called over the secure radio. Mulbah pressed the earpiece in tighter and tried to keep his smile from his tone.

"Yes, Lieutenant?"

"These *people*"—she spat the word out like a curse—"trying to touch my suit, *bass*. One man ran his hand up my leg and I almost kick him out the building. If I weren't in the suit, *bass*, I would have killed him."

Mulbah frowned at this little bit of news. It would be suicide for anyone not in armor to try and molest a woman in a CASPer, but apparently there were still some idiots who hadn't been chlorinated from the gene pool just yet. He sighed.

"Did you get a name?"

"My Tri-V says he's the Prime Minister of Mali," she replied. "It's why he still breathes."

"Thank you for not killing the prime minister, Lieutenant," Mulbah said, loud enough to draw the attention of all the politicians within earshot. Pretending not to notice their sudden focus on his conversation, he continue, "However, the next time someone touches you, feel free to…oh, I don't know, break their ribs or something."

"Got it, *bass*," Sunshine said.

Mulbah, now struggling to hide his smile, looked around the room and saw quite a few faces quickly turning away. Message sent, he headed toward President Forh, who was chatting up a tall, thin woman Mulbah didn't immediately recognize.

"There he is now, the man who made all of this possible," President Forh said as Mulbah approached. The politician had a huge grin upon his face. "Colonel, have you met Siobhe Mwanza?"

Mulbah's eyes widened as he finally recognized the famous actress who had starred in a number of movies featured on the Tri-V in recent years, including one blockbuster that defied all expectations. Congolese by birth, but raised in America, her childhood was very similar to his own.

"Charmed," she smiled sweetly at him. "You are becoming very famous in the Congo. My mother speaks of you often."

"I'm flattered," Mulbah bowed his head slightly. "I never wanted to be famous."

"No, but sometimes doing great things leads to fame," she reminded him. "Mister President, Colonel Luo, it was a pleasure to meet you both."

"And you too, miss," Mulbah replied and watched her for a very long time before he managed to tear his eyes away from her retreating form. He found the president smiling at him. Mulbah quirked an eyebrow. "What?"

"I've never seen you flirt before," the president admitted.

"I didn't flirt!"

"Yes, you did."

"No."

"I watched you do it."

"That was being polite, not flirting," Mulbah countered.

"I beg to differ."

"What?"

"Nothing, Colonel," the president waved a hand dismissively. "You keep your wily ways a secret, old man."

"Old man?" Mulbah laughed. "Mister President, we're the same age!"

"In years, perhaps," President Forh chuckled. "In terms of experience? You are fairly ancient."

"You have me there, sir," Mulbah admitted as he looked around. "Almost time to sign, isn't it?"

"I think a few of the others are still jockeying for position," President Forh said as he followed Mulbah's gaze. "This is a truly historic event, and everyone wants their name at the top."

"Except the Nigerians," Mulbah reminded the president, whose eyes narrowed at the reminder. "I had to threaten them just to come."

"But they came," the Liberian president stated. "That's all which matters. If they sign or not, it's their problem. But their *junta* won't want to lose any semblance of authority in the eyes of their people, so they'll sign. They'll complain later, stating we forced them into it, but for now we just need the appearance that our part of Africa is unified behind this."

A single bell chimed overhead, signaling the end of the reception. The president and Mulbah grinned at one another, both realizing the historic moment for what it was. They followed the group as the room began to empty into the larger conference room, where fourteen seats were lined up near a podium at the front of the room. Meanwhile, dozens more seats were set out for the audience. Mulbah was surprised at the lack of press attendance for the historic moment. While there were many recording devices out, Mulbah did not see any members of the press with an Information Guild mark on their ID badge.

*That's weird,* he thought as the leaders of the thirteen other African nations signing the accords took their seats at the front of the crowd. Spontaneous applause broke out from those in attendance, and soon everyone was clapping and whistling. It was a joyous moment, even if the look on the Nigerian faces promised the future would be difficult.

*It always will be difficult,* Mulbah thought as the applause began to die down. Africa was a continent of tribes, not countries. Forging a unified ideology might be next to impossible, but the Accords should strengthen the bonds between the various nations representing their tribes. At least, it would provide mutual defense should one of them try to attack another. And it had teeth since it would be enforced by the Kakata Korps.

"I welcome you all to this summit," President Forh said as he stood behind the podium. More applause, and Mulbah began to wonder if they were trying to outdo one another with their enthusiasm. He quickly squashed his inherently cynical line of thinking and leaned back, allowing his slate to record the speech to relay out to the rest of the Korps back at HQ.

As the president continued his welcome speech, Mulbah's mind drifted away to the problem which loomed over Earth as a whole. Fractious at best, humanity was known throughout the galaxy as a very chaotic and unpredictable species. He knew this was part of the reasoning behind the Mercenary Guild's occupation. What he did not understand was just why the Galactic Union went along with it. Allowing 36 races to determine the fate of thousands, and possibly tens of thousands, of races was foolhardy.

*Might truly does make right,* he thought and held back a chuckle. As much as Peepo and the rest of the Mercenary Guild liked to proclaim they were simply doing what was best for the galaxy, Mulbah had a sneaky suspicion it was more self-interest than anything else. Humans were too good at war, having practiced it on a large scale throughout history. Adapt and overcome should have been the moniker which all Human mercenary organizations operated under. No other description was closer to the truth.

"In conclusion, we the people of Earth denounce those who would hold our world hostage at the point of a knife," President Forh declared, slamming a clenched fist down upon the podium. Mulbah nodded, agreeing wholly with what the man was saying. "Throughout history, many foreigners have placed their boot upon the neck of the African. Even today, the aliens in the Mercenary Guild would try and stop the rise of a powerful and united Africa. Alien invader, foreign occupier, the neck cares not on which foot the boot is worn. We *will* fight to defend our lives, our homes, our very freedom!"

Whoa, Mulbah silently whistled to himself, impressed. *Didn't see that coming. I wonder how Peepo's going to take this?*

"Upon this document I sign my name, with the support of the people of Liberia, and we declare we shall no longer live in fear of the oppressor." President Forh's animated expressions would have made for excellent viewing upon a Tri-V. Mulbah was happy he was recording the speech. He couldn't wait to hear the opinion of the other Korps mercenaries. This was how legacies were cemented. "I, President Justin Forh of Liberia, declare the occupation of Earth is illegal under Galactic Law and will sign this document in support of this claim. With the support of the newly created West Africa Defense League, we will take this claim to the ruling body of the Galactic Union with proof this is an illegal occupation."

*Proof?* Mulbah was curious. As far as he knew, there was no absolute proof, only hearsay and rumor, outside of what he himself had. If President Forh had other evidence that what the Mercenary Guild was doing violated Galactic Law, this was the first he'd heard of it.

With a flourish, the president put pen to paper. The room broke out in fervent applause as the president of Côte d'Ivoire followed, practically elbowing the president of Burkina Faso out of the way in the process. Some good-natured laughter erupted, though Mulbah had seen the look the two had given one another beforehand.

Suddenly, the familiar sound of a sonic boom ripped through the entire complex, shaking the windows and causing a few of the overhead fixtures to swing. Many of the politicians screamed and ducked while security forces rushed into the room, grabbing their charges but unsure where to take them. With no obvious signs of a threat, they were frozen, uncertain.

"Leopard Six, Lion Six Actual, over," Mulbah said as he covered the earpiece so he could hear better over the screams of guests and politicians alike. The timing sucked, but he had anticipated this. Aliens might be aliens, but they were often predictable as well. "Initiate Stonewall. I repeat, initiate Stonewall. Confirm, over."

"Stonewall is confirmed, Colonel," Samson said a few seconds later. Like Mulbah, he had been waiting for this moment and was prepared. "Red building, three down from Parliament, south side of the street. Executing Stonewall now, Lion Six. Sunshine is already on location. ETA for the Leopards is eight minutes, Goshawks in ten."

"Copy, Leopard Six. Tell Zion to move his ass."

"Roger. *Bass?*"

"Yes, Captain?"

"It has been a big honor, *bass.*"

"Same here, my friend. Lion Six Actual, out."

Mulbah closed his eyes and waited as the sea of people moved around him; the mass was buzzing with tension and energy. The inevitable was finally happening and he wasn't sure how to take it. He should have been nervous or afraid, but all he felt was relief. Was the strike going to hit the mansion itself or were they going to try to take the politicians alive? Mulbah guessed alive, since they were still breathing, but he knew time was short.

"Colonel, what's going on?" President Forh asked as he managed to squeeze between a few of his presidential guards, a worried expression on his face. "The guards report that dozens of shuttles just appeared above the city. Your lieutenant just ran down the street and won't let anybody come near a red brick building."

"The fight just came to us, Mister President," Mulbah told him in a soft voice as he opened his eyes. He let out a weary sigh.

"What? Who is attacking you?"

"Not you, us," Mulbah clarified. "I'm pretty sure it's every alien merc still on Earth, sir."

\* \* \* \* \*

# Part Three

# A Mighty Roar

# Chapter Seven

**SOGA HQ, Sao Paolo, Brazil**

The small Veetanho took a calming breath and tried to stay focused on the task at hand. He had picked up reports the attacks had begun as his shuttle finished docking at the landing port, and instead of picking up a new contract, he would now try to stop the fight before it really got going. He paused as he was met by a group of MinSha at the office door.

"I'm expected," Thorpi said. The lead MinSha looked him over once and checked him for weapons, which was a first, before turning to allow him access to the Secretary's former office. The door opened, and Thorpi strode into the room, followed closely by a MinSha guard who was eyeing the young officer warily. Seated behind the expansive desk was his high mother and the leader of the Mercenary Guild, General Peepo. She did not appear to be pleased at his arrival.

"You utter fool," she hissed, setting down the slate she was reading when he walked in. "You utter, pathetic waste of flesh and air."

"Good morning to you as well, mother," Thorpi said with a gentle flick of his ear. It was subtle, but enough to convey either respect or derision. It was a risky and bold move, but he no longer cared. "How goes your plot against my employer?"

"My...what are you talking about?" she demanded.

"As we speak, the first assault shuttles are landing in Monrovia," Thorpi said in a firm voice. "I was just wondering how well your attack is going."

"You already know," Peepo growled dangerously. "How?"

"Radio chatter got quiet about an hour ago," Thorpi answered. "Which means an attack is imminent. Your favored daughter also did not tell me anything directly, but her comment about timing made me consider all the possibilities which could occur. Like all of her younger siblings, she underestimated this poor, sad excuse for a creche sister. For example, the probability you would seek to eliminate my employer once he completed your goals. But you underestimated the resolve of the Liberians. Colonel Luo and his men know what you are planning and have adapted accordingly."

"Your insolence is noted," Peepo stated. "Have you come to simply gloat about your intellectual prowess?"

"I was here to meet with you and ask you to reconsider your plan, but I think that moment has passed," Thorpi replied. "However, I did manage to prepare the Korps before your attack began. I saw what you were doing, prepared for it, and I was right, wasn't I? The Korps was nothing more than another pawn in your long game."

"You have become too Human, creche daughter," Peepo stated as she stood up from behind her desk. "Passing yourself off as male to appease your Humans, thinking you are more than you were born to be. I *made* you. I created you. You were supposed to be a favored daughter, but something went wrong. A genetic failure to our species. You weren't good enough to be favored. You will never be good enough to be anything more than an aberration."

"I'm good enough to thwart your plans," Thorpi answered in as calm of a voice as he could manage. One of them wasn't walking out of the room alive, and Thorpi was not yet certain who it would be. "The Korps are ready for your attack. I know about the sickness with the Tortantulas and the Besquith. Your Zuul will suffer horribly at the hands of the Korps. The sky will be painted with their blood."

Quick as lightning Peepo snatched the smaller Veetanho by the throat, lifting him off his feet. Thorpi kicked and struggled, but the strength of the high mother was too great for him. She squeezed tighter, and Thorpi couldn't breathe.

"The 'illness' with the Besquith and Tortantula was dealt with months ago," she informed him as his eyes began to burn from the lack of oxygen to his brain. "You're behind on the times, creche daughter. I simply kept them out of the fight to continue this illusion. The Four Horsemen are planning to strike Earth soon. I know all that is going on. I know about your 'plans.' I've let you play in the shadows long enough, failed spawn. It is time for you to see the light."

Without loosening her grip, Peepo carried Thorpi to the window overlooking the city of Sao Paolo. She smashed the back of his head into the window once, twice. Blood ran freely down the back of his head as she relaxed her grip. Peepo turned Thorpi around and pressed his face against the glass.

"You see Earth as something more than what it is," she told him, her tone filled with loathing and disgust. "The Humans cannot be brought to heel soon enough. Their world is weak and polluted, their people lazy. Their mercenaries are dishonest and do not follow the natural order of things. They ignore the status quo. We will either subjugate them for the coming fight, or they will be eradicated. There can be no other options."

"You're wrong," Thorpi wheezed, his voice slightly muffled against the glass. "You're wrong about them."

"How am I wrong?" Peepo demanded. "Everything I've said is true."

"You have all the facts," Thorpi managed to gasp before Peepo used her powerful muscles to squeeze the smaller Veetanho's throat once more. "But you have come to the wrong conclusion."

"Everything is going perfectly to plan," Peepo whispered into Thorpi's ear. Her breath was hot against his sensitive fur. "*My* plan. It's just too bad you're not going to live long enough to see it come to fruition."

Peepo slammed Thorpi's head into the window three more times before she finally felt the vertebrae in his neck snap like a dry twig. Thorpi twitched for a moment before going still. Peepo let go, and the body slumped to the floor. She cast an eye at the MinSha.

"Get someone in here to clean this mess up," she said as she turned away, wiping her paws off as she strode back to her desk. She activated her comms, and it was immediately answered. "Administrator? It is time. Begin your blackout of Earth."

There was no response, but Peepo did not need one. The Information Guild was reliable, unlike some others she had the misfortune of dealing with.

* * *

**Assault Shuttle *Dranga-12*, 42 Kilometers Above Monrovia, Liberia District, Earth**

Subcommander Druss heard the warning call over the howling of the assault shuttle's engines and knew the element of surprise no longer existed, if it ever had.

The Zuul mercenary commander was suddenly pressed into his padded seat as the shuttle accelerated and began to pull more Gs. Around him, he could faintly hear the whines of his mercs as the additional gravity wreaked merry hell upon their senses. They were hardened veterans, but none had anticipated the Humans would put up much resistance, especially given the area's history.

The Maki piloting their shuttle suddenly took the shuttle into a hard turn, causing Druss' brain to do strange things. The commander somehow managed not to vomit.

"Hold on!" the Maki pilot warned, a few moments too late, as the shuttle somehow righted itself and blasted through the air, thrusters on full as it attempted to put some distance between itself and whatever was chasing them. The violent shaking of the airframe grew, and Druss guessed that everything they had been told about the Liberian defenses was terribly out of date.

As the chaff from the *Excelsior*-class shuttle tried to distract the active-seeking missile from taking it down, a second wave of missiles, with their radar controller set to passive-search only, were launched from a different site deep in the heart of Chocolate City. They were from the modified PAC-V missile launch system, which the Korps had dubbed the PAC-VL the moment they laid eyes on it since it was now, after all, Liberian. These missiles, courtesy of Donahue and his company, had a lower heat signature and were miniscule in size when compared to their active counterparts. These were the real threat and four of the twelve assault shuttles never knew what hit them as they struggled to avoid the active sensors of the launch sites.

Debris and alien body parts rained from the sky, most of which fell into the bay just off the Liberian coast. Over 100 Zuul died within a single minute of entering Liberian air space as the alien mercenaries bore the brunt of the defense network that had been emplaced weeks earlier.

The surviving shuttles managed to make it into the inner confines of Monrovia and the pilots found their landing site easily—a large set of soccer fields not too far from the Executive Presidential Mansion. As predicted, it wasn't even lightly defended. The Maki pilots had but a moment to ponder this strange phenomenon as the shuttles landed.

Settling into the thick mud, the rear entrance of the shuttle dropped open. The air outside was humid and sticky, which made the already miserable Zuul even more so. Their fur felt damp and the body armor each mercenary wore chafed. Even their weapons, normally easily wielded, felt slick in their hands. Panting, they unbuckled their harnesses and prepared to disembark from the assault shuttle.

As Subcommander Druss and his surviving Zuul mercenaries piled out, a new sound filled their ears. It reminded the alien commander faintly of a mourning howl, but orders of magnitude louder. In fact, Druss realized as he looked upwards, it sounded very similar to artillery. His threat sensors suddenly pinged as it confirmed incoming artillery on their position. It was going to hurt.

"Incoming!" he roared as the world around the shuttles began to explode as the 155mm shells struck the dense mud and detonated. Subcommander Druss cursed as shrapnel and overpressure waves tore through his troops, and dozens of his mercs died with each shell's explosion. He hit the watery muck and wished, not for the first time, he had never heard of General Peepo or any of these misbegotten, thrice-damned Humans.

\* \* \*

### Lion Gate Entrance, Freeport of Monrovia, Liberia District, Earth

"Lion Six Actual, out," Mulbah said as he ended the conversation. Samson killed the comms and sighed. It was time. He triggered the base-wide alert.

"Imminent assault on HQ," the general broadcast began. "Initiate Operation Stonewall. Repeat, Operation Stonewall is now in effect. All personnel report to your pre-assigned positions."

Samson set the warning to auto-play but muted it for his suit as he brought up the tactical overlay. He saw 1st Company was already in their CASPers and ready to reinforce the Executive Presidential Mansion, which everyone had expected would likely be one of the primary targets for the Mercenary Guild when the time came. Zion and the rest of 3rd Company were supposed to join them.

"Move your ass, Zion," Samson growled as he finished the warm-up sequence on his CASPer. The Mk 7 suit lumbered to life and the captain quickly exited the warehouse. He watched in glee as the air-defense missiles Donahue had sold the Korps launched into the sky. Dozens upon dozens of the deadly surface-to-air missiles disappeared as they sought their targets.

Bounding twenty meters a leap, Samson hurried to get past the Barclay Training Center before anybody decided it was a good landing area. It was *too* perfect, given it was the only open space within a kilometer of the Presidential Mansion, and it was the primary reason Mulbah and Thorpi had decided to have the first artillery barrage hit there.

Checking his display, he was pleased to see he was the last member of 1st Company to cross the artillery fire zone. Accelerating, he launched himself over a cluster of houses which were just outside the presidential complex and landed solidly on the last bit of concrete before the tall gate which protected the compound.

Vaulting the gate with ease, Samson was met by the rest of the 1st Company. He saw they were all loaded for Oogar. Scanning the compound, he was able to determine the defensible positions Thorpi had pointed out during the prep period. The reinforced concrete barriers weren't the best, but they were better than nothing.

"Find your assigned positions and dig in," Samson ordered his men. He switched to a private frequency. "Top, make sure everyone holds fire until they have a clear shot, *ken*? Don't want to let them know we here too early, *menh*."

"Yes, *bass*," First Sergeant Simbo said. "Who you think we gonna get?"

"Don't know," Samson admitted. "They'll be tough, though. You watch."

He took a position behind the large concrete barrier which had been erected just past where Mulbah had saved the life of the nation's president during the assassination attempt. Now 1st Company was there to buy time for the evacuation of all the leaders who had joined the Defense League.

"Stay sharp, boys," Samson said after switching back to the company frequency. His old childhood accent began to slip through the longer he spoke. "They come soon."

\* \* \*

### Kakata Korps HQ, Freeport of Monrovia, Liberia District, Earth

Antonious looked at the landing shuttles on his Tri-V and chuckled darkly. The SAMs had been an unpleasant surprise for the aliens, and the following artillery bombardment had ruined their day. He checked in on the base defenses as a proximity alarm began to wail across the compound.

"Six more assault shuttles, inbound," Antonious muttered as he walked his Mk 8 CASPer across the parade field to the prepared defensive position. He looked over at Master Sergeant Oti's CASPer and grunted as the Mk 7 began to stride forward. "Wait, *menh*. Those might not be Zuul."

"Who you think they might be?" Oti asked, pausing.

"Not Zuul," Antonious reiterated as the shuttles landed on the airfield near the edge of the base. These shuttles were better armored, seemed slightly larger in size, and had different markings across their hulls. He zoomed in as much as he could and began transmitting the information across to the rest of 2nd Company. His Tri-V displayed the symbols and his Mk 8 helpfully transcribed them. He swore softly. "Definitely not Zuul. Defense positions Delta! Move it, *jockos*!"

The shuttles opened and Antonious began to shake inside his suit as he recognized a veritable horde of Tortantulas pouring forth from the shuttles. The aliens were supposed to be out of action, according to all the intelligence reports Thorpi had, yet here they were. Antonious figured either the Veetanho had played them and set them up for his mother or he had been conned by his mother as well. Not knowing the major as well as the others, Antonious put the odds at an even 50/50.

"Boomsticks, this is Jackal Six, over," Antonious called over the secure frequency.

"I really wish you mercs would quit calling us that," a voice complained a few seconds later. Antonious smirked in spite of their situation.

"Copy, Boomsticks," Antonious replied. "Request for fire, over."

"That'll give away our position sooner than the colonel wanted, Jackal Six," the soldier on the other end reminded him.

"I understand, Boomsticks. But if you don't readjust your firing grid, you're going to let us get eaten by a bunch of car-sized spiders, over."

"Tortantulas?"

"Got it in one, *menh*," Antonious stated. "Prepare for shot at the following coordinates on my command, over."

Antonious fed them the coordinates via his CASPer. A moment later the artillery team responded back.

"That's…very close to your position, Jackal Six," they warned him. "Confirm, over."

"Confirm last. Fire, *craw craw* boy."

"Roger, Jackal Six," the voice nervously responded. "Shot, over."

"Boomsticks, Jackal Six. Shot, out," Antonious responded as his CASPer tracked the incoming artillery shells. Since it was such a short distance and there were no buildings taller than four meters between the artillery pieces and the fire zone, it was a mercilessly short flight time.

"Jackal Six, Boomsticks. Splash, over."

*Any second now,* Antonious thought as the familiar howl of incoming artillery sounded in his ears. Less than 400 meters away from the Jackal's position near the storage hangar, the Tortantulas were funneling through a narrow point in the road, which slowed their forward progress as the low-slung temporary housing units blocked their path slightly.

The Korps had faced off with a small unit of Tortantulas before and learned a few things from watching their behaviors. The first thing the Kakata Korps had recognized was the presence of a Flatar rider meant the Tortantula was, more than likely, one of the leaders of the horde. However, killing them off tended to bring about wanton carnage from the surviving solo Tortantulas. The trick, the Korps learned, was to kill the Flatar and the solos with a massive artillery barrage, leaving the larger Tortantulas alive to be picked apart later by a concentration of fire. This meant snipers and artillery, the latter of which the Korps usually did not have.

The single artillery shot landed near the front of the Tortantulas at the choke point, the 155mm round detonating and wiping out a cluster of the riderless aliens in a heartbeat. The blast knocked a couple more off their legs and left several more crippled and unable to continue. A feral stopped and began to feed upon its fallen comrades, a sight which turned Antonious' stomach. Others, urged on by the Tortantula/Flatar teams, pushed past the writhing injured with nothing but a glance.

"Boomsticks, Jackal Six. Adjust fire north-northeast, plus 40 meters. Shot, over," Antonious said in a monotone voice, his eyes locked onto the firing grid. The first shot, while close, had only killed the Tortantulas without the riders. This was good, but Antonious wanted to kill the leaders in the rear as well.

"Jackal Six, Boomsticks. Shot, over."

"Shot out," Antonious confirmed.

"Jackal Six, Boomsticks. Splash, over."

The second artillery round smashed directly into the rear mass of Tortantulas, most of whom had riders. A giant plume of dust, Tortantula parts, and smoke rose into the air. Panicking, some of the Tortantulas tried to push forward through the ferals, which led to the riderless aliens attempting to turn around and kill what was threatening them.

Antonious nodded. *Perfect.*

"Boomsticks, Jackal Six. Rounds on target. Fire for effect, over."

He waited for the subsequent arty fire for a long moment. Given the short distance, it should have arrived almost immediately after he called it in. But, there was nothing. Antonious blinked and repeated the rolling barrage request. The artillery unit did not respond. He swore softly as he realized counterbattery fire had found his fire support quicker than he had anticipated. The HQ artillery corps was likely wiped out, leaving only the battery protecting the Executive Presidential Mansion and the eastern approach.

Antonious brought his laser rifle up to his shoulder and knelt behind the prepared defenses of the warehouse. The Tortantulas were wise to the trap and had split into two groups, with one moving to the east while a larger one headed west toward the old concrete pier. The eastern path was prepped for any potential enemy, with the Liberian Army waiting in the slums of Bushrod Island to attack from the rear, while the Jackals were responsible for any excursions to the west. He swallowed and tried to quash any fear which might be heard in his voice. The men needed him to be strong. Everyone needed to believe he was fearless, brave.

"All troops at HQ, this is Captain Karnga. Army, cover the eastern group. You know what to do. One group is going to the west, *jockos*. 2nd Company, let's move."

\* \* \*

### Camp Johnson Road, Monrovia, Liberia District, Earth

Zion and the rest of 3rd Company ran down Camp Johnson Road as fast as they could, passing the occasional car as they made their way to the Executive Presidential Mansion. More than a little embarrassed Samson made it into position before he did, Zion was determined to make up for the lost time.

Responsible for the front entrance and Camp Johnson Road, which ran in front of the mansion, Zion knew eventually one of the assaulting merc companies would try to take the easy way down the street to attack the complex. The problem he saw with the large building was it was rather indefensible, even with the additional concrete barriers the Korps had put into place over the previous two weeks. The steep decline in front of the Executive Presidential Mansion would be a death trap for any who took refuge there. It was designed to funnel people in and make them surrender the high ground, something that would mean certain death to anyone who tried to defend from there.

No, Zion knew his best chance at providing a delaying action would be to take the fight to whoever they had to face. The idea of assaulting the attackers sounded bizarre, but the longer he mulled it over, the more he liked it. There was the distinct probability they could catch the alien mercs before they got too close to the Executive Presidential Mansion as well, which would be an added bonus. The longer the Korps kept the president—and now, the other leaders from around Africa—safe and out of the Mercenary Guild's control, the better the odds they could escape.

"Goshawks, let's move," Zion said as he spotted a new group of shuttles in the sky. These weren't shot at by the PAC-VLs; Donahue had warned them the launch sites would be quickly targeted by the Mercenary Guild once their location was revealed. He switched to a private frequency. "Samson, it's Zion. More shuttles are landing over by the old Tubman High School. The front of the mansion can't be defended, like Thorpi expected, so 3rd is going to head out. Good luck, Captain."

"You too, lawyer boy," Samson replied.

Zion bounded off, followed closely by the rest of the 3rd Company as they went looking for a fight.

\* \* \*

**Executive Presidential Mansion, Monrovia, Liberia District, Earth**

The Reaper drone buzzed low overhead, scanning the grounds around the compound as the Zuul moved onward from the soccer pitch. Samson watched the feed in grim amusement. The dog-like mercenaries had paid the butcher's bill trying to escape the trap the Korps had laid at the Barclay Training Center and had suffered severe losses at the soaked soccer pitch.

While he didn't have an exact count, Samson estimated the attacking merc company had lost 50% of their troops before they had even managed to clear the pre-planned artillery bombardment zone.

The drone feed suddenly cut out as a Zuul spotted it and shot it with his laser rifle. Samson grunted. He had known the drone would get taken out eventually, just not so soon. The captain would now have to rely on the third-rate cameras which provided security around the compound. While decent, they paled in comparison to the equipment the Korps used. Samson cursed as he realized he was unable to determine just how far away they were from the gate.

*Should have used upgraded cameras for security,* he mentally chided himself. *Hindsight is 20/20.* "Leopards, here they come. Fire only when you have a clear shot, *ken?*"

Seconds ticked by and despite the cool air in his suit, Samson began to sweat. Being in combat was one thing. Assaulting an enemy position was easy, because he did not usually have time to worry. Defending, on the other hand, was not something he was used to doing. Much like Antonious and the Jackals, 1st Company lived for the assault. Let Zion and the 3rd handle defensive positions along the eastern drag.

*Them running off and punching aliens in the face is weird,* he thought as he began to pick out the distinct shapes of Zuul on the other side of the steel barrier. It was obvious what they were about to do, since the only way to "kill" the CASPers protecting the mansion was through the gate. The main question was whether they were using satchel charges or shaped incendiary devices.

Multiple explosions ripped apart the gate near the rear of the compound, creating a large breach in the wall. As the dust began to clear, Samson could faintly see the ocean beyond, before the gap was filled with Zuul in combat armor pushing through the opening and into the killing grounds.

"Fire!" he ordered, and thirteen CASPers opened fire almost simultaneously, their magnetic accelerator cannons ripping through the first wave of Zuul mercenaries. The aliens fell but the next group was undaunted, returning fire with deadly accuracy as they slipped behind some of the outer concrete barriers that had been set up in case the attack had come from a different direction. One CASPer immediately turned yellow on his Tri-V screen. It was still operational but Private Asselmo in Alpha Four wouldn't be running any marathons anytime soon. "Leopards, hit them with K-bombs!"

All five CASPers of Bravo Squad stepped back from the front line and knelt down behind the concrete. Angling back a little, they began to pop modified K-bombs into a high-trajectory flight path. The first wave of the Zuul heard the familiar whistle of the incendiary devices and moved to find new cover. Unfortunately, the Zuul still flooding through the hole in the wall missed the memo and were caught out in the open as the K-bombs began to detonate.

Flames erupted from the bombs as they struck the ground, and the Zuul were unable to move away from the white-hot flames in time. The alien howls of agony nearly drowned out the gunfire.

"Keep feeding them rounds!" Samson barked as the Zuul started to fall back slightly, trying to find some relief from the withering gunfire and the heat of the flames. For the time being, it appeared the Leopards held the upper hand, though Samson knew this wouldn't last forever. It just needed to last long enough.

"They will learn to love the taste of hate!"

\* \* \*

### West Pier, Freeport of Monrovia, Liberia District, Earth

Antonious sprinted down one of the smaller side roads to cut off the Tortantula's advance. His Mk 8 was lighter and had an agility his previous suit couldn't match. However, his previous CASPer had been able to carry more ammunition and K-bombs, and he sacrificed some armor as well. However, the used suit Mulbah had purchased and retrofitted for full pinlink connectivity meant instead of remaining behind and doing nothing, Antonious was able to join the fight and lead his men from the front.

He had no idea where Greg Donahue or Mattis Aerospace had dug up a Mk 8 Command CASPer, but he wasn't one to look a gift horse in the mouth. Especially when it was something as precious and amazing as the mecha was turning out to be.

Accessing the last recon drone orbiting the HQ, he saw the mass of Tortantulas which had split off and headed west were pushing all the way to the edge of the old concrete docks by the bay. He blinked, surprised. He wasn't aware the Tortantulas even liked water. Judging by their frames and weight, though, he doubted they would enjoy the experience if they fell in.

*Could they swim?* He thought it unlikely but suddenly had a desire to know. *Only one way to find out.*

His Tri-V showed an up-to-date map of the docks, and he saw there was another potential chokepoint. Accessing his pinlink, he pinged certain spots with red to mark the areas he wanted the rest of the Jackals to cover and sent the data to his company.

"Cut them off there," he told his men over the secure channel. "We make them swim, *ken?*"

"Yes, *bass!*" they replied in unison. Almost every member of 2nd Company had been there since the Korps first started bringing in new mercenaries after the nearly-failed kidnapping attempt on Troubadour Station. It had allowed for a bond neither of the other two companies had managed, especially given the losses they had suffered. Undermanned they might be, and not the fastest when it came to drills, but the Jackals knew how to fight as a team.

Antonious launched himself high into the air and saw the group of Tortantulas had split into two smaller groups in order to navigate the narrow confines of the dock area. A Flatar spotted him and took a shot with his pistol, but fortunately missed. Landing badly, he stumbled and nearly crashed into one of the leftover containers that hadn't been cleared from the converted port.

"Stupid, stupid," he muttered and watched as the rest of the Jackals got behind cover. He updated the Tri-V data and set up firing lines. If they were to have any chance, they would need to stop the Tortantulas now, before they could rejoin the second group moving out onto Bushrod Island to the east. "Lock and load! We got aliens!"

"Paint the sky!" Master Sergeant Oti called out.

"First Squad, form the line!" Antonious ordered as the lead element of the Tortantulas appeared in front of them. The Jackals had timed their approach perfectly. Now they needed to finish the job. "Second, be ready to plug the gaps! Ain't none of them ugly *craw craws* making it past us today!"

Directing their fire on the lead Tortantulas, the Jackals tried to create a clog in the narrow funnel between the old shipping containers and the edge of the dock. The Tortantulas with Flatar riders tried to stop the tide and change direction but the mass of bodies was packed in too tightly; there wasn't enough room for the large aliens to maneuver.

Even with his magnetic accelerator cannon blazing away, Antonious was able to direct fire from the company and make minor adjustments while they fought. Being fully outfitted with pinplants was not something he'd thought he would ever be comfortable with, yet now that he was fully one with his CASPer, there was no way he could ever go back to fighting the old way. The controls were too good, and his ability to direct his men greatly increased.

*If we live through this, everyone in the company needs one of these,* he thought.

One of the suits from First Squad turned red as a Flatar managed to put a round through him. The impact drove the CASPer backward and to the ground. The shot had instantly killed young PFC Diaby and rendered his suit inoperable. Every member of the Korps was familiar with how deadly and accurate the Flatar laser pistols could be.

"K-bombs!" Antonious ordered and immediately Second Squad dropped down to a single knee behind the main line created by First. The soft *whoomp* of K-bombs mounted on the shoulders of the Second Squad being launched was a pleasing sound to Antonious. It meant death was about to rain down on his enemy's head.

The first bombardment shattered the charge of the Tortantulas. The alien mercenaries, struggling to push past the bombs detonating in their midst, were forced over the edge of the dock and into the water. More followed as the pressure of the mass charge found somewhere to move, even if it was unwittingly. Too late did the Flatar realize where their riderless Tortantulas were being driven.

Antonious spotted one old, grizzled-looking Flatar who had some sort of bionic apparatus on his head. This one appeared to know what he was doing and was directing the Tortantulas to avoid the sea while simultaneously firing at the CASPers. His laser rifle snapped up and Antonious quickly squeezed off a few rounds. One shot glanced off the thick, armored thorax of the Tortantula the veteran Flatar was riding. This got the alien's attention, and the Flatar, evidently not impressed with Antonious or his shooting, fired back in return.

The captain yelped in surprise as the shot caromed off a rusted metal shipping container and glanced across his chest. Panicking, Antonious looked down and saw he was still alive. The shot had somehow not had enough power after the deflection, so instead of a smoking hole, there was simply a black scorch mark. He breathed a sigh of relief.

"Too close, *menh*," he whispered. He took careful aim and put a round directly into the head of the offending Flatar. The small, furry alien's head evaporated in a fine mist as the large caliber round struck true, leaving only the cybernetic part of the head attached to the body. "Fuck off, *craw craw* boy."

"*Bass*, we hit them with more bombs, *ken*?" Oti asked.

"Do it," Antonious ordered. "End this quick, then move back to the front gate."

They lofted more K-bombs high into the air, which landed in the midst of the Tortantula swarm. Spidery legs were blasted everywhere as the last of the smaller group were either killed outright or pushed into the waters by their dying brethren. Flatar struggled to climb the concrete walls of the docks but the concentrated fire of the Jackals was simply too much. One by one the small furry aliens disappeared over the edge and fell three meters into the polluted waters.

"Keep killing them," Antonious ordered as First Squad began to walk toward the last few Tortantula. What had originally seemed like a large horde was now shown to be a rather small collection of Tortantulas, with only a few riders. The majority of the alien mercs had apparently taken the less obvious route onto Bushrod Island. The Jackals had killed, at most, maybe two dozen.

"Seemed like there was more, *bass*," Oti said, the same thought going through his head. "They're going to go to the Lion's Gate now, *ken*?"

"Yeah," Antonious grunted as the last Flatar was killed with a single shot from a laser carbine. He checked the status of the other companies and grimaced. Samson and the 1st were getting absolutely hammered at the Executive Presidential Mansion, and there was little he or the Jackals could do to help them. "We go to the Lion's Gate and kill more of these guys. Protect the base as long as we can. Move it, *jockos*!"

\* \* \*

### PAC-VL Command Site, Chocolate City, Liberia District, Earth

"Oh, shit," Greg Donahue muttered as fighters screamed across the sky. The alien design sent chills down his spine as he watched them bank effortlessly as the aircraft made a run toward the Executive Presidential Mansion a few kilometers away, pulling G forces which would have made a Human black out. "Fucking MinSha…"

Shooting down the unprepared assault shuttles had been a walk in the park. The alien mercs had obviously not been expecting it and had paid for it dearly.

"How long until we're reloaded?" Donahue asked the burly Ghanaian soldier nearby. He had seen the massive giant of a man during the recruitment drive, and the American had snagged him to be his NCO for the missile launch team. It didn't matter that the soldier from Ghana could barely read or write. Donahue had made him the task master of their little group, and in this, Dior Mtumbe was a brilliant people person.

"Good now, *bass*!" Dior replied. "Them *boyos* work hard, yeah?"

"Perfect!" Donahue exclaimed, pleased. Dior was proving to be a godsend who could motivate even the laziest to work. "Clear the launch vehicles!"

*"Tsamaea tseleng, litšoene,"* Dior screamed at the loading team, brandishing a billy club. Donahue had no clue what the big man was saying but it appeared to be effective as the men scattered like frightened dogs. *"Kapa u shoele ka mor'a moo!"*

Donahue waited as the command vehicle was fed data from the passive radar system that had been set up to receive from the CASPers around the city. Using the location of the suits and the data they sent, the command system was able to determine the flight path of the fighters. It cautioned that launching would cause the fighters to be shot down over civilian population.

Donahue swallowed. It would be pointless if he ended up killing civilians, which was who he was trying to protect. Checking the projected flight path, he saw it would be Mulbah and the Command Squad who were going to have to eat the fire from the fighter's first pass.

"Good luck, Mulbah," he whispered as he prepared a new firing solution.

\* \* \*

### University of Liberia, Monrovia, Liberia District, Earth

Of all the places they could have stashed his command CASPer, the School of Forestry was the last place on Earth anyone outside the Korps would have suspected.

Suggested by Zion and seconded by Antonious, the school was a separate building off the main administration building. Other than the mechanics garage, it was the only building with enough clearance for the CASPer to be safely stashed inside without damaging the ceiling. The Command Squad was inside in standby mode, watching his suit just in case the Mercenary Guild decided to attack. They complained about the tediousness of hauling the suit all the way out to the school from HQ but now Mulbah was doubly glad they had.

"Staff Sergeant Ange," Mulbah radioed, huffing as he reached the building. He hated cardio with every fiber of his being and couldn't wait to get inside the suit. "Everything ready?"

"We're all powered up and ready, *bass*," Casimir confirmed. "The LT is here already. Just waiting on you."

"Yeah, I know," Mulbah grumbled. He would have been there ten minutes earlier, but Lieutenant Sunshine had neglected to consider the possibility of carrying him while she ran to the rendezvous. He couldn't blame her, really. He hadn't thought to ask her for a lift, even if it could be considered demeaning.

He reached the Forestry building and paused, heaving for air as he doubled over. Unwittingly or not, too much paperwork and not enough exercise had left him with a slight pooch in the midsection. When combined with his natural hatred of cardio, Mulbah had gotten out of shape.

"Running sucks," he gasped as the faint scream of jet engines filled his ears. He glanced up and saw a trio of unfamiliar fighters tearing through the sky toward him. Or more accurately, toward the Parliament Building across the street from the Executive Presidential Mansion. "Oh fuck."

The fighters began firing, and their rounds tore easily through the ancient stucco and plaster covering the outer walls of the Parliament Building. Mulbah could hear the impacts from the large caliber rounds chewing into the building and whispered a brief prayer that it had been evacuated when the alert was first given. Otherwise there were going to be a lot of unnecessary casualties.

Finally able to breathe, Mulbah pulled open the door to the Forestry school and was greeted with the barrel of a laser rifle pointed right at his face. Behind it loomed a solid black CASPer. The rifle shifted away almost immediately. It dawned on him he probably should have told them he was there before yanking open the door. He was lucky he hadn't been killed.

"Sorry, *bass*," Private Ibara apologized, turning his CASPer slightly. "Been seeing some shady looking people wandering around. Didn't want anybody thinking they could get lucky with our stuff."

"No problem," Mulbah said and trotted over to his CASPer. "We've got fighters overhead and troops on what looks like three different assault vectors from the feeds I'm getting. 2nd Company has HQ under control for now, and 1st is holding at the president's mansion. 3rd is headed toward Tubman High School. The Liberian Army is assisting on Bushrod, but they're dragging ass so they're probably not going to be much help to the Jackals."

"What's our plan, *bass*?" Casimir asked.

"Support Captain Tolbert and the Leopards until we get the signal that all the diplomats are safe and away," Mulbah said as he climbed into his CASPer. Activating the suit's computer systems, the entire mecha shook slightly as it powered up. He began to run through the pre-op and cursed himself. "Should have left it in standby like you guys."

"*Bass*, what about Donahue and his missiles?" Sunshine asked, her tone filled with worry. "Why did he not shoot the ships down?"

"Probably because they're over a civilian area right now," Mulbah said as he tested the arms, then the legs. The suit responded perfectly. Satisfied, he turned to look at the others. "He wouldn't want the jets to crash in the city. Probably waiting for them to get clear. Plus, they're not the priority targets. The assault landing shuttles are."

"He needs to do it quick then," Sunshine pointed out as the highlighted a section of the map on her Tri-V and sent it to Mulbah. "Because Captain Karnga is about to hit the wall."

Mulbah glanced at the map and grimaced. If he had known there would be Besquith and Tortantulas involved, he would never have split the Korps up this much. It would have been easier to simply sacrifice himself and allow the rest of the Korps to defend from HQ after taking care of the Presidential Mansion.

"That's a whole lot of hurt on its way in," he muttered. His suit showed green on his Tri-V and everything felt right in the world. It was time for the command squad to get to work. "Okay, let's move. We've got aliens to kill."

\*\*\*

### The Lion's Gate, Freeport of Monrovia, Liberia District, Earth

The Jackals moved rapidly along the back routes across the base. Antonious and the rest of 2nd Company knew there was no possible way for the Liberian Army to hold off the Tortantulas they were about to run into. He knew the best-case situation would be for the army soldiers to die before they were eaten by the ravenous spider-like alien mercs.

Antonious slipped on a piece of stray lumber and tumbled to the ground. Somehow, he contorted his suit and managed to slide a bit on the concrete before popping back upright and continuing on. A quick diagnostic of his suit was comforting. His CASPer had protected everything, except for his dignity.

"Nice, *bass*," Master Sergeant Oti called out, apparently believing Antonious had done the maneuver on purpose. Not wanting to shatter the illusion, he grunted in reply.

"Yeah, got me some practice. We got to hurry."

"Yes, *bass*!"

"Incoming!" someone screamed. Antonious had just enough time to look up at the sky before his threat detector lit off. A trio of fighters were coming in hot and low. Antonious paused and tried to target them but the fighters were already gone before he could pull the trigger. Irritated at himself, he radioed the American who was supposed to be preventing fighters from harassing them.

"PAC Command, this is Jackal Six, over."

"Yes, Captain, I know about the goddamned fighters!" Donahue sounded frustrated. There was angry yelling in the background which was easily heard over the open mic. Somebody was not happy with the performance of their crew, Antonious realized. "They just cleared the city, so *now* we can fucking shoot at them!"

"Just checking, PAC Command." Antonious chuckled. "Jackal Six, out."

"He sounded pissed, *bass*," Oti commented in a dry voice.

"Ya think?" Antonious shook his head. "To the gate, *jockos*. We got people to save."

"Contact," Sergeant Obaye called out from the front. "Got lots of Torts clustering near the shantytown across the street from the Lion's Gate, *bass*. They…oh *nkama. Bass*, those aliens are eating people, *menh*."

"What?" On an intellectual level, Antonious knew Tortantulas often ate their enemy. However, it did not sit well with him knowing his fellow countrymen were being devoured by car-sized spiders with crazed chipmunks riding them. "Are you sure?"

"Yes, *bass*," Obaye confirmed. "The army guys are getting eaten. It's a slaughter!"

"Engage the enemy," Antonious ordered as the image of men being devoured by the giant spider-like aliens came unbidden to his mind. He shook off the thought and tried to focus. "Try not to shoot them army boys, *ken*?"

"Got it, *bass*," Obaye replied.

"You heard Obaye, *jockos*," Antonious called out as they reached the Lion's Gate.

Next to the entrance was the recently repaired ten-meter-high concrete lion statue. Antonious was pleased to see the Liberian national flag was once more hanging from the lion's mouth. Even the graffiti, which had once littered the base of the statue, had been cleaned.

"Kill the Tortantulas!"

*"Paint the sky!"* came the battle cry as the nine surviving CASPers of 2nd Company charged forward.

Caught unaware while in the throes of their slaughter, the Tortantula/Flatar teams had little warning before the CASPers crashed into them. Arm blades swinging, Antonious decapitated one Flatar who was unfortunate enough to look up and see what the commotion was all about. Pivoting on the balls of his feet, he nimbly danced aside as the Tortantula tried to strike back. Antonious fired off a few rounds from his laser rifle into what he presumed was the Tortantula's face, and the giant alien mercenary slumped to the ground. More of the large spider-like creatures turned, and the captain realized charging into the group of Tortantulas, while brave, was a decidedly stupid idea.

However, the butchery of the Liberian Army slowed as the Tortantulas recognized the greater threat in their midst, and they turned to face the new menace.

Antonius recalled the weak points of the Tortantulas were the spindly legs. "Jackals, hit their legs. Watch for the Flatar. You see one of them *jockos* you shoot them, *ken*?"

Every single surviving member of the 2nd Company was too busy fighting for their lives to responded verbally.

Antonious drove the point of his arm blade through the head of a nearby Tortantula looking away from him, and the suit enhanced his strength many orders of magnitude beyond what he normally could have managed. The tip punched through the armored head of the alien mercenary and into the concrete below. The Tortantula shuddered and slumped forward. He jerked his arm clear and looked around.

Not seeing a rider, Antonious shot the nearest Flatar with his laser rifle. The rider screamed in pain and fell off his mount, dead before it hit the ground. The Tortantula reacted quickly, grabbing at his CASPer with its leading two legs. Panicking slightly, Antonious sliced at the legs as he backed away. The Tortantula seemed immune to pain as it continued toward him, even though the ends of its appendages had been cut off. He thrust his rifle into the gaping maw of the alien and fired off another burst, one-handed. Blood and ichor sprayed back as he finally succeeded in deterring the massive creature.

Momentarily satisfied, Antonious decided it was time to create some space between the two groups.

"Jackals! Back to the gate!" he ordered as he shot another Tortantula in the abdomen. The alien hissed in pain but did not fall. Antonious fired several more shots, and after nine direct hits, it finally fell to the ground, dead. He ejected the battery and slapped in a fresh one as he muttered to himself, "These *jockos* are hard to kill."

\* \* \*

**PAC-VL Command Site, Chocolate City, Liberia District, Earth**

"Finally!" Donahue pumped his fist in celebration as the guidance system locked onto one of the fighters. Their erratic flight paths had made them difficult. It didn't help that he'd had to remain on passive scanning so as to not give away the command site's location. "Target lock! Fire Two! Fire Three!"

Two small missiles launched from tubes over a kilometer away, their exhaust ports flaring as they accelerated to four times the speed of sound. The first missile chased a fighter as it swerved through the sky above Monrovia, ignoring the metallic chaff it deployed. The pilot tried flares next, and the lead missile followed the white-hot flare and detonated near it. The fighter leveled out before making a sweeping turn to the right, the threat having passed. That was a mistake.

The second missile was following the first. With passive sensors only, it received all the pertinent data from the lead missile and was able to triangulate the position of the target. With twice the speed and agility of its deceased cousin, the warhead closed on the tail of the fighter without much difficulty.

The MinSha pilot had a brief moment of warning before the second missile struck the rear fuselage of the fighter. Skin-to-skin impact kills were rare, given the capabilities of modern Galactic technology, so when the PAC-VL burrowed into the armor of the aircraft, the pilot had just enough time to register something was wrong before fifty pounds of high-explosive composite in the warhead detonated, blowing the craft from the sky.

Donahue had a moment to cheer before he realized the command site had drawn the ire of the two surviving fighters. They swung low over the city, their cannons blazing, and heavy incendiary rounds tore apart the inflatable buildings which hid their vehicle. Screams erupted outside as the men working the site were killed by the cannon fire.

Time was short. Donahue set everything in the command site to automatic and stumbled out the rear and into the warm mud. Blood and body parts were scattered everywhere, a terrible sight to even the hardened merc's eye. He looked away as the high-pitched whine of the fighters grew louder. Glancing up, Donahue spotted them closing in on his position once more. There was no more time. His luck had run out.

"Bless us, O Lord, in this moment..." he whispered as the aircraft opened fire.

* * *

**Executive Presidential Mansion, Monrovia, Liberia District, Earth**

*Damn it,* Samson thought as Donahue's PAC-VL command site was taken down by the fighters. As good as the 100-year-old anti-air missiles were, the fighters of the Mercenary Guild were simply too much for the ancient technology.

His Tri-V beeped as it detected the fighters coming in over the bay. Scanning, he saw they were the high-G fighters preferred by the MinSha. Instead of three, however, he could only find two. Either Donahue and his missiles had gotten lucky, or one of them had backed off and gone elsewhere. *I hope we got lucky, and they shot one down,* Samson thought.

"Find cover!" he shouted across the general frequency as streams of high-velocity rounds began to tear up the ground around them. One suit from Alpha Squad immediately went red as a cluster of rounds punched through the CASPer's armor. His Tri-V identified the dead merc as the squad leader, Sergeant Seku Washington. "Damn it! Don't stick your fucking heads up!"

The fighters screamed overhead, causing a few of the suits to angle upwards as they tracked their flight. Samson was about to yell at them when a round punched through the armor of another CASPer. He heard the gasp as bright red blood exploded out of the front of the suit. Another suit turned red on his Tri-V.

Samson tracked the direction of the shot and saw the Zuul were pressing the attack once more, flames from the phosphorous-laden K-bombs having dissipated enough for the alien mercs to move. The Zuul pushed forward and Samson, rapidly running out of space, had a decision to make.

"Lion Six Actual, this is Leopard Six," he said as he flipped frequencies. Firing his MAC at an exposed Zuul soldier, he grinned as the alien was torn apart. "Are the packages clear of the building, over."

"They're clear, Samson," Mulbah replied a heartbeat later. "Stay alive. The longer you fight, the more time we have to get them away."

"Copy, *bass*. Leopard Six, out," Samson confirmed. Changing back to the 1st Company frequency, he ordered, "Keep them *craw craw* boys busy, *ken*? Alpha Squad, fall back to the patio. Use the barriers, *ken*? Bravo, provide fire cover. Don't worry about the paint of them walls, *menh*."

\* \* \*

### Tubman Memorial Plaza, Monrovia, Liberia District, Earth

Joining up with Zion and the men of 3rd Company, Mulbah spotted a pair of exhaust trails over one of the launch sites to the north. He watched as one of the alien fighters was torn from the sky and then winced as secondary explosions signaled the end of their missile defense system. Unsure whether or not Donahue and his men escaped, he whispered a silent prayer for them.

"Contact!" Zion called as the first wave of alien mercs appeared. Using the wide, squat buildings for cover, Mulbah aimed at the telltale shapes of the Besquith advancing on their position. "Light 'em up!" Zion ordered, and a wave of laser and gunfire ripped through the plaza.

Mulbah squeezed off two shots from his laser rifle as he searched for the Besquith leader. Unfortunately, the aliens were moving so fast toward them that he had a hard time identifying the leader. With the Besquith, it was usually the largest and boldest Alpha leading from the front, but when the massive, dangerous aliens charged, they all looked pretty much the same—*huge!*

The Besquith started to drop as Zion and 3rd Company laid down a suppressive fire unlike anything Mulbah had ever seen. Each shot was well placed and the sheer volume caused the first wave of Besquith to falter and seek cover. He could hear Zion cackle over the radio. It was a disturbing sound.

"*Bass*, those fighters are coming back around," Sunshine warned him. Mulbah looked at his Tri-V and saw she was correct. The fighters, having taken care of the PAC-VL command site, were now swinging east to assist the Besquith against the Korps.

Fighters to his back, Besquith to his front…Mulbah and the Korps were quickly running out of options.

"Command Squad! On me!" Mulbah ordered as he turned and faced the attacking fighters. Planting his CASPer's right foot back for balance, Mulbah readied himself. He activated his MAC and targeted the fighters. "Bring those fighters down!"

All five suits of the Command Squad fired their MACs simultaneously. The aircraft returned fire and their cannons, while not as accurate, were far more destructive. Mulbah heard the impacts of the rounds on the ground and buildings around them. One suit turned red, and Private Ibarra grunted softly over the radio before he dropped to the ground, a smoking hole in the stomach region of his CASPer.

"Shit," Mulbah growled. Ibarra had been one of his first hires after they had returned from saving the Korteschii from the lizard raiders. Despite the man's constant refusal to be promoted beyond the rank of private, he had been a brilliant font of useless information, all of it hysterical.

"Got him!" Sunshine exclaimed, and Mulbah glanced up in time to see one of the two fighters suddenly veer off, smoke pouring from its engines. It rapidly descended and disappeared from view. Mulbah targeted the surviving fighter and led it with his MAC. Rounds from his cannon stitched up the side of the aircraft's fuselage but he was unable to determine if it would be enough to bring it down. The aircraft disappeared from his view. He watched as Sunshine went down a side street on the far side of the plaza, hoping for a better shot.

"Damn it, Sunshine," Mulbah barked. "Get back in formation!"

"It's coming back, *bass*," Sunshine proclaimed excitedly as she returned to the firing line.

Mulbah nodded inside his suit. "Of course it's coming back!" he shouted. "The bastard is still flying, and we're not dead yet!"

\* \* \*

### Executive Presidential Mansion, Monrovia, Liberia District, Earth

Samson was running low on MAC rounds so he switched to his laser rifle as the Zuul threatened to overrun their position. While his accuracy was better with the rifle than the MAC, the action on the smaller weapon slowed his rate of fire. During a gunfight against a numerically superior opponent, this was a problem, he was fast learning.

"Bravo, fall back to the mansion," Samson ordered as he shot another Zuul directly between the eyes. "Alpha, give cover fire. Simbo, watch your left!"

"Yes, *bass*!" Simbo replied and pivoted nimbly in his suit. A small squad of Zuul were attempting to flank their position, and he fired off a few K-bombs to dissuade them. He shot at several who decided to charge forward, killing the ones who were no longer protected by the concrete.

"Medic!" a voice cried out as Bravo Four turned yellow on the Tri-V. PFC Doré—*no, that's Private Dau, one of the new recruits,* Samson corrected himself—was on his back and screaming in pain. Somehow his CASPer's legs had been blown off and the damage was bad enough to cause massive hemorrhagic bleeding from his belly as well. Within seconds of turning yellow the suit changed to red, and Private Dau's screams came to an end.

"*Merde,*" Samson swore in French, a habit he'd recently picked up from one of the newer recruits. The Leopards were losing men at an unsustainable rate. The way it was going, he could see no way to protect the underground tunnels long enough to allow the politicians and their lackeys to escape. He grunted and started firing rapidly, dropping Zuul mercs in rapid order.

"*Bass*, we gon' lose this fight!" a voice cried out over the radio. Samson recognized Private Asselmo's voice immediately.

"Carry harder, *menh*," Samson told him as a fighter swung around for another pass at them. "Carry harder."

\* \* \*

**Lion's Gate, Freeport of Monrovia, Liberia District, Earth**

"Fuck me!"

One of the Tortantulas broke through the line of CASPers, grabbed Antonious by his mecha's leg, and tossed him twenty feet through the heavy steel gate. He crashed onto and through the metal bars and his Tri-V flickered as his CASPer's right leg turned yellow. The solid impact drove the oxygen from his lungs, and he gasped, panicky, as his lungs screamed for air.

Regaining control of his diaphragm after a few terrifying seconds, Antonious realized he was still alive. This was a positive. The long, metal rod from the gate sticking through the lower part of his suit's leg was not. It had, fortunately, missed his calf, though not by much. The steel rubbed against his haptic suit inside the CASPer, reminding him just how fortunate he was. It was something that normally would have bothered him had he not been in the middle of a life-or-death fight against car-sized spiders with homicidal, well-armed chipmunks riding them.

Scrambling to his feet, he pulled the rod from his leg, then he slashed wildly at the Tortantula charging at him. His arm blade sliced off one of the large mandibles near the alien's mouth, and it screeched in pain and stabbed at him with one of its legs. Barely managing to get an arm up in time to block the attack, the blade sliced the foreleg in half all the way up to the first joint. The Tortantula jerked back far enough for Antonious to angle his K-bomb launcher directly into the mouth of the injured alien. He fired one grenade at point-blank range.

The large explosive detonated the instant it struck the Tortantula's face, liquifying the front half of the alien in the blink of an eye. The body stumbled back, already dead before it hit the ground. Antonious had no time to celebrate his victory, though. Explosions in close quarter combat cut two ways, and a large piece of shrapnel embedded itself in his chest.

"Shit," he muttered. Wincing in pain, he noticed a large splinter of the grenade had penetrated the frontal armor of the Mk 8 CASPer just below where he figured his heart was. The piece of shrapnel was not deep enough to kill but moving with it in place was nothing short of agonizing.

Antonious could still fight, though, which was all that mattered. Staggering upright, he tried to target one of the Tortantulas but discovered his targeting array was off. The impact on his suit had jarred it out of alignment. Cursing and wincing in pain, he tried to do a quick reboot of the targeting systems.

More of his men fell as the Tortantulas broke through. He was down to seven working suits, not counting his own damaged one. Time was running out, and they had barely put a dent in the Tortantula's numbers.

His system changed from yellow to green as his targeting array came back online. Swinging to his left, ignoring the stabbing pain in his chest, Antonious fired his MAC at a cluster of Tortantulas threatening to flank his men. The aliens backed off as the withering hail of gunfire tore into them. While he wasn't sure whether or not any died, he knew for certain the Tortantulas would use a little more caution the next time.

"Zion? Mulbah?" Antonious wheezed as fresh pain washed over him. "It's Antonious. I need help...at the Lion's Gate."

"You okay?" a concerned voice replied. It was Samson, which was surprising; Antonious hadn't realized his old friend was still alive.

"Hurt...bad," he managed to say as he stepped back, tired. He dropped to a knee and continued firing at the Tortantulas. Around him, CASPers began to fall as the overwhelming weight of the alien advance slowly ground them down. The remnants of the Liberian Army were either scattered or dead. Some Tortantulas were no longer attacking, instead feeding upon the bodies of the dead around them. "Need help."

"Antonious? It's Mulbah. Hang tight. Command Squad is on the way. ETA...three minutes."

"Got it, *bass*," Antonious wheezed as breathing became more difficult. Darkness began to creep in on his peripheral vision but he pushed it aside. He needed to kill more aliens and hold the gate. He switched back to his company's radio frequency. "Three minutes, *jockos*. Hold, gods damn you all. Fucking *hold*!"

\* \* \*

### Balli Island, Monrovia, Liberia District, Earth

Balli Island during the dry season was the fastest route through the city for the CASPers. Since it was end of the wet season, however, Mulbah and the rest of the

Command Squad soon became bogged down in the thick mud. Much like Donahue had predicted with the missile sites scattered around in nearby Chocolate City, the Liberian soil made everything more difficult.

"Are you serious? Right now?" Mulbah complained as he struggled to move more than five meters per jump through the muck. They needed to get back to the HQ before the last of 2nd Company was wiped out, but the environment was simply not cooperating.

"I'm free," Corporal Obassi announced from the front as he cleared the last bit of mud on Balli Island. "Want me to wait, *bass*?"

"Yes!" Mulbah nearly shouted as he struggled to get one of his legs unstuck. Going in piecemeal would allow the Tortantulas converging on 2nd Company to wipe them out easily. "We're almost through."

Finally, after what seemed like an eternity but was probably only an extra few minutes, the entirety of the Command Squad was free of the island's watery mud and moving toward the Freeport. Clearing the Mesurado River was a little more difficult, given the high waters, but they made it to the next checkpoint on Providence Island by simply sticking to the riverbank instead of trying to island hop through the marshy grounds.

Mulbah cursed his own stubbornness. He should have done this in the first place, instead of trying to follow the preplanned path. Adapting to a situation and improvising quickly was not something he was best at.

With nothing but paved road and old lean-to shacks standing between him and his base, Mulbah increased his speed. His squad dutifully followed suit, knowing precisely what he was doing and the plan of attack. They had to hurry, else the sacrifices made by Antonious and the rest of the Jackals would be in vain.

They quickly caught sight of the fight, and it was apparent the Tortantulas weren't expecting any threats from the rear. Mulbah looked through assault plans before deciding to simply tear into the aliens while they remained blissfully unaware.

"Light 'em up!" he commanded, and the squad began firing their laser rifles and MACs into the seething mass of Tortantulas. The giant spider-like aliens, caught off-guard by the new threat, were slow to respond. The rear rank of Tortantulas fell as MAC rounds tore into them.

A shot from a grey and white Flatar atop one of the largest Tortantulas Mulbah had ever seen in his life killed Corporal Obassi in the blink of an eye. The round penetrated straight through the chest armor of the man's CASPer and removed the corporal's head. The armor was peeled open like a rotten tomato and the CASPer stumbled to the ground, crashing heavily onto the concrete. Sparks flew as it slid to a halt. Blood flowed and Mulbah looked away, horrified at the sight of his dead employee.

He returned fire but hit a different Tortantula as the screams of men filled his ears. The soldiers of the Liberian Army had been massacred by the alien mercs, and between them and the oncoming Besquith, the only thing Mulbah could even begin to consider a modicum of victory had been the losses inflicted upon the Zuul. In this regard, Samson and 1st Company had earned their pay.

"Sunshine!" Mulbah called out as he realized the end was near.

"Yes, *bass*?" the young woman asked as she targeted the last of the fighters and took a potshot at it. One of its wings dipped and they saw smoke appear from behind it.

"Holy shit," Mulbah grunted. "Nice shot."

"Luck," she replied.

"Lieutenant Sunshine," Mulbah began again as he stepped away from the fight and allowed the Command Squad to pincer the Tortantulas and give 2nd Company breathing room. "You are ordered to go to the storage warehouse and supply your CASPer with fuel and rations. You are then ordered to get the hell out of here and off this planet."

"*What?*" The young mercenary fairly screamed at him. It was the reaction he expected, yet it still made him proud, knowing the girl wanted to stay and fight with the rest of the Korps. "I'm not leaving you, *bass*!"

"Are you disobeying a direct order, Lieutenant?"

"No, *bass*," she countered immediately. He could hear the anger in her tone. "Just disagreeing with it."

"I'll live with that," Mulbah told her. "You *must* get off the planet. You have to stay alive. Hate me all you want, but it is vital you stay alive and get off this planet."

"And what, *bass*?" she asked him.

"Tell the universe what happened here," he said quietly. "You *must* stay alive and get off-world."

"Yes, *bass*," she said in a miserable voice. She turned and headed toward the storage warehouse inside the base, away from the Tortantulas and her friends. She paused as her CASPer detected a fighter. She scanned the sky and saw it was descending directly at the Executive Presidential Mansion—and Samson.

"Samson!" she called out over the comms. "There's a fighter coming right at you! I think he's going to crash!"

\* \* \*

### Executive Presidential Mansion, Monrovia, Liberia District, Earth

"Oh shit," Samson muttered as he spotted the fighter gliding toward his position. He turned his MAC and fired his last few rounds at it. They struck true, but physics was not on Samson's side. Recognizing that momentum was going to carry the fighter into his ranks, he could do little other than warn his men and hope they all survived. "Incoming! Find cover!"

Unfortunately, Alpha Squad did not heed his warning. The men were clustered together, their suits providing cover for one another as they struggled to hold the approaching Zuul at bay. This made protecting one another easier, but also made them a larger target for the pilot of the failing fighter to aim for.

The fighter slammed into the group of CASPers at over two hundred knots. The aircraft exploded violently and disintegrated upon impact. Two CASPers were consumed by the fighter's fuel as the hot gasses expanded outward in a blue flame, cooking the two mercs inside instantly. The remaining three CASPers of Alpha Squad had enough time to know they were about to die before the larger parts of the fighter sliced into them, butchering the men and suits alike. CASPers were tough and had good armor, but when enough force was applied, anything could be defeated.

The mansion caught fire as jet fuel sprayed onto the outer walls. Burning hot, the fire quickly spread.

Bravo Squad, along with Samson, had managed to avoid the majority of the fighter's impact, and they were still alive, for the time being at least. Now it was up to them to hold the Zuul off until they received the all-clear from Mulbah.

It did not look promising.

* * *

**Tubman Memorial Plaza, Monrovia, Liberia District, Earth**

The last MAC burst fired by the company merely slowed the Besquith for a few moments, allowing Zion and the remaining survivors of 3rd Company a brief respite as they pulled back from the area.

Zion was exhausted. 3rd Company was in relatively decent shape compared to the rest of the Korps, but he also knew they had been extremely lucky so far. The Besquith had seemed timid in their approach, preferring to advance using cover instead of launching themselves into the prepared CASPer positions. This was both good and bad, he knew. Good, because it meant he still had the majority of his mercs available. But bad because this meant the Besquith Alpha knew precisely what he or she was doing.

"Fall back and provide cover," he ordered as he shot at the exposed leg of a Besquith. The round punched through and the alien howled in rage and pain. The alien did not slow down, however, and Zion watched in dismay as it found cover around the back side of another building. Instinct screaming, he redirected the defenses to watch for a flanking maneuver. "Watch the left!"

The warning came too late as four Besquith that had managed to close in on the exposed left flank ripped into two of the CASPers. The drivers fought valiantly against the alien mercs, using every weapon at their disposal, but the Mk 7s were designed for sieges, not close quarters combat.

It was not an accident these CASPers were targeted, Zion knew, as the Besquith continued to move around the building and out of the prepared kill zone. He swore silently and tried to figure out a way to adjust the squads before realizing that without artillery support, his prepared kill zone was nothing more but a speed bump for the Besquith. The Korps had to find another way.

"Master Sergeant Nuhu!" Zion barked as he watched another Besquith make it around the corner. "The left flank is going to get hammered! Take a squad and cover it!"

"On it, *bass*," the company's senior NCO replied instantly. Three CASPers peeled off a moment later, following the master sergeant as they moved to provide support for the faltering flank. Zion looked back at his Tri-V and grimaced as the display shifted to show just how many Besquith there were still.

"Running out of ideas here, *bass*," Zion hissed in a quiet voice as he shot another Besquith between the eyes. Still they came, unyielding.

\* \* \*

### Executive Presidential Mansion, Monrovia, Liberia District, Earth

Samson's suit had multiple holes in it, courtesy of the Zuul sniper rifles who had finally managed to acquire better firing angles on the CASPers. However, the heavier armor of the Mk 7 continued to serve him well. Around him, though, he was rapidly losing mercs as Alpha Squad was almost wiped out to a man when the alien fighter crashed into their final line of defense. Only young Private Fields remained. It was either a dead man at the stick or an insanely brave merc who had taken their dying aircraft into the midst of the CASPers. Either way, the Leopards were well below half-strength now, with only the company medic unscathed. At the rate the Zuul were continuing to push, however, Samson doubted this would remain so.

The Leopards had done what they needed to do. The last politician had escaped, leaving the Korps alone in the city, along with the Zuul, Besquith, and the Tortantulas. Of the three, Samson had never thought he'd find himself glad to be facing a horde of Zuul. If the Tortantulas or Besquith had the numbers the dog-like aliens had shown up with, the Korps would have been devastated instead of simply reeling.

It was time.

"Fall back, protect the tunnels," he radioed to the surviving members of 1st Company. His breathing was labored and forced because a piece of the suit was squeezing his ribs. He ignored the warning symbols on his Tri-V and started backing into the large building. Even with the raised ceilings, he and the other Leopards were forced to duck slightly. The cramped quarters would favor the numerous Zuul. It was why he and the others needed to bring the entire building down on top of the tunnels below.

His Tri-V flashed. The Liberian Army had just slammed the Besquith with the final volley of artillery the Korps had, leaving dozens dead and more wounded. Whatever Zion and the surviving members of 3rd Company were doing, it was more than enough to keep the vicious Besquith at bay. Samson couldn't have been any prouder of the lawyer.

He leaned out and shot two Zuul who were trying to advance on their positions. One toppled over, obviously dead, but the second was merely wounded and managed to get safely to cover. Samson cursed under his breath as he saw his laser rifle was running low on charges. He only had what was in the current magazine and two spares, nothing more. The end of the road was nearing, and they had not yet achieved their objective.

"Keep fighting!" Samson ordered. "Keep fighting until they dead, or we are!"

\* \* \*

### Warehouse Zero, Freeport of Monrovia, Liberia District, Earth

Sunshine grew more and more frustrated with each passing breath. Intellectually she knew the warehouse was not deliberately set out to be a maze, but with each passing moment and unlabeled aisle she stumbled upon, it was obvious somebody within 2nd Company had a wild and crazy idea about organization.

Schematics appeared on her screen, as well as a map out of the city. She shook her head. This was not how she wanted her time in the Korps to end. She was loyal, though, and followed orders. Until Mulbah told her otherwise, she would do as told.

"Fucking *menh*," she swore softly. The warehouse was *huge*. How had she ever found her way around here before she had joined the Korps? She racked her brains and tried to remember.

Two rights, then a left, a long path, then another...right? Or was it left?

\* \* \*

**Executive Presidential Mansion, Monrovia, Liberia District, Earth**

Only three CASPers of 1st Company remained, yet the Zuul were still numerous and ferocious in their seemingly unending assault.

Samson was down to his last magazine and was taking sporadic shots. His rate of fire had dropped as he tried to make sure every shot took out an enemy. Out of the corner of his eye he saw both First Sergeant Simbo and Private Fields still up and shooting. Samson had expected his old friend to still be alive, since the First Sergeant was made up of scar tissue and spite, but the fact Fields was still alive shocked him a bit. He was glad, though, since it meant there was one more body to continue the fight, even if the rookie had very little actual combat experience.

"Top, I'm low on ammo." He managed to put a round directly between the eyes of an unfortunate Zuul attempting to throw a grenade. A second explosion a few moments later created a lull in the fighting as a large gap appeared in the Zuul line. "How're you holding up, *menh*?"

"Yellow, *bass*," Simbo responded between shots. "One more magazine until I'm red."

"We got these blades on our suits," Samson reminded him. "Just keep the young boy over there shooting, *ken*?"

"Got it, *bass*," Simbo answered and plugged another Zuul. "We shoulda kept score, *menh*."

"Yeah," Samson grunted. "I'd be winning."

"No, *bass*, it be me."

"Bullshit."

"I don't lie, *bass*."

"I'm dry," Samson announced as he fired his last round; it was a miss. He looked around at the ruined CASPers and tried to see if any were within range that had some spare magazines. Finding none, he sighed and looked over at Private Fields. The young newcomer was firing steadily, making each shot count. Samson was astonished to see the rookie making good selections with each squeeze of the trigger. His little incident in the Tanzerouft must have left an impression.

"What now, *bass*?" Simbo asked. "We surrender?"

"We don't surrender," Samson said. "*Bass* said we stay and fight until we can fight no more."

"Rourke's Drift," Simbo muttered, surprising Samson. He didn't know the first sergeant had even heard of it. "Only this time, we them white boys."

"Them white boys won that time," Samson reminded him. He recalled something Mulbah had told him when the plan had first been proposed. "I don't think we're winning this. *Bass* say this is our Little Big Horn."

"Don't know that one," Simbo admitted with a dry chuckle.

"Me either."

"*Bass*," Private Fields suddenly cut in. "I know you want me to use the chain of command, but since it's just us left, I wanted you to know I'm almost out of ammo. All I got left is K-bombs."

"You got K-bombs left?" Samson asked, astonished. He checked the count on how many the young private had fired and saw, according to his tally, Fields should be completely out. "How?"

"Sergeant Washington told us to carry extras even though it's against regs," Private Fields stated. "So we all got an extra five."

"All of Alpha Squad has this?" Simbo asked him.

"Yes, First Sergeant!"

"That sneaky mother..." Samson's voice trailed off as his respect for the dead squad leader grew. Washington had known there would be one hell of a fight coming and had prepared his men accordingly. An idea came to mind. It was a bad one, but better than nothing. Plus, it would permanently hide the underground tunnels from the Zuul. It would take some digging to locate them later. By then, it would be too late. "Private, can you eject those bombs without detonating them?"

"Yes, *bass*, no problem."

"Eject four and tie them all together," Samson ordered. "Keep one in the pipe. Take any from them dead boys if they got 'em and do the same."

"Yes, *bass*."

"Why you want to keep one in the hole, *bass*?" Simbo asked, curious.

"To make them duck when we do something real stupid, *menh*."

"Why the hell not?" Simbo asked, understanding Samson's thought process almost immediately. He laughed and waved a hand toward the burning building. "Not like we haven't already burned the shit out of this place, *ken*?"

\* \* \*

### Lion's Gate, Freeport of Monrovia, Liberia District, Earth

Deep in his chest, Mulbah felt a familiar rage begin to build as he struggled to corral his mercenaries into a coherent defense. They were fast running out of options. Then again, he only needed to hold out for a little while longer.

A loud rumble ripped through the air, causing him to look up. He spotted five more objects descending from the upper atmosphere and tried not to laugh at the absurdity of it. He had 38 mercenaries total, and Peepo was acting as if this were a fight against the entirety of the Four Horsemen. Not normally a jovial man, he found a wicked sense of gallows humor seemed to overwhelm him at the oddest of times.

It reminded him somewhat of when he'd been held captive by the Zuparti the year before. They'd beaten him, with the help of some hulking Lumar, for what had felt like days before his rescue had come. During that time, he had drifted into a weird kind of half-life where everything serious was funny and his life meant nothing and everything simultaneously. It was a sensation he never wanted to experience again.

He shook his head to clear it; melancholy did not suit him. Fighting did. He turned and shot a stray Tortantula in the face once, twice, before it fell to the ground. For good measure he put two more rounds into the exposed weak spot at the back of the alien's neck. It twitched one more time before he was certain it was dead.

"All Kakata Korps, this is Lion Six," he called over the comms, broadcasting on a general channel for all his surviving mercenaries after checking his clock. Time was running short but they only needed a few more minutes before he could be certain everyone was away. "Keep fighting. You might be hurting. You might be tired, sore, injured. I don't care about your aches or pains. Fight. *Fight*, damn you all. We need to give them more time. I *order* you to fight for your country, your people, and your fucking families!"

\* \* \*

**Executive Presidential Mansion, Monrovia, Liberia District, Earth**

"Damn it, *bass*," Samson muttered as he listened to Mulbah. "We're doing as much as we can."

"K-bombs set, *bass*," Private Fields said as he crouched behind one of the few undamaged concrete barriers. "They all on stringers, too."

Samson nodded as he aimed his stolen laser rifle at a Zuul and fired. The Zuul yelped and dropped like a stone. He checked the cartridge and saw he only had enough charges for five more shots. "Good. We're really running out of time here."

"The fire is gonna get us?" Simbo asked as he picked up a solid piece of concrete and hurled it at the Zuul. It missed and exploded in a cloud of dust and rock upon a portion of the still-standing fence. The first sergeant cursed and found another chunk of concrete to throw.

"Or the Zuul," Samson confirmed as he checked the timer. Everything was set. He checked the positions of the Zuul. The alien mercs remained in small pockets as they surrounded the entire mansion. There was no escape for the men of 1st Company. Not that Samson or Mulbah had really expected it, given how far away from the HQ they had to be to ensure the leaders of the Defense League could escape.

Still, Samson had clung to a small hope that some of his men would escape. The fighters had been a rude surprise, though. Not to mention the arrival of the Besquith *and* the Tortantulas. Nobody had really believed they would be used; it was common knowledge both races had been hit with *something* biological. To see them deployed into battle had been a gut-wrenching moment for every member of the Korps.

"Timer set for thirty seconds," Samson announced to them. "Leopards...I think this is the part where we all die or something."

"*Menh*, this is some fucking bullshit right here," Private Fields groused. "I don't want to die a virgin."

"No virgin, Fields," Simbo called out in a teasing voice. "'Cause I'm pretty sure you're about to get fucked, *boyo*."

"That's not right..."

Samson shook his head and hurled the daisy-chained K-bombs through the window of the burning mansion. The bombs hit the floor and stayed together, as he had hoped. He coughed and looked at his Tri-V. It was time. "Let's do this! *Paint the sky!*"

The three CASPers broke out from their cover and charged into the surprised Zuul. Their rapid fire faltered as the heavy mecha crashed into them, arm blades slicing through the soft spots of their armor. The alien mercenaries recovered faster than Samson hoped but not fast enough to stop many of them from dying.

Fields' suit was tripped up and the young private went sprawling. He landed heavily on a concrete barrier. He tried to push himself up off the barrier but it quickly became evident he was stuck. A Zuul, sensing the CASPer was vulnerable, ran forward and slapped their version of a sticky bomb on the exposed back of the suit.

Samson was too far away to help and was forced to listen to Fields' panicked cries before the multiple detonations of Zuul grenades cut him off for good. In a rage, Samson swung the arm of his CASPer in a wide circle, decapitating three Zuul in one strike before slamming a fist through another. The confused expression on the alien's face would have been comical had Samson not been lost in the depths of his rage.

Fields' CASPer blew up spectacularly, creating a flash hot enough to set a nearby Zuul's fur on fire. Samson struggled to fight off the dog-like aliens but they pressed the attack.

Dark memories came to his mind as he fought on, and days long past flitted through his thoughts. When he had fought as a child against different warlords who had angered his *bass*. He could still taste the coppery tang of his blood as he bit his lips while crying, trying to make sure he killed other children before he himself died. Recalling the rank stench of burned gunpowder and rotting corpses, his stomach turned as he found killing aliens to be much easier.

Killing shouldn't be easy, he knew in his heart. It was a lesson he had strived to teach his own children. It might be necessary, but it should never be easy. Being a mercenary was not something just anybody could do. It required a mindset Samson wondered if he truly ever had.

A solid impact and explosion near the small of his back knocked him to the ground. He struggled to get up but found his legs weren't working. Looking down, he was surprised to see he had a large hole in his belly and blood was pouring out. Oddly, it didn't hurt at all. His systems were screaming at him and the Tri-V was showing the lower half of his suit was red. He tried to chuckle but it was too tiring.

The CASPer grew hotter around him. Had he fallen into the fire? That would be bad. Dying was no big deal. Being cooked before dying, though, would be horrible. Cooked Human flesh was one of the more disgusting odors he had ever had the misfortune of smelling. It was one of the reasons Samson studiously avoided the Korps' HQ whenever Mulbah had barbecue days.

*Ow, it hurts,* menh. It suddenly dawned on him just what was going on. Another glance down showed him there was too much blood inside his CASPer for it to be anything else. Something had pierced his suit and gone straight through some major blood vessels, potentially an artery had been severed. There was no sensation in his legs at all and breathing was growing difficult with each flutter of his faltering heart. He tried to stab the legs of an approaching Zuul but his arm was too weak. He was done.

I'm dying? Damn it.

\* \* \*

**Tubman Memorial Plaza, Monrovia, Liberia District, Earth**

Zion yelped as a claw from one of the Besquith embedded itself in his CASPer's armor. He turned and the massive furred arm, and body attached to it, was dragged along. Zion brought up his blade and sliced the Besquith's arm off in one stroke. The claw remained stuck in his armor, so he deftly sliced the blade through the face of the alien. The Besquith fell to the ground, bleeding from two ghastly wounds, unlikely to recover.

3rd Company continued to fight the Besquith in the middle of the plaza, turning the formerly immaculate memorial site into a ruined collective of trashed buildings and mangled metal sculptures. The grass was torn up completely, which was Zion's fault more than the Besquiths, and alien blood was everywhere. The Besquith were putting up a terrific fight, but the CASPer's ability to keep the fighting at a distance favored the Humans inside, since the Besquith preferred to fight in close-quarters combat.

"Zion? You still alive?" Mulbah called out over the comms.

"Yeah, for now," Zion replied as he turned and shot another Besquith in the hip. The massive alien slid to the ground before reaching out and grasping the leg armor of another member of 3rd Company. Taking careful aim, Zion put a round through the head of the alien before it could disembowel Sergeant Kepah. Claws dragged down the leg of the sergeant as the Besquith died rather messily.

"Good call on Sunshine," Mulbah informed him. "She's going to avenge us all."

"If you say so." Zion grunted as a Besquith managed to get in close and rip open a CASPer cockpit. Before he could shoot and kill the alien, the Besquith managed to stick its head in and rip the pilot's face off. On Zion's Tri-V, he saw Corporal Wallace would not be going home that night, his suit suddenly going red as life support signs failed. Blood dripped down the gaping maw of the Besquith as it launched itself off the fallen CASPer and crashed into another.

"Goshawks, tighten up!" Zion ordered as the formation became ragged. Outgoing fire slackened as a few CASPers turned to deal with the threat in their midst. Suddenly it clicked in Zion's head just what Mulbah had said. "Wait. Colonel, what did you do?"

"I sent her away," Mulbah explained. "She has information which needs to get off-planet and into the hands of a Peacemaker."

"You sent her away?" Zion asked, shocked. "But .."

"You want her to stay alive?" Mulbah interrupted.

"Yes, sir."

"Then delay the Besquith for as long as possible," Mulbah instructed. "Don't be in a hurry to die. That's how you can help her."

"Got it," Zion confirmed. "Goshawk Six, out."

*I didn't even get to say goodbye,* he thought as the Besquith continued their relentless attack. He raised his rifle and shot a Besquith in the chest. Instead of falling, though, the alien merc pushed ahead and landed a heavy blow on Master Sergeant Nuhu's left arm.

Sparks flew as the Besquith went into a rage, claws scraping along the CASPer's armor as it struggled to get inside. Master Sergeant Nuhu tried to use his undamaged arm to swipe at the Besquith but his reluctance to release his laser rifle hampered him.

Screaming furiously, the wounded Besquith finally managed to crack the cockpit open like an egg to get at the pilot. Nuhu's cries for help were abruptly cut off in a wet gurgle as the Besquith's fangs ripped open his throat. Blood sprayed out of the cockpit as the CASPer staggered backward. More Besquith closed in on the gory scene and Zion knew they had mere moments before 3rd Company was overwhelmed.

"I'm sorry, Christian," Zion whispered as he targeted the small area just below the jumpjets of his CASPer. He squeezed the trigger, and the tiny spot ruptured.

Inside the containment tank was the fuel which powered the CASPer's jumpjets. Like Zion, Master Sergeant Nuhu had not used any fuel while they moved into their defensive position upon leaving the Kakata Korps HQ. The highly volatile fuel exploded as it reacted with the oxygen in the atmosphere.

The hypergolic fuel expanded rapidly, superheating the air as it converted the rich oxygen into energy. The fireball expanded in less than one-tenth of a second before the concussive blast followed. The blast grew, violently tearing into the ranks of the Besquith gathered around Master Sergeant Nuhu's dying form. White-hot flames fused the Besquith to the concrete where they were standing before blasting away their flesh and soft tissue, leaving only their ghastly skeletal remains behind.

Unfortunately, the explosion also took out two members of 3rd Company, cooking the men inside their mechas before they even had a chance to blink from the bright blast. They died just as quickly as the Besquith, without feeling much pain.

The shockwave from the explosion pushed the surviving Besquith back, creating a large open space between them and the surviving CASPers. Zion, knowing an opening when he saw one, knew there was only a short time for him to get his surviving mercs back to HQ.

"Goshawks! Back to the base!" he ordered as he provided covering fire. The CASPers turned and fell back toward their headquarters, forcing the Besquith to pay dearly for every inch of ground they claimed.

\* \* \*

**Warehouse Zero, Freeport of Monrovia, Liberia District, Earth**

Tears ran freely down Sunshine's face as she finished refueling her CASPer. It had been torturous for her to listen to the deaths of Samson and the rest of 1st Company. The mercenaries she called her family were dying in droves while she was safe inside and preparing to flee. All because Mulbah wanted her to get off the planet and to safety.

Intellectually, she understood and even agreed with him. Zion had mentioned to her they had information which needed to get to the Peacemakers. The only problem was all she had on her person was what she knew, which, admittedly, wasn't much. If she understood anything about Mulbah, however, she was certain the colonel had already figured out how to get the information to whoever it was supposed to get to. All she needed to do was get out of Monrovia alive.

"Probably uploaded the data into my CASPer," she muttered as she finished the refueling process. Not knowing what else to take, nor where her final destination lay, she grabbed some dried ration packs just in case. These would keep her alive, though the taste was atrocious. Still, it was better than some of the stuff she had been forced to eat while living with Major General Sparkles.

Loaded up, she clambered back into her CASPer and sealed the cockpit. Taking a deep breath, she double-checked her systems. All systems green. With the amount of fuel she currently carried, she could easily make it over 250 kilometers before worrying about refueling the suit. Without a combat loadout, she knew she could potentially stretch it to over 400.

Being armed with only two reload magazines for her laser rifle and nothing more made her slightly nervous. If any of the three merc races caught up to her, she wouldn't be able to put up much of a fight. None of the scenarios she had run with Zion predicted anything like this, not even the Moloq one. She swallowed and remembered something she had heard once, long ago, though she could not remember from where.

Adapt, then overcome.

She would adapt to the change of plans. It was simple. As a member of the Kakata Korps, she was expected to be the best they had to offer. A beacon of hope for Africa. Scourge to those who wished to enslave humanity. A chance at redemption for all men and women alike. She would overcome the odds, and kill every single individual who came in her way.

First, however, she needed to get the hell out of Monrovia.

Exiting the warehouse, the sounds of intense fighting could be head from the direction of the Lion's Gate. If she had understood Antonious correctly, the Tortantula and their Flatar riders had slaughtered the regular Liberian Army as they valiantly sacrificed themselves to give the Korps more time to repel the assault. She didn't dare bring up the status of the company on her suit, not after she had barely managed to convince herself to follow the colonel's orders.

Mulbah was there with the Command Squad, fighting alongside the Jackals as they struggled to hold onto the main gate to the Korps' headquarters. It was where she *should* be. The colonel needed an update, and while she knew he would yell at her for not leaving yet, Sunshine needed to know precisely how he was planning on transferring the data to her CASPer while she was on her way out of the city. There were ways, but if it was a large data file dump then she might need to stay in one area.

"Colonel, it's Lieutenant Sunshine," she radioed as she stepped out into the daylight and looked toward the sea. It startled her at how blue the ocean was on her Tri-V. Pollution in the Freeport had traditionally been high, but with the Korps purchasing it and renovating most of the dockside area, the levels of grime and muck in the water had all but disappeared.

"You're supposed to be on the road already, Lieutenant," Mulbah scolded her after a few moments of silence. "What's the delay?"

"Sir, I...I don't know where the information is," she admitted. "Is it in your offices?"

"No...but thanks for reminding me about the other thing," Mulbah stated, his tone weary. "Near your position there's a makeshift holding cell. In it is the Blevin. I need you to...I need you to let her go."

"Let her go?" Sunshine was startled. From everything Zion had told her, the Blevin was supposed to be executed for murdering PFC Doré. What had changed? "You sure, *bass*?"

"No," Mulbah said irritably. "But if I hated everyone who was ever hired to do merc guild business, I'd never learn to do anything else again. No, just let her go. She'll be on her own but I'm pretty sure she can take care of herself."

"And the data, *bass*?" she reminded him. "Where do I get it?"

"I uploaded it...to your CASPer two days ago, the moment I figured an attack was imminent."

"Oh."

"Just get yourself off-planet," he told her. "Find the Peacemakers."

"Do you want me to rip out the CPU of the CASPer once I find a way?" she asked.

"Uh...sure, yeah, that would help," Mulbah told her. "Not to sound rude, Sunshine, but I'm—ouch, you little fucker, that hurt!—a little busy right now. Get your ass out of here!"

"Yes, *bass*," she said. She opened her mouth to say more but was cut off by Mulbah.

"You're a good merc, Lieutenant," he told her. "I wish I had more like you. Take care, and remember to paint the skies with our songs of glory in colors even the ancestors themselves would be envious of."

"I will, *bass*," Sunshine managed to say through a choking sob. "Lion Eight, out."

Killing the comms, she hurried down to find the prison cell holding the Blevin. Perhaps she could save one life this day, besides her own.

\* \* \*

### Lion's Gate, Freeport of Monrovia, Liberia District, Earth

"Good luck, Sunshine," Mulbah whispered into the dead comm. He had killed her link the moment she had signed off for multiple reasons. Primarily it was to ensure the Mercenary Guild couldn't trace her after she left the area. Also, he didn't want her listening in should the battle suddenly turn bad.

2nd Company was hurting. Their already-undermanned squads took a huge hit when the Tortantula massed their attacks. Only through the sheer determination of Antonious and the fortuitous arrival of the Command Squad did the Lion's Gate still stand. They were still going, but Antonious was injured and Mulbah wasn't sure how much longer the tough merc could hold on.

Checking his Tri-V, he saw 3rd Company was heading back to the Freeport with a host of Zuul and Besquith in pursuit. The Besquith numbers were down, and there weren't nearly as many Zuul as they had expected, which was mostly due to Samson and the stalwarts of 1st Company, who had been wiped out to a man in order to ensure the world leaders who had been at the defense summit escaped through the tunnels beneath the mansion.

Only a few others outside of the presidential security detail knew where the exit to those tunnels lay, and it was a secret Mulbah was more than willing to take to the grave with him. As long as the president and others made their way out, General Peepo wouldn't be able to throw Africa into its deepest existential crisis since the Congo Civil War. A true decapitating strike would have thrown Western Africa into a darkness from which it might never have recovered.

Mulbah knew they had been lucky Peepo hadn't started the fight by hitting the mansion with a kinetic. Using the alien mercenaries, as bloody as the fighting turned out to be, was better than watching Africa burn.

Another CASPer jostled his arm, bringing him back to the present. His eyes took in the scene and his analytical brain broke down the combat situation. It soon became apparent they were all about to die.

"Boss? It's Zion," a familiar voice crackled over the radio. "We're two minutes out. Those Torts still roughly where they were when you hit them?"

"Roughly," Mulbah confirmed.

"Hit 'em with K-bombs in one hundred seconds," Zion instructed. "We'll hit them as the flames die. And for the love of God, quit shooting your MACs when the bombs explode."

"You sure, Zion?"

"Hell no!" Zion barked, laughing over the comms. "But it's either that or they eventually kill you, then come for us. This way we can take more of them with us before we all die."

"Copy, captain," Mulbah grinned savagely. "One hundred seconds and counting." He switched frequencies. "Command Squad, 2nd Company, hear me and listen! Countdown to launch K-bombs in ninety-five seconds. Everyone launch everything for five seconds, then stop. On my signal, show them the pain and *paint the fucking sky!*"

"Paint the sky!"

* * *

Antonious was on one knee now, blood pouring freely from his chest wound. He had quit moving some time before with his left arm resting on the base of the great stone lion, keeping him upright. Exhaustion hit him in waves which were growing stronger with each passing breath. He could feel his heartbeat weakening, and there was a dull, constant roar in his ears with each *thud-thud* in his chest.

*Tired.* It was the only real coherent thought in his head. Fighting the deadly siren of sleep, Antonious forced his head up as the rest of the 2nd Company shouted something. *Paint the sky,* he thought. *Yeah, we do that. The Kakata Korps does that. We paint the sky with the blood of our enemies. Why do I hurt so much?*

A counter appeared in the lower right-hand corner of his Tri-V. It read 54. He didn't really know what it meant but assumed it had something to do with what his men had been yelling moments before. However, the details escaped him. He grinned at this and shook his head, which caused a new wave of agony to wash over him. Antonious was excellent at adapting, no matter what.

"Paint the sky," he whispered in a hoarse voice, his throat raw and bloody. His mouth tasted of copper and metal. Breathing hurt. Moving anything other than his feet was difficult, at best. Pain was everywhere. Was this what dying gloriously in combat felt like? If it was, he decided as he tried to look at his Tri-V display that he couldn't recommend it to anyone.

The subtle *whoomp* of K-bombs being launched could faintly be heard over the buzzing noise growing louder by the second in his ear. He shook his head and tried to remember what was so important about the noise. He knew what they were, this wasn't the issue. The question was *why*. Was there something else he was supposed to do?

The sound faded and explosions could be heard. Antonious remembered they were in a fight against alien mercenaries, protecting Monrovia as well as the Korps' HQ. He had a duty, and he would be damned if he were to fail his men. Failure was not an option for him. Not now, not ever.

Coughing up blood, Antonious fumbled for the trigger to deploy his K-bombs. His fingers were wet with blood and the controls were slippery. Dizzy, he cursed under his breath and tried again. This time he found the proper sequence and launched all twenty of his K-bombs

Antonious fell to the ground, dead, his last bit of energy spent.

\* \* \*

As the initial blast of the K-bombs subsided, Zion and the remaining members of the 3rd Company charged into the confused mass of Tortantulas. The spider-like aliens were momentarily stunned from the concussive blasts of the

K-bombs, which gave Zion the perfect opening to wreak havoc upon them. Even the few Flatar riders were dazed at the ferocity of the Goshawk's attack as they hammered into the unprotected flank of the Tortantulas. Feral Tortantulas screamed as their legs and abdomens were sliced open by the whirling dervish of blades, while heads were split asunder by the terrifyingly accurate gunfire from the CASPers' MACs.

For the barest of moments, Zion had hope. The very thought of not only winning this fight, but surviving as well, had never been brought up while discussing the defense of Monrovia or the Korps' HQ. The arrival of the Besquith and Tortantulas had been a shock, and after seeing the Zuul wipe out Samson and 1st Company, Zion doubted anybody would walk out of the carnage alive.

Optimism flared wildly in his chest. They could *win*. What had been unthinkable minutes earlier was now within their grasp. The Besquith were reeling. The Zuul were utterly devastated from the attack on the Executive Presidential Mansion; their numbers had been reduced from thousands to a mere hundred. The Tortantulas had not suffered the losses of the others, but the Flatar riders had been whittled down enough that the larger Tortantulas were having a hard time controlling the ferals in their midst.

It was a tenable situation, Zion recognized. If the combined weight of Mulbah, his squad, and the surviving mercs of 2nd Company hit the Tortantulas at the precise moment, it would be a hammer striking a piece of iron against the anvil. The Korps could win. *No*, he thought as he shot a random Tortantula square in the face, *we will win*.

His threat detector chirped and he looked up. Twenty K-bombs were on a direct course at both the Tortantulas and the CASPers in their midst. Hope faded as he saw his imminent death in those descending explosives.

"Fuck me..."

\* \* \*

"Oh shit," Mulbah muttered as his suit detected the launch of the K-bombs the same time Zion's did. Whirling around, he saw they had come from Antonious. He opened his mouth to scream at the company captain before realizing the tough playboy was already dead. He cursed his own stupidity for not overriding the suit once he had recognized Antonious was dying.

Turning back, he managed to catch a glimpse of the first K-bomb detonation within the seething crowd of Tortantulas and CASPers. Screams filled his ears as alien and Human alike were mauled by the massive blasts as the bombs ripped through the melee with indiscriminate violence. Body parts flew everywhere; an horrific visage unlike anything he had ever seen before filled his Tri-V screen.

There was little else he could do. Keying his mic, he gave one final order.

"Charge!"

Mulbah and the surviving members of the 2nd Company tried to fight their way into the maelstrom. There was nothing left for them to accomplish now, since the president and other world leaders had successfully been evacuated from the city, and Sunshine had escaped.

He wanted to tell her what had been done, what he and Thorpi had agreed to do without her knowledge. The Veetanho had explained there were different ways to transmit data without the usual suspects questioning anything, and with Mulbah's blessing, he had done just that with the young girl. She would be a courier for them, taking the incriminating evidence with her to deliver to the Peacemaker Guild. They were the only ones who could help save Earth.

Mulbah fought hard for as long as possible. Men and alien alike died by the droves as the Korps gave as good as they received. The problem quickly became apparent, though. Mulbah had always known the relative small size of the Korps would be their undoing one day. He just never thought it would happen while he was still on Earth.

A claw struck him, knocking him off-balance. He fought off another Tortantula and shot it in the face for good measure. Another raked the back of his suit, causing him to drop to a knee as he tried to stay upright. Pivoting, he shoved the MAC directly into the face of the offending alien and fired a full burst. Rolling to his left, he sliced the leg off another Tortantula and tried to keep a third from impaling him with a foreleg. He only succeeded marginally as this Tortantula managed to penetrate his CASPer's armor.

Gasping in pain, Mulbah looked at the massive fangs which were frantically chewing their way into his cockpit. The rank breath of the terrifying alien mercenary could be felt against his cool skin through the newly-created holes of his CASPer. He struggled but felt solid strikes against his suit's armor as the frenzied alien tried to crack it open to pull him out and eat him. He wasn't having it, though, and punched the Tortantula as hard as he could.

The spider-like alien stumbled back and Mulbah had a moment of space to catch his breath. He let out a primal scream of defiance. From behind him, an unearthly howl responded to his challenge. He turned and felt his skin grow cold and clammy. His stomach dropped as he recognized the newly arrived alien mercs.

The Besquith had arrived and it was time for the Korps to pay the butcher's bill.

Mulbah fired his MAC directly into the gaping maw of the lead Besquith from point-blank range. The high-velocity rounds created a small kinetic shockwave as they passed through the meaty part of the Besquith's head, which in turn formed a small amount of back pressure. As the round passed out the back of the alien's furry cranium, the vacuum and shockwave combined to expand the rear half of the Besquith's skull into a fine mist.

Mulbah shoved the dead creature off him and scrambled back to his feet. It was clear the aliens had caught them in a maneuver very similar to the trap the Korps had laid out for the Tortantulas twice now. He didn't have much time to stop the wholesale slaughter of his men.

A warning light appeared on his Tri-V. The Besquith had somehow managed to dislodge his magnetic accelerator cannon from its mount upon dying, leaving him with just his laser rifle. He was fresh out of K-bombs as well.

Cursing, he turned and deflected the blow of another Besquith with an arm blade. The creature slid along the ground, its claws struggling to find purchase before it launched back at Mulbah. He brought his rifle up but the alien was too big and too fast. The rifle was torn from his grip and tossed aside like a chew toy.

Mulbah shoved his entire fist into the large mouth of the rampaging Besquith and sliced open the alien's throat from the inside out. Blood sprayed out like a fountain and the Besquith stumbled, obviously confused. Mulbah took a step forward and punted the beast square between the legs as hard as he could, just for good measure.

The dead Besquith flew back and landed solidly on the ground. Mulbah had but a moment of respite before three more attacked.

The number of mercenaries still alive for the Kakata Korps were rapidly dwindling. 3rd Company, already devastated by Antonious' accidental late release of the K-bombs, had finally been cut down to the last by the sheer weight and ferocity of the Tortantulas in their quest for slaughter. No longer fearful of being attacked on both sides by the CASPers, they were able to turn their full attention to the surviving Humans in their midst. With the element of surprise gone, the CASPers stood zero chance in the confined quarters against the Tortantulas.

2nd Company, even with the loss of their captain, were still putting up one hell of a fight, Mulbah noticed as he brought his arm blades up to block another attack by the trio of Besquith. Of all the companies in the Korps, the Jackals being the last standing in a pitched battle was not something he could have imagined months before. Antonious and his senior NCO, First Sergeant Oti, had done a terrific job training them after Taranto.

Of the Command Squad, Mulbah saw no sign. He swallowed, his mouth dry, as he realized there were only eight of the Korps left.

*Not counting Sunshine, at least,* he thought as he drove the point of a blade across the face of one particularly aggressive Besquith. A deep cut appeared across the Besquith's lower jaw but it only seemed to anger the alien more. It raked a pair of long claws across his chest armor and multiple systems in his suit started to chirp warnings. The CASPer was taking too much damage to continue on.

Screams filled his ears as the number of surviving Human mercenaries dropped to five. Each loss was another shot to his soul, his heart ached with each death. There was nothing more he could do. He had failed his mercs, his country, and possibly even the world by trusting the Mercenary Guild. There would be no coming back. He knew for the rest of his short life, the souls of his dead would weigh upon him.

Tossed bodily to the ground, Mulbah only had a moment to realize the battle was over at long last. All the CASPers around him were a smoking, bloody ruin of meat and metal. On his Tri-V display, every single suit showed red. 38 mercenaries, men he had vetted, hired, trained, and led into combat, all dead. Thousands of Liberian Army infantry, wiped out. The only thing he had succeeded in was allowing for the world leaders who had been at the Executive Presidential Mansion to escape. Even then, it had been the sacrifice of Samson and the rest of the Leopards who had achieved that distinction, not Mulbah.

Laying on his back, he could see the sun overhead. He was surprised for a moment at just how bright it was outside before realizing his cockpit was filled with more than a few holes, allowing him to see unfiltered daylight. The jagged, odd-looking foreleg of a Tortantula stabbed at one of the holes in the cockpit to make it bigger. The leg also pierced his skin at the collarbone. He felt it snap beneath the weight of the creature, and he screamed in pain.

The CASPer, ever helpful, administered a mild analgesic to counter the pain and allow him to keep fighting. However, the alien mercenaries had other ideas. Standing on top of his suit, the Tortantula held him down and called out for one of the Besquith to help.

"This is their leader," the Tortantula told the Besquith as it approached. "Keep him alive while you pull him out. His slaughter will be of legend."

The Besquith snarled but obeyed, punching the suit to make the holes bigger.

Mulbah squinted as more daylight struck his face. A jagged claw withdrew and a second solid punch made the hole larger. Fangs larger than his head could be seen through the opening, covered in blood and saliva. Mulbah felt a shiver of fear run down his spine as he saw his death drawing near.

He tried to bring an arm blade up to bear but a heavy weight slammed it back down to the concrete. The Tri-V failed as power in the suit died completely. Struggling to move, Mulbah found the bloodshot eye of a small creature looking in on him. It was the same Flatar rider he had tried to kill earlier, before it had managed to kill Corporal Obassi.

*How long ago was that?* he wondered. It felt like days but he doubted more than two hours had passed since the battle had begun. It never ceased to amaze him just how the Human brain could compress time. Even facing death, his mind remained analytical.

He had no real fear of death. It was his sense of failure which bothered him more. While the Korps had achieved their mission by getting the world leaders out of harm's way, along with the president, it had come at a high cost. They had sacrificed it all to give them a little bit of a head start. Between this, and Sunshine's apparent escape, Mulbah could convince himself this was a win for the good guys.

"Well, go on. Get him out of there," the Flatar ordered, and the Besquith managed to rip the canopy from the CASPer. Claws dug into his chest, and he cried out in pain as blood began to flow freely. Lifted out of the suit and held up into the air, Mulbah was completely limp in the alien's grasp. He had no more strength left, no more fight. He was beaten.

"Colonel Mulbah Luo," the Besquith growled and licked Mulbah's bloodied face. The alien's breath was rank. The mercenary commander wished he had the energy to make a snarky remark about it. "You will be a delicious snack."

"No," the Flatar said and pointed his miniature gun at the back of the Besquith's head. "He will hear the charges against him and be found guilty before he joins the slaughtered. There must be a trial. Peepo's orders."

"A show trial," Mulbah whispered through his split lips. The impact of the punches from the Besquith had done more damage than he realized. Blood flowed from his scalp and began to clot near his left eye, obscuring his vision. He tried to laugh but only managed a weak cough. More blood dribbled down his chin. His lungs burned, and everything hurt.

"Colonel Luo, you have been found guilty for crimes against the Mercenary Guild," the Flatar intoned, looking at Mulbah's face dispassionately. It was obvious to him the Flatar found being this close to the Human distasteful, though the mercenary commander did not know why. "Have you anything to say?"

"Fuck the guild," Mulbah spat and winced as his collarbone rubbed against itself. It was definitely a compound fracture, he realized as bone grated against bone. *That's not going to heal in a hurry.*

"As expected," the furry alien's head nodded slowly. "You disappoint me. I had hoped for something better. Set him down and ready him for the slaughter."

The Besquith let him go and Mulbah collapsed to the hot concrete. The rough pavement scratched at his cheek. Groaning, he rolled onto his stomach and tried to pick himself up off the ground with his uninjured arm. His bare hands burned on the blacktop. It was hot, too hot for the time of the year. The temperature hadn't really changed much, yet it felt like the weather had gotten hot and sticky since the attack first began.

His haptic suit was in tatters. Between the Besquith who had ripped him from the cockpit and the breakdown of the CASPer, he was surprised he was still clothed. Not that he cared. Aliens staring at his naked body wasn't nearly as bad as his ex-wife laughing at him the one time he had gone swimming in the Atlantic. It was the first and only time he had ever worn a Speedo.

He peered around the concrete with his working eye. There was a bit of dirt pushing through part of the broken road. Fascinated, he reached out and took a bit of soil from his homeland into his fingers and squeezed. It was harsh, yet familiar. He brought it to his face and inhaled. The dirt smelled horrible, but it was still home. Wanting to laugh but afraid his ribs would hurt more, he simply let it fall from his hand in large clumps.

*Home?* He had never really looked at Liberia as his home. He had lived there, had his company there, and created opportunity for many families there. Yet never did he ever think of the country as his *home*. Not until this moment, in his final breaths, did it even occur to him death would come for him in the land of his birth.

Looking up, he could see the ruined stone statue of the massive lion which protected the Lion's Gate. Stray shots from the Flatar had gouged deeply into the stone, but the lion's face was still recognizable. The tattered flag of Liberia was still in its mouth, frayed but whole. He smiled thinly, the pain momentarily forgotten as the familiar red, white, and blue could be seen. It was good enough for the people to see, to continue their struggle, for hope to remain. Earth, and Liberia by extension, would be free one day. Not today, perhaps. But soon.

The Flatar's pistol blocked his view. Mulbah found himself staring down the long barrel of the gun. Beyond lay the cold, flinty eyes of the furry alien. The look flooded Mulbah's heart with ice. It was not the first time a gun had been shoved into his face, but he knew without a doubt he was going to die.

"Your race is soft and weak," the Flatar said as its grip tightened on the handle of his gun. "This is why you will always lose. Without your suits, you are nothing."

"We haven't lost yet," Mulbah said. "We are still here. Here we shall remain."

The Flatar snarled at him. "For now, Human. For now."

There was a bright flash and Colonel Mulbah Luo, Commanding Officer of the Kakata Korps, died as abruptly as his Korps had lived.

\* \* \* \* \*

# Epilogue

Sunshine stopped and turned her CASPer around to watch as the last of the alien assault shuttles lifted off and jetted away from the capitol. Everywhere near the city was obscured by black, oily clouds of smoke. The land of her birth was in ruins; its capitol destroyed. War had returned to Liberia with a vengeance, and she wept because of this. Not for the fighting itself, but because in every war there would be innocent casualties. Her sadness was for the fact she had been sent away from the fight. She would not be able to help her boss in the struggle against the aliens.

Sunshine almost turned back again to rejoin the fight. It would mean she would disobey a direct order from her boss, but it would be worth it. She might not be able to save them, but knowing she would fight and die with men who looked at her as something other than a prostitute would have been worth it. Consequences be damned. The survivor inside her was tired of running, of being afraid. There was payback to be had.

For the barest of moments, she hesitated. In a Mk 7 CASPer, it was highly unlikely she would be able to turn the tide of the battle. This, and her strict loyalty to both Zion and Colonel Luo, pushed her onwards. Her given oath drove her, and a primal instinct led the way.

Sunshine knew she had to head northeast, into the Sahara. Within the barren wastelands the training caches should still be there, unless nomads had found and removed them. A possibility, sure, which would lead to her death if they were missing. While her death would definitely be bad, the knowledge of failing her mission would drive her insane.

The suit would guide her to the caches of supplies she would need to complete the trip. She knew in her bones, though, that her persistence would take her to the end of the journey. She would find a transport off-world and get whatever information the colonel had put in the CASPer to whoever could stop the Mercenary Guild from killing all of Earth.

A bright flash suddenly filled her Tri-V screen. The filters cut down the glare, but for a few minutes purple blobs clouded her vision. Sunshine blinked, trying to clear her vision. Her irritation changed to confusion as her eyes finally adjusted and the blots disappeared. Spinning her CASPer around, she turned to see what had caused the light.

"Oh no," she gasped.

One hundred kilometers away from the direction of Monrovia, a giant mushroom cloud could be seen. Her Tri-V quickly showed that it was not a nuclear explosion, but the result of a kinetic strike. There was no radiation the suit could detect, although the mushroom cloud was reading high temperatures as it climbed steadily into the sky.

Sunshine swallowed as the initial sonic wave washed over the area. It was fairly flat but it was far enough above sea level for her to see the effect the wave had on the local fauna. Her suit helpfully provided her with information, and she knew the concussive wave would follow in roughly five minutes. While she knew she *should* be okay, Sunshine was well aware that being further away would be even better. She pushed onward in the hopes of finding safety.

The Peacemaker Guild were the only ones who could help Earth now. How, though, would she find them? From what Mulbah had said, and Zion later confirmed, the Peacemaker Guild had stayed silent during the entire time the planet had been under the Mercenary Guild's rule. The so-called intergalactic police, in her eyes, were very similar to the corrupt officials of Liberia.

Tears flooded her eyes. It was hopeless. She did not even know where to go other than the caches in the desert. She turned away from the dead, blasted city of Monrovia and looked into the dense foliage beyond. It was another two hundred kilometers of jungle overgrowth before the land would begin to dry out and become the Sahara. After that, it was almost 6,000 kilometers to the closest star port, which was on the Sinai Peninsula. Unless she could find a way across the Mediterranean or the Atlantic, Egypt was her destination.

She sobbed now. There simply was no way for her CASPer to make it there without refueling points. She knew there were a few depots out in the Sahara, but as the Tri-V brought up the path she needed to take in order to survive the journey, it became readily apparent the journey would take almost three months. She would have to conserve her fuel, not bound using her jumpjets, in order to make it between three of the depots as well.

"I am a merc," she whispered as she shoved away the fear and anguish. Strength filled her as she remembered who she truly was. "I am strong. I am not afraid of death. I live to paint the sky for my ancestors. I can do this."

Ahead of her, a tawny-colored shape moved behind a small cluster of rubber trees. Sunshine instinctively brought up her laser rifle but held her fire, curious. There was very little in the jungles of Liberia which could hurt a CASPer, even an older Mk 7. Another flash of golden-brown to her left caused her to swivel on point. Her eyes widened as the form began to take shape.

It was a lion, and not just any lion. It was a female, large in size and sleek in build. Bright golden eyes matched the shiny fur coat perfectly. In that moment it dawned on the young woman, perhaps Oti's stories about the lions of Liberia wasn't so farfetched after all?

Whatever the case may be, the lion did not seem displeased with Sunshine's presence in its hunting grounds. The lion looked back at her, golden eyes staring at the CASPer before it began to pad slowly into the jungle, northward. She watched it until it had almost disappeared from view. The lioness paused and looked back over its shoulder at her, as if beckoning for the young girl to follow.

"Well, you're going the same way I am," Sunshine murmured thoughtfully as she met the lionesses' eyes. While she knew the creature could not see her face through the CASPer cockpit, the feeling the lioness was looking directly into her soul was a sensation Sunshine could not shake.

She shoved the horrific memory of the mushroom cloud over Monrovia from her mind as best as she could. The dead were just that, living in her memory, now and forever. Fate could not be changed no matter how hard she wished otherwise.

Days turned into a week, then two, and yet the lioness continued unerringly to guide her. It would disappear during the hot daytime hours, leaving Sunshine alone to rest and recover. Traveling at night conserved power and energy consumption, even though the desert was cold at night. At one point the lioness disappeared for three entire days. Just as Sunshine had given up hope, it had reappeared, well-fed and rested. Wherever it had run off to, the mercenary figured the lioness was doing well enough that Sunshine wouldn't have to split her meager rations with the lioness.

One month passed. Occasionally Sunshine would spot nomads wandering through the wide desert whenever she spotted an oasis, but for the most part she was alone, save for the lioness. She tried to be inconspicuous but it was difficult, since the nomads oftentimes had never seen a CASPer before. The majority of them would turn and head the other direction, believing her to be some sort of devil or another. A few just maintained a safe distance.

Two months, and it was more of the same. She began to wonder why she even hurried during the night. It was highly doubtful anyone would be looking for her. Her radio had been virtually silent since the clouds over Monrovia. There was nobody out here, not in the vast and seemingly endless sea of sand dunes. To pass the time, Sunshine began to talk to herself. Cheerful at first, but the longer she stayed trapped within her own psyche, the more despondent she became. It wasn't her fault, merely a lack of external mental stimulation, which caused her to lose herself within her own mind.

As dawn broke for the final time, she cried out in despair as the suit ground to a halt atop a large rise. She had found the last cache almost a week before and had continued to tirelessly march across the Sahara. All external power of the CASPer died save for the Tri-V. It managed to inform her the town ahead was the failed city built around the Toshka Project before it, too, shut down. Struggling to manually open the cockpit's hatch, she finally managed to shove it open. She fell to the ground with the grace of a bull in a china shop and landed solidly on a rocky surface. Sunshine felt the pain in her elbow but ignored it as she looked for her guide. A soft and helpless whimper escaped her lips.

The lioness had disappeared sometime before dawn. The CASPer was out of fuel and there were no more caches that she knew of. She had reached the end of the journey, one way or the other. Ahead of her, Sunshine could see a small town resting on the banks of a narrow canal, not far from her dune. Here was where the lioness had meant for her to be, apparently. Dropping to her knees, she covered her face and tried not to cry. It was over 400 kilometers to the space port on the Sinai Peninsula. She had merely reached one of the many reservoirs which fed into the Nile River. There was no way she could do it.

She had failed. "I'm sorry, *bass*."

Sunshine looked out at the small village. There were some children wandering around, but most appeared to be clustered around an unusual looking object at the western edge of the town. It seemed to be a safe place to try and build up enough credits to refuel her CASPer. If they had any sort of refueling capabilities, she could eventually continue on her journey and follow the final orders given to her. How long would it be before she could continue, however, was a mystery. She shook as she struggled to get her breathing under control.

"I'm sorry I failed you all."

The barest hint of noise behind her caused her muscles to stiffen in anticipation. Something was there with her, watching. It wasn't the lion, she was certain. It felt too small to be the feline. But then, what, exactly? She was almost afraid to look. What—or more importantly, *who*—could sneak up on anyone in the middle of the desert?

"Little kita," a light voice said from her left. It was humorous and yet, held a slight rebuke in its tone. "Brave and strong, yet fearful and alone. I am impressed by your strength and determination. My friend told me you were coming. I greet you."

"What?" Sunshine asked, turning slightly. There was nothing to be seen but sand and a few small, scraggly bushes. Her mind was playing tricks on her. There could be no other explanation. She was going to die, alone, with madness clouding her mind.

Suddenly she saw the creature who was talking to her. It was perched atop her CASPer's shoulder, looking down at her. It was vaguely familiar, but Sunshine could not say why. *Is that...a cat?*

"Who are you? *What* are you?"

"I am Tsan, and I am here to help. Welcome to our negotiation."

# # # # #

## About the Author

A 2015 John W. Campbell Award finalist, Jason Cordova has traveled extensively throughout the U.S. and the world. He has multiple novels and short stories currently in print. He also coaches high school varsity basketball and loves the outdoors.

He currently resides in Virginia.

Catch up with Jason at https://jasoncordova.com/.

\* \* \* \* \*

## Author's Note:

While this novel is a work of fiction, the accounts of the child slaves and child soldiers in the book are based on actual events from over a dozen brave young men, aged 9-17, who shared their trials and tribulations with the author. Not all the boys were physically scarred. Some hid their hurts well, but all of them have the emotional and psychological wounds that oftentimes never heal. It is the author's belief these boys only shared their experiences as an attempt to help heal these wounds.

Slavery is a horrid thing, and these young men survived something that is incomprehensible in western society. It is the author's hope that these boys continue their journey to becoming men and never give up the strength which got them this far. They have already won the battle against evil, but only time will tell if they realize it.

Jason Cordova
Clifton Forge, VA

\* \* \* \* \*

**Connect with Chris Kennedy Publishing**

Website: http://chriskennedypublishing.com/

Facebook: https://www.facebook.com/ckpublishing/

\* \* \* \* \*

Do you have what it takes to be a Merc?

Take your VOWs and join the Merc Guild on Facebook!

Meet us at: https://www.facebook.com/groups/536506813392912/

\* \* \* \* \*

The following is an

**Excerpt from Book One of the Salvage Title Trilogy:**

# Salvage Title

---

# Kevin Steverson

Available Now from Theogony Books

eBook, Paperback, and Audio Book

### Excerpt from "Salvage Title:"

The first thing Clip did was get power to the door and the access panel. Two of his power cells did the trick once he had them wired to the container. He then pulled out his slate and connected it. It lit up, and his fingers flew across it. It took him a few minutes to establish a link, then he programmed it to search for the combination to the access panel.

"Is it from a human ship?" Harmon asked, curious.

"I don't think so, but it doesn't matter; ones and zeros are still ones and zeros when it comes to computers. It's universal. I mean, there are some things you have to know to get other races' computers to run right, but it's not that hard," Clip said.

Harmon shook his head. *Riiigghht,* he thought. He knew better. Clip's intelligence test results were completely off the charts. Clip opted to go to work at Rinto's right after secondary school because there was nothing for him to learn at the colleges and universities on either Tretra or Joth. He could have received academic scholarships for advanced degrees on a number of nearby systems. He could have even gone all the way to Earth and attended the University of Georgia if he wanted. The problem was getting there. The schools would have provided free tuition if he could just have paid to get there.

Secondary school had been rough on Clip. He was a small guy that made excellent grades without trying. It would have been worse if Harmon hadn't let everyone know that Clip was his brother. They lived in the same foster center, so it was mostly true. The first day of school, Harmon had laid down the law—if you messed with Clip, you messed up.

At the age of fourteen, he beat three seniors senseless for attempting to put Clip in a trash container. One of them was a Yalteen, a member of a race of large humanoids from two systems over. It wasn't a fair fight—they should have brought more people with them. Harmon hated bullies.

After the suspension ended, the school's Warball coach came to see him. He started that season as a freshman and worked on using it to earn a scholarship to the academy. By the time he graduated, he was six feet two inches with two hundred and twenty pounds of muscle. He got the scholarship and a shot at going into space. It was the longest time he'd ever spent away from his foster brother, but he couldn't turn it down.

Clip stayed on Joth and went to work for Rinto. He figured it was a job that would get him access to all kinds of technical stuff, servos, motors, and maybe even some alien computers. The first week he was there, he tweaked the equipment and increased the plant's recycled steel production by 12 percent. Rinto was eternally grateful, as it put him solidly into the profit column instead of toeing the line between profit and loss. When Harmon came back to the planet after the academy, Rinto hired him on the spot on Clip's recommendation. After he saw Harmon operate the grappler and got to know him, he was glad he did.

A steady beeping brought Harmon back to the present. Clip's program had succeeded in unlocking the container. "Right on!" Clip exclaimed. He was always using expressions hundreds or more years out of style. "Let's see what we have; I hope this one isn't empty, too." Last month they'd come across a smaller vault, but it had been empty.

Harmon stepped up and wedged his hands into the small opening the door had made when it disengaged the locks. There wasn't enough power in the small cells Clip used to open it any further. He put his weight into it, and the door opened enough for them to get inside. Before they went in, Harmon placed a piece of pipe in the doorway so it couldn't close and lock on them, baking them alive before anyone realized they were missing.

Daylight shone in through the doorway, and they both froze in place; the weapons vault was full.

\* \* \* \* \*

Get "Salvage Title" now at:
https://www.amazon.com/dp/B07H8Q3HBV.

Find out more about Kevin Steverson and "Salvage Title" at:
http://chriskennedypublishing.com/.

\* \* \* \* \*

The following is an
**Excerpt from Book One of the Earth Song Cycle:**

# Overture

## Mark Wandrey

Now Available from Theogony Books

eBook and Paperback

### Excerpt from "Overture:"

Dawn was still an hour away as Mindy Channely opened the roof access and stared in surprise at the crowd already assembled there. "Authorized Personnel Only" was printed in bold red letters on the door through which she and her husband, Jake, slipped onto the wide roof.

A few people standing nearby took notice of their arrival. Most had no reaction, a few nodded, and a couple waved tentatively. Mindy looked over the skyline of Portland and instinctively oriented herself before glancing to the east. The sky had an unnatural glow that had been growing steadily for hours, and as they watched, scintillating streamers of blue, white, and green radiated over the mountains like a strange, concentrated aurora borealis.

"You almost missed it," one man said. She let the door close, but saw someone had left a brick to keep it from closing completely. Mindy turned and saw the man who had spoken wore a security guard uniform. The easy access to the building made more sense.

"Ain't no one missin' this!" a drunk man slurred.

"We figured most people fled to the hills over the past week," Jake replied.

"I guess we were wrong," Mindy said.

"Might as well enjoy the show," the guard said and offered them a huge, hand-rolled cigarette that didn't smell like tobacco. She waved it off, and the two men shrugged before taking a puff.

"Here it comes!" someone yelled. Mindy looked to the east. There was a bright light coming over the Cascade Mountains, so intense it was like looking at a welder's torch. Asteroid LM-245 hit the atmosphere at over 300 miles per second. It seemed to move faster and faster, from east to west, and the people lifted their hands to shield their eyes from the blinding light. It looked like a blazing comet or a science fiction laser blast.

"Maybe it will just pass over," someone said in a voice full of hope.

Mindy shook her head. She'd studied the asteroid's track many times.

In a matter of a few seconds, it shot by and fell toward the western horizon, disappearing below the mountains between Portland and the ocean. Out of view of the city, it slammed into the ocean.

The impact was unimaginable. The air around the hypersonic projectile turned to superheated plasma, creating a shockwave that generated 10 times the energy of the largest nuclear weapon ever detonated as it hit the ocean's surface.

The kinetic energy was more than 1,000 megatons; however, the object didn't slow as it flashed through a half mile of ocean and into the sea bed, then into the mantel, and beyond.

On the surface, the blast effect appeared as a thermal flash brighter than the sun. Everyone on the rooftop watched with wide-eyed terror as the Tualatin Mountains between Portland and the Pacific Ocean were outlined in blinding light. As the light began to dissipate, the outline of the mountains blurred as a dense bank of smoke climbed from the western range.

The flash had incinerated everything on the other side.

The physical blast, travelling much faster than any normal atmospheric shockwave, hit the mountains and tore them from the bedrock, adding them to the rolling wave of destruction traveling east at several thousand miles per hour. The people on the rooftops of Portland only had two seconds before the entire city was wiped away.

Ten seconds later, the asteroid reached the core of the planet, and another dozen seconds after that, the Earth's fate was sealed.

\* \* \* \* \*

Get "Overture" now at:
https://www.amazon.com/dp/B077YMLRHM/

Find out more about Mark Wandrey and the Earth Song Cycle at:
https://chriskennedypublishing.com/

\* \* \* \* \*

Made in the USA
Columbia, SC
21 September 2019